# THE GIRL FROM HONEYSUCKLE FARM

BY
JESSICA STEELE

MILLS & BOON®

First published in Great Britain 2009
Paperback edition 2010
Harlequin Mills & Boon Limited,
Eton House, 18-24 Paradise Road, Richmond, Surrey TW9 1SR

© Jessica Steele 2009

ISBN: 978 0 263 86888 3

Harlequin Mills & Boon policy is to use papers that are natural, renewable and recyclable products and made from wood grown in sustainable forests. The logging and manufacturing process conform to the legal environmental regulations of the country of origin.

Printed and bound in Spain
by Litografia Rosés, S.A., Barcelona

**Jessica Steele** lives in the county of Worcestershire, with her super husband, Peter, and their gorgeous Staffordshire bull terrier, Florence. Any spare time is spent enjoying her three main hobbies: reading espionage novels, gardening (she has a great love of flowers), and playing golf. Any time left over is celebrated with her fourth hobby: shopping. Jessica has a sister and two brothers, and they all, with their spouses, often go on golfing holidays together. Having travelled to various places on the globe, researching backgrounds for her stories, there are many countries that she would like to revisit. Her most recent trip abroad was to Portugal, where she stayed in a lovely hotel, close to her all-time favourite golf course. Jessica had no idea of being a writer until one day Peter suggested she write a book. So she did. She has now written over eighty novels.

# CHAPTER ONE

PHINN tried hard to look on the bright side—but could not find one. There was not so much as a glimmer of a hint of a silver lining to the dark cloud hanging over her.

She stared absently out of the window of her flat above the stables, barely noticing that Geraldine Walton, the new owner of the riding school, while somehow managing to look elegant even in jeans and a tee shirt, was already busy organising the day's activities.

Phinn had been up early herself, and had already been down to check on her elderly mare Ruby. Phinn swallowed down a hard lump in her throat and came away from the window, recalling the conversation she'd had with Kit Peverill yesterday. Kit was Ruby's vet, and he had been as kind as he could be. But, however kind he had been, he could not minimise the harshness that had to be faced when he told her that fragile Ruby would not see the year out.

Phinn was quite well aware that Ruby had quite a few health problems, but even so she had been very shaken. It was already the end of April. But, however shaken she had been, her response had been sharp when he had suggested that she might want to consider allowing him to put Ruby down.

'No!' she had said straight away, the idea not needing to be considered. Then, as she'd got herself more collected, 'She's not in great pain, is she? I mean, I know you give her a painkilling injection occasionally, but…'

'Her medication is keeping her relatively pain-free,' Kit had informed her. And Phinn had not needed to hear any more. She had thanked him for his visit and had stayed with Ruby for some while, reflecting how Ruby had been her best friend since her father had rescued the mare from being ill treated thirteen years ago, and had brought her home.

But, while they had plenty of space at Honeysuckle Farm in which to keep a horse, there had been no way they could afford to keep one as a pet.

Her mother, already the breadwinner in the family, had hit the roof. But equally there had been no way that Ewart Hawkins was going to let the emaciated mare go back to the people he had rescued her from. And since he had threatened—and had meant it—to have them prosecuted if they tried to get her back, her owners had moved on without her.

'Please, Mummy,' Phinn remembered pleading, and her mother had looked into her pleading blue eyes, so like her own, and had drawn a long sigh.

'You'll have to feed and water her, *and* clean up after her,' she had said severely. 'Daily!'

And Ewart, the battle over, had given his wife a delighted kiss, and Phinn had exchanged happy grins with her father.

She had been ten years old then, and life had been wonderful. She had been born on the farm to the best parents in the world. Her childhood, given the occasional volcanic explosions from her mother when Ewart had been particularly outrageous about something, had been little short of idyllic. Any major rows between her parents, she'd later realised had, in the main, been kept from her.

Her father had adored her from the word go. Because of some sort of complication at her birth, her mother had had to stay in bed, and it had been left to Ewart to look after the newborn. They had lived in one of the farm cottages then, only moving to the big farmhouse when Grandfather and then Grandmother Hawkins had died. Phinn's father had bonded with his baby daughter immediately, and, entirely uninterested in farming, he had spent hour after hour with his little girl. It had been he who, advised by his wife, Hester, that the child had to be registered with the authorities within forty-two days of her birth, had gone along to the register office with strict instructions to name her Elizabeth Maud—Maud after Hester's mother.

He had never liked his mother-in-law, and had returned home to have to explain himself to his wife.

'You've called her—*what*?' Hester had apparently hit a C above top C.

'Calm down, my love,' he had attempted to soothe, and had gone on to explain that with a plain name like Hawkins, he had thought the baby had better have a pretty name to go in front.

'Delphinium!'

'I'm not having my beautiful daughter called plain Lizzie Hawkins,' he'd answered, further explaining, 'To be a bit different I've named her Delphinnium, with an extra "n" in the middle.' And, to charm his still not mollified wife, 'I'm rather hoping little Phinn will have your gorgeous delphinium-blue eyes. Did you know,' he went on, 'that your beautiful eyes go all dark purple, like the Black Knight delphinium, when you're all emotional?'

'Ewart Hawkins,' she had threatened, refusing to be charmed.

'And I brought you a cabbage,' he'd said winningly.

The fact that he had brought it, not bought it, had told her that he had nipped over some farmer's hedge and helped himself.

'Ewart Hawkins!' she'd said again, but he had the smile he had wanted.

Hester Rainsworth, as she had been prior to her marriage, had been brought up most conventionally in a workaholic family. Impractical dreamer, talented pianist, sometime poet and would-be mechanical engineer Ewart Hawkins could not have been more of an opposite. They had fallen in love—and for some years had been blissfully happy.

Given a few ups and downs, it had been happiness all round in Phinn's childhood. Grandfather Hawkins had been the tenant of the farm, and on his death the tenancy had passed to her father. The farm had then been her father's responsibility, but after one year of appalling freak weather, when they had spent more than they had earned, Hester had declared that, with money tight, Ewart could be farmer and house-husband too, while she went out and found a job and brought some money in.

Unlike his hard-working practical father, Ewart had had little interest in arable farming, and had seen absolutely no point in labouring night and day only to see his crops flattened by storms. Besides, there'd been other things he'd preferred to do. Teach his daughter to sketch, to fish, to play the piano and to swim just for starters. There was a pool down at Broadlands, the estate that owned both Honeysuckle Farm and the neighbouring Yew Tree

Farm. They hadn't been supposed to swim in the pool, but in return for her father going up to the Hall occasionally, and playing the grand piano for music-lover Mr Caldicott, old Mr Caldicott had turned a blind eye.

So it was in the shallows there that her father had taught her to dive and to swim. If they hadn't taken swimwear it had been quite all right with him if she swam in her underwear—and should his wife be home when they returned, he'd borne her wrath with fortitude.

There was a trout stream too, belonging to the Broadlands estate, and they hadn't been supposed to fish there either. But her father had called that a load of nonsense, so fish they had. Though, for all Phinn had learned to cast a fine line, she could never kill a fish and her fish had always been put back. Afterwards they might stop at the Cat and Drum, where her father would sit her outside with a lemonade while he went inside to pass time with his friends. Sometimes he would bring his pint outside. He would let her have a sip of his beer and, although she thought it tasted horrible, she had pretended to like it.

Phinn gave a shaky sigh as she thought of her dreamer father. It had been he and not her mother who had decorated her Easter bonnet for the village parade. How proud she had been of that hat—complete with a robin that he had very artistically made.

'A robin!' her mother had exclaimed. 'You do *know* it's Easter?'

'There won't be another bonnet like it,' he had assured her.

'You can say that again!' Hester had retorted.

Phinn had not won the competition. She had not wanted to. Though she had drawn one or two stares, it had not mattered. Her father had decorated her hat, and that had been plenty good enough for her.

Phinn wondered, not for the first time, when it had all started to go so badly wrong. Had it been before old Mr Caldicott had decided to sell the estate? Before Ty Allardyce had come to Bishops Thornby, taken a look around and decided to buy the place— thereby making himself their landlord? Or…?

In all fairness, Phinn knew that it must have been long before then. Though he, more recently, had not helped. Her beautiful blue eyes darkened in sadness as she thought back to a time five, maybe six years ago. Had that been when things had started to go awry? She had come home after having been out for a ride with Ruby, and after attending to Ruby's needs she had gone into the big old farmhouse kitchen to find her parents in the middle of a blazing row.

Knowing that she could not take sides, she had been about to back out again when her mother had taken her eyes from the centre of her wrath— Ewart—to tell her, 'This concerns you too, Phinn.'

'Oh,' she had murmured non-committally.

'We're broke. I'm bringing in as much as I can.' Her mother worked in Gloucester as a legal assistant.

'I'll get a job,' Phinn had offered. 'I'll—'

'You will. But first you'll have some decent training. I've arranged for you to have an interview at secretarial college. You—'

'She won't like it!' Ewart had objected.

'We all of us—or most of us,' she'd inserted, with a sarcastic glance at him, 'have to do things we don't want to do or like to do!'

The argument, with Phinn playing very little part, had raged on until Hester Hawkins had brought out her trump card.

'Either Phinn goes to college or that horse goes to somebody who can afford her feed, her vet and her farrier!'

'I'll sell something,' Ewart had decided, already not liking that his daughter, his pal, would not be around so much. He had a good brain for anything mechanical, and the farmyard was littered with odds and ends that he would sometimes make good and sell on.

But Hester had grown weary of him. 'Grow up, Ewart,' she had snapped bluntly.

But that was the trouble. Her father had never grown up, and had seen no reason why he should attempt it. On thinking about it, Phinn could not see any particular reason why he should have either.

Tears stung her eyes. Though it had been the essential Peter Pan in her fifty-four-year-old father that had ultimately been the cause of his death.

But she did not want to dwell on that happening seven months ago. She had shed enough tears since then.

Phinn made herself think back to happier times, though she had not been too happy to be away from the farm for such long hours while she did her training. For her mother's sake she had applied herself to that training, and afterwards, with her eye more on the salary she would earn than with any particular interest in making a career as a PA, she had got herself a job with an accountancy firm, with her mother driving her into Gloucester each day.

Each evening Phinn had got home as soon as she could to see Ruby and her father. Her father had taught her to drive, but when her mother had started working late, putting in extra hours at her office, it was he who had suggested that Phinn should have a car of her own.

Her mother had agreed, but had insisted *she* would look into it. She was not having her daughter driving around in any bone-rattling contraption he'd patched up.

Phinn had an idea that Grandmother Rainsworth had made a contribution to her vehicle, and guessed that her mother's parents might well have helped out financially in her growing years.

But all that had stopped a few months later when her mother, having sat her down and said that she wanted to talk to her, had announced to Phinn's utter amazement that she was moving out. Shocked, open-mouthed, Phinn had barely taken in that her mother intended leaving them when she'd further revealed that she had met someone else.

'You mean—some—other man?' Phinn had gasped, it still not fully sinking in.

'Clive. His name's Clive.'

'But—but what about Dad?'

'I've discussed this fully with your father. Things—er—haven't been right between us for some while. I'll start divorce proceedings as soon as everything settles…'

Divorce! Phinn had been aware that her mother had grown more impatient and short-tempered with her father just lately. But—*divorce*!

'But what—'

'I'm not going to change my mind, Phinn. I've tried. Lord knows I've tried! But I'm tired of the constant struggle. Your father lives in his own little dream world and…' She halted at the look of protest on her daughter's face. 'No, I'm not going to run him down. I know how devoted you are to him. But just try to understand, Phinn. I'm tired of the struggle.

And I've decided I'm not too old to make a fresh start. To make a new life for myself. A better life.'

'Th-this Clive. He's part of your fresh start—this better life?'

'Yes, he is. In due time I'll marry him—though I'm not in any great hurry about that.'

'You—just want your—freedom?'

'Yes, I do. You're working now, Phinn. You have your own money—though no doubt your father will want some of it. But…' Hester looked at her daughter, wanting understanding. 'I've found myself a small flat in Gloucester. I'll write down the address. I'm leaving your father, darling, not you. You're welcome to come and live with me whenever you want.'

To leave her father had been something Phinn had not even thought about. Her home had been there, with him and Ruby.

It was around then, Phinn suddenly saw, that everything had started to go wrong.

First Ruby had had a cough, and when that cleared she'd picked up a viral infection. Her father had been marvelous, in that he'd spent all of his days looking after Ruby for her until Phinn was able to speed home from the office to take over.

The vet's bill had started to mount, but old Mr Duke had obligingly told them to pay what they could when they could.

Phinn's days had become full. She'd had no idea

of the amount of work her mother had done when she was home. Phinn had always helped out when requested, but once she was sole carer she'd seemed to spend a lot of her time picking up and clearing up after her father.

And time had gone by. Phinn had met Clive Gillam and, contrary to her belief, had liked him. And a couple of years later, with her father's approval, she had attended their wedding.

'You want to go and live with them?' her father had asked somewhat tentatively when she had returned.

'No way,' she'd answered.

And he had grinned. 'Fancy a pint?'

'You go. I want to check on Rubes.'

It seemed as though her mother's new marriage had been a signal for everything to change. Mr Caldicott, the owner of the Broadlands estate, had decided to sell up and to take himself and his money off to sunnier climes.

And, all before they knew it, the bachelor Allardyce brothers had been in the village, taking a look around. And, all before they could blink, Honeysuckle Farm and neighbouring Yew Tree Farm, plus a scattering of other properties, had all had a new landlord—and an army of architects and builders had started at work on Broadlands Hall, bringing its antiquated plumbing and heating up to date and generally modernising the interior.

She had spotted the brothers one day when she was resting Ruby, hidden in the spinney—property of Broadlands. Two men deep in conversation had walked by. The slightly taller of the two, a dark-haired man, just had to be the Tyrell Allardyce she had heard about. There was such a self-confident air about the man that he could have been none other than the new owner.

Phinn had seemed to know that before she'd over-heard his deep, cultured tones saying, 'Don't you see, Ash...?' as they had passed within yards of her.

Ash was tall too, but without that positive, self-assured air that simply exuded from the other man. Listening intently, he must have been the younger brother.

Tyrell Allardyce, with his brother Ashley, had called at Honeysuckle Farm one day while she was out at work. But from what her father had told her, and from what she had gleaned from the hotbed of local gossip, Ty Allardyce was some big-shot fi-nancier who worked and spent most of his time either in London or overseas. He, so gossip had said, would live at Broadlands Hall when his London commitments allowed, while Ashley would stay at the Hall to supervise the alterations and gen-erally manage the estate.

'Looks like we're going to be managed, kiddo,' her father had commented jocularly.

Highly unlikely!

Further village gossip some while later had suggested that Mrs Starkey, housekeeper to the previous owner of Broadlands, was staying on to look after Ashley Allardyce. It seemed—though Phinn knew that, village gossip being what it was, a lot of it could be discounted—that Ashley had endured some sort of a breakdown, and that Ty had bought Broadlands mainly for his brother's benefit.

Phinn thought she could safely rule that out—the cost of Broadlands, with all its other properties, must go into millions. Surely, if it were true that Ashley had been ill, there were cheaper ways of finding somewhere less fraught than London to live? Though it did appear that the younger Allardyce brother *was* living at the Hall. So perhaps Mrs Starkey, whom Phinn had known all her life, was looking after him after all.

Everything within this last year seemed to be changing. To start with, old Mr Duke had decided to give up his veterinary practice. It was a relief that she had just about settled with him the money she'd owed for Ruby's last course of treatment. Though it had worried Phinn how she would fare with the new man who had taken over. Mr Duke had never been in any hurry for his money, and Ruby, who they calculated had been about ten years old when they had claimed her, was now geriatric in the horse world, and rarely went six weeks without requiring some treatment or other.

Kit Peverill, however, a tall mousy-haired man in his early thirties, had turned out to be every bit as kind and caring as his predecessor. Thankfully, she had only had to call him out twice.

But more trouble had seemed to be heading their way when, again clearing up after her father, she'd found a letter he had left lying around. It had come from the Broadlands estate, and was less of a letter but more of a formal notice that some effort must be made to pay the rent arrears and that the farm must be 'tidied up'—otherwise legal proceedings would have to be initiated.

Feeling staggered—she'd had no idea that her father had not been paying the rent—Phinn had gone in search of him.

'Ignore it,' he had advised.

'Ignore it?' she'd gasped.

'Not worth the paper it's written on,' he had assured her, and had gone back to tinkering with an old, un-roadworthy, un-fieldworthy quad bike he had found somewhere.

Knowing that she would get no sense out of him until his mind-set was ready to think of other things, Phinn had waited until he came into supper that night.

'I was thinking of going down to the Cat for a pint—' he began.

'I was thinking we might discuss that letter,' Phinn interrupted.

He looked at her, smiled because he adored her, and said, 'You know, little flower, you've more than a touch of your mother about you.'

She couldn't ignore it. One of them had to be practical. 'What will we do if—er—things get nasty—if we have to leave here? Ruby…'

'It won't come to that,' he'd assured her, undaunted. 'It's just the new owner flexing a bit of muscle, that's all.'

'The letter's from Ashley Allardyce…'

'He may have written it, but he will have been instructed by his big brother.'

'Tyrell Allardyce.' She remembered him very clearly. Oddly, while Ashley Allardyce was only a vague figure in her mind, his elder brother Ty seemed to be etched in her head. She was starting to dislike the man.

'It's the way they do things in London,' Ewart had replied confidently. 'They just need all the paperwork neatly documented in case there's a court case. But—' as she went a shade pale '—it won't come to that,' he repeated. 'Honeysuckle Farm has been in Hawkins care for generations. Nobody's going to throw us off this land, I promise you.'

Sadly, it had not been the first letter of that sort. The next one she had seen had come from a London firm of lawyers, giving them formal notice to quit by September. And Phinn, who had already started to dislike Tyrell Allardyce, and although she had never hated anyone in her life, had known that she hated Ty that he could do this to them. Old Mr Caldicott would never, ever have instructed such a letter.

But again her father had been unconcerned, and told her to ignore the notice to quit. And while Phinn had spent a worrying time—expecting the bailiffs to turn up at any moment to turf then out—her father had appeared to not have a care in the world.

And then it had been September, and Phinn had had something else to worry about that had pushed her fear of the bailiffs into second place. Ruby had become quite ill.

Kit Peverill had come out to her in the middle of the night, and it had been touch and go if Ruby would make it. Phinn, forgetting she had a job to go to, had stayed with her and nursed her, watched her like a hawk—and the geriatric mare had pulled through.

When Phinn had gone back to work and, unable to lie, told her boss that her mare had been ill, she had been told in return that they were experiencing a business downturn and were looking to make redundancies. Was it likely, should her horse again be ill, that she would again take time off?

Again she had not been able to lie. 'I'll go and clear my desk,' she'd offered.

'You don't have to go straight way,' her employer had told her kindly. 'Let's say in a month's time.'

Because she'd known she would need the money, Phinn had not argued. But she never did work that full month. Because a couple of weeks later her world had fallen apart when her father, haring around the fields, showing a couple of his pals what a reconstructed quad bike could do, had upended it, gone over and under it—and come off worst.

He had died before Phinn could get to the hospital. Her mother had come to her straight away, and it had been Hester who, practical to the last, had made all the arrangements.

Devastated, having to look after Ruby had been the only thing that kept Phinn on anything resembling an even keel. And Ruby, as if she understood, would gently nuzzle into her neck and cuddle up close.

Her father had been popular but, when the day of his funeral had arrived, Phinn had never known he had so many friends. Or relatives, either. Aunts and uncles she had heard of but had seen only on the rarest of occasions had come to pay their respects. Even her cousin Leanne, a Hawkins several times removed, had arrived with her parents.

Leanne was tall, dark, pretty—and with eyes that seemed to instantly put a price on everything. But since the family antiques had been sold one by one after Hester had left, there had been very little at

Honeysuckle Farm that was worth the ink on a price ticket. Thereafter Leanne had behaved as decorously as her parents would wish.

That was she'd behaved very nicely until—to his credit—Ashley Allardyce had come to the funeral to pay his respects too. Phinn had not been feeling too friendly to him, but because she did not wish to mar the solemnity of the occasion with any undignified outburst—and in any case it was not him but his elder brother Ty who was the villain who went around instigating notices to quit—she'd greeted Ashley calmly, and politely thanked him for coming.

Leanne, noticing the expensive cut of the clothes the tall, fair-haired man was wearing, had immediately been attracted.

'Who's he?' she'd asked, sidling up when Ashley Allardyce had gone over to have a word with Nesta and Noel Jarvis, the tenants of Yew Tree Farm.

'Ashley Allardyce,' Phinn had answered, and, as she'd suspected, it had not ended there.

'He lives around here?'

'At Broadlands Hall.'

'That massive house in acres of grounds we passed on the way here?'

The next thing Phinn knew was that Leanne, on her behalf, had invited Ash Allardyce back to the farmhouse for refreshments.

Any notion Phinn might have had that he would

refuse the invitation had disappeared when she'd seen the look on his face. He was clearly captivated by her cousin!

The days that had followed had gone by in a numbed kind of shock for Phinn as she'd tried to come to terms with her father's death. Her mother had wanted her to go back to Gloucester and live with her and Clive. Phinn had found the idea unthinkable. Besides, there was Ruby.

Phinn had been glad to have Ruby to care for. Glad too that her cousin Leanne frequently drove the forty or so miles from her own home to see her.

In fact, by the time Christmas had come, Phinn had seen more of her cousin than she had during the whole of her life. Leanne had come, she would say, to spend time with her, so she would not be too lonely. But most of Leanne's time, from what Phinn had seen, was being spent with Ash Allardyce.

He had driven Leanne back to the farmhouse several times, and it had been as clear as day to Phinn that he was totally besotted with her cousin. Phinn, aware, if village talk were true, of his recent recovery from a breakdown, had only hoped that, vulnerable as he might still be, he would not end up getting hurt.

Because of a prior arrangement Leanne had spent Christmas skiing in Switzerland. Ash had gone too. For all Phinn knew his notice-to-quit-ordering brother might have made one of his rare visits to Broadlands and spent his Christmas there, but she hadn't seen him, and she'd been glad about that. The notice to quit had never been executed. It had not needed to be.

Since Phinn had no longer had a job, she'd no longer needed a car. Pride as much as anything had said she had to clear the rent arrears. She had formed a good opinion of Ash Allardyce, and did not think he would discuss their business with Leanne, but with him becoming closer and closer to her cousin, she had not wanted to risk it. She did not want any one member of her family to know that her father had died owing money. She'd sold her car and sent a cheque off to the lawyers.

Though by the time all accounts had been settled—and that included the vet's last bill—there had been little money remaining, and Phinn had known that she needed to get a job. A job that paid well. Yet Ruby had not been well enough to be left alone all day while she went off to work.

Then Leanne, on another visit, having voiced her opinion that Ash was close to 'popping the question' marriage-wise, had telephoned from Broadlands Hall to tell her not to wait up for her, that she was spending the night there.

It had been the middle of the following morning when Leanne, driving fast and furiously, had

screeched to a halt in the middle of the farmyard.
Phinn, leaving Ruby to go and find out what the rush
was about, had been confronted by a furious Leanne,
who'd demanded to know why she had not told her
that Broadlands Hall did *not* belong to Ash Allardyce.

'I—didn't think about it,' Phinn had answered de-
fensively. Coming to terms with her beloved father's
death and settling his affairs had taken precedence.
Who owned Broadlands Hall had not figured very
much, if at all, in her thinking at that particular time.
'I told you Ash had a brother. I'm sure I did.'

'Yes, you did!' Leanne snapped. 'And so did Ash.
But neither of you told me that Ash was the *younger*
brother—and that he doesn't own a *thing*!'

'Ah, you've met Ty Allardyce,' Phinn realised.
And discovered she was in the wrong about that too.

'No—more's the pity! He's always away somewhere—away abroad somewhere, and likely to be
away some time!' Leanne spat. 'It took that po-faced
housekeeper to delight in telling me that Ash was
merely the estate *manager*! Can you imagine it?
There was I, happily believing that any time soon I
was going to be mistress of Broadlands Hall, only
to be informed by some jumped-up housekeeper
that some poky farm cottage was more likely to be
the place for me. I don't think so!'

Phinn doubted that Mrs Starkey would have said
anything of the sort, but as Leanne raged on she

knew that once her cousin had realised that Ash was not the owner of Broadlands, it wouldn't have taken her very long to realise the ins and outs of it all.

'Come in and I'll make some coffee,' Phinn offered, aware that her cousin had suffered something of a shock.

'I'll come in. But only to collect what belongings of mine I've left here.'

'You—er—that sounds a bit—final?' Phinn suggested at last.

'You bet it is. Ten minutes and the village of Bishop Thornby has seen the last of me.'

'What about Ash?'

'What about him?' Leanne was already on her way into the house. 'I've told him—nicely—that I'm not cut out for country life. But if that hasn't given him something of a clue—tell him I said goodbye.'

Ash did not come looking for her cousin, and Honeysuckle Farm had settled into an unwanted quietness. With the exception of her mother, who frequently rang to check that she was all right, Phinn spoke with no one other than Ruby. Gradually Phinn came to see that she could do nothing about Leanne having dropped Ash like a hot brick once she had known that he was not the one with the money. Phinn knew that she could not stay on at the farm for very much longer. She had no interest in trying to make the farm a paying concern. If her father had not been able to do it with all his expertise, she did not see how she could. And, while she had grown to quite like the man whom Leanne had so unceremoniously dumped, the twenty-nine-year-old male might well be glad to see the back of anyone who bore the Hawkins name.

She had no idea if she was entitled to claim the tenancy, but if not, Ash would be quite within his rights to instigate having her thrown out.

Not wanting the indignity of that, Phinn wondered where on earth she could go. For herself she did not care very much where she went, but it was Ruby she had to think about.

To that end, Phinn took a walk down to the local riding school, run by Peggy Edmonds. And it turned out that going to see Peggy was the best thing she could have done. Because not only was Peggy able to house Ruby, she was even—unbelievably—able to offer Phinn a job. True, it wasn't much of a job, but with a place for Ruby assured, Phinn would have accepted anything.

Apparently Peggy was having a hard time battling with arthritis, and for over a year had been trying to find a buyer for what was now more of a stables than a riding school. But it seemed no one was remotely interested in making her an offer. With her arthritis so bad some days that it was all she could do to get out of bed, if Phinn would like to work as a stable hand, although Peggy could not pay very much, there was a small stall Ruby could have, and she could spend her days in the field with the other horses. As a bonus, there was a tiny flat above one of the stables doing nothing.

It was a furnished flat, with no room for farm-house furniture, and having been advised by the house clearers that she would have to pay *them* to empty the farmhouse, Phinn got her father's old friend Mickie Yates—an educated, eccentric but loveable jack-of-all-trades—to take everything away for her. It grieved her to see her father's piano go, but there was no space in the tiny flat for it.

So it was as January drew to a close that Phinn walked Ruby down to her new home and then, cutting through the spinney on Broadlands that she knew so well, Phinn took the key to the farmhouse up to the Hall.

Ash Allardyce was not in. Phinn was quite glad about that. After the way her cousin had treated him, dropping him cold like that, it might have been a touch embarrassing.

'I was very sorry to hear about your father, Phinn,' Mrs Starkey said, taking the keys from her.

'Thank you, Mrs Starkey,' Phinn replied quietly, and returned to the stables.

But almost immediately, barely having congratu-lated herself on how well everything was turning out—she had a job and Ruby was housed and fed—the sky started to fall in.

By late March it crash-landed.

Ruby—probably because of her previous ill-treatment—had always been timid, and needed peace and quiet, but was being bullied by the other much younger horses. Phinn took her on walks away from them as often as she could, but with her own work to do that was not as often as she would have liked.

Then, against all odds, Peggy found a buyer. A buyer who wanted to take possession as soon as it could possibly be achieved.

'I'll talk to her and see if there's any chance of her keeping you on,' Peggy said quickly, on seeing the look of concern on Phinn's face.

Phinn had met Geraldine Walton, a dark-haired woman of around thirty, who was not dissimilar to her cousin in appearance. She had met her on one of Geraldine's 'look around' visits, and had thought she seemed to have a bit of a hard edge to her—which made Phinn not too hopeful.

She was right not to be too hopeful, she soon discovered, for not only was there no job for her, neither was there a place for Ruby. And, not only that, Geraldine Walton was bringing her own staff and requested that Phinn kindly vacate the flat over the stable. As quickly as possible, please.

Now, Phinn, with the late-April sun streaming

through the window, looked round the stable flat and knew she had better think about packing up her belongings. Not that she had so very much to pack, but... Her eyes came to rest on the camera her mother, who had visited her last Sunday, had given her to return to Ash on Leanne's behalf.

Feeling a touch guilty that her mother's visit had been a couple of days ago now and she had done nothing about it, Phinn went and picked up the piece of photographic equipment. No time like the present—and she could get Ruby away from the other horses for a short while.

Collecting Ruby, Phinn walked her across the road and took the shortcut through the spinney. In no time she was approaching the impressive building that was Broadlands Hall.

Leanne Hawkins was not her favourite cousin just then. She had been unkind to Ash Allardyce, and, while Phinn considered that had little to do with her, she would much prefer that her cousin did her own dirty work. It seemed that her mother, who had no illusions about Leanne, had doubted that Ash would have got his expensive camera back at all were it not for the fact that he, still very much smitten, used it as an excuse to constantly telephone Leanne. Apparently Leanne could not be bothered to talk to him, and had asked Phinn to make sure he had his rotten camera back.

Phinn neared the Hall, hoping that it would again be Mrs Starkey who answered her ring at the door. Cowardly it might be, but she had no idea what she could say to Ash Allardyce. While she might be annoyed with Leanne, Leanne was still family, and family loyalty said that she could not say how shabbily she personally felt Leanne had treated him.

Phinn pulled the bell-tug, half realising that if Ash was still as smitten with Leanne as he had been, he was unlikely to say anything against her cousin that might provoke her having to stand up for her. She…

Phinn's thoughts evaporated as she heard the sound of someone approaching the stout oak door from within. Camera in one hand, Ruby's rein in the other, Phinn prepared to smile.

Then the front door opened and was pulled back—and her smile never made it. For it was not Mrs Starkey who stood there, and neither was it Ash Allardyce. Ash was fair-haired, but this man had ink-black hair—and an expression that was far from welcoming! He was tall, somewhere in his mid-thirties—and clearly not pleased to see her. She knew very well who he was—strangely, she had never forgotten his face. His good-looking face.

But his grim expression didn't let up when in one dark glance he took in the slender, delphinium-blue-eyed woman with a thick strawberry-blonde plait hanging over one shoulder, a camera in one hand and a rein in the other.

All too obviously he had recognised the camera, because his grim expression became grimmer if anything.

'And you are?' he demanded without preamble.

Yes, she, although having never been introduced to him, knew very well this was the man who was ultimately responsible for her father receiving that notice to quit. To quit the land that his family had farmed for generations. It passed her by just then that her father had done very little to keep the farm anything like the farm it had been for those generations.

'I'm Phinn Hawkins,' she replied—a touch belligerently it had to be admitted. 'I've—'

His eyes narrowed at her tone, though his tone was none too sweet either as he challenged shortly, 'What do you want on my land, Hawkins?'

And that made her mad. 'And you are?' she demanded, equally as sharp as he.

She was then forced to bear his tough scrutiny for several uncompromising seconds as he studied her. But, just when she was beginning to think she would have to run for his name, 'Tyrell Allardyce,' he supplied at last. And, plainly unused to repeating himself, 'What do you want?' he barked.

'Nothing you can supply, Allardyce!' she tossed back at him, refusing to be intimidated. Stretching out a hand, she offered the camera. 'Give this to your brother,' she ordered loftily. But at her mention of his brother, she was made to endure a look that should have turned her to stone.

'Get off my land!' he gritted between clenched teeth. 'And—' his tone was threatening '—don't *ever* set foot on it again!'

His look was so malevolent it took everything she had to keep from flinching. 'Huh!' she scorned, and, badly wanting to run as fast as she could away from this man and his menacing look, she turned Ruby about and ambled away from the Hall.

By the time she and Ruby had entered the spinney, some of Phinn's equilibrium had started to return. And a short while later she was starting to be thoroughly cross with herself that she had just walked away without acquainting him with a few of the do's and don'ts of living in the country.

Who did he think he was, for goodness' sake? She had *always* roamed the estate lands freely. True, there were certain areas she knew she was not supposed to trespass over. But she had been brought up using the Broadlands fields and acres as her right of way! She was darn sure she wasn't going to alter that now!

The best thing Ty Allardyce could do, she fumed, would be to take himself and his big city ways back to London. And stay there! And good riddance to him too! She had now met him, but she hoped she never had the misfortune of seeing his forbidding, disagreeable face ever again!

CHAPTER TWO

SOMEHOW, in between worrying about finding a new home for herself and Ruby, Phinn could not stop thoughts of Ty Allardyce from intruding. Though, as the days went by and the weekend passed and another week began, Phinn considered that to have the man so much in and out of her mind was not so surprising. How *dared* he order her off his land?

Well, tough on him! It was a lovely early May day—what could be nicer than to take Ruby and go for a walk? Leaving the flat, Phinn went down to collect her. But, before she could do more than put a halter on the mare, Geraldine Walton appeared from nowhere to waylay her. Phinn knew what was coming before Geraldine so much as opened her mouth. She was not mistaken.

'I'm sorry to have to be blunt, Phinn,' Geraldine began, 'but I really do need the stable flat by the end of the week.'

'I'm working on it,' Phinn replied, at her wits'

end. She had phoned round everywhere she could think of, but nobody wanted her *and* Ruby. And Ruby fretted if she was away from her for very long, so no way was Ruby going anywhere without her. Phinn had wondered about them both finding some kind of animal sanctuary, willing to take them both, but then again, having recently discovered that Ruby was unhappy with other horses around, she did not want to give her ailing mare more stress. 'Leave it with me,' she requested, and a few minutes later crossed the road on to Broadlands property and walked Ruby through the spinney, feeling all churned up at how it would break her heart—and Ruby's—to have to leave her anywhere.

The majestic Broadlands Hall was occasionally visible through gaps in the trees in the small wood, but Phinn was certain that Ty Allardyce would by now be back in London, beavering away at whatever it was financiers beavered away at. Though just in case, as they walked through fields that bordered the adjacent grounds and gardens they had always walked through—or in earlier days ridden through—she made sure that she and Ruby were well out of sight, should anyone at the Hall be looking out.

Hoping not to meet him, if London's loss was Bishops Thornby's gain and he *was* still around, Phinn moved on, and was taking a stroll near the pool where she and her father had so often swum when she did bump into an Allardyce. It was Ash.

It would have been quite natural for Phinn to pause, say hello, make some sort of polite conversation. But she was so shaken by the change in the man from the last time she had seen him that she barely recognised him, and all words went from her. Ash looked terrible!

'Hello, Ash,' she did manage, but was unwilling to move on. He looked positively ill, and she searched for something else to say. 'Did you get your camera all right?' she asked, and could have bitten out her tongue. Was her cousin responsible in any way for this dreadful change in him? Surely not? Ash looked grey, sunken-eyed, and at least twenty pounds lighter!

'Yes, thanks,' he replied, no smile, his eyes dull and lifeless. But, brightening up a trifle, 'Have you seen Leanne recently?' he asked.

Fleetingly she wondered if Ash, so much in love with Leanne, might have found cause to suspect she was money-minded and, not wanting to lose her, not told her that it was his brother who owned Broadlands. But she had not seen her cousin since the day Leanne had learned that Ash was not the one with the money and had so callously dropped him.

'Leanne—er—doesn't come this way—er—now,' Phinn answered, feeling awkward, her heart aching for this man who seemed bereft that his love wanted nothing more to do with him.

'I don't suppose she has anywhere to stay now that you're no longer at Honeysuckle Farm,' he commented, and as he began to stroll along with her, Phinn did not feel able to tell him that the only time Leanne had ever shown an interest in staying any length of time at the farm had been when she'd had her sights set on being mistress of Broadlands Hall. 'I'm sorry that you had to leave, by the way,' Ash stated.

And her heart went out to this gaunt man whose clothes were just about hanging on him. 'I couldn't have stayed,' she replied, and, hoping to lighten his mood, 'I don't think I'd make a very good farmer.' Not sure which was best for him—to talk of Leanne or not to talk of Leanne—she opted to enquire, 'Have you found a new tenant for Honeysuckle yet?'

'I'm—undecided what to do,' Ash answered, and suddenly the brilliant idea came to Phinn that, if he had not yet got a tenant for the farm, maybe she and Ruby could go back and squat there for a while; the weather was so improved and it was quite warm for early summer. Ruby would be all right there. But Ash was going on. 'I did think I might take it over myself, but I don't seem able to—er—make decisions on anything just at the moment.'

Ash's confession took the squatting idea from Phinn

momentarily. Leanne again! How *could* she have been so careless of this sensitive man's fine feelings?

'I'm sure you and Honeysuckle would be good for each other—if that's what you decide to do,' Phinn replied gently.

And Ash gave a shaky sigh, as if he had wandered off for a moment. 'I think I'd like to work outdoors. Better than an indoor job anyway.' And, with a self-deprecating look, 'I tried a career in the big business world.'

'You didn't like it?'

He shook his head. 'I don't think I'm the academic type. That's more Ty's forte. He's the genius in the family when it comes to the cut and thrust of anything like that.' Ash seemed to wander off again for a moment or two, and then, like the caring kind of person he was, he collected himself to enquire, 'You're settled in your new accommodation, Phinn?'

'Well—er…' Phinn hesitated. It was unthinkable that she should burden him with her problems, but the idea of squatting back at Honeysuckle was picking at her again.

'You're not settled?' Ash took up.

'Geraldine—she's the new owner of the stables— wants to do more on the riding school front, and needs my flat for a member of her staff,' Phinn began.

'But you work there too?'

'Well, no, actually. Er...'

'You're out of a job *and* a home?' Ash caught on.

'Ruby and I have until the end of this week,' Phinn said lightly, and might well have put in a pitch for his permission to use Honeysuckle as a stop-gap measure—only she chanced to look across to him, and once more into his dull eyes, and she simply did not have the heart. He appeared to have the weight of the world on his shoulders, and she just could not add to his burden.

'Ruby?' he asked. 'I didn't know you had a child?'

He looked so concerned that Phinn rushed in to reassure him. 'I don't.' She patted Ruby's shoulder. 'This lovely girl is Ruby.'

His look of concern changed to one of relief. 'I don't know much about horses, but...'

Phinn smiled. There wasn't a better-groomed horse anywhere, but there was no mistaking Ruby's years. 'She's getting on a bit now, and her health isn't so good, but—' She broke off when, turning to glance at Ruby, she saw a male figure in the distance, coming their way at a fast pace. Uh-oh! Ash hadn't seen him, but she didn't fancy a row with Ty Allardyce in front of him. 'That reminds me—we'd better be off. It's time for Ruby's medication,' she said. 'Nice to see you again, Ash. Bye.'

And with that, unfortunately having to go towards

the man she was starting to think of as 'that dastardly Ty Allardyce', she led Ruby away.

'Bye, Phinn,' Ash bade her, seeing nothing wrong with her abrupt departure as he went walking on in the opposite direction.

With Ruby not inclined to hurry, there was no way Phinn could avoid the owner of the Hall, who also happened to be the owner of the land she was trespassing on. They were on a collision course!

Several remarks entered her head before Ty Allardyce was within speaking distance. Though when he was but a few yards from her—and looking tough with it—her voice nearly failed her. But in her view she had done nothing wrong.

'Not back in London yet, I see!' she remarked, more coolly than she felt.

'Why, you—' Ty Allardyce began angrily, but checked his anger, to demand, 'What have you been saying to my brother?'

While part of Phinn recognised that his question had come from concern for Ash, she did not like Ty Allardyce and never would. 'What's it got to do with you?' she challenged loftily.

His dark grey eyes glinted, and she would not have been all that surprised had she felt his hands around her throat—he looked quite prepared to attempt to throttle her! 'It has everything to do with me,' he controlled his ire to inform her shortly. 'You Hawkins women don't give a damn who you hurt...'

'Hawkins women!' she exclaimed, starting to get angry herself. 'What the devil do you mean by that?'

'Your reputation precedes you!'

'Reputation?'

'Your father was devastated when your mother dumped him. My—'

Mother *dumped* him! Phinn was on the instant furious, but somehow managed to control her feeling of wanting to throttle *him* to butt in with mock sarcasm. 'Oh, really, Allardyce. You truly must try to stop listening to village gossip...'

'You're saying he *wasn't* devastated? That his reason for not paying the rent had nothing at all to do with the fact that your mother took up with some other man and left your father a total wreck?'

Oh, Lord. That quickly squashed her anger. She did not doubt that her father *had* been capable of conveying his marriage break-up as his reason without exactly saying so. But his marriage break-up had had nothing to do with him not paying the rent—the fact the rent had not been paid had been more to do with her mother's hands no longer being on the purse strings. It was true, Phinn had discovered, that the rent had only ceased to be paid when her mother had left.

'What went on between my father and mother is

nothing at all to do with you!' Phinn stated coldly, wanting her anger back. 'It's none of your business…'

'When it comes to my brother I'll make it my business. You've seen him! You've seen how gutted he is that your cousin ditched him the same way your mother ditched your father. I'm not having another Hawkins anywhere near him. Get off my land and stay off it! And,' he went on icily when she opened her mouth, 'don't give me "Huh!" This is your last warning. If I catch you trespassing again I'll have you in court before you can blink!'

'Have you quite finished?'

'I hope never to have to speak to you again,' he confirmed. 'You just leave my brother alone.'

'Be glad to!' she snapped, her eyes darkening. 'I don't know what Bishops Thornby ever did to deserve the likes of you, but for my money it was the worst day's work he ever did when old Mr Caldicott sold this estate to you!' Thereafter ignoring him, she addressed the mare. 'Come on, Rubes. You're much too sweet to have to stand and listen to this loathsome man!'

With that, she put her nose in the air and saun-tered off. Unfortunately, because of Ruby's slow gait, she was prevented from marching off as she would have wished. She hoped the dastardly Allardyce got the idea anyway.

Her adrenalin was still pumping when she took Ruby back to her stall. Honestly, that man!

Phinn wasted no time the next day. Once she had attended to all Ruby's needs, she made the long walk up to Honeysuckle Farm. She walked into the familiar farmyard, but, having been away from the farm for around three months, as she stood and stared about she was able to see it for the first time from a different perspective. She had to admit to feeling a little shaken.

Rusting pieces of machinery littered the yard, and there was a general air of neglect everywhere. Which there would be, she defended her father. Had he lived he would have repaired and sold on the rusting and clapped out pieces. Had he lived…

Avoiding thoughts that some of the machinery had lain there rusting for years, and not just since last October when her father had died, and the fact that the place had become to be more and more run-down over the years but that until today she had never noticed it, Phinn went to take a look at the old barn that had used to be Ruby's home.

The secure door latch had broken years ago, but, as her father had so laughingly said, they had nothing worth stealing so why bother repairing it? That his logic was a touch different from most people's had all been part of the man she had adored. It hadn't been that he was idle, he'd just thought on a different and more pleasurable level.

The barn smelt musty, and not too pleasant. But

it was a sunny day, so Phinn propped the doors open wide and went in. Everything about the place screamed, *no!* But what alternative did she have? Ruby, her timid darling Ruby, would by far prefer to be up here in the old barn than where she was. Had Phinn had any idea of Ruby's fear of the other horses she would never have taken her there in the first place. Too late now to be wise after the event!

Looking for plus points, Phinn knew that Ruby would be better on her own, away from the younger horses. As well as being timid, Ruby was a highly sensitive mare, and with their mutual attachment to each other, Honeysuckle was the best place for them. Another plus: it was dry—mainly. And there was a field. Several, in fact. Overgrown with weeds and clutter, but in Phinn's view it wouldn't take her long to clear it and put up some sort of temporary fencing.

With matters pertaining to Ruby sorted out in her head, Phinn crossed the yard, found a ladder, and was able to gain entry into the farmhouse by climbing up to a bedroom window. Forcing the window did not take a great deal of effort, and once in she went through to what had once been her own bedroom.

It smelt musty, but then it hadn't been used in months. There was no electricity, so she would have to do without heat or light, but looking on the brighter side she felt sure that Mickie Yates would cart her few belongings up for her. Mickie had been a good friend of her father's, and she knew she could rely on him not to tell anyone that she was squatting—trespassing, Allardyce would call it if he knew—at Honeysuckle.

Phinn left Honeysuckle Farm endeavouring not to think what her mother's reaction to her plan would be. Appalled would not cover it.

By Thursday of that week Phinn was trying to tell herself that she felt quite enthusiastic about her proposed move. She had been to see Mickie Yates and found him in his workshop, up to his elbows in muck and grease, but with the loveliest smile of welcome on his face for her.

Whatever he thought when she asked for use of him and one of his vehicles to transport her cases and horse equipment on Friday she did not know. All he'd said was, 'After three suit you, Phinn?'

She knew he would be having his 'lunch' in the Cat and Drum until two fifty-five. 'Lovely thank you, Mickie,' she had replied.

It was a surprisingly hot afternoon, and Phinn, not certain when she would be in the village again, decided to walk Ruby to the village farrier. It would be even hotter at the forge, so she changed out of her more usual jeans and top, exchanging them for a thin, loose-fitting sleeveless cotton dress. Donning some sandals, she felt certain that by now grumpy Allardyce *must* be back in London, where he surely more particularly belonged.

Perhaps after their visit to Idris Owen, the farrier and blacksmith, a man who could turn his hand to anything and who had been another friend of her father's, Phinn and Ruby might take another stroll in the shady spinney.

Knowing that she should be packing her belongings prior to tomorrow's move, she left her flat—and on the way out bumped into Geraldine Walton. Geraldine seemed difficult to miss these days. But for once Phinn was not anxious about meeting her.

'You do know I shall want the flat on Saturday?' Geraldine began a touch stiffly, before Phinn could say a word.

'You shall have it,' she replied. 'Ruby and I are moving tomorrow.'

Geraldine's severe look lightened. 'You are? Oh, good! Er…I hope you've found somewhere—suitable?'

Phinn ignored the question in her voice. Villages being villages, she knew she could not hope to keep her new address secret for very long. But, her new address being part of the Broadlands Estate, the longer it was kept from Ty Allardyce the better. Not that she was aware if Geraldine even knew him, but there was no point in inviting more of his wrath—and a *definite* court summons—if they were acquainted.

'Most suitable,' she replied with a smile, and, aiming to make the best of what life was currently throwing at her, she went to collect Ruby.

Idris greeted Phinn with the same warm smile she had received from Mickie Yates. Idris was somewhere around fifty, a huge mountain of a man, with a heart as big. 'How's my best girl?' he asked, as he always did. No matter what time of day she visited, he always seemed to have a pint of beer on the go. 'Help yourself,' he offered, as he checked Ruby's hooves and shoes.

Phinn still did not like beer any better than she had when she had first tasted it. But it was blisteringly hot in there, and to take a healthy swig of his beer—as encouraged so to do in the past by her father—was now traditional. She picked up the pot and drank to her father's memory.

When he was done, Idris told her that she owed him nothing, and she knew he would be upset if she insisted on paying him. So, thanking him, she and Ruby left the smithy and headed for the small wood.

Keeping a watchful eye out for the elder Allardyce, Phinn chatted quietly to Ruby all the way through the spinney, and Ruby, having a good day for once, talked back, nodded and generally kept close.

Once out of the shaded spinney, they strolled towards the pool with the heat starting to beat down on them. Ruby loved the warmth, and Phinn, catching a glimpse of the pool, had started to think in terms of what a wonderful day for a swim.

No, I shouldn't. She attempted to ignore that part of her that was seeing no earthly reason why she shouldn't take a quick dip. She glanced about—no one in sight. They ambled on, reaching the pool and some more trees, and all the while Phinn fought down the demon temptation.

She would never know whether or not she would have given in to that demon had not something happened just then that drove all other thoughts from her head. Suddenly in the stillness she heard a yell of alarm. It came from the dark side of the pool. It was the cry of someone in trouble!

In moments she had run down the bank and did not have to search very far to see who was in trouble—and what the trouble was! Oh, God! Her blood ran cold. Across from the shallow end was a dark area called the Dark Pool—because that was precisely what it was: dark. Dark because it was overhung with trees and the sun never got to it. Not only was it dark, it was deep, and it was icy. And everyone knew that you must *never* attempt to swim there. Only someone *was* in there! Ash Allardyce! He was flailing about and quite clearly close to drowning!

All Phinn knew then was that she had to get to him quickly. There was a small bridge spanning the narrow part of the pool, but that was much farther down. And time was of the essence. There was no time to think, only time to act. Her father had taught her lifesaving, and had taught her well. Up until then it was a skill she had never needed to use.

Even as these thoughts were flashing thought her mind Phinn was kicking off her sandals and pulling her dress over her head. Knowing she had to get to Ash, and fast, and all before she could query the wisdom of what she was doing, Phinn was running for the water and taking a racing dive straight in.

After having been so hot, the water felt icy, but there was no time to think about that now. Only time to get to Ash. Executing a sprinting crawl, Phinn reached him in no time flat, gasped a warning, 'Stay still or you'll kill us both,' turned him onto his back and, glad for the moment that he was twenty pounds lighter than he had been, towed him to the nearest bank, which was now on the opposite side from where she had first seen him.

How long he had been struggling she had no idea. 'Cramp!' he managed to gasp, and managed to sit up, head down, his arms on his knees, exhausted, totally drained of energy.

It had all happened so quickly, but now that it was over Phinn felt pretty drained herself, and had an idea she knew pretty much how a mother must feel when she had just found her lost child. 'You should have had more sense,' she berated him with what breath she could find. 'Everybody *knows* you don't swim in *that* part of the pool.' Suddenly she was feeling inexplicably weepy. Shock, she supposed. Then she remembered Ruby, and looked to the other bank. She could not see her. 'I'll be back,' she said, and took off.

Not to swim this time—she didn't feel like going back in there in a hurry—but to run down to the small bridge. It fleetingly crossed her mind as she ran to wonder if Ash had perhaps been a touch suicidal to have chosen to swim where he had. Then she recalled he had said he'd had a cramp, and she began to feel better about leaving him. She had been brought up *knowing* that a deep shelf had been ex- cavated on that side of the pool for some reason that was now lost in the mists of time. The water was deep there—nobody knew how deep, but so deep as to never heat up, and was regarded locally with the greatest respect. Ash, who hadn't been brought up in the area, could not possibly have known unless someone had told him. Well, he knew now!

Phinn ran across the bridge, and as she did so she saw with relief that Ruby had not wandered off and that she was quite safe. Phinn's relief was short- lived, however, because in that same glance she saw none other than Ty Allardyce. Phinn came to an abrupt halt.

Oh, help! He was facing away from her and had not yet spotted her. He was looking about—perhaps searching for his brother? He was close to Ruby. Then Phinn saw that he was not only close to Ruby, he had hold of her rein. Phinn knew then that it was not his brother he was searching for but Ruby's owner—and that Ruby's owner was in deep trouble!

As if aware of someone behind him, Ty Allardyce turned round. Turned and, as if he could not believe his eyes, stared at her.

And that was when Phinn became aware of how she was dressed—or rather *undressed*. A quick glance down proved that she was as good as naked! Standing there in her wet underwear she was conscious that her waterlogged bra and briefs were now transparent, the pink tips of her breasts hardened and clearly visible to the man staring at her.

Her face glowed a fiery red. 'A gentleman would turn his back,' she hissed, with what voice she could find.

Ty Allardyce favoured her with a hard stare, but was in no hurry to turn around. 'So he would—for a lady,' he drawled.

Phinn wanted to hit him, but she wasn't going any closer. And he, surveying her from her soggy braided hair down to the tip of her bare toes, took his time, his insolent gaze moving back up her long, long shapely legs, thighs and belly. By this time her arms were crossed in front of her body. Strangely, it was only when his glance rested on her fiercely blushing face that he gave her the benefit of the term 'lady' and, while still holding Ruby's rein, turned his back on her.

In next to no time Phinn had retrieved her dress and sandals and, having been careless how her dress had landed, found that her hands were shaking when she went to turn it right side out.

But once she had her dress over her shoulders, she felt her former spirit returning. She had to go close up to him to take Ruby's rein, and, as embarrassed as she felt, she somehow managed to find an impudent, 'Lovely day for a dip!'

His reply was to turn and favour her with one of his hard stares. It seemed to her as if he was deciding whether or not to pick her up and throw her in for another dip.

Attempting to appear casual, she moved to the other side of Ruby. Not a moment too soon, she realised, as, not caring for her insolence, 'That's it!' he rapped, his eyes angry on her by now much paler face. 'I've warned you twice. You'll receive notice from my lawyers in the morning.'

'You have my address?' she enquired nicely—and felt inclined to offer him her new address; but at his hard-eyed expression she thought better of it.

Ty Allardyce drew one very harsh, long-suffering

breath. 'Enough!' he snarled. 'If you're not on your way inside the next ten seconds, I shall personally be escorting you and that flea-bitten old nag off my land!'

'Flea-bitten!' she gasped. How *dared* he?

'Now!' he threatened, making a move to take Ruby's rein from her.

'Leave her alone!' Phinn threatened back, her tone murderous as she knocked his hand away. She was not sure yet that she wasn't going to hit him— he was well and truly asking for it! Emotional tears sprang to her eyes.

Tears he spotted, regardless that she'd managed to hold them back and prevent them from falling. 'Of for G—' he began impatiently. And, as if more impatient with himself than with her, because her shining eyes had had more effect on him than her murderous threat, 'Clear off, stay off—and leave my brother alone!'

Only then did Phinn remember Ash. A quick glance to the other side of the pool showed he had recovered and was getting to his feet, which told her she could safely leave him. 'Wouldn't touch either of you with a bargepole,' she told Ty loftily, and turned Ruby about and headed in the direction of the spinney.

With everything that had taken place playing back in her mind, Phinn walked on with Ruby. She had no idea how long it was since she had seen Ash in trouble—ten perhaps fifteen minutes? A glance to her watch showed that it did not care much for under-water activity and would never be the same again.

She felt ashamed that she had very nearly cried in front of that brute. *Flea-bitten old nag!* But she started to accept—now that she was away from him, away from the pool—that perhaps she had started to feel a bit of reaction after first seeing Ash in difficulties, taking a header in to get him out, and then, to top it all, being confronted by Ty Allardyce.

Yes, it must be shock, she realised. There was no other explanation for her thinking, as she had at the time, that Ty Allardyce had been sensitive to a woman's tears.

Sensitive! She must be in shock still! That insensitive brute didn't have a sensitive bone in his body! How could he have? He had actually called her darling Rubes a flea-bitten old nag! Oh, how she wished she had hit him.

Well, one thing was for sure. She would take great delight in marking any lawyer's letter that arrived for her tomorrow 'address unknown', before she happily popped it in the post box to be sent speedily straight back whence it came!

# CHAPTER THREE

AS SOON as she had settled Ruby, Phinn went to the stable flat, stripped off, showered and washed the pool out of her hair. Donning fresh underwear, a pair of shorts and a tee shirt, she wrapped a towel around her hair and made herself a cup of tea. She admitted that she was still feeling a little shaken up by the afternoon's events.

Although, on reflection, she wasn't sure which had disturbed her the most: the unexpectedness of coming upon Ash Allardyce without warning and her efforts to get the drowning man to the bank, or the fact that his hard-nosed brother had so insolently stood there surveying her when she had stood as near to naked as if it made no difference.

He quite obviously thought she had taken advantage of the hot weather to strip off to her underwear and have a swim in waters that belonged to his lands. And he hadn't liked that, had he? He with his, 'Clear off, stay off—and leave my brother alone!'

She cared not whether Ash ever told him the true facts of her swim. She had always swum there—weather permitting. Though she did recall one marvellously hysterical time when it had come on to rain while she and her father had been swimming, and he had declared that since they couldn't get any wetter they might as well carry on swimming.

Barefooted, she padded to get another towel and, because her long hair took for ever to dry naturally, she towelled it as dry as she could, brushed it out, and left her hair hanging down over her shoulders to dry when it would.

Meantime, she packed her clothes and placed a couple of suitcases near the door, ready for when Mickie Yates would come round at three tomorrow afternoon. Now she had better start packing away her china, and the few ornaments and mementoes she had been unable to part with from her old home.

The mantelpiece was bare, and she had just finished clearing the shelves, when someone came knocking at her door. Geraldine coming to check that she was truly leaving tomorrow, Phinn supposed, padding to the door. She pulled it open—only to receive another shock!

Finding herself staring up into the cool grey eyes of Ty Allardyce, Phinn was for the moment struck dumb. And as he stared into her darkening blue eyes, he seemed in no hurry to start a conversation either.

The fact that she was now dry, and clad in shorts and top, as opposed to dripping and in her underwear as the last time he had studied her, made Phinn feel no better. She saw his glance flick to her long strawberry-blonde hair, free from its plait, and pulled herself sharply together.

'As I live and breathe—the lesser-spotted superior Allardyce,' she waded in. 'Now who's trespassing?'

To his credit, he took her remark equably. 'I should like to talk to you,' he said for openers.

'Tough! Get off my—er…' *damn* '…doorstep.'

His answer to her command was to ignore it. And, much to her annoyance, he did no more than push his way into what had been her sitting room-cum-kitchen.

'You're leaving tomorrow?' he suggested, his eyes moving from her suitcases to the boxes of packed teacups, plates and ornaments.

Phinn fought to find some sharp comeback, but couldn't find one. 'Yes,' she replied, belligerent because she saw no reason to be any other way with this man who wanted to curtail her right to use and respect his grounds as her own.

'Where are you going?' he enquired, and she hated it that, when she could never remember any man making her blush before, this man seemed to be able to do so without the smallest effort.

'I—er…' she mumbled, and turned away from

him, walking towards the window in a vain hope
that he had not noticed she had gone red.

'You're looking guilty about something,' he commented, closing the door and coming further into the
room, adding, as she turned to face him, 'I do hope,
Miss Hawkins, that I'm not going to wake up on
Saturday morning and find you camping out on my
front lawn?'

The idea amused her, and despite herself her lips
twitched. And she supposed that 'Miss Hawkins'
was one better than the plain 'Hawkins' he had used
before. But she quickly stamped down on what she
considered must be a quirk in her sense of humour.
'To be honest, that was something I hadn't thought
of doing,' she replied.

'But?'

This man was as sharp as a tack! He knew full
well that there was a 'but'. 'But nothing,' she replied
stiffly. She didn't want a spanner thrown into the
works of her arrangements at this late stage. But Ty
Allardyce continued to look back at her, his mind
fully at work, she didn't doubt. 'Well, I've things
to do. Thank you for popping by,' she said coolly,
moving towards the door, knowing full well that this
wasn't a social call, but at a loss to know what else
one would call it.

'What you would need,' he stated thoughtfully,
his glance lighting briefly on her long length of leg

in the short shorts, 'is somewhere you can lay your head, and somewhere where at the same time you can stable that—'

'Her name is Ruby,' Phinn cut in, starting to bridle. 'The flea-bitten old nag, as you so delight-fully called her, is Ruby.'

'I apologise,' he replied, and that surprised her so much she could only stand there and blink. And blink again when he went on. 'Do you know, I really don't think I can allow you to go back to Honeysuckle Farm? It—'

'How did you know I intended to go there?' she gasped in amazement. Surely Mickie hadn't...?

He hadn't. 'I didn't know. That is I wasn't sure until you just this minute confirmed it.'

'Clever devil!' she sniffed. Then quickly realised that she was in a hole that looked like getting bigger and bigger—if she couldn't do something about it. 'Look,' she said, taking a deep breath, 'I know you're cross with me—full-time, permanently. But I wouldn't harm the place. I'd—'

'Out of the question,' he cut in forthrightly.

'Why?' she demanded, when common sense told her she was going about this in totally the wrong way.

'There aren't any services up there for a start.'

'I won't need any. I've got a supply of candles. And it's too warm for me to need heating. And...'

'And what if it rains and the roof leaks?'

'It doesn't. I was up there the other…' Oh, grief—just think before you speak!

'You've been inside?' he demanded. 'You still have a key?'

'Yes and no.' He looked impatient. She hated him. 'Yes, I've been inside. And, no, I haven't got a key.'

'You got in—how?'

It wouldn't have taken much for her to tell him to get lost, but she was still hopeful of moving back to Honeysuckle Farm tomorrow. 'I—um—got in through one of the bedroom windows,' she confessed.

'You climbed in…' He shook his head slightly, as if hardly believing this female. 'You include breaking and entering in your list of skills?'

'I'm desperate!' she exclaimed shortly. 'Ruby's not well, and—' She broke off. Damn the man. It must still be shock—she was feeling weepy again. She turned her back on him, wanting to order him out, but ready to swallow her pride and plead with him if she had to.

But then, to her astonishment and to her disbelieving ears, she discovered that she did not have to plead with him at all. Because, staggeringly, Ty Allardyce was stating, 'I think we can find you somewhere a bit better than the present condition of Honeysuckle Farm to live.'

Things like that just did not happen for people like Delphinnium Hawkins—well, not lately anyhow. She stared at him open-mouthed. He didn't like her. She definitely didn't like him. So why? 'For Ruby too?' she asked slowly.

'For Ruby too,' he confirmed.

'Where?' she asked, not believing it but desperately wanting to.

'Up at the Hall. You could come and live with—'

'Now, wait a minute!' she cut in bluntly. 'I don't know what you think I am, but let me tell—'

'Oh, for heaven's sake!' He cut her off irritably. Then, taking a steadying breath, let her know that she could not be more wrong. 'While I'll acknowledge you may have the best pair of legs I've seen in a while—and the rest of you isn't so bad either…' She refused to visibly blench, because he must be referring to the sight he'd had of her well-proportioned breasts, pink tips protruding. 'I have better things to do with my free time than want to bed one of the village locals!'

Village locals! Well, that put her in her place. 'You should be so lucky!' she sniffed. But, with Ruby in mind, she could not afford to be offended for very long. 'Why would you want me living up at the Hall?'

'Shall we sit down?' he suggested.

Perhaps her legs would be less on display if she sat down. Phinn moved to one chair and he went and occupied the other one. Then, waiting until she looked ready to listen, he began, 'You did me a service today that will render me forever in your debt.'

'Oh, I wouldn't say that.' She shrugged off his comment, but realised then that he now knew all about his brother's attack of cramp. 'See where trespassing will get you!'

'Had you not trespassed…had you not been there—' He broke off. 'It doesn't bear thinking about,' he said, his jaw clenching as if he was getting on top of some emotion.

'Ash wasn't to know that that part of the pool is treacherous. That you have to stick strictly to the shallows if you want to swim,' she attempted lightly.

But Ty was not making light of it, and seemed to know precisely how tragic the consequences could have been. 'But you knew it. And even so—according to Ash when he was able to reflect back—you did the finest and fastest running racing dive he'd ever seen. He said that you dived straight in, not a moment's hesitation, to get him out.'

'Had you arrived a little earlier than you did, I'd have happily let *you* go in,' she murmured, starting to feel a touch embarrassed. With relief she saw, unexpectedly, the way Ty's mouth had picked up at the corners and knew her attempt at humour—her intimation that she would quite happily have let him take his chances on drowning—had reached his own sense of humour.

Though he was not to be drawn away from the seriousness of their discussion it seemed, because he continued. 'You saved my brother's life with not a thought for your own, when you knew full well about that treacherous side of the pool. You went straight in.'

'I did stop to kick my sandals off and yank my dress over my head,' she reminded him, again attempting to make light of it.

But then wished that she hadn't, when grey eyes looked straight into hers and he commented, 'I have not forgotten,' adding in a low murmur, 'I doubt I ever shall. I thought you'd been skinny-dipping at first.' He brought himself up short. 'Anyhow, Ash—for all he's lost a lot of weight—is still quite heavy. Had he struggled, you could both have drowned. Dear God—' He broke off again, swallowing down his anguish.

Seeing his mental torment, and even if she didn't like him, Phinn just had to tell him, 'Ash didn't struggle. It wasn't an attempt at suicide, if that's what you think. It was cramp, pure and simple. The water's icy there. There's a deep shelf… He…'

Ty Allardyce smiled then. It was the first smile he had ever directed at her and her heart went thump. He was *so* handsome! 'I know he wasn't attempting to take his own life,' he agreed. 'But from that remark it's obvious that you've observed that my brother is…extremely vulnerable at the moment.'

Phinn nodded. Yes, she knew that. 'I know you blame me in part, but truthfully there was nothing I could have done to stop it. I mean, I didn't know that Leanne would—er—break it off with him the way she did.'

'Perhaps I was unfair to blame you,' Ty conceded. 'But to get to other matters—Ash tells me you have a problem, with no job and no home for you and your—Ruby. I,' he stated, 'am in a position to offer you both.'

A home *and* a job? Things like this just did *not* happen. 'I don't want your charity!' she erupted.

'My God, you're touchy!' Ty bit back. But then, looking keenly at her, 'You're not…? Are you in shock? Starting to suffer after-effects from what happened today?'

Phinn rather thought she might be. And—oh, grief—she was feeling weepy again. 'Look, can you go back to being nasty again? I can cope with you better when you're being a brute!'

He wasn't offended, but nor was he reverting to being the brute that always put her on her mettle. 'Have you any family near?' he asked, quite kindly.

This—his niceness—was unnerving. So unnerving that she found she was actually telling him. 'My mother lives in Gloucester, but…'

'I'll drive you there,' he decided. 'Get—'

'I'm not—' she started to protest.

'Stop being argumentative,' he ordered. 'You're

in no condition to drive.' And, when she would have protested further, 'You'll probably get the shakes any minute now,' he went on. 'It will be safer all round if I'm at the wheel.'

Honestly—this man! 'Will you stop trying to bulldoze me along?' she flared crossly. 'Yes, I feel a bit shaken,' she admitted. 'But nothing I can't cope with. And I'm not going anywhere.'

'If I can't take you to your mother, I'll take you back to the Hall with me.' He ignored what she had just said.

'No, you won't!' she exploded, going on quickly. 'Apart from anything else, I'm not leaving Ruby. She's—'

'She'll be all right until you pick her up tomorrow,' he countered. 'You can—'

'You can stop right there. Just *stop* it!' she ordered. 'I'm not going anywhere today. And when I do go, Ruby goes with me.'

Ty Allardyce observed the determined look of her. And, plainly a man who did not take defeat lightly, he gave her a stern expression of his own. 'I'll make you some tea,' he said, quite out of nowhere—and she just had to burst out laughing. That just made him stare at her.

'I'm sorry,' she apologized, and, quickly sobering, 'I know tea is said to be good for shock, but I've had some tea and I don't want more. And please,' she went on before he could argue, 'can we just accept that I know you truly appreciate my towing Ash back onto terra firma this afternoon and then forget all about it?'

Steady grey eyes bored into her darkened blue ones. 'You want to go back to me being the brute up at the Hall who keeps trying to turf you off his land?'

Phinn nodded, starting to feel better suddenly. 'And I'll go back to being the—er—village local…' Her lips twitched, and she saw his do the same before they both sobered, and she went on. 'The village local who thinks you've one heck of a nerve daring to stop me from doing things I've always done on Broadlands land.'

He nodded, but informed her, 'You're still not going back to Honeysuckle Farm to live.'

'Oh, come on!' she exclaimed. 'I have to leave here tomorrow. Geraldine wants the flat for a member of her staff, and I've promised I'll move out.'

'That, as I've mentioned, is not a problem. There's a home and a job waiting for you at the Hall.'

'And a home for Ruby too?'

'At the moment the stable is being used for storage, but you can clear it out tomorrow. It's dry in there and—'

'It has water?'

'It has water,' he confirmed.

'You have other horses?' she asked quickly, and, at his questioning look, 'Ruby's a kind of rescue mare. She was badly treated and has a timid nature. Other horses tend to gang up on her.'

'You've no need to worry on that score. Ruby will have an idyllic life. There's a completely fenced-off paddock too that she can use.'

Phinn knew the paddock, if it was the one she was thinking of. As well as being shaded in part by trees, it also had a large open-ended shed a horse could wander into if it became too hot.

All of a sudden Phinn felt weepy again. She would be glad when this shock was over and done with! Oh, it did sound idyllic. Oh, Ruby, my darling. 'This is a—a permanent job?' she questioned. 'I mean, you're not going to turf me out after a week?'

'It wouldn't be a permanent position,' he replied. Though he added before she could feel too deflated, 'Let's say six months definite, with a review when the six months are up.'

'I'll take it,' she accepted at once, not needing to think about it. She would have six months in which to sort something else out. Trying not to sound too eager, though unable to hold back, she said, 'I'll do it—whatever the job is. I can cook, clean, garden— catalogue your library...'

'With a couple of part-time helpers, Mrs Starkey runs the house and kitchen admirably, and Jimmie Starkey has all the help he needs in the grounds.'

'And you don't need your library catalogued?'

she guessed, ready to offer her secretarial skills but suspecting he had a PA in London far more competent than she would be to take care of those matters.

'The job I have for you is very specialised,' Ty Allardyce stated, and before she could tell him that she was a little short in the specialised skills department, he was going on. 'My work in London and overseas has been such that until recently I've been unable to spend very much time down here.'

At any other time she might have thrown in a sarcastic *We've missed you*, but Ty Allardyce was being deadly serious, so she settled for, 'I expect you keep in touch by phone.'

He nodded. 'Which in no way prepared me for the shock I received when I made what was meant to be a snatched visit here a couple of weeks ago.'

'Ah—you're talking…Ash?'

'You've noticed the change in him?'

Who could fail to? 'He's—not ill?'

'Not in the accepted sense.'

'Did Leanne do this to him?' She voiced her thoughts, and saw his mouth tighten.

'I couldn't believe that some money-grabbing female could so wreck a man, but—' He broke off, then resumed, 'Anyhow, I felt there was no way I could return to London. Not then. Not now—without your help.'

'I'll do anything I can, naturally.'

'Good,' he said. 'The job is yours.'

She stared at this man who she had to admit she was starting to like—though she was fully prepared to believe that shock did funny things to people, but still felt no further forward. 'Er—and the job is what, exactly?'

'I thought I'd just said,' Ty replied, 'I want you to be Ash's companion.'

Her mouth fell open. 'You want me to be your brother's *companion*?' she echoed.

'I'll pay you, of course,' Ty answered, seeing absolutely nothing untoward in what he was proposing.

'You want me to be his paid companion?' she questioned again, as it started to sink in. 'His—his minder?'

'No, not minder!' Ty answered shortly. 'I've explained how things are.'

'Not really you haven't,' Phinn stated, and was on the receiving end of an impatient look.

'The situation is,' he explained heavily, 'that while I can do certain parts of my job in my study, via computer and telephone, other matters require my presence in London or some other capital. I've been down here for two weeks more than I originally intended already. And, while I have a pressing need to get back to town, I still don't feel ready to leave Ash on his own.'

Phinn thought about it. 'You think I might be the person to take over from you for a while?'

'Can you think of anyone better than someone who has actually risked their own life for him, as you did today?'

'I don't know about that,' she mumbled.

'Ash likes you. He enjoyed talking to you the other day.'

'Um—that was the day you told me to leave him alone, to—'

'I was angry,' Ty admitted. 'I didn't want another Hawkins finishing off what your cousin had done to him. But that was before I was able to reason that he was still so ensnared by her that other women just don't exist for him. Frankly, Ash wouldn't fancy you even if you *did* use your beauty to try to hook him.'

Beauty? Hook him? Charming! At that point Phinn was in two minds about whether or not she wanted the job. She felt sorry for Ash—of course she did. As for her cousin…she was feeling quite angry with Leanne. But…then Phinn thought of Ruby, and at the thought of a stable *and* a paddock there was no question but that she wanted the job.

'I haven't the first idea what a paid companion is supposed to do… I mean, what would I have to do? You wouldn't expect me to take him down to the pub and get drunk with him every night, I hope?'

'You like beer?' he asked sharply.

'No!' she shot straight back.

'You'd been drinking this afternoon,' he retorted, obviously not caring to be lied to. 'There was a smell of beer on your breath.'

'Honestly!' she exclaimed. And she was thinking of *working* for this man who could sniff out beer at a hundred paces! But what choice did she have? 'If you must know, I hate the stuff. But I've been having a courtesy swig out of Idris Owens' beer tankard ever since I was ten years old—it's a sort of tradition, each time I go to the farrier. It would have been churlish to refuse his offer when I took Ruby to have her hooves checked over by him this afternoon.'

For a moment Ty Allardyce said nothing, just sat there looking at her. Then he said quietly, 'Rather than hurt his feelings, you quaffed ale that you've no particular liking for?'

'So what does that make me?' she challenged, expecting something pretty pithy in reply.

But, to her surprise, he replied in that same quiet tone. 'I think it makes you a rather nice kind of person.' And she was struck again by the change in him from the man she had thought he was.

'Yes, well…' she said abruptly—grief, she'd be going soft in the head about him in a minute. Buck up, she instructed herself. This man could be iron-hard and unyielding without any trouble. Hadn't she witnessed that for herself? 'So I'm—er—to take over the sort of guardianship of Ash from you while you—um—go about your business?'

'Not quite,' Ty replied. 'What I believe Ash needs just now is to be with someone who will be a sensitive ear for him when he needs to talk. Someone to take him out of himself when he looks like becoming a little melancholy.'

'You think I've got a sensitive ear?'

Again he looked steadily at her. 'You'll do,' he said. And he would have left it at that, but there were questions queuing up in Phinn's mind.

'You think it will take as long as six months for Ash to—um—get back to being his old self?'

'Hopefully nowhere near as long. Who knows? Whatever—I'm prepared to guarantee stabling and a place for you to rest your head for the whole six months.'

'Fine,' she said.

'You'll start tomorrow?'

And how! 'You'd better let me have your phone number,' she requested, overjoyed, now it had had time to sink in, that by the look of it Ruby was going to have a proper stable and a paddock all to herself.

'Why would you want my phone number?' Ty asked shortly.

'Oh, for goodness' sake!' she erupted at her new boss. 'So I can ring Ash and ask him to come and pick me up with my belongings. I can bring Ruby over later.'

'You want to inspect her accommodation first?'

'I'd—er—have put it a little more tactfully,' she mumbled. 'But, yes, that's the general idea. I could still ask Mickie if you don't want Ash to do it.'

'Who's Mickie?'

'He lives in the village. He's a bit eccentric, but he has a heart of gold. He—er—' She broke off—that was more than he needed to know.

She quickly realised that she should have known better. '"He—er—" what?'

Phinn gave a resigned sigh. 'Well, if you must know, I'd already arranged for Mickie to take my cases and bits and pieces up to Honeysuckle Farm for me tomorrow.'

Ty Allardyce shook his head, as though she was a new kind of species to him. 'Presumably he would have kept quiet about your whereabouts?'

'Well, there you are,' she said briskly, about nothing, and then fell headlong when, in the same bracing tone, she said, 'Had I not sold my car, I...' Her voice trailed away. 'Well, I did,' she added quickly. And then, hurriedly attempting to close the interview—or whatever it was, 'So I'll get Mickie to—'

'You sold your car?' Ty Allardyce took up.

'Yep.' He didn't need to hear more.

And nor did he, she discovered. Because what

this clever man did not know he was astute enough to decipher and guess at. 'According to my lawyers, you paid a whole whack of back rent before you handed in the keys to the farm,' he commented slowly. Adding, 'Had I thought about it at all, I'd have assumed that the money came from your father's estate. But—' he looked at her sharply '—it didn't, did it?'

She shrugged. 'What did I need a car for? I thought I'd got a steady job here—no need to look for work further afield. Besides, I couldn't leave Ruby on her own all day.' Phinn halted, she'd had enough of talking about herself. 'Have you told Ash that you were going to offer me a job?'

Ty looked at her unspeaking for some moments, and then replied, 'No.'

She saw it might be a little awkward if Ash objected strongly. 'How do you think he'll take my moving in to be his companion?' No point in ducking the question. If Ash did not want her there, then the next six months could be pretty miserable all round.

'My brother feels things very deeply,' Ty began. 'He has been hurt—badly hurt. In my view it would be easier for him if he didn't know the true reason for your being at the Hall.'

'I wouldn't be able to lie to him,' Phinn said quickly. 'I'm not very good at telling lies.'

'You wouldn't have to lie.'

Phinn looked into steady grey eyes and felt somewhat perplexed. 'What, then?' she asked. 'I can't just ring him out of the blue and ask him to come and get me.'

'It won't be a problem,' Ty assured her. 'Ash knows that you and Ruby have to leave here. I'll tell him that, apropos of you having nowhere to go, I called to thank you for what you did today and offered you a temporary home.'

Phinn's eyes widened. 'You think he'll believe such philanthropy?' she queried—and discovered that her hint of sarcasm was not lost on him.

'My stars, I pity the poor man who ends up with *you*!' he muttered under his breath, but then agreed, 'Normally I doubt he'd believe it for a moment. But, apart from him not being too concerned about anything very much just now, he's as grateful to you as I am that you were where you were today.' The matter settled as far as he was concerned, he took out his wallet, extracted his business card, wrote several numbers on it and, standing up, handed it to her.

Phinn glanced at the card in her hand and read that he had given her his office number, his mobile number, the phone number of his London home and the one she had asked for—the number of the Hall.

'No need to have gone raving mad,' she commented. She had only wanted one telephone number, for goodness' sake!

'Just in case,' he said, and she realised he meant her to ring him if she felt things were going badly for Ash. 'Feel free to ring me at any time,' he added.

'Right,' she agreed, and stood up too. She found he was too close and, feeling a mite odd for no reason, took a step away.

'How are you feeling now?' he thought to ask before he turned to the door.

'Feeling?' For a moment she wasn't with him.

Without more ado he caught hold of both of her hands. When, his touch making her tingle, she would have snatched her hands back, he held on to them. 'You're not shaking,' he observed—and then she *was* with him.

'Oh, I think the shock has passed now,' she informed him, only then starting to wonder if this man—this complex kind of man—had stayed talking with her as long as he had so as to be on hand if she looked like going into full-blown shock. 'You're kinder than I thought,' she blurted out, quite without thinking—and abruptly had her hands dropped like hot coals.

'Spread that around and I'll have to kill you,' he said shortly. And that was it. He was gone.

Starting to only half-believe that Ty Allardyce had been in the flat and made that staggering, not to say wonderful job and accommodation offer for her and Ruby, Phinn went quickly to the window that overlooked the stableyard.

He was there. She had not dreamt it. Ty Allardyce was in the stableyard talking to Geraldine Walton. What was more, Geraldine was smiling her head off. Never had Phinn seen her look more animated or more pleasant.

Phinn added 'charm' to Ty Allardyce's list of accomplishments, and wondered what he was talking to Geraldine about. Keeping out of sight, she watched for a minute or so more, and then the two of them disappeared.

While they were gone she observed that there was a pick-up vehicle in the yard that did not belong to the stables. She assumed that Ty Allardyce had driven over in it.

She soon saw that her assumption was correct. When he and Geraldine Walton appeared again, he was hauling a bale of straw and Geraldine was wheeling a bale of hay. Phinn watched as the two bales were loaded onto the pick-up. She kept out of sight as the two disappeared again, and then reappeared with the special feed Phinn herself had bought for Ruby, who needed it on account of her teeth not being what they once had been.

Feeling little short of amazed, Phinn watched as the two chatted a little while longer, before Ty got into the pick-up and drove away.

Was he a mover or was he a mover? My heavens, it had all been cut and dried as far as he was con-

cerned before he had even left Broadlands! Ty
Allardyce needed someone trustworthy to keep his
brother company while he returned to the business
he had already neglected for far too long, and he had
it all planned out before he had come to see her!

While he might not have cared for her standing
up to him over her right to trespass, it was plain that
in his view, when it came to being trustworthy with
his brother, there was no higher recommendation
than that she had that day taken a header into the
pool to get his brother out when Ash had got into difficulties. Plan made, all that he'd needed to do was
come and see her and—as it were—make her an
offer she couldn't refuse.

That he had known in advance that she would not
refuse his offer was evidenced by the fact he had
driven over in the pick-up. Efficient or what? Since
he would be at the stables, he might as well collect
a few things and save an extra journey later.

Feeling a little bit stunned by the man's effi-
ciency, Phinn went out to check on Ruby. Inevitably,
it seemed, she bumped into Geraldine Walton.

'You didn't say you were starting work up at the
Hall?' Geraldine commented, and seemed more
relaxed than she had before.

Phinn felt a little stumped as to how to reply.
There was no way she was going to reveal to
anyone the true nature of her job at the Hall. On the

other hand, given that Geraldine could be tough when she had to be, she did not want to part with bad feelings.

'I'm just hoping my secretarial skills aren't too rusty,' she answered lightly. It was the best she could do at a moment's notice, and she hoped it would suffice as a white lie. 'Must go and check on Ruby,' she added with a smile, and went quickly on.

Ruby came over to her as soon as she saw her, and Phinn told her all about the move tomorrow, and about the nice new paddock all to herself. Ruby nuzzled into her neck appreciatively—and Phinn came near to feeling relaxed for the first time in an age.

She stayed talking to Ruby for quite some while, and was in fact still with her when she thought that perhaps she had given Ty plenty of time in which to tell his brother that from tomorrow on they were to have a house guest.

Realising she had left her mobile phone and the phone numbers Ty had given her back in the flat, she parted from Ruby briefly while she nipped back to the accommodation she would be vacating in the morning.

Finding the card, she dialled the number of the Hall and, for no known reason expecting that Ash would be the one to answer her call, was a little non-plussed to hear Ty's voice. 'Allardyce,' he said, and she knew straight away that it was him.

'Oh, hello, Ty—er—Mr Allardyce,' she stumbled, feeling a fool.

'Ty,' he invited, and asked, 'Did you want to speak with Ash?'

'If I may,' she replied primly. And that was it. A few minutes later Ash was on the line.

'I wanted to ring you,' he said, before she could say a word. 'We hadn't got your number, but I wanted to thank you so much, Phinn, for what you did today. I didn't get a chance before. When I think—'

'That's all right, Ash,' she butted in. 'Er—actually, Ty stopped by to thank me. Um—I think you must have told him about my need to move from here?'

'I'm glad I did. Ty says he knows we can never repay you, but that he's offered you and your horse temporary accommodation here until you can sort something out.'

'You don't mind?'

'Good Lord, no! Ty's suggested I get busy sorting out the old stable in the morning.'

'I'll come and help!' Phinn volunteered promptly. 'Actually, I'm without wheels, so if you could come and collect me and some of my stuff, it…?'

'I owe you—big-time. Nine o'clock suit?'

Phinn went to bed that night with her head buzzing. She barely knew where to start when she thought of all that had happened that day. Drinking beer in the forge! That ghastly picture of Ash in trouble! His complex brother! His amazing offer! All in all, today had been one almighty day for huge surprises.

Strangely, though, as she lay in the dark going over everything in her head, it was Ty Allardyce who figured most largely in her thoughts. He could be hard, he could be bossy—overbearing, even—but he could be kind too. Complex did she say? Ty Allardyce was something else again.

She remembered the way he had taken her hands in his, and recalled the way she had tingled all over. Don't be ridiculous, she instructed herself. Just look forward to going to Broadlands Hall to be a companion to Ash so that Ty can get back to the work he so obviously loves.

From her point of view, things couldn't be better. When she thought about it, a return to Honeysuckle Farm had been a far from ideal solution. Both she and Ruby would fare much better at Broadlands. They were truly most fortunate.

But—Phinn fidgeted in her bed—why was she feeling just a little disturbed? As if there was something not quite right somewhere?

# CHAPTER FOUR

PHINN was up and about long before Ash called for her the next day. She had tended to Ruby's requirements earlier, and spent her time waiting for Ash in folding Ruby's blankets and in getting the mare's belongings together.

Turning Ruby out into the field for the last time, Phinn cleaned out her stall so that Geraldine would have nothing to complain over. But even though she felt sure Ruby's new accommodation would be adequate, she still wanted to look it over before she moved her.

A little after nine Ash drove into the yard and found her waiting for him. He looked dreadfully tired, Phinn thought, as though his nights were long and tortuous.

'Ready?' he asked, pushing out a smile.

'There's rather a lot to cart over,' she mentioned apologetically.

They had almost finished loading the pick-up

when Geraldine Walton appeared, and Phinn introduced the two. 'You manage the estate, I believe?' Geraldine commented pleasantly, clearly having been in the area long enough to have picked up village gossip.

'Something like that,' Ash muttered, and hefted the last of Phinn's cases into the back of the pickup. 'That it?' he asked Phinn.

She smiled at him and, feeling that he had perhaps been a little off with Geraldine, smiled at her too. 'I'll be over for Ruby later,' she confirmed.

'She'll be fine until then. No need to rush back. I'll keep an eye on her,' Geraldine promised.

A minute or so later and Ash was driving the pickup out of the stableyard. Her job, Phinn realised, had begun. 'Er—Ty gone back to London?' she enquired—more to get Ash to start talking than because she had any particular interest in his brother.

But Ash took his glance from the road briefly to give her what she could only describe as a knowing look as he enquired, 'Didn't he phone you before he left?'

There was no reason why he should phone, as far as Phinn was aware, and she almost said as much—but that was before, on thinking about that knowing look, the most astonishing thought hit her! It couldn't be—could it?

She tried to look at the situation from Ash's angle. Given that she was unable to tell Ash that the real reason she was coming to live at the Hall was in order to keep an eye on him and, unbeknown to him, be his companion, did Ash think that there was more in his brother's invitation for her to stay at the Hall than his gratitude after yesterday's events?

She opened her mouth to tell Ash bluntly that there was nothing going on between her and his brother Ty, nor likely to be, but the moment had passed. Then she was glad she had said nothing; she had obviously got it wrong. In actual fact, when she thought of the glamorous females that Ty probably dated, she was doubly glad she had said nothing. Far better to keep her mouth shut than to make a fool of herself.

Ash drove straight to the stable. There were bits and pieces of packing cases outside, she noticed as they drove up. 'I was supposed to have the stable empty before you got here, but I—er—got kind of sidetracked,' Ash excused.

'Well, with two of us I don't suppose it will take us very long,' Phinn said brightly, more concerned with having a look inside than anything else just then.

Taking into account that there were more packing cases inside, plus an old scrubbed kitchen table and other items which she guessed had come out of the Hall when it had been modernised, the stable was more than adequate—even to the water tap on one wall. Indeed, once she had got it all spruced up, brushed out, and with fresh straw put down, it would be little short of luxury for Ruby.

'Roll your sleeves up time!' she announced.

'You don't want to go into the house and check on your room first?'

Where she laid her head that night was immaterial to Phinn just then. Her first priority was to get Ruby settled. 'I'm sure it will be fine,' she answered. 'Will you help?'

Reluctantly at first, Ash started bundling boxes out of the way. And then gradually he began to take over. 'Leave that one,' he ordered at one stage, when she tried to manhandle what had been some part of a kitchen cabinet. 'I'll move that.' And later, 'What we're going to have to do is to take this lot down to the tip.'

Sacrilege! Phinn took out her phone and pressed out Mickie Yates's number. With luck she'd get him before he went for lunch, and she needed to talk to him anyway.

She was in luck. He was home. 'Mickie? Phinn Hawkins.'

'I haven't forgotten,' he replied, a smile in his voice. 'Three o'clock.'

'Change of plan,' she stated. 'I'm—er—working and staying at the Hall for a while.' She could feel Ash's eyes on her, and felt awkward. 'The thing is, we're clearing out the stable for Ruby. Can you find homes for some kitchen units and the like that still have some life in them, do you think?'

'Today?'

'That would be good.'

'An hour?'

'That would be brilliant.'

'See you, lovely girl.'

Putting her phone away after making the call, Phinn looked up to find that Ash was staring at her. 'You're working here?' he enquired.

She went red. Grief—what *was* it about these Allardyce brothers? 'Shut up—and help me move this,' she ordered—and to her great delight, after a stunned moment she saw a half-grin break on Ash's features. It seemed an age since she had last seen him smile.

She was delighted, but a moment or two later she distinctly heard him comment, 'She blushes, and Ty says he'll try and get back tonight…' And then she heard him deliberately sing a snatch of 'Love Is in the Air'.

'Ash,' she warned.

'What?' he asked.

What could she say? 'Nothing,' she replied.

'Sorry,' he apologized. 'Am I treading all over your tender feelings?'

There was no answer to that either. 'Now, where did I put that yard broom?' she said instead, but knew then she had to believe that Ash thought that there might be something going on between her and his elder brother.

What? After only seeing her once? Though on second thought, how did she know that since Ty did not want Ash to know the real reason she was there, Ty had *not* instigated or at least allowed Ash to nurture such thoughts? He could quite truthfully have told Ash that, apart from the time she had called at the house with his camera, they had bumped into each other on a couple of other occasions and stopped for a chat.

That, 'Get off my land!' and a threat to summons her for trespass hardly constituted 'a chat' was neither here nor there. But it was plain Ash thought that there was more to Ty inviting her to live under his roof and offering to stable her horse than appeared on the surface. Hadn't she herself asked Ty, 'You think he'll believe such philanthropy?' Clearly Ash did not. What Ash had chosen to believe was that she was some kind of would-be girlfriend to his brother. And, bearing in mind that she could not tell Ash the truth, there was nothing she could do to disabuse him of the idea.

Having reached the conclusion that Ash was not so down as she had at first thought, she saw the more cheerful mood he had been in while they had been busy start to fall away once the stable was empty of impedimenta and Mickie Yates had called and carted everything away.

'I think I'll take a shortcut through the spinney and collect Ruby,' Phinn said lightly. Straw was down; water was in the trough they had unearthed and scrubbed.

'I'll drive you there if you like?' he offered, but she knew that his heart was not in it.

For a moment she wondered if the fact that Geraldine had the look of her cousin and it would upset him had anything to do with it. If so, perhaps it would be kinder not to trigger memories of Leanne should Geraldine be about.

'No need,' she answered gently. But, bearing in mind that he had seemed happier when working, she went on. 'Though if you're strolling down anywhere near the paddock you might check if it's Ruby-friendly for me.'

Ash nodded and went on his way. By then Phinn was learning to trust Ty enough that if he thought the paddock was suitable for Ruby, there would be no stray barbed wire or plant-life dangerous to horses.

She was feeling sorely in need of a shower and a change of clothes, but Ruby still had to be Phinn's first priority. She wanted her away from the other horses, and so went as quickly as she could to get her.

First she was met by Geraldine—a smiling Geraldine—who offered to supply her with hay and straw from her own supplies. 'You can have it for the price I pay for it,' she offered pleasantly.

Thanking her, feeling cheered, Phinn went looking for Ruby, and was instantly rewarded when Ruby spotted her straight away and came over to her as fast as she could. 'Come on, darling,' Phinn murmured to her softly. 'Have I got a lovely surprise for you.'

Ruby did not have much of an appetite, and after staying with her for a while as she got used to her new surroundings, Phinn left her and went over to the house.

She went in though the kitchen door and at once saw Mrs Starkey, who was at the sink scrubbing new potatoes. She smiled when she saw her. 'Come in, Phinn, come in. Your room's all ready for you.'

'I hope I haven't put you to a lot of trouble?' Phinn apologised.

'None at all! It will be nice having you in the house,' Mrs Starkey answered cheerfully, more than happy, it seemed, in her now streamlined kitchen. 'Dinner's usually about seven-thirty, but I've made you a sandwich to tide you over. Or you could have some soup, or a salad, or…'

'A sandwich will do fine, Mrs Starkey. What I need most is a shower and a change of clothes.'

Mrs Starkey washed and dried her hands. 'Come on, then. I'll show you your room. Ashley came in earlier with your belongings and took them up for you. I hope it's all right? I've had your cardboard boxes put in the storeroom, but…'

'That's lovely.' Phinn thanked her, and as they climbed the winding staircase asked, 'Where is Ash? Do you know?'

For a brief second or two the housekeeper lost her smile. 'I think he's taken himself off for a walk. He didn't want anything to eat, and he barely touched his breakfast.' She shook her head. 'I don't know,' she said, more to herself than anything as they went along the landing.

Phinn was unsure what, if anything, to answer. But she was saved having to make a reply when Mrs Starkey halted at one of the bedroom doors.

'Here we are,' she said, opening the door and standing back for Phinn to go in. 'I hope it's to your liking.'

Liking! 'Oh, Mrs Starkey, it's lovely!' she cried. And it was.

'I'll leave you to get settled in and have your shower.' Mrs Starkey seemed as pleased as Phinn herself.

Phinn stood in the centre of the recently refurbished room and turned very slowly around. The huge, high-ceilinged, light and airy room, with its own modernised bathroom, was more of a bedsitting room than anything. One wall had been given over to built-in wardrobes, with a dressing table in between—far more wardrobe space than she would ever need, Phinn mused. And there was a padded stool in delicate cream and antique gold in front of the dressing table area that had a light above it.

The bed was a double bed, with a cream and antique gold bedcover. At the foot of the bed was a padded cream ottoman, and further in front of that a padded antique gold-coloured chaise longue. A small round table reposed to the side of it, and to the side of that stood a small matching padded chair.

Remembering her cold and draughty bedroom at Honeysuckle Farm, where she would have been returning today but for the turn of events, Phinn could only stare in wonder. She took another slow turn around again—and she had thought Ruby's accommodation luxurious!

Feeling a little stunned, and thinking that she would not want to leave when her six months at Broadlands Hall were over, Phinn went to inspect the bathroom. She was not disappointed. There must be a snag, she pondered. And, stripping off, stepped into the shower—certain that the plumbing or some such would prove faulty.

It proved not faulty. The water was fine, as hot or not as she would have wished.

Refreshed from her shower, Phinn quickly dressed in some clean clothes and, with her thoughts on introducing Ruby to the paddock, swiftly left her room—she could unpack later. She went to the kitchen.

'Tea or coffee?' Mrs Starkey asked as soon as she saw her. And only then did Phinn realise that she felt quite parched.

'Actually, I'd better go and see to Ruby. But I'll have a glass of water,' she answered. No time to wait for tea or coffee.

'Juice?' Mrs Starkey offered, and as Phinn glanced at the motherly woman she suddenly felt as if she had come home.

'Juice would be lovely,' she replied gratefully. And while she drank her juice she saw Mrs Starkey fold her sandwich up in a paper napkin.

'Our John never used to have a moment to breathe either,' she remarked, handing over the sandwich with a smile.

'Thank you, Mrs Starkey,' Phinn said, and had her empty glass taken out of her hand when she would have taken it over to the sink and washed it, and the sandwich pressed in its place.

Life was suddenly good. Phinn all at once realised that she was feeling the best she had felt since her father had died. Now, who did she thank for that? Ty, Ash, Mrs Starkey—or just the passage of time?

Whatever—just enjoy.

Another plus was that Ruby appeared a little hungry. Some of her special feed had gone anyway.

Phinn took her down to the fenced-off paddock, checked she had water, and sat on the fence eating her sandwich while Ruby found her way around.

After a while Phinn got down from the fence. Ruby was not her only concern, but this was her first day, and apart from having to clear out the stables and make everything ready, Phinn had not got into any sort of pattern as yet. But she was mindful that she should be looking out for Ash.

Leaving Ruby, Phinn went looking for him. He had gone for a walk, Mrs Starkey had said. But that had been hours ago.

Phinn had gone some way, and was near to the pool when through the trees she caught a glimpse of something blue. If memory served, Ash had been wearing a blue shirt that morning. Should she leave him or keep him company?

The matter was solved when she recalled that she was being *employed* to keep Ash company. She went forward, making sufficient noise so as not to suddenly startle him. She found him sitting on the bank, his expression bleak, and her heart went out to him. How long had he been sitting there, staring at the water without really seeing anything but her cousin?

'Can you believe this glorious weather?' she asked, for something to say.

'Get Ruby over okay?' Ash roused himself to ask.

'The paddock's a dream!'

'Good,' he replied politely, and made no objection when she decided to sit down beside him.

Sitting down beside him was one thing. Now she had to think of something to talk about! 'Are you really the estate manager?' she asked, playing the companion role by ear.

'It doesn't need much managing,' he replied.

'You reckon?'

'You know differently?' he countered, and she sensed an interest—slight, but a spark of interest nevertheless.

'No. Not really,' she answered hurriedly. 'Only…'

'Only?'

'Well, I couldn't help noticing the other day when I was walking through Pixie End Wood that there are one or two trees that need taking out and new ones planting in their place.'

'Where's Pixie End Wood?'

Phinn worked on that spark of interest. 'If I'm not too busy with Ruby tomorrow I'll take you there, if you like?'

He nodded, but she knew his interest was waning. 'How's Leanne?' he asked, totally unexpectedly.

Oh, Ash. Phinn knew, just as she knew that there was nothing she could do to help, that Ash was bleeding a little inside. 'We're not in contact,' she replied. 'It's like that with relatives sometimes. You rarely ever see each other except for weddings and—' She broke off, spears of sad memory still able to dart in unexpectedly and stop her in her tracks.

'I'm sorry.' Ash, like the normally thoughtful person he was, sensed what she had not been able to say. The last time Leanne had surfaced had been to attend Phinn's father's funeral. 'Come on,' he said, shaking off his apathy in the face of Phinn having a weak moment. 'Let's go and see how Ruby likes her new digs.'

By early evening Phinn was in her room again, wondering at her stroke of luck at being at Broadlands. Because her watch had stopped working she was having to guess at the time, but she thought it had been around six that evening when she and Ash had returned to the house. She had come straight to her room and begun finding homes for her belongings.

She had been surprised, however, when opening a drawer in her bedside table, to find an envelope with her name on it. When she had opened it, it had been to extract a cheque written and signed in Ty's firm hand, for what she presumed was her first month's wages.

She felt a little hot about the ears when, never having been paid in advance before, she wondered if Ty had guessed at the parlous state of her finances. The fact that the cheque was for more than she would have thought too made her realise the importance he gave to his brother's welfare. In his view Ash needed a companion when Ty could not be there himself—and he was prepared to pay up-front for that cover.

Knowing that she was going to do her best to fulfil that role, Phinn, surmising that 'companions' probably ate with the family, went to assess her wardrobe. She had several decent dresses, but she had no wish to be 'over the top'. Jeans were out, she guessed, so she settled for a smart pair of white trousers and topped them with a loose-fitting short blue kaftan.

It seemed an age since she had last used anything but moisturiser on her face, but she thought a dab of powder and a smear of lipstick might not be a bad idea. Why, as she was studying her finished appearance, she should think of Ty Allardyce she had no idea.

She hadn't seen him since yesterday. Nor had she heard him come home. Would he be there at dinner? Did she want him there at dinner? Oh, for goodness' sake—what the blazes did it matter where he was? He—

Someone tapping on her door caused her to break off her thoughts.

And, on her answering the door, who should be standing there but none other than the subject of her thoughts? She felt suddenly shy.

'Hungry?' Ty enquired easily.

She at once discounted that she was in any way shy of him. 'Mrs Starkey said dinner was around seven-thirty,' Phinn responded. Shy or not, she glanced away from those steady grey eyes and raised her left hand to check the time on her wrist. No watch!

'It's seven forty-five,' Ty informed her.

'It isn't!' she exclaimed. Where had the day gone?

'You look ready to me,' he observed. And, stepping back, he clearly expected her to join him.

A smile lit the inside of her. Ty must have come up the stairs purposely to collect her. 'Busy day?' she enquired, leaving her room and going along the landing with him.

'Not as physically busy as you, from what I hear. Ash tells me you put him to shame.'

She shook her head. 'Once Ash got into his stride it was he who did the lion's share of lumping and bumping,' she stated, and saw that Ty looked pleased.

'And your friend Mickie Yates came and took everything away?'

'You don't mind?'

'Good Lord, why would I?' Ty replied, and startled her completely when, totally away from what they had been talking about, he shot a question at her. 'Where's your watch?'

Taken by surprise, she answered, 'It got wet,' quite without thinking. And was halfway down the stairs when Ty stepped in front of her, turned and halted—causing her to have to halt too.

'You mean you forgot to take it off when you did your Olympian dive yesterday?'

'I can't think of everything!' she exclaimed. 'It will be all right when it dries out,' she added off-handedly, knowing that it would never work again, but not wanting to make an issue of it. It hadn't been an expensive watch, after all.

'As you remarked—you're no good at telling lies.' He neatly tripped her up.

What could she do? Say? She gave him a cheeky grin. 'The paddock is lovely,' she informed him.

He shook his head slightly, the way she noticed he did when he was a little unsure of what to make of her.

Dinner was a pleasant meal, though Phinn observed that Ash ate very little. For all that the ham salad with buttered potatoes and a rather fine onion tart was very palatable, he seemed to be eating it for form's sake rather than because he was enjoying it.

'Did you find time to get into the estate office today?' Ty, having included her in all the conversation so far, put a question to his brother.

'Who wants to be indoors on a day like today?' Ash replied. 'I'll see what I can do tomorrow,' he added. Ty did not press him, or look in any way put out. And then Ash was confessing, 'Actually, I think Phinn would make a better estate manager than me.'

Phinn opened her mouth, ready with a disclaimer, and then noticed Ty's glance had switched to her. He was plainly interested in his brother's comment.

'I'm beginning to think that nothing Phinn does will surprise me,' he said. 'But—' he glanced back to Ash '—why, particularly?'

'Apparently I'm being taken on a tour of Pixie End Wood tomorrow. Phinn tells me there are a couple of trees there that need felling, and new ones planting.'

Ty's glance was back on her, and she was sure she looked guilty. She knew that he was now aware that her trespassing had not been limited to the few places where he had witnessed it.

When, after dinner, a move was made to the drawing room, Phinn would by far have preferred to have gone to the stable. But, even though she felt that Ty would not expect her to be on 'companion duty' when he was home to keep his brother company, she was aware that there were certain courtesies to be observed when living in someone else's home.

And so, thinking that to spend another ten minutes with the Allardyce brothers wouldn't hurt, she went along to the drawing room with them. But she was hardly through the door when she stopped dead in her tracks.

'Grandmother Hawkins' table!' she exclaimed, all the other plush furnishings and antique furniture fading from her sight as she recognised the much-loved, much-polished, small round table that had been theirs up until 'needs must', as her father had called their impecunious moments, and the table had been sold.

'Grandmother Hawkins?' Ash enquired. 'You mean you once owned that table?'

Grandmother Hawkins had handed it down to Phinn's parents early in their marriage, when they'd had little furniture of their own. They had later inherited the rest of her antiques. 'It's—er—lovely, isn't it?' she replied, feeling awkward and wishing that she hadn't said anything.

'You're sure it's yours? Ty bought it in London.'

'I'm sure. We sold it—it wasn't stolen. We—er…' She had been about to say how it had been about the last one of their antiques to go, but there was no need for anyone to know of their hard-up moments. 'It was probably sold to a dealer who sold it on.'

'And you recognise it?'

'I should do—it was my Saturday morning job to polish it. I've been polishing it since I was about three years old.' A gentle smile of happy remembering lifted her mouth. 'My father's initials are lightly carved underneath. We both got into trouble when he showed me how to carve mine in too. My mother could never erase them—no matter how much she tried.'

'The table obviously holds very happy memories for you,' Ty put in quietly.

'I had the happiest of childhoods,' she replied, and suddenly felt embarrassed at talking of things they could not possibly be interested in.

'You were upset when your father sold it?' Ty enquired, his eyes watching her.

She looked at him in surprise, the blue top she wore reflecting the deepening blue of her eyes. How had he known it was her father who had sold the table and not her mother? 'He was my father!' she protested.

'And as such could do no wrong?' Ty suggested quietly.

She looked away from him. It was true. In her eyes her father had never been able to do anything wrong. 'Would you mind very much if I went and took a look at Ruby?'

She flicked a quick glance back to Ty, but his expression was inscrutable. She took that to mean that he would not mind, and was on her way.

Ruby had had the best of days, and seemed truly happy and content in her new abode. Phinn stayed with her, talking softly to her as she did every evening. And as she chatted to her Phinn started once more to come near to being content herself.

She was still with Ruby when the mare's ears pricked up and Phinn knew that they were about to have company.

'How's she settled in?' Ty asked, coming into the large stable and joining them.

'I think we can safely say that she loves her new home.'

Ty nodded. Then asked, 'How about you?'

'Who could fail to love it here? My room's a dream!'

He looked pleased. 'Any problems I should know about?' he asked. 'Don't be afraid to say—no matter how small,' he added.

'It's only my first day. Nothing untoward, but—' She broke off, caught out by the memory of Ash giving her that knowing look that morning.

'What?' Ty asked.

My heavens, was he sharp! 'Nothing,' she answered. But then she thought that perhaps she *should* mention it. 'Well, the thing is, I think Ash seems to have got hold of the idea that—um—you and I—are—er—starting some sort of…' Grief, she knew she was going red again.

'Some sort of…?' Ty questioned, not sparing her blushes.

And that annoyed her. 'Well, if you must know, I think he thinks we're starting some sort of romantic attachment.' There—it was out. She waited for him to look totally astounded at the idea. But to her astonishment he actually started to grin. She stared at him, her heart going all fluttery for no good reason.

Then Ty was sobering, and to her amazement he was confessing, 'My fault entirely, I'm afraid.'

'Your fault?'

'Forgive me, Phinn?' he requested, not for a moment looking sorry about anything. 'I could tell the way his mind was working when I told him I'd asked you to stay with us for a while.'

Phinn stared at him. 'But you didn't tell him—?' she gasped.

'I thought it better not to disabuse him of the notion,' Ty cut in.

'Why on earth not?' she bridled.

'Now, don't get cross,' Ty admonished. 'You know quite well the real reason why you're here.'

'To be Ash's companion.'

'Right,' Ty agreed. 'You're here to keep him company—but he's not to know about it. From where I'm viewing it, Ash has got enough to handle without having the added weight of feeling under too much of an obligation for what you did for him yesterday. He's indebted to you—of course he is. We both are,' Ty went on. 'The alternative—what could have happened had you not been around and had the guts to do what you did—just doesn't bear thinking about. But he's under enough emotional pressure. I just thought it might take some of the pressure from him if he could more cheerfully think that, while things might be going wrong for him in his personal life, I—his big brother—was having a better time of it and had invited you here more because I was smitten than because of what we both owe you.'

Despite herself, Phinn could see the logic of what Ty had just said. She remembered how down Ash had seemed when she had come across him on the bank today. She recalled that bleak expression on his face and had to agree. Ty's brother did not need any extra burden just now.

'As long as you don't expect me to give you a cuddle every now and then,' she retorted sniffily at last.

She saw his lips twitch and turned away, and, feeling funny inside, showed an interest in Ruby.

'As pleasant as one of your cuddles would surely be, I'll try to hold down my expectations,' Ty replied smoothly, and for a minute she did not like him again, because again he was making her feel a fool. All too plainly the sky would fall in before he would want to be anywhere near cuddling distance with *her*.

'Are you home tomorrow?' she turned to enquire, thinking that as it was Saturday he might well be.

'Want to take me to Pixie End Wood too?'

She gave him a hostile look, bit down on a reply of *Yes, and leave you there*, and settled for, 'You intimated you'd neglected your work in London. I merely wondered if you'd be going back to catch up.'

'You don't like me, do you?'

At this moment, no. She shrugged her shoulders.

'I can take you or leave you,' she replied, to let him know that she was not bothered about him one way or the other. But flicking a glance to him, she saw she had amused him. Not in the least offended, he looked more likely to laugh than to be heartbroken.

'How's the…Ruby?' He made one of his lightning switches of conversation.

Ah, that was different. Taking the talk away from herself and on to Ruby was far preferable. 'She's happy—really settled in well. She's eaten more today than she has in a while. And this stable, the paddock—they're a dream for her.'

'Good,' Ty commented, and then, dipping his hand into his trouser pocket, he pulled out a wristwatch and handed it to her. 'You'll need one of these until your own dries out,' he remarked.

Having taken it from him, Phinn stared at the handsome gentleman's watch in her hand. 'I can't…' she began, trying to give it back to him.

'It's a spare.' He refused to take it. 'And only a loan.'

She looked at him, feeling stumped. The phrase 'hoist with her own petard' came to mind. She had told him her watch would be all right again once it had dried out—but he knew that, no matter how dry it was, it would never be serviceable again.

'I'll let you have it back in due time.' She accepted it with what dignity she could muster, and was glad when, with a kind pat to Ruby's flank, Ty Allardyce bade her, *'Adieu,'* and went.

Phinn stayed with Ruby, wondering what it was about the man that disturbed her so. In truth, she had never met any man who could make her so annoyed with him one second and yet on the point of laughter the next.

Eventually she said goodnight to Ruby and returned to the house, musing that it had been thoughtful of Ty to loan her a watch. How many times that day had she automatically checked her left wrist in vain?

The evidence of just how thoughtful he was was again there when, having gone up the stairs and into her room, Phinn discovered that someone had been in there.

She stood stock still and just stared. The small round table that had been by the antique gold chaise longue had been removed. In its place, and looking every bit as if it belonged there, was the small round table that had been in the drawing room when last she had seen it.

'Grandmother Hawkins' table,' she said softly, and felt a warm glow wash over her. Welcome home, it seemed to be saying. She did not have to guess who had so thoughtfully made the exchange. She knew that it had been Ty Allardyce.

Phinn went to bed liking him again.

# CHAPTER FIVE

PHINN sat on the paddock rail around six weeks later, keeping an eye on Ruby, who'd had a bout of being unwell, and reflecting on how Broadlands Hall now seemed to be quite like home. She knew more of the layout now. Knew where Ty's study was—the place where he always spent some time when he was there.

Most of the rooms had been smartened up, some replastered and redecorated. The room next for redecoration was the music room—the room in which she had often sat listening with Mr Caldicott while her father played on his grand piano. The music room door was occasionally left open, when either Wendy or Valerie, who came up from the village to clean, were in there, giving the room a dusting and an airing. Apparently the piano had been left behind when all Mr Caldicott's other furniture had been removed. Presumably Ty had come to some arrangement with him about it.

Phinn patted Ruby's neck and talked nothings to her while at the same time she reminded herself that she must not allow herself to become too comfortable here. In another four or so months, probably sooner if she were to get anything established for Ruby, she would have to begin looking for a new home for the two of them.

But meantime how good it was to not have that worry hanging over her head as being immediate. What was immediate, however, was the vet's bill that was mounting up. Last month's pay cheque had already gone, and the cheque Ty had left on Grandmother Hawkins' table for her to find a couple of weeks ago was mostly owed to Kit Peverill.

'Don't worry about it,' Kit had told her when she had settled his last veterinary bill. 'There's no rush. Pay me as you can.'

He was kind, was Kit, and, having assumed she had come to the Hall to work in the estate office, he had called to see Ruby as soon as he could when Phinn had phoned. She could not bear to think of Ruby in pain, but Kit had assured her that, though Ruby suffered some discomfort, she was not in actual pain, and that hopefully her sudden loss of appetite would pick up again.

Kit had been kind enough to organise some special food for Ruby, and to Phinn's surprise Geraldine Walton had arrived one day with a load of straw. Ash had been off on one of his 'walk-abouts' that day. But soon after that Geraldine had—again to Phinn's surprise—telephoned to say she had a surfeit of hay, and that if Ash was available perhaps he would drive over in the pick-up and collect it.

Having discovered that Ash was at his best when occupied, Phinn had asked him if he would mind. 'Can't you manage without it?' he had enquired, clearly reluctant.

'Yes, of course I can,' she'd replied with a smile. 'I shouldn't have asked you.'

He had been immediately contrite. 'Yes, you should. Sorry, Phinn, I'm not fit company these days. Of course I'll go.' Muttering, 'With luck I shall miss seeing the wretched woman,' he went on his way.

From that Phinn gleaned that it was not so much the errand he was objecting to, but the fact that he did not want any contact with the owner of the riding school and stables. Which gave her cause to wonder if it was just that he had taken an aversion to Geraldine. Or was he, despite himself, attracted to her and a little afraid of her because of what another woman with her colouring had done to him?

Phinn had kept him company as much as she could, though very often she knew that he wanted to be on his own. At other times she had walked miles with him all over the estate lands.

She had talked with him, stayed silent when need be, and when he had mentioned that he quite liked drawing she had several times taken him sketching down by the trout stream. Which had been a little painful to her, because it was there that her father had taught her to sketch.

She had overcome her sadness of spirit when it had seemed to her that Ash appeared to be less stressful and a shade more content when he lost himself as he concentrated on the sketch he was creating.

But Ash was very often quite down, so that sometimes she would wonder if her being there made any difference to him at all. A point she had put to Ty only a week ago. Cutting her nose off it might have been, had he agreed with her and suggested that he would not hold her to their six-month agreement. But it was nothing of the sort!

'Of course you've made a difference,' Ty assured her. 'Apart from the fact I feel I can get back to my work without being too concerned over him, there is a definite improvement from the way he was.'

'You're sure?'

'I'm sure,' he replied, and had meant it. 'Surely you've noticed that he's taking more of an interest in the estate these days? He was telling me on the phone only the other day how you had both met with some forester—Sam…?'

'Sam Turner,' she filled in. 'I was at school with

his son Sammy. Sammy's followed in his father's footsteps.' And then, getting carried away, 'Ash and I walked the whole of Pixie End Wood with Sam and Sammy…' She halted. 'But you probably know that from Ash.'

Ty hadn't answered that, but asked, 'Is there anybody you don't know?'

For the weirdest moment she felt like saying, *I don't know you.* Weird or what? Anybody would think that she *wanted* to know him—better. 'I was brung up around here,' she replied impishly—and felt Ty's steady grey glance on her.

'And a more fully rounded "brung-up" female I've never met,' he commented quietly.

'If I could decide whether that was a compliment or not, I might thank you for it,' she replied.

'It's a compliment,' he informed her, and she had gone about her business wondering about the other women of his acquaintance.

By 'fully rounded' she knew he had not been talking about her figure—which if anything, save for a bosom to be proud of, she had always thought a little on the lean side. So were his London and 'other capitals' women not so generally 'fully rounded'? And was being 'fully rounded' a good thing, or a bad thing? Phinn had given it up when she'd recalled that he had said that it was a compliment.

But now, sitting on the rail mulling over the

events of these past weeks, she reflected that Ty, having employed her so that he could go about his business, seemed to come home to Broadlands far more frequently than she had thought he would. Though it was true that here it was Friday, and he had not been home at all this week.

Phinn felt the most peculiar sensation in her insides as she wondered, today being Friday, if Ty would come home tonight? Perhaps he might stay the whole weekend? He didn't always. *Some filly up in London*, her father would have said.

But she did not want to think about Ty and his London fillies. Phinn titled her head a fraction and looked to Ruby, who was watching her. 'Hello, my darling Rubes,' she said softly, and asked, 'What do you say to an apple if I ask Mrs Starkey for one?'

Mrs Starkey was continuing to mother her, and Phinn had to admit she did not object to it. Occasionally she would sit and share a pot of tea with the housekeeper, and Phinn would enquire after Mrs Starkey's son, John, and hear of his latest doings, and then go on to talk of the various other people Phinn had grown up knowing.

Bearing in mind her own mother had taken up golf, and was more often out than in, Phinn *had* made contact with her to let her know of her move. After her mother's third-degree questioning Phinn had ended the call with her mother's blessing.

About to leave her perch and go in search of an apple for Ruby, Phinn just then heard the sound of a car coming up the drive and recognised Kit Peverill's vehicle. She had asked him to come and look Ruby over.

Ruby wasn't too sure about him, but was too timid by nature to raise any strong objections. Instead she sidled up to Phinn and stayed close when he had finished with her.

'She'll do,' he pronounced.

'She's better!' Phinn exclaimed in relief.

'She's never going to be better, Phinn,' Kit replied gently. 'You know that. But she's over this last little upset.'

Phinn looked down at her feet to hide the pain in her eyes. 'Thank you for being so attentive,' she murmured, and, leaving Ruby, walked to his vehicle with him to collect some medication he had mentioned.

'It's always a pleasure to see you, Phinn,' he commented, which took her out of her stride a little, because he had never said anything like it before. Indeed, she had always supposed him to be a tiny bit shy, more of an animal person than a people person. But she was to discover that, while shy, he was not so shy as she had imagined. And that he quite liked people too as well as animals, when he coughed, and followed up with, 'Er—in fact, I've been meaning to ask you—er—how do you feel about coming out with me one night—say, tomorrow night?'

Phinn kept her eyes on the path in front while she considered what he had said. 'Um…' She just hadn't thought of him in a 'date' situation, only a 'vet' situation. 'We—I'm…' Her thoughts were a bit muddled up, but she was thinking more about how long she would want to leave Ruby than of any enjoyment she might find if she dated this rather pleasant man.

'Look, why not give me a ring? I know you won't want to be away from Ruby for too long, but we could have a quick bite over at the Kings Arms in Little Thornby.'

Phinn was on the point of agreeing to go out with him, but something held her back. Perhaps she would go if Ty came home this weekend. Surely she was not expected to stay home being a companion to Ash if Ty was there to keep him company?

'*Can* I give you a ring?' she asked.

After Kit had gone, Phinn thought it time she attended to her duties, and went looking for Ash. The sound of someone busy with a hammer attracted her towards the pool, and she headed in that direction where, to her amazement, she found Ash on the far side, hammering a large signpost into the ground. In bold red the sign proclaimed 'DANGER.

KEEP OUT. TREACHEROUS WATER'. Close by was another post, from which hung a lifebelt.

Ash raised his head and saw her. 'Thought I was useless, didn't you?' he called, but seemed the happiest she had seen him since her cousin had done a brilliant job of flattening him.

What Phinn thought was that he was an extremely bruised man, who loved well, but not too wisely, and was paying for it.

'I think you're gorgeous,' she called back with a laugh, and felt a true affection for him. Had she had a brother, she would have liked one just like Ash.

Ash grinned, and for the first time Phinn saw that perhaps her being there *was* making a bit of a difference. Perhaps Ash was starting to heal. Phinn went to get Ruby an apple.

It started to rain after lunch, and although Ruby did not mind the rain, it was heavy enough for Phinn to not want to risk it for her. After stabling her she went indoors, and was coming down the stairs after changing out of damp clothes when the phone in the hall rang.

Phinn had spotted Mrs Starkey driving off in her car about fifteen minutes ago, and, with Ash nowhere to be seen, she picked up the phone with a peculiar sort of hope in her heart that the caller would not be Ty, ringing to say that he wouldn't be home this weekend.

An odd sort of relief entered her soul when the caller was not Ty but Geraldine Walton again, with an offer of more straw. 'I'm running out of space under cover here, so if Ash could pop over he'd be doing me something of a favour,' Geraldine added.

'It's very good of you think of me,' Phinn replied, feeling for certain now that Ash was more the cause for the call than the fact that Geraldine had more straw than she knew what to do with. Geraldine had said not one word about having surplus stocks when she had wandered over yesterday to settle what she owed her! 'Ash isn't around just now. But I'd be glad of the straw,' she accepted.

Phinn was about to go looking for Ash, and found she did not have to when he came crashing in through the front door. 'It's bucketing down out there!' he exclaimed, shaking rain from his arms.

'You don't fancy going out again?'

'Need something?' he enquired, at once willing to go on an errand. He hadn't heard what the errand was yet!

'Geraldine Walton has more straw…' Phinn did not have to say more. Though this time Ash did not seem quite as reluctant as he had before.

'I'll wait for this to give over first,' he said, and, as she herself had done, he went up to change.

The house seemed so quiet when, a half-hour

later, keys to the pick-up in hand, Ash left for Geraldine Walton's stables.

Feeling restless suddenly—even Mrs Starkey was out—Phinn was about to go and have a chat to Ruby when, as she was walking past, she saw that the music room door was again open. Either Wendy or Valerie must have left it ajar.

About to close the door and walk on by, Phinn, with her hand on the door handle, found she was hesitating. She had nowhere near the natural talent her father had had for the piano, but he had instructed her well.

It was an age since she had last played. An age since she had last wanted to play. Phinn pushed the door open wider and took a few steps into the room.

She took a few more steps, and a few more, and was then looking down at the piano keys—the lid having been left open because that was best for the piano.

The keys invited. She stretched out a hand and played one note—and then another. And as she stood there she could almost hear her father say, 'Come on, kiddo, let's murder a little Mozart.'

A sob caught the back of her throat. She coughed away the weakness, but felt drawn to sit down on the piano stool. And that was all it took.

She was rusty from lack of practice, but the notes were there—remembered. Her father had loved Mozart. She played Mozart in his memory, remembering the good times they had shared, remembering his laughter. Oh, how he'd loved to laugh…

How long she sat there, 'murdering' Mozart's Concerto Number Twenty-Three, Phinn had no idea. Nor did she have any idea quite when memories of her father started to merge with thoughts of Ty Allardyce.

Nor, when she had just come to the end of the adagio, did she know how long Ty Allardyce had been standing there, watching her. For she felt rather than saw him, and looked up, startled. And then she was startled *and* totally confused. She took her hands from the keys immediately.

'How long have you been standing there?' she gasped, feeling choked suddenly.

'Long enough to know you're a sensitive soul with a splendid touch. And a talent you have been keeping very well hidden.'

She abruptly stood up and, feeling highly emotional just then, moved away from the piano. 'It needs tuning!' she said, purely because she was otherwise bereft of words. She made for the door, but had to halt when Ty blocked her way. 'I'm sorry,' she apologized, for using the instrument. 'You don't mind…?' Her all at once husky voice trailed away, words still defeating her.

'Don't be sorry. I didn't know you could play.' He seemed slightly staggered by his discovery. But he collected himself to tell her, 'Out of tune or not—that was quite beautiful.'

Tall and dark, he looked down at her, still blocking her way. 'I—thought everyone was out...' she began, but he was stretching out a hand to her cheek.

'What's this?' he asked gently, looking down into the deep blue of her eyes. Then, so tenderly she could scarcely believe it, Ty touched her skin and wiped away a stray tear that had rolled down the side of her face uninvited by her. And Phinn at that moment felt too utterly mesmerised to move. Who would have suspected him of such tenderness? 'Sad memories?' he asked softly.

'I—haven't played since my father died,' she replied, her voice still holding that husky note.

'You're still mourning him,' Ty stated.

'We were close. But it's getting better,' she said, and for the first time she felt that it really was.

'Oh, come here,' Ty murmured and, taking a hold of her, he pulled her into his arms. 'I think it's high time someone gave you a hug,' he voiced from above her head.

And, most peculiarly, Phinn found that she was snuggling into his hold and truly liking the feel of his broad manly chest against her face. But she stirred against him. She did not want to move, but this could not be right.

'You've come home for some peace and tranquillity,' she began. 'Not to…' She pulled back from him. 'I'm all right now,' she said.

Ty let her go and stepped back, his grey eyes searching her face. She smiled up at him, to prove that she was indeed all right, and he smiled back. 'If I promise to get the piano tuned, will you promise to come in here and play whenever you want to—regardless of who's in and who's out?' Phinn stared at him numbly, and he smiled and made her feel weepy again, when he assured her, 'This is your home now.'

Too full suddenly to say a word, Phinn quickly went by him—out from the music room, along the hall, and straight up the stairs to her room. She had acknowledged that Ty did strange things to her long before she got there.

Collapsing onto the bedroom chair, she found her thoughts were not of her father, as they so often had been, but of Ty Allardyce and the complex man he was.

After having been ready at one time to throw her off his lands, he was now telling her that this, Broadlands Hall, was her home! Obviously he was only referring to it being her temporary home, but still the same, Ty just saying what he had had the effect of making her feel less rootless—albeit only temporarily.

She remembered that oh, so tender touch to her

cheek, remembered the gentle way he had held her in his arms, and, most oddly, felt that she wanted to be back in his arms, back being held by him again.

But if he was a complex man, what about her? Only then did she realise how overwhelmingly pleased she was that he was home!

Which—the fact that it pleased her to know he was there—made it seem somewhat illogical to her that she felt reluctant to go down and see him again. Shy? Her? Never! She glanced at her watch. His watch. And felt decidedly not herself. What on earth was the man doing to her, for goodness' sake?

Nothing! Nothing at all, she told herself stoutly. Grief, it was just that, having been around men pretty much all her life—her father's friends, mainly—she had never met any man quite like Tyrell Allardyce.

Still the same, since he was home to keep his brother company—if Ash was back—Phinn saw no good reason to go down.

She did, however, leave her room briefly to go and check on Ruby. But she returned to her room and, when clothes had never particularly bothered her before—what she wore being immaterial so long as it was clean and respectable—she spent some time wondering if she should perhaps put on a dress for a change.

Ten minutes later, having dithered on the yes or

no question for more than long enough, Phinn decided she must be going mental! Smart trousers and a top had been good enough all this week. Why on earth would she want to wear a dress just because Ty was home?

At seven twenty-five, wearing the smart trousers and a top, Phinn went down the stairs to the drawing room, where the two brothers were in idle conversation.

Her glance went straight to Ty, who looked across the moment she came in. He made no mention of her piano-playing activities, and she was grateful for his sensitivity there.

'Would you like something to drink, Phinn?' he enquired courteously. She shook her head. She wasn't shy; she knew that she wasn't. She just felt not herself somehow. 'Then perhaps we'd better go and see what Mrs Starkey has in store for us,' he said with a smile.

What Mrs Starkey had in store, after a superb cheese soufflé starter, was trout with almonds as a main course—which gave Ash cause to remark to his brother, 'Phinn took me fly-fishing yesterday.' Lack of space had dictated that her father's piano had to go, but Phinn had been unable to part with his fishing equipment. 'You know—the trout stream I sketched? It's hidden behind Long Meadow,' Ash continued.

'Long Meadow?' Ty queried, with a glance to Phinn.

'Been there years,' she obliged.

'You should see Phinn cast a line!' Ash went on. And then reported, 'She's promised to teach me to tie a fly.'

Ty's gaze was on her again, with that expression on his face that she was getting to know. 'Is there nothing you cannot do?' he asked lightly.

'Heaps of things,' she replied, and felt obliged to mention, since this clever man must know full well that her casting skills had been learned while trespassing in waters that belonged to the estate, 'Old Mr Caldicott used to appreciate the odd trout.'

Ty looked from her to the trout on his plate. 'You caught these yesterday?'

But even while she was shaking her head, Ash was chipping in. 'Not Phinn. Me. Phinn went all girly on me and put her catch back. Though...' Ash looked down at his own plate '...I don't remember mine being this big.'

'You'll never make a fisherman, Ash,' Phinn butted in, aware that all the fishermen *she* knew exaggerated sublimely. She guessed that Mrs Starkey's errand that afternoon had included a visit to the fishmonger's in town.

And while Ash was grinning, Ty asked him what else he had been up to that week. 'Walked a lot. Fished a lot,' Ash answered. 'Ran an errand for Phinn. Oh, and prior to the specialists you arranged getting here to survey and check out the Dark Pool, I took delivery of that danger notice we talked about and hammered it in. Looks all right too—even though apart from us it's only trespassers that are likely to see it.'

Ty looked to Phinn, and as her lips twitched on recalling the way he had threatened to have her summonsed for trespassing, his rather pleasant-shaped mouth picked up too, and there seemed to be only the two of them there, in a kind of small, intimate moment between them.

And then Ash was going on. 'Phinn thinks I'm gorgeous, by the way.'

Phinn shared a grin with Ash, feeling just then that they had become firm friends. But, happening to glance back at Ty, she saw that he was suddenly looking more hostile, if anything. Certain then that she had imagined any kind of an intimate moment with him, she could only wonder what she had done wrong now.

For courtesy's sake, in front of Ash, she pretended that she was unaffected whichever way Ty looked at her, or however hostile he was. What had happened to the tender, understanding man of that afternoon?

Phinn ate her way through the rest of her meal, but could not wait to be able to leave the dining room. The moment the meal was at an end, she was getting to her feet.

'If you'll excuse me?' she said politely to no one in particular. 'I'll go along and check on Ruby.' Both men were on their feet too. Phinn did not wait to find out whether they objected or not.

Having been stewed up inside for the last half-hour, Phinn calmed down as she tended to Ruby. And the calmer she became, gradually she began to see what Ty's hostile look had been all about. Ash, because of her cousin, had got himself into quite a state. Ty, seeing her and Ash getting on so well— and for all his previous opinion that his brother was so ensnared by her cousin that other women did not exist—must now be afraid that another of the Hawkins clan was getting to him. There was no other explanation for that hostile look.

Well, he need not worry. She and Ash were friends and nothing more. And, conscious of how concerned Ty had been, and probably still was, about Ash, she had one very good way of putting him straight.

Though before she could go and see him she spotted Ruby's ears pricking up, and had a fair idea then that she wouldn't have to wait that long.

Nor did she. And as Ty stepped into the stable, before she could say anything, he got in first. 'I wanted a word with you.'

For one dreadful moment Phinn thought he was going to ask her to leave. But even with that sinking feeling in the pit of her stomach, pride stormed in to make her aggressive. 'I didn't do it—whatever it was!' she stated, showing a fair degree of hostility of her own.

Ty stared at her in some surprise. 'Heaven help us!' he grunted. 'Do you always meet trouble halfway?'

'I'm in trouble?' she questioned belligerently.

'You will be if you don't shut up and let me get a word in!'

She opened her mouth, and then closed it. Then opened it again to tell him, 'Whatever it is, don't raise your voice and frighten my horse!'

'Oh, God, you're priceless,' Ty muttered, and, putting his hand into his trouser pocket, he pulled out something and handed it to her. 'Here,' he said, 'I got you this.'

Having taken it from him, Phinn looked and was stunned at what he had given her. 'A watch!' she gasped. And not just any old watch, but a most beautiful watch!

'The one you have on is much too big for your delicate wrist,' he commented.

But just then Phinn suddenly noticed the maker's name, and warm colour rushed to her face. 'You got this especially for me?' she questioned—it must have cost a mint! Hurriedly she thrust it back at him. 'No, thank you,' she told him primly.

'No?' He seemed quite taken out of his stride—as if it had never occurred to him that she would not accept it. 'What do you mean, no?' he questioned shortly.

'It's too expensive!'

'Don't be ridiculous!' he rapped.

And that infuriated her. 'Don't you call me ridiculous!' she hissed, even in her fury mindful of Ruby. 'My watch—if that's meant to be a replacement—cost only about forty pounds. I wouldn't even hazard a guess at the price you paid for that one.' And, as Ty continued to stare at her, 'If you want this one back—' she began, starting to undo the clasp.

Ty's hand coming to hers to stay her action caused a tingle to shoot through her body. 'Keep it on,' he ordered. Then all at once his tough expression changed. 'Have I offended you, Phinn?' he asked softly.

And just then, right at that very moment, Phinn knew—quite absurdly—that she was in love with him. Just like that she knew.

Again, from the pure emotion of the moment, she went red. Though she somehow managed to keep her head to tell him, 'Right is right and wrong is wrong. And that—' indicating the watch in his hand '—is wrong.'

Ty studied her for long silent moments. Then, slipping the watch back into his pocket, 'I don't think I've ever met anyone with quite such high morals as you,' he stated.

'Then you've been mixing with totally the wrong company,' she replied with an impish grin, though was uncertain that she wanted to be considered too much of a goody-goody. Although, on thinking about it, to have trespassed quite happily all over his land without the smallest compunction did, she felt, rather tarnish her goody-goody halo a little bit. 'Anyhow, I rather wanted to have a word with you too.' She looked from him, scared for a moment that this new love she felt for him might somehow be visible to him.

'What's wrong?' he asked sharply.

'Nothing's wrong!' she snapped back, moving away from Ruby—if they were going to have a row, she would prefer that her Rubes, so sensitive to atmosphere, did not know about it. 'The thing is,' she went on more calmly—time now to let him know that *this* Hawkins wasn't after his brother, or him either for that matter, time to let him know that she had other fish to fry. 'Er…' How to get started? 'Will you be here tomorrow night?' She said it the only way she could: bluntly.

Ty eyed her for a couple of solid seconds. 'You're asking me for a date?' he enquired, his expression completely serious.

Phinn rolled her eyes heavenward. 'It's not your birthday!' she answered snappily but then, probably because a date with Ty sounded like just so much bliss, 'I have other irons in the fire,' she informed him snootily. 'Kit, the vet, has asked me out tomorrow night.'

'The vet? He's been here?'

'Several times, actually. Ruby has been unwell.'

'She's better now?' he asked tersely.

Phinn declined to go into details of the anxiety of it all, but agreed that Ruby was well again. 'So, given that I wouldn't want to leave her for too long, I presume I'm allowed some time off—if you're at home?'

Ty studied her as though he did not care very much for this conversation. But then suddenly he smiled. It was a silky kind of smile; one she had no belief in!

And she knew that she was right not to have belief in it when, his voice as silky as his smile, he said, 'My dear Miss Hawkins, how could you have forgotten?'

She quickly racked her brains, but could think of nothing she had forgotten. 'Forgotten what?'

'That you can't possibly go out with him.'

'Why can't I?' she demanded belligerently.

He smiled again. Love him she might, but she still wanted to swipe that smile off his face. 'How can you go out with another man,' he enquired pleasantly, 'when you know full well that you're supposed to be my girlfriend?'

For a stunned couple of seconds, Phinn stared at him, speechless. And then it was that she remembered that Ty did not want Ash to know that the real reason she was there was to keep him company, and that she had gone along with that. She had also agreed that Ash had enough of a burden weighing on him, and had agreed too, she supposed, to let Ash believe what he obviously believed—that she was there more as Ty's friend than his. In fact his girl-friend—would-be—sort of.

In actual fact, now she came to think of it, she did not feel too put out that her dating facility had been curtailed. But she gave Ty a look of disgust for his trouble anyway, and, muttering an old family saying, 'Well, give me a kiss and lend me tuppence!' which was meant to convey her disgust, she turned sharply away from him.

Then nearly died of fright when, spinning her back round to him, Ty replied, 'Anything to oblige,' with a wicked kind of gleam in his eyes. And the next thing Phinn knew Ty had hauled her into his arms and his head was coming down.

Desperately she tried to avoid his lips, but with one hand moving up to the back of her head he held her still. Then his mouth settled over hers and she was lost.

Unhurriedly, he eased her lips apart, and while her heart hammered frantically away inside her, he held her close up against him. And Phinn never wanted it to end.

A discreet kind of cough from the doorway made

her jerk away from Ty. But he still had an arm about her waist as they both turned to see a grinning Ash standing there.

'Sorry to interrupt,' he said, not looking sorry at all, but looking very much like the Ash she had known before her cousin had so unceremoniously dumped him. 'But the vet's been on the phone. I didn't know if it would be important or not, now that Ruby seems better, but I said you would call him back.'

'Oh, thanks, Ash,' Phinn replied, trying to gather her scattered wits. And, needing to be on her own, 'I'll go and call him now,' she added.

But so much for being on her own to sort her feelings out. 'I'll come with you,' Ty offered, and while Ash went on his way, actually whistling 'Love Is in the Air', Phinn left the stable hoping that Ty had no idea of what the tune was.

She was still feeling all of a fluster from Ty's kiss—which she had to admit, reluctantly, that she might have inadvertently invited—when, with Ty still by her side, they reached the house.

They were in the hall and within a yard of the phone when, with Phinn making no attempt to slow her speed, Ty caught a hold of her arm. 'Make the call from here,' he ordered. 'Tell him you're spoken for.'

And bang went her feeling of being all mixed up inside. 'Like blazes, I will!' she erupted, not taking kindly to being so bossed about—after he had kissed her so wonderfully too! If she rang Kit Peverill at all, it would be in the privacy of her room and on her mobile.

But, with Ty still holding her arm, the matter was settled when the phone just then rang. Ty stretched forward and picked it up. 'Allardyce,' he said, and while he listened Phinn was thinking it might be some business call and she could make her escape. 'Phinn's here now,' she heard him say. And then he was handing the phone to her and insisting, 'Tell him.'

Phinn sent him a malevolent look, which bounced straight off him, and took hold of the phone. She guessed the call must be from Kit, and wished Ty Allardyce would clear off because, although he had let go of her arm, he was still standing there, clearly bent on listening to her every word.

'Hello,' she managed pleasantly, after taking a calming breath.

'I hope you don't mind me ringing again, Phinn,' Kit replied, a touch diffidently. 'Only I'm on call, and I thought I'd leave you my on-call number so I wouldn't miss you when you rang. Er—have you thought any more about tomorrow night?'

She felt uncomfortable, and that feeling was not helped when Ty Allardyce seemed immune to her killing looks. 'The thing is, Kit…' she began. 'I—um—I'm sorry.'

'You can't make it?' He sounded disappointed. 'Perhaps some other time? If...'

'Well, to be honest—' since the deed had to be done, she now wanted it done and out of the way '—your invitation—er—sort of caught me on the wrong foot. That is—I've just—er—started seeing someone.' There—it was done.

'Oh,' Kit mumbled. 'Oh, all right.' And, 'Er—if it doesn't work out...'

'Of course,' she replied, but could not help but feel awful, even if she now knew that she did not want to date Kit. But, as she put the phone down, it did not make her any less cross with Ty Allardyce. 'Satisfied?' she asked him waspishly.

And he smiled, a more genuine smile this time. 'Don't be mad at me, Phinnie,' he said charmingly. 'You know he doesn't mean anything to you.'

'How do I know?' Smile or no smile she was at her belligerent best. 'We—Kit and I—we might have been—er—made for each other.'

But Ty was shaking his head. 'I kissed you, Phinn. But you kissed me back.' And, as warm colour stained her cheeks, 'You wouldn't have done that had the vet been in there with so much as half a chance.'

Phinn stared at him open-mouthed. 'How did you get to know so much about women?' she exclaimed in disgust. But then, as jealousy nipped for the first time ever in her life, 'Don't tell me!' she ordered. 'I don't want to know!' And with that she turned about and stormed angrily away.

But the truth of the matter was, he was right. He thought she had high morals, and while she did not know about that, what she *did* know was that he was right in that she would not have returned his kiss had she felt anything at all for Kit Peverill. More, having fallen in love with Ty Allardyce, she knew without doubt that the idea of being in any man's arms other than his was absolutely abhorrent to her.

Now, why had she gone and fallen in love with him? Of all the idiotic things to do, wasn't that the cruncher? Kiss her he might—if invited. And she could not deny her inviting words were probably enough for any red-blooded male—be she his pretend girlfriend or no. But when it came to the love stakes idiotic was what it truly was. Because worldly, sophisticated men like Tyrell Allardyce just did not fall in love with lippy, trespassing 'village locals' like her.

Phinn returned to the stable to chat to Ruby. She had only just discovered her feelings for Ty, but one way and another she was finding it all very disheartening.

Though, whatever else happened during the remainder of her time at Broadlands, all Phinn knew—with Ty Allardyce knowing so very much about women—was that she was going to have to keep her feelings for him extremely well hidden!

# CHAPTER SIX

SATURDAY began with a miserable wet dawn, but Phinn could not be down. She'd had a restless night, and awoke to know that her love for Ty was no figment of her imagination. It was still there this morning and, while she would take great care that he would never know of it, it gave her a feeling of joy to know that he was here, at home.

She did not want to think of how it would be when he went back to London, but decided that for the moment she would just enjoy knowing that he was sleeping under the same roof.

Phinn showered and dressed early and, with her hair pulled back in a band, slipped quietly out of the house.

It was while she was talking to Ruby that Phinn realised she must have begun to fall in love with Ty as far back as when he had offered them a home. Incredible as it seemed, it must have been then. She clearly recalled thinking then that there was something not right about it somewhere. Now she knew what it was—some sixth sense had been trying to warn her that before too long she was going to get hurt.

Too late now to do anything about it. She was in love with him, and that love was here to stay. She knew that.

When Phinn went back to the house, both Ty and Ash were at breakfast. All at once feeling a sudden eagerness to see Ty again, she hastened up the stairs to wash and tidy signs of the stable from her before going quickly down again.

'Ty wants to take a walk around the estate. Coming with us?' Ash asked.

Normally she would have liked nothing better. But, sensitive to the two brothers, she thought that perhaps they might need some brotherly time together, and they would probably talk more easily if she were not there.

'I've a date with…' Pure wickedness made her look at Ty—there was a glint in his eyes that said he was listening, and was daring her to have a date with the vet. 'With a pitchfork, a wheelbarrow and, by special request, Jimmie Starkey's compost heap.'

'Whatever turns you on,' Ash replied, and, with a smile, 'If you prefer mucking out the stable to a morning spent in fascinating company…'

Phinn grinned at him, affection for him in her look, and real pleasure in her heart as she noticed how his appetite had started to pick up. With luck that twenty or so pounds he had lost would soon be put back on again.

'Did you sleep well?' Ty butted in sharply.

Taken by surprise, Phinn turned to him, startled. 'Do I look haggard?' she queried.

One sleepless night and she looked a wreck!

His answer was to study her for all of one full minute. And, just when she was thinking that she was going to go red at any second, 'You look quite beautiful,' he answered, so entirely unexpectedly and sounding so much as if he meant it, that she did blush.

She recovered quickly, however, and, having realised that his remark had to be because Ash was there, and that Ty was merely playing his role of being interested in her, she told him lightly, 'I'm still not coming with you.'

Up in her room after breakfast, she went and stared at her face in the mirror. She wanted to be beautiful. She wanted Ty to think she was beautiful. But did a straight nose, wide and quite nice delphinium-blue eyes, eyebrows that were a shade darker than her strawberry-blonde hair, a dainty chin and a fairly nice forehead—oh, and a complexion that, yes, had been remarked on in the past as 'quite something'—constitute beauty? Her phone rang and put an end to her daydreaming.

It was her mother, her morning's golf having been cancelled because Clive had a heavy cold. 'How are things, darling? And how's Ruby?' It was good to chat to her mother, and they talked for some while, with her mother ending, 'When are we going to see you?'

Promising to try and pay them a visit soon, Phinn rang off, reflecting that her mother had a very different life now from the one she had had with her father. But this wasn't getting Ruby's stable sorted.

The early-morning rain had cleared when, changed into old jeans and a tee shirt, Phinn turned Ruby out into the paddock and went back to the stable. Before she could start work, though, Ty Allardyce appeared. How she loved him! Her heart raced. How he must never know.

'The weather's cleared for your walk,' she offered, friendly, polite—that was the way. But, forget it. Ty, it seemed, had come looking for a fight.

'Have you been in touch with Peverill?' he questioned bluntly, coming to stand but a yard from her. What happened to *You look quite beautiful*? Phinn thought.

'Since my telephone conversation with him last night, you mean?'

Ty gave her an impatient look. 'I passed your room—you were on the phone with someone.'

What big ears you have! For one delicious moment, Phinn had the weird notion that Ty had sounded jealous. See where falling in love got you—it made you weird in the head! All he was bothered about was the thought that she might blow their cover by going out with the vet after all.

Despite her inner turmoil, Phinn smiled at him sweetly. 'You don't really mind if I chat on the phone to my mother occasionally? It's ages since I last saw her.'

Ty's annoyed look instantly fell away. 'I've been a brute again, haven't I?' He did not expect an answer.

He got one anyway. 'You can't help it. It's your nature,' Phinn replied—and just had to laugh. She didn't believe it for a moment. What *was* his nature was a big brother's need to look out for his younger brother—and if that included taking her to task if he thought she was going to put a spoke in the wheel of the progress he had made so far, he would.

But Ty was unoffended by her remark, and actually seemed amused by it. Then, taking on board what she had just said about not having seen her mother for ages, and remembering she had sold her car, he was serious as he suggested, 'There are several vehicles here if you'd like to go and visit your mother.' And, as an afterthought, 'I'll take you to see her myself, if you prefer.'

'Wouldn't dream of it,' Phinn replied, thinking again what a complex man he was. He had come to see her ready to sort her out, and here he was offering to spend some of his precious weekend taking her family visiting!

'Or why not invite her and her husband here for a meal? Your mother could see where—'

Phinn stopped him right there. 'Do you know, Ty,' she butted in, 'when you forget to be a brute, you sometimes surprise me by being really, really nice?'

He looked taken aback. But then, as if noting from her solemn-eyed expression that she was being sincere, his tone changed when he quietly stated, 'You do realise that if you carry on in that vein, you're in serious danger of being kissed again.'

Oh, my, how he could make her heart race! Phinn teetered on the brink of saying, *Promises, promises*— but instinctively knew that such a remark was bound to guarantee that Ty *would* kiss her. And, while heart and soul she would welcome his kisses, she knew that that way lay danger: danger of Ty, with his experience.

Which was why she forced herself to take a step away from him. 'One kiss in twenty-four hours is more than enough for us village locals,' she told him primly.

His lips twitched. 'You're never going to let me forget that "village locals" comment, are you?'

'Not if I still know you when you're a hundred,' she replied cheerfully. And offered nicely, 'If you want to help I'm sure I can rustle up another pitch-fork from somewhere.'

He looked amused. 'You certainly know how to say goodbye to a man,' he said, declining her offer, and went.

After that, the day seemed to fly by. Ty and Ash came back from their inspection of the estate, with Ty approving of Sam Turner's suggestions for keeping Pixie End Wood healthy.

After a quick lunch he said he had arranged to call in at Yew Tree Farm. 'Anyone like to come?' he asked.

'You and Phinn go,' Ash suggested. 'If Phinn will loan me her rods, I fancy having another go at casting.'

'Oh, I don't—' Phinn began. Ash was welcome to borrow her fishing equipment, but Ty wouldn't want her with him when he went to call on his tenants at Yew Tree Farm.

'That's fine,' Ty cut in. 'See you in half an hour then, Phinn.'

She opened her mouth to protest, saw Ty was looking at her with something of a stern expression, and, probably because deep down she wanted to spend some time with him, 'Offhand, I can't think of anything I'd rather do,' she remarked.

Of course Ty thought she was being saucy, but she did not care. Did not care either that he would probably just as soon go on his own. But if he wanted Ash to think that they were more friendly than they were, who was she to argue?

'Ruby all right?' Ty queried when, thirty-five

minutes later, with Ash in possession of her father's fishing equipment, Phinn sat beside Ty in his car and they set off.

Ruby, in Phinn's view, was a nice safe topic. 'She's feeling great today,' she replied happily.

'But doesn't always?'

'Poor love, she's getting on a bit. Sometimes she's fine for weeks on end, but just lately—well, she's had more bad days than good.'

'And that's where the vet comes in?'

Not so safe a topic. 'Kit has been brilliant.' She gave the vet his due. 'Most attentive.'

'I'll bet,' Ty muttered. Then, plainly not interested in the vet, 'Tell me about Phinn Hawkins,' he requested.

'You know everything.'

'I very much doubt that,' he replied.

'What do you want to know?'

'You could start by telling me your first name?' he suggested.

And have him laugh his socks off? Not likely! 'You know my first name.'

'Phinn doesn't begin with a "D",' he countered. She wondered how on earth he knew that her first name began with a "D". 'Your father's initials were "E.H." The only other initials carved into the underside of Grandmother Hawkins' table are "D.H".'

'You checked?' she asked, startled.

'I spotted the initials when I purchased the table, obviously. Since I was the one who upended it to take it to your room, I couldn't very well miss seeing them again.'

'I never did thank you for that lovely gesture. I did—do—appreciate it.'

'So, what does the "D" stand for?' Stubbornly, she refused to answer. 'You're not going to deny the "D" is yours, I hope?'

'So, about me. I was born at Honeysuckle Farm and was adored by my parents and grandparents. Because my mother was quite poorly after having me—some complication or other—my father looked after me, and he never stopped even when she was well again.'

'As he adored you, you in turn adored him?' Ty put in.

'Absolutely! He was wonderful. A gifted pianist. A…'

'It was he who taught you to play?'

'Yes.' She nodded, remembering those hours at the piano. 'Just as he taught me so many other things.'

'Go on,' Ty urged, when she drifted off with her thoughts for a second or two.

'You can't possibly be interested.'

'I wouldn't have asked had I not been interested,' he replied—a touch sharply, she felt. She mustn't go reading into it that he might be interested in any personal way in Phinn Hawkins. 'What "many other things" did he teach you?'

'Apart from how to trespass all over Broadlands?'

'He taught that one well,' Ty commented—but she sensed amusement rather than censure in his tone.

'He also taught me to respect the property I was trespassing on. Not to fish out of season, where to swim and where not to swim.'

'How to perform a flat-out racing dive?'

'We owe that one to him,' she murmured.

'That alone forgives him anything he ever did wrong,' Ty said quietly, and they both knew they were talking of her rescue dive. 'The courage it took to do it, though, was all your own,' he added.

But Phinn loved him, and did not want him to relive a time when he might have lost his beloved brother in what was a very heart-tearing memory for him. 'Anyhow,' she said brightly, 'having bought me many books he thought I should be reading, and having many times taken me out of school when he thought they were neglecting areas they should be teaching me, he would take me round museums and art galleries. We went everywhere—concerts, opera... And when town got too much we would come home and walk through the woods, and he would teach me about trees and animals. Teach me how to sketch, how to fish, tie a fly and appreciate Mozart.' She smiled as she confessed, 'I learned by myself how to take a swig of my father's beer down at the pub without pulling a face at the foul taste.' Her smile became a light laugh as she added, 'I supposed I learned by myself too, how to cuss and swear. I was less than four years old, it seems when I apparently came out with a mouthful that nearly sent my grandmother into heart failure and saw my mother banning my father from taking me anywhere near the Cat and Drum.'

There *was* a smile in Ty's voice when he suggested, 'You grew out of cussing very quickly, I take it?'

'In record time, I think you could say—and the ban was lifted,' she answered with a grin. 'And that is more than enough about me. Your turn.'

'Turn?' he queried, as if he had no idea what she meant.

'Oh, don't be mean! I've just talked my head off about me!'

'You can't…'

'Possibly be interested? That's my line! And I am.'

'Interested in me?'

'In a purely reciprocal way,' she replied—she who was avid to know every last little thing about him. 'According to Ash, you're a genius when it comes to business.'

'Business is quite good at the moment,' he replied—rather modestly, Phinn thought.

'You mean it's thriving?'

'It occupies a lot of my time.'

'But you love it?'

'It adds that bit of adrenalin to my day,' he admitted, adding, 'I'm out of the country all of next week.'

Her heart sank. It was being greedy, she knew, but if Ty was going to be out of the country all next week, then there was absolutely no chance whatsoever that he would come down to Broadlands any weekday evening.

'Ash will miss you,' she said, but could easily have substituted her own name.

'He'll be all right,' Ty answered. 'With you here I can safely go away, knowing that he could never have a better guardian.'

Feeling that they were getting away from the subject of him, Phinn was just about to ask him which university he had attended when she suddenly became aware that they were driving through the land farmed by Nesta and Noel Jarvis, the tenants of Yew Tree Farm. And the further they drove on, with flourishing fields on either side of the road, the more the contrast between Yew Tree Farm and Honeysuckle Farm hit her full square. Yew Tree Farm was thriving! The Jarvises must have had the same hard times that Honeysuckle had experienced. But where Honeysuckle had gone under, Yew Tree had somehow survived—had borne the fall in wheat prices, the rising cost of fuel, and had continued to make the farm the success it was today.

Neighbours of Honeysuckle, they had suffered the same vagaries of weather, all the wet summers, and must have endured the same machinery breakdowns, yet—they were thriving!

Phinn was reduced to silence as Ty steered his vehicle into the farmyard. No air of neglect here. No heaps of rusting machinery. Remembering Honeysuckle and its neglected air the last time she had seen it, she did not want to get out of the car. Perhaps she could stay where she was. Ty had said he was merely going to call in—perhaps his business would not take that long.

But, no, he was coming round to the passenger side and opening the door. Already he had a hand on her arm. 'If your business is private...' she suggested.

Ty looked at her, and seemed to guess from her expression that something was amiss, because, 'What is it?' he asked. But before she could tell him both Nesta and Noel Jarvis, having heard their vehicle, had come out to greet them.

Not wanting to cause a fuss, Phinn shook her head at Ty and, with his hand on her arm, stepped from the car. She pinned a smile on her face as Mr and Mrs Jarvis recognised her.

'You know Phinn, of course,' Ty commented as he shook hands with the couple.

'Phinn, my dear, how are you?' Nesta Jarvis asked. They had known Phinn all her life, and had both been at her father's funeral. 'We heard you were working at Broadlands now. How are you getting along?'

'We would be lost without her, Mrs Jarvis,' Ty commented, and enquired of Noel Jarvis, 'Busy time of year for you, I expect?'

They did not overstay their welcome, but while Ty politely refused an offer of refreshments and went into the study with Noel, Phinn stayed and had a cup of tea with Nesta. They passed the time with Nesta enquiring after her mother, and Phinn enquiring after the Jarvises' son and two daughters. The girls had married and moved away, while the son, Gregory, had married and now lived in a farm cottage, working with his father.

Phinn was still in a quiet frame of mind when, having said farewell to the Jarvises, she sat beside Ty on the journey back to the Hall.

Then suddenly Ty was steering the vehicle into a lay-by and pulling up. Phinn turned in her seat to look at him. 'Are you going to share it with me, Phinn?' he asked quietly, seriously.

She could have told him that there was nothing to share, but at the very least she owed him an apology. She swallowed on a knot of emotion, then with a shaky sigh began. 'I hated you when you gave us notice to quit. But you were right. We weren't paying the rent—and the place was a tip.'

'That wasn't your fault,' Ty put in quietly.

But she wasn't having that. 'You asked if there was nothing I couldn't do—well, I well and truly messed up there! I should have made more of an effort, but I didn't. And it's taken going to Yew Tree Farm today and seeing what a well-run farm should look like for me to see it.'

'Don't beat yourself up about it, Phinn,' Ty instructed her seriously. 'You had a home to run. Nobody would have expected you to be out riding a tractor all day.' She still felt she should have done more. Though it was a fact that Ty certainly made her feel better when he asked, 'Would your father have been happy for you to take on *his* work?'

Put like that, no, he would not. Her father might not have shown much interest in running the farm, but she knew he would have taken great exception had she attempted to take over. Her mother had often called her her father's playmate, and Phinn knew she would have taken the fun out of what had been his last days had she said that she had work to do each time he asked her to go somewhere with him. He had disliked it intensely when she had left the farm each day to go to her job at the accountants.

'How do you always know how to say just the right thing?' she asked Ty, and he smiled a gentle smile.

But, as her heart seemed to skip a beat, his smile deepened and he murmured conspiratorially, 'I'll bet Noel Jarvis can't play the piano like your father could.'

Oh, Ty. She loved him so. 'I bet he couldn't have trimmed my Easter bonnet like my dad did either,' she said, and was able to laugh. She loved Ty the more that he did not think her odd, but seemed to *know* that her dad trimming her Easter bonnet had been something rather special.

'All right now?' he asked.

She nodded. 'Yes,' she said. 'And—thank you.' And she felt the world was a wonderful place when, leaning across to her, Ty placed a brief kiss on her cheek.

'Let's go home—and see if Ash has caught any more trout.'

What they did find when they reached the house was that there was a beat-up old car on the drive. And as they went in Phinn clearly heard what to her was the unmistakable sound of a piano tuner at work.

She stopped dead in her tracks. 'Mr Timmins?' she queried of Ty, who had halted with her.

'Mr Timmins,' he agreed with a grin.

Phinn sailed up to her room. Mr Timmins never worked on Saturday afternoons for *anyone*! But, remembering Ty's wonderful grin, she felt just then that *she* would do anything for Ty too.

All too soon Saturday gave way to Sunday. It was a joy to her that Ty had decided not to leave for

London until very early on Monday morning, but to Phinn the hours on Sunday went by in a flash.

That evening after dinner, while she *wanted* to stay in the drawing room, where Ty was, she made herself get to her feet.

'I'm for bed,' she said, to no one in particular. And, because she just had to look at him, 'Have a good trip next week,' she bade Ty.

He stood up and walked to the door with her— purely for Ash's benefit, she knew. 'See you hopefully on Friday,' he murmured when they halted at the door, out of earshot of Ash.

Phinn nodded. 'Bye, you,' she said, and looked up into a pair of steady grey eyes.

'Bye yourself,' he said softly, and, to make her heart go positively wild, he bent down and, otherwise not touching her, gently kissed her on the mouth.

Phinn wheeled away from him without a word. Only when she got to her room and closed the door did she put her fingertips to the lips he had kissed. Oh, my!

It was not the same Broadlands without Ty there. The summer had temporarily disappeared, and it did nothing but rain on Monday. Bearing in mind that Ash still had a tendency to be a bit down occasionally, mainly in the afternoon, Phinn sought him out and offered to give him a fly-tying lesson.

But on Tuesday *she* was the one who was down.

Ruby was ill again. Kit Peverill was as good as ever, and recommended a new medicine for Ruby. New and expensive.

'I'd like her to have it,' Phinn told him, wanting the best for her Rubes, even if she had no idea how she was going to pay for it.

'Don't worry about settling your account straight away,' Kit said kindly, just as if he knew she was near to broke.

But she did worry about it. Before Kit had asked her out, the fact she sometimes owed him money had not unduly bothered her. She'd always known that she would pay him some time. But now that he had asked her out it seemed to make it more of a personal debt to him, somehow. And she did not like it.

By Thursday, however, Ruby was starting to pick up again, her new medication obviously suiting her. Phinn knew then that, whatever the cost, there was no way Ruby was going to stop taking it.

It was raining again at lunchtime, and while on the one hand Phinn was delighted with Ruby's progress, she could not lose that niggle of worry about owing the vet money.

Ash came and found her in the stables, and he did not seem very bright either. Phinn had an idea. It was too wet to take Ash off for a good long walk, but there was somewhere else she could take him.

'If you were very good, Ashley Allardyce, I

might think of taking you down to the pub for a pint,' she told him, managing to sound more bright than she felt.

Ash looked at her, considered the proposition and, with not much else happening in his life just then, accepted. 'If you promise to behave yourself, I might come,' he said. And, since they would both be soaked if they walked anywhere very far in the present downpour, 'The pick-up okay?'

The Cat and Drum was full of its usual lunchtime regulars. 'Take a seat over there,' Phinn instructed him. 'I'll get the drinks.'

'No, I'll get them,' Ash insisted.

'Actually, Ash, I rather wanted to have a private word with the landlord.'

'Devious maid,' Ash accused, though he didn't seem to mind that there had been a motive behind her invite to the pub. 'Make mine a pint.'

Telling Bob Quigley that she would like a quick word with him, Phinn delivered Ash his pint and returned to have a discussion with the landlord.

Phinn had finished her discussion with him when, as she half turned, she saw that Ash was deep in conversation with none other than Geraldine Walton!

Far from being the grumpy kind of man he had been with Geraldine when she had first introduced the two, Phinn observed that Ash seemed in no particular hurry to cut short the conversation they were having.

In fact, to Phinn's mind, Ash seemed suddenly to be very much lifted from his earlier mood.

In no hurry either to interrupt them, and wondering if Geraldine usually stopped by the Cat at lunchtime or if she had been passing and had recognised the pick-up parked outside, Phinn was glad just then to be accosted by Mickie Yates.

'What are you doing in this iniquitous place, young lady?' he greeted her warmly.

'Mickie!' she exclaimed, and kissed his whiskery cheek.

Chatting with Mickie took up a good five minutes—but Ash and Geraldine were still finding things to talk about. Don't hurt him! Phinn thought, finding protective feelings for Ash rushing to the surface. But then she reminded herself that, while Geraldine could not afford to be a softie and run a successful business, the owner of the riding school and stables was nowhere as hard-hearted and avaricious as her cousin Leanne.

Rather than have Ash look over and think he might be obliged to come back to her, Phinn stayed turned away from him. Jack Philips, an old friend of her father, came up to her, and then Idris Owen joined in, in to collect fresh supplies to take back to his forge. She could have chatted with them all day.

Eventually a much more cheerful Ash came over to them. When they at last left the pub, he asked if she had seen Geraldine Walton there, and Phinn replied, 'I did, actually. I hope you don't think me rude, but I didn't want to be impolite to my father's old friends and come over.'

'If you'd accepted all the drinks they offered you'd be staggering,' was all he replied.

Ruby continued to make progress, and Kit Peverill visited early on Friday morning to check her over and give her an injection. And still it rained. But with Ruby settled, a long day was stretching out in front of Phinn. Ty might be home tonight—but how to fill in those yawning hours between now and then? Then she had another idea.

One of the outbuildings had come in for modernisation when Ty had purchased Broadlands, and now served as the estate office. But so far Phinn had not seen the inside of it, and doubted that Ash had spent very much time in there either.

Bearing in mind, if village gossip had been correct, that Ash might have endured some kind of breakdown when working in an office environment, Phinn was wary of suggesting anything that might set him back in any way, but after she had spent some quality time with Ruby, Phinn went looking for him. She found him in the drawing room, staring out of the window at the rain.

'It's a lovely spot here,' she commented when, having heard her come in, Ash looked round.

'It is,' he agreed.

'I've just walked past the estate office. It struck me—I've never seen the inside of it.'

'I wish I didn't have to,' Ash muttered, explaining, 'I've been very neglectful. The paperwork is piling up in there.'

'Hmm…' Phinn murmured, and then offered lightly, 'Do you know, Ash? Today just might be your lucky day.' And, at his querying look, 'It just so happens that I'm a qualified secretary, with a certificate that says I'm good in office administration.'

Ash looked at her in surprise. 'No?'

'Yes,' she replied. And then offered, 'I bet together we could lick your paperwork into shape in no time.'

'You're on!' He grabbed at the offer.

Before she could think further they were out of the house, had the office door unlocked and the lights switched on against the dull day. In no time they were hard at it, tackling the paperwork.

They worked steadily through the rest of the morning, with Phinn keeping an eye on Ash in case the work they were doing was having any ill effect. It wasn't. In fact the more of the backlog they cleared, the brighter Ash seemed to become.

'Oh, Ty's already dealt with that,' he said at one point, having unearthed a letter from Noel Jarvis, enquiring about the possibility of Noel and his son purchasing Yew Tree Farm. 'It seems he phoned Ty in London when his letter here went unanswered.'

'That's probably why we went there last Saturday,' Phinn commented.

'It was,' Ash confirmed. 'Apparently the previous owner of Broadlands always refused to split up the estate. But with Ty saying I can have Honeysuckle Farm if I want it, he's quite happy to sell Yew Tree to the Jarvises. Ty said they have kept it in splendid shape all these years, and ought to have it—' He broke off. 'Oh, Phinn, I'm sorry. I wasn't meaning that Honeysuckle...'

'Don't apologise, Ash,' Phinn said quickly, feeling that she had grown up quite a lot recently. As short a while ago as last week she would have been upset to hear anyone compare Honeysuckle with Yew Tree unfavourably. But last Saturday, when she had felt so awful about the very same thing, Ty had made her feel better.

True, Honeysuckle was a mess. But she could have done little about that—not if she hadn't wanted to make her father's life less fun than it had been. Ty—darling Ty—had put that into perspective for her.

Oh, she did so hope he would come home tonight. It had been an unbearably long week without him. She didn't know if she would be able to take it if he did not come back tonight. She just could not face thinking of the emptiness if he did not come home the entire weekend either!

After a break, while she went and spent some time with Ruby, Phinn returned to the office feeling quite pleased with how much she and Ash had cleared between them. Only some pieces of filing and a few letters to type now, and the office would be more or less as up to date as it was ever going to be.

Phinn was in actual fact tearing away, typing the last of the letters, when—Ash having wandered off to 'get some oxygen to my brain'—the door opened. Her eyes on the page to the left of her, while her fingers raced over the keyboard, she assumed it was Ash returning.

She finished the letter and, as Ash had not made any kind of comment, looked up—and held in a gasp of breath. It was not Ash who had come in but Ty!

Warmth and joy filled her heart. She could not think of a thing to say, and just hoped she had not gone red.

Grey eyes held blue eyes, and then Ty was shaking his head slowly. 'Phinnie Hawkins,' he murmured, 'you never cease to amaze me.'

'Good,' she said impishly, but for no reason felt a touch embarrassed suddenly. 'I used to work as a secretary.'

Again he shook his head slightly. 'You worked as well as kept house?'

Like millions of other women, she didn't doubt.

'You thought all my day consisted of was a little light dusting?' she derided.

'The inside of that farmhouse was shining when I went there,' Ty documented. He paused, and then added, 'But, in addition to keeping the place immaculate, it was *you* who earned to put food on the table.'

Instantly her derision fell from her. She wasn't having that. 'Actually, my father was very clever. He could make, mend, repair and sell things. He was a good provider!' she said stoutly. She wished she hadn't mentioned that her father had sold things as soon as she'd said it. Ty already knew where one of their antiques had gone.

But, as if not wanting to fall out with her, Ty replied seriously, 'You don't have to defend him to me, Phinn. How could he be anything *but* a fine man to have produced such a lovely daughter?'

Phinn looked at him wide-eyed. Oh, my—did he know how to make a girl feel all flustered inside! And yet he had sounded as if he meant it—that 'lovely daughter' bit. 'Okay, so now that we all know you graduated from charm school with honours, what can we do for you?'

'I saw the light on. I thought it was Ash in here,' Ty remarked, and then asked, 'How's he been this week?'

'He's all right,' Phinn assured him. 'He's occasionally a bit down, but generally I think he's picked up quite a bit. Anyhow, I've been watching him today, and he seems fine with the office work.'

'You've been in here most of the day?'

'A lot of it. We've cleared most of the backlog—' Phinn broke off as just at that moment Ash came back.

'What do you think of my new PA?' he asked Ty. And, not waiting for him to answer, 'She's great,' he complimented her. With a smile to her, he looked at his brother to tell him cheerfully, 'In fact, were she not spoken for, I would seriously ask her to consider *me*!'

Phinn smiled happily. She knew that Ash was only teasing, but it was good to see him so uplifted. But when, smiling still, she glanced at Ty, she caught a glimpse of something in his expression that suggested he was not best pleased with his brother's comment.

A second later, however, and she knew that she was mistaken. Because Ty was telling his brother good-humouredly, 'Keep your hands off, Ash,' and then seemed about to depart.

Just to show how little she cared where he went, she said, 'This is the last letter, Ash.' Pretending to be more interested in the job in hand than in either of the Allardyce brothers. 'If you'd like to sign them, I'll take a walk down to the postbox.'

Getting ready to go down to dinner that night, Phinn was again beset by an urge to wear a dress.

Crackers—absolutely! She'd lived in trousers for so long now—apart from that one very memorable occasion down at the pool—that she was bound to evoke some sort of comment if she went down wearing something Ash would call 'girly'.

As usual both Ty and Ash were down before her, and, taking her place at the dining table, Phinn felt a flicker of anxiety. She wanted to have a word with Ty later, but was unsure how he would react.

'Did Phinn tell you she frogmarched me down to the pub for a pint yesterday lunchtime?' Ash asked Ty.

Ty turned to her, his grey eyes taking in her wide blue eyes and superb complexion. 'Nothing Phinn does surprises me any more,' he answered lightly. But, with his glance still on her, he asked, 'Are you leading my brother into bad ways?' his mouth curving upward good-humouredly.

'It's my opinion that Ash is perfectly capable of getting into mischief without my help,' she replied, and loved Ty so when he smiled at her. She looked away, got herself under control, and then asked, 'How was your trip?'

The meal passed with Ash asking questions about business and Ty saying that they didn't want to bore Phinn to death—when in truth she wanted to know everything about him. When pressed, he gave a light account of what he had been doing that week.

Phinn started to feel nervous when the meal came

to an end and the three of them ambled from the dining room. She felt comfortable enough now not to have to pay a courtesy ten-minute visit to the drawing room with them before she went to see Ruby.

As the two men turned towards the drawing room, and she made to go the other way, she called out, 'Ty!' He halted, and while Ash halted too at first, he must have realised that this was a private moment, because with a hint of a smile on his face he carried on walking.

'Phinn?' Ty encouraged, his eyes on her suddenly anxious face.

'The thing is. Well, I need to see to Ruby now. But—er—can I have a word with you later?'

Ty's expression became grim on the instant. 'If you're thinking of leaving, forget it!' he rapped sharply.

And that rattled her. She was uptight enough without that. 'Forget what I said about charm school!' she erupted, and stormed angrily away from him.

His voice followed her. 'I'll be in my study.'

'Huh!' she snorted in disgust.

As usual, being with Ruby for any length of time calmed her. And really, now that she was calm enough to think about it, Ty sounding so well and truly against her leaving Broadlands was rather flattering.

'So we'll stay, Rubes, my darling,' she told the old mare. 'Not that we've anywhere else to go. I know you like it here—and between you and me, but don't tell him, it would break my heart to leave.'

All of which put Phinn in a mellow frame of mind when she was ready to go back to the house. Nipping into the downstairs cloakroom to wash her hands, brush any stray bits of straw from her and push tendrils of strawberry-blonde hair from her forehead, Phinn rehearsed what she was going to ask. She didn't know why she felt so nervous. There was no way Ty could refuse.

She left the cloakroom hoping that Ty, aware by now of the length of time she spent with Ruby each evening, would be in his study as he'd said, and that she would not have to go looking for him.

As she went along the hall, she saw that the study door, which was usually closed, now stood open. *Oh, Ty!* She saw it as a sign of welcome, and again felt all squishy inside about him at his thoughtfulness.

Reaching the door, she tapped lightly on it, and her heart did a now familiar flutter as Ty came to the door and invited her in.

'Take a seat,' he offered, indicating a dark brown leather button-back chair and closing the door.

'It won't take that long,' she replied, as he turned to his computer and closed down the work he had been doing.

'You've changed your mind about leaving?' he questioned sternly.

'That was in your head—never in mine!' she replied, wishing she felt better.

'You're certainly looking guilty about something,' he answered shortly.

'No, I'm not!' she exclaimed. Needing some breathing space suddenly, she decided to take the seat he had offered a few seconds ago.

'Has the vet been here?' Ty demanded, taking the office chair and turning it to face her. When Phinn went red—purely because this interview was about money and the vet's bill she couldn't pay, he accused, 'What have you been up to?'—and she could have hit him!

'I haven't been up to anything! And of *course* the vet's been here! Ruby hasn't been well! And if I'm flushed it's not because I'm guilty of anything, but because I'm embarrassed! Honestly!' she fumed.

'Embarrassed? You?'

'Oh, shut up and listen,' she flared, doubting that any of his other employees had ever told him to shut up. But Ty did just that, for he said not another word, and she began floundering to find the right way to say what she had to. Then she realised that after the way this interview had started it just could not get any worse, and so she plunged. 'Is it all right with you if I take a part-time job?'

'You've got a job!' Ty shot back at her forthrightly, before she could blink.

'I know that!' she erupted. 'But this would only be part-time—in the evenings.'

'With the vet?' he charged, before she could draw another breath.

*'No!'* she protested, exasperated. He seemed to have the vet on the brain! 'I just thought that—well, Ruby will be all right on her own for a few hours, and Ash is looking so much better now… His appetite's picked up and he's generally not so— er—bruised as he was, say a month ago. And what with you coming home some evenings to keep him com—'

'If it's not Peverill, who else have you been in contact with?' Ty cut in.

She didn't want to tell him! All this in answer to what to her mind had been a perfectly simple question! Stubbornly she refused to answer. But Ty, at his most unfriendly, was waiting—and not yielding an inch.

'Oh—if you must know—' she exploded, nettled. 'Er…' Oh, damn the man! 'As Ash mentioned, we went down to the pub yesterday,' she said shortly.

Ty's expression did not lighten any. 'I'm all ears,' he invited.

She sent him a cross look, but had to go on. 'Well, the thing is, I was talking to Bob Quigley…'

'Bob Quigley? Another of your chums?'

'He's the landlord of the Cat and Drum,' she supplied impatiently. Now that she had got started, she wanted it all said and done quickly. Heavens above, it was only a tiddly request, after all!

'So you were talking to Bob Quigley down at the pub…?'

Phinn was about to mention how Ash had seemed to be getting on very well with the new owner of the riding school and stables, but she checked and decided not to—all the quicker to get her request over and done with. 'Well, the upshot of it is, that—well…' She was as impatient with herself as Ty obviously was. 'He—the landlord Bob—offered me a job.'

Ty looked at her with raised brows. 'Behind the bar?' He seemed more amused than anything.

'Yes,' she muttered.

Ty took that on board. 'Know anything about being a pub barmaid?' he enquired coolly, his amused look fading.

'Not the first thing,' she admitted. 'But when I asked Bob if he was fully staffed, he said he would give me a job any time.'

'I'll bet he did!' Ty barked bluntly.

'I wish you'd stop blowing hot and cold!'

'How do you expect me to react? Presumably it's not the company you're after, so what it boils down to is that I'm not paying you enough!'

Feeling contrite suddenly, she said, 'It's not that…' She was embarrassed again, and looked away from him. 'The thing is…'

She glanced back to Ty, and was totally undone when, as if seeing her embarrassment, he changed tack and asked gently, 'What, Phinn? Tell me.'

Phinn took a couple of shaky breaths. 'Well, the thing is, I'm starting to owe the vet big-time. And he's okay about that,' she added quickly. 'He knows that I'll pay him as soon as I can. But…'

'But?' Ty encouraged when she ran out of steam.

'Well, I've owed Kit before. And I didn't mind owing him before. But—well, now that he's asked me out, it—er—makes my debt to him sort of personal, and—well, I'd rather work a couple of hours each evening down at the Cat than leave my account unpaid.'

Ty leaned back in his chair, his expression softening. 'Oh, Phinn Hawkins, what am I going to do with you?' he asked. And then, not really wanting an answer, 'You'd desert us in the evenings, all because Peverill has taken a shine to you?'

She guessed Ty was making light of it because he could see how uncomfortable she was feeling. 'That's about it,' she mumbled. 'Kit's told me there's no hurry, that he knows I'll pay him when I can. But I feel kind of—awkward about it, and…'

'Oh, we can't have that,' Ty said, shaking his head,

but finding a smile for her. 'Quite obviously I shall give you a raise.'

'No!' she protested, feeling hot all over. 'I consider I'm overpaid by you as it is.'

'And *I* consider, dear Phinn,' Ty said to make her bones melt, 'that Ash and I would be totally lost without you.'

'Rubbish!'

'Not so. You've no idea how just by being here you brighten the atmosphere. You're so good with Ash—sensing his mood…'

'Tosh!'

'Not to mention that the office has never been straighter than it is today,' he went on, as if she hadn't spoken. 'And, given that I didn't take you on to do secretarial work, that makes me in *your* debt.'

'No!' she denied woodenly.

'You deserve a bonus at least.'

'No!' she maintained.

'Look here, Phinnie.' Ty changed tack again. 'See it from my point of view. You must know that I truly cannot have my girlfriend out working when I come home especially to see her.'

How that made her heart pump overtime! He had so truly sounded as if he really meant it. Thank goodness for common sense. But taking anything personal out of the equation, she could see that Ash might think it a touch peculiar if when Ty came home, *she* went out.

'I...' she said helplessly, and started to feel more anxious than ever.

'Don't worry at it, Phinn,' he instructed. 'I can see exactly why you don't want to owe Peverill—and I think you're quite right. But from my point of view you're doing more than enough here without taking on extra work. So I'll ring the vet and tell him to send Ruby's accounts to me.'

'What for?' she asked, feeling more than a shade bewildered.

'I'll settle them.'

'No, you won't!' she bristled hotly.

'Yes, I will,' he replied firmly—no argument. And, to show that the interview was over, he turned from her and reactivated his computer.

Phinn stared at him. He was not looking at her, and she guessed that since he had been abroad and out of his office all week he wanted her to go so that he could catch up on the week's business events.

With the utmost reluctance, feeling that she could argue with him until she was blue in the face and it would do no good, Phinn, with a heavy sigh but not another word, left his study.

She was on her way upstairs when the unpalatable truth hit her. Ty had appreciated her reason for not wanting to owe the vet because, as he had said, the vet had taken a shine to her. But by that same token Ty had just as good as told her that it was all right for her to owe the vet's bill to Tyrell Allardyce because—quite clearly—he, Ty, had *not* taken a shine to her.

She went to bed mourning that he had not—nor ever would. And spent a sleepless night aware that she was far too unsophisticated to appeal to the sophisticated tastes of Ty Allardyce.

# CHAPTER SEVEN

THE weather improved over the weekend and, having been in touch with Bob Quigley to thank him but to tell him she would not be needing a job after all, Phinn was sitting on the paddock rail on Sunday morning watching Ruby. Joy filled Phinn's heart at how well her mare was doing. Then she heard male voices as Ty and Ash came from the house.

A short while later, however, and Ty had left his brother and had come looking for her. He reached her, but for a moment or two said nothing—just observed her in her jeans and tee shirt, with her hair bunched back from her face in a rubber band.

This man she loved so much had the most uncanny knack of making her feel shy! She flicked her glance from him, paying particular attention to climbing down from the fence.

'What have I done wrong now?' she asked, once she was standing beside him.

'Who said you'd done anything wrong?' Ty countered lightly.

'Well, you haven't come over just for a bit of a chat,' she replied, feeling that there must be a reason for Ty coming to seek her out.

He shrugged. 'Could be I thought that—purely to give some authenticity to our relationship—perhaps I should take you out to dinner one evening.'

Her heart spurted again; there was nothing she would like better. But their 'date' wouldn't be for her benefit, but for Ash's. So she stayed outwardly cool to reply, 'We haven't got a relationship.'

'Stop being difficult!' Ty admonished. 'You know how sensitive Ash is. He'll start to wonder soon why you and I—'

'There is no you and I. And anyway, Mrs Starkey is the best cook in these parts. I'd sooner eat her dinners than anyone else's.'

'Difficult, did I say!' Ty grunted. 'Does any man *ever* get to date you?'

'The vet nearly did—once,' she retorted. And oddly, at that shared memory, they both seemed to find it funny—and both grinned.

'Oh, Miss Hawkins,' Ty murmured—which meant nothing, but she thought that perhaps he did quite like her. Then he sobered, and said, 'Actually, Phinn, Ash and I are on our way up to Honeysuckle Farm. Would it be too painful for you to join us?'

After seeing the way Yew Tree Farm had been run last Saturday—the way a farm should be run—Phinn rather thought that to see dilapidated Honeysuckle again would be extremely painful.

'I'd rather not,' she replied quietly, realising that Ash was not the only Allardyce who was sensitive. Ty was sensitive too—in this case to her feelings.

As was proved when he accepted without fuss that she would not visit the farm with them. 'There's every chance that Ash will take over the farm,' he commented.

'I'm sure he'll make a very good job of it,' she replied.

'You don't mind?'

'I'd rather Ash was there than anyone else,' she answered. Ty just stood and looked at her for long, long moments. 'What?' she asked, wondering if she had a smut on her nose.

'D'you know, Phinn Hawkins, you're beautiful inside as well as out?'

*Oh, Ty!* She wasn't sure that she wasn't going to buckle at the knees, so she turned from him and propped her arms on the fence, looking to where Ruby was happily looking back at her.

'I'm still not going out with you!' she threw over her shoulder—and had to hang firmly on to the rail when Ty did no more than move her bunched hair to one side and planted a warm kiss to the back of her neck—and then departed.

The hours dragged by while Ty was away with Ash, but positively galloped when they came back. And again that Sunday Ty decided to leave it until Monday morning before, extremely early, he left Bishops Thornby for London.

Phinn ached with all she had for him to come back on Monday evening, but it was Wednesday before she saw him again. Ash had gone on his own to spend some more time up at Honeysuckle, and she and Ruby had spent a superb day, with Ruby so much better and the weather perfect.

In fact it was late afternoon when, leaving Ruby in the paddock, Phinn decided to check in the office to see if anything there needed to be attended to. She had her back to the main house and was walking towards the office when she first heard a footfall and then—incredibly—someone behind her calling her name. But not the name she was used to!

'Delphinnium!' The call was soft, the voice male.

She froze. On the instant stood rooted. Then, shocked, she spun swiftly around. There stood Ty, with a grin cracking his face from ear to ear. 'How did you know?' she gasped in amazement. Where had he sprung from? She hadn't heard him arrive!

Ty, enjoying her utter stupefaction, continued to grin. 'I was driving near the church when I saw the vicar,' he answered. 'Very obligingly, he let me look at the baptismal register.'

Starting to recover, she came out fighting. 'If you breathe a word to anyone…' she threatened.

'What's it worth to stay quiet?' Ty asked, not a bit abashed. But, interested, he enquired, 'Where did you get a name like that anyhow?'

'Blame my father,' she sighed. 'I was supposed to be Elizabeth Maud, only he disobeyed his instructions when he went to register my birth—and thereby guaranteed that his only daughter would remain a spinster throughout the whole of her life.'

'How so?' Ty enquired, looking intrigued.

'With a name like mine, there is absolutely no way,' Phinn began to explain, 'that I'm going to stand up in a white frock in front of any vicar and have my intended roll in the aisle laughing to hear me declare that "I, Delphinnium Hawkins, take you, Joe Bloggs…"'

Ty looked amused, seemed happy to be home, and that gave her joy. 'Your name will be our secret,' he said conspiratorially. And then, while Phinn had drifted off on another front to wonder at the goings-on in this man's clever brain that, when he must have other much more high-powered matters going on in his head, he had paused to check out her name, he was asking, 'Talking of frocks—not necessarily a white one—have you got one?'

'You want to borrow it?' she asked, covering the fact that she was feeling a touch awkward. Was what he was actually saying that he was fed up with seeing her so continually in trousers?

His lips twitched at her retort, but he replied seriously enough. 'Apart from the fact that it's more than high time those fabulous legs had an airing, I've some people coming to dinner on Saturday—a couple of them will be staying overnight.'

'I can have my dinner with Mrs Starkey if—' she began, and saw a sharp look of hostility enter his expression.

'What the blazes are you talking about?' he cut in shortly.

'You won't want me around if you're entertaining,' Phinn tried to explain.

'Give me strength!' Ty muttered. 'If you haven't got it yet, *you*, *Delphinnium* Hawkins, are part of my family now!' he informed her angrily.

'Not the hired help?' Being short-tempered wasn't his prerogative. 'And don't call me Delphinnium!'

'You're asking for trouble!'

'Trouble is my middle name—and nobody asked you to adopt me!'

Ty gave an exasperated sigh. 'Sometimes I don't know whether I should wallop your backside or kiss you until you beg for mercy!' he snarled.

And, having made him so angry, when he had previously looked so happy, Phinn was immediately contrite. 'Don't be cross with me, Ty,' she requested nicely. 'I'm sorry,' she apologised, and, because he did not look ready to easily forgive her, she went closer and stretched up—and kissed him.

She felt his arms come about her. But he held her only loosely, but his anger was nullified. 'Now who's been to charm school?' he asked.

And she grinned. 'For you, I'll come to your table on Saturday. And for you—I'll wear a dress.'

His grey eyes stared down into her blue ones. 'You'd better clear off before I start some kissing of my own,' he growled. But he let her go, and Phinn, her heart drumming, cleared off quickly to the paddock gate.

Ty came home again on Thursday evening, and again on Friday, and by Saturday Phinn knew the names of the two people who would be staying with them overnight. They were brother and sister, Will and Cheryl Wyatt. Cheryl had apparently just sold her apartment and was between accommodation. She was staying with her brother until she found the right property to purchase.

Ruby was off-colour again on Saturday, so Phinn was out of the house with her when the brother and sister arrived, and missed seeing them.

Having gone to her room to clean up, Phinn decided she was in no hurry to go down again—which gave her plenty of time to stand under the shower. She shampooed her hair too, and later, robe-clad and with a towel around her hair, she surveyed her wardrobe. Her dresses were not too plentiful, and were mainly Christmas or birthday presents from her mother. But, again thanks to her mother, what dresses she had were of good quality.

Having surveyed them for long enough, the one that stood out from all the others was a plain heavy silk classic dress in a deep shade of red. She did not own any inexpensive fun jewellery, but felt the low neckline called for something. The dress definitely called for her hair to be other than pulled back in a band or plaited into a braid. And suddenly Phinn started to feel nervous. Which was odd, because she had never felt nervous about meeting new people before!

All the other people expected at dinner, as well as being his friends, were people Ty did business with, and nerves were still attacking as the time neared when she knew she must go downstairs. Standing before the full-length mirror, she surveyed the finished product. Good heavens—was that her?

She felt like herself, but gone was the lean and lanky, perpetually trouser-clad female she was used to. In her place was a tall, slender woman who curved in all the right places.

Her dress was shorter than she remembered—just above the knee. It seemed strange, ages since she had even last seen her knees. Was the neckline too low? Not by today's standards, she knew, but she wasn't used to revealing a bit of cleavage. Perhaps Grandmother Hawkins' pearls—rescued by her mother before her father could sell them—would bring the eye away from her bosom?

Phinn had used only a discreet amount of make-up, but somehow her wide eyes seemed to be much wider. Because there was no way the watch Ty had loaned her went with her outfit, the pearls were her only jewellery.

Her eyes travelled up to her hair, now confined by pins into an elegant twist on the top of her head.

All in all, she did not think she had dressed 'over the top'. She guessed that Ty's friends would be on the sophisticated side, and did not want to let him down. He had more or less asked her to wear a dress, hadn't he? Or—a dreadful thought struck her—had he? Had he just been teasing? They had been talking about 'a frock', hadn't they, when he had asked her if she possessed one?

Had he been joking? He hadn't actually *asked* her to wear a dress, she recalled. Would he be amazed to see her in anything but trousers?

Phinn was just about to make a rapid change into her more usual dinnertime garb when all at once she heard someone tap on her door.

For all of five seconds she was in a fluster. She had no clue who was on the other side of the door, but, glancing at the watch on her bedside table, Phinn saw that it was not yet seven.

She went to the door and opened it the merest trifle. She looked out. Ty stood there. Ty, magnificent in dinner jacket and bow tie. She opened the door wider, feeling better suddenly, with no need to hide what she was wearing. She was glad that Ty had hinted that she might feel more comfortable in a dress. By the look of it, even though it was with friends, tonight's dinner was a semi-formal affair—she would have felt very under-dressed had she stuck to her usual trousers and top.

'Oh, my…!' Ty breathed, his eyes travelling over her as she stood framed in the doorway. 'You look sensational!'

The compliment pleased her, warmed her. 'You're not looking so bad yourself,' she responded, and laughed. She was wearing higher heels than normal, but he still stood above her.

'I feel I should lock you away in a glass case somewhere,' he answered, and—*ooh*, she loved him so.

'That good, eh?' she queried impishly. And in that moment, for her, there did not seem to be any other people in the world except thc two of them.

'Stunning,' he replied. 'I'd like to—' Just then the sound of someone at the door came, and Ty broke off. 'Saved by the bell,' he said humorously. 'Ash will see to it. Actually, Phinn, I notice you aren't wearing a watch. If you feel lost without one, I thought you might agree to borrow this.' And, putting his hand into his dinner jacket pocket, he withdrew the watch he had tried to give her before.

'You were supposed to have taken that back to the jewellers!' she exclaimed.

'I tried. They wouldn't have it,' he lied—quite blatantly.

'Tyrell Allardyce!' she admonished.

'Yes, sweet Delphinnium?' he replied—and she just had to laugh.

She took the watch from him. 'I'll return it to you tomorrow,' she said.

'Agreed,' he answered, without argument.

And she smiled. 'If I wasn't wearing lipstick, I'd kiss you,' she commented.

'Don't let that stop you,' he encouraged.

'I hear voices. I believe your guests are waiting for you.'

'Damn,' he said—and so started the most wonderful evening of her life.

Ty's friends-cum-business associates ranged in age from late twenties to late forties. There were seven of them in all, and Phinn tried to remember their names as the introductions were made—with not one of them questioning who she was and why she was there.

There were ten seated at the large round dinner table. Phinn was seated opposite Ty, which suited her well, because it gave her the opportunity of glancing at him every so often. Funnily enough, it seemed to her that every time she looked across to him that Ty was looking back at her.

She realised then that her imagination must be working overtime, so concentrated on chatting to Will Wyatt, who was around the same age as Ty, and who was seated on her right. She chatted equally to the man on her left, an older man named Kenneth.

In talking to the two men, and feeling quite at ease with them, Phinn discovered that she had more general knowledge than she had realised. She knew that she had her father to thank for that because, aside from taking her to museums and art galleries, it had been her father who had encouraged her to ask questions and form her own opinions. It had been her father with whom she had discussed the merits and de-merits of painters and writers. And it was all there in her head—just waiting to be tapped.

'What do you think of Leonardo?' Kenneth asked at one point.

'A true genius,' Phinn answered, always having much admired Leonardo da Vinci—and then she and Kenneth were in deep discussion for the next ten minutes, until Will Wyatt accused Kenneth of monopolising her.

'I have the advantage of being married—to my

good lady here,' Kenneth replied, looking to his wife, who was deep in conversation with the man to the left of her. 'Therefore Phinn is quite safe with me. You, on the other hand, young Will...'

In no time the three of them were laughing. It was then that Phinn happened to glance across to Ty. He was not laughing. He wasn't scowling either. He was just—looking. Feeling all mixed-up inside, Phinn stayed looking at him, her brain seeming to have seized up. Then Cheryl Wyatt, seated to the left of Ty, placed a possessive hand on his arm to draw his attention—and all of a sudden, as Ty glanced to Cheryl and smiled, Phinn was visited by another emotion. An emotion that had visited her briefly once before and was one she did not like. Jealousy.

It was the only small blip of the evening.

Wendy and Valerie, Mrs Starkey's usual helpers in the house, had been roped in to help serve the meal. But when everyone adjourned to the drawing room afterwards, Phinn took off kitchenwards.

She was in the throes of telling Mrs Starkey how well everything had gone when Ty appeared, on the very same errand.

'Thank you, Mrs Starkey. Everything was perfect,' he said, and Mrs Starkey beamed with pride. Phinn guessed she and her staff would be well rewarded for their efforts, and moved towards the kitchen door.

She went out into the hall feeling a touch awkward suddenly. A moment later Ty was joining her, and they were strolling back along the hall.

'I don't want you to think—' she began in a rush, but was stopped when Ty placed a hand on her arm and halted her. 'I—er…' She faltered. He waited, saying nothing, just standing there looking down at her as if he liked looking at her. 'I know—er—I mean I know I'm not the hostess here…'

'A very lovely hostess you would make,' he put in lightly.

Which did little to ease her feeling of awkwardness. 'I wanted to thank Mrs Starkey—' She broke off. 'I didn't know if…'

'If I would think to do so?' Ty looked kindly down at her. 'Who else would I expect to do the honours for me, little Phinn, but an adopted member of my family?'

'Oh, Ty,' she said softly, and didn't know just then quite how she felt.

If Ty included her as his family because he felt under some kind of obligation, because through her he still had a brother, then she did not want to be part of his family. If, on the other hand, he regarded her as family because he enjoyed having her under his roof—albeit temporarily—then there was nothing she would like better than to be considered part of his family. But she could never explain that to him—not without the risk of showing him how very much she loved him.

She opted to change tack. 'By the way, I meant to thank *you*. Kit Peverill says you rang him and asked him to forward all the accounts for Ruby's care to you.'

'You've seen Peverill?' Ty asked sharply. 'Has he been here?'

Phinn looked at him, exasperated. 'You're never the same two minutes together!' she erupted. 'Of *course* he's been here. I've an elderly horse. I want a vet who's local—a vet who knows me, who knows Ruby, who I can trust to drop everything but emergencies when I call!' She gave a heated sigh, and, having got that off her chest, an impish look came into her eyes. 'Hmm…Kit said, incidentally, that he hadn't known that *you* were the man I had just started seeing until your call about the account. He rather put two and two together and assumed… Anyhow, at just that point his phone rang with an emergency, and he'd gone before I could tell him differently. Er…'

'There's more?'

'It's just that this is a small village, and while I'm sure Kit won't gossip, he'll only have to say some small thing in passing about me having a boyfriend and it will be all over the place before you can blink.'

Phinn half supposed she'd expected Ty to be

cross—for all it was more his doing than hers. But he wasn't cross—not at all. He merely replied equably, 'I reckon my shoulders are broad enough to take it.'

'Fine,' Phinn murmured, and moved on. But when they came to the part of the hall where he would turn into the drawing room to join his guests, she halted briefly to ask, 'Would you mind if I went along to see Ruby?'

'You'll be missed,' Ty replied.

Her heart gave a giddy flip at the ridiculous idea that Ty, personally, would miss her. 'There goes that charm again!' she scorned humorously, and headed for the outside door.

She was not the only one outside, Phinn soon discovered, because she was on her way to the stable when Will Wyatt called out, 'Where are you off to?'

She turned, startled. 'What are you doing out here?' she asked lightly.

'When you disappeared I thought I might as well ease my sorrows with a cigar,' Will replied. 'Wherever you were dashing off to, can I come too?' he asked.

Charm, she rather thought, was catching. 'Do you like horses?'

'Love them!' he said promptly, and as promptly stamped out his cigar.

Ruby had picked up again, but Phinn knew from

experience that it did not mean that she would stay up. Phinn introduced her to Will Wyatt, who was lovely and gentle with her, and she warmed to him.

They were still with Ruby when her ears twitched, and a few seconds later Ty appeared, with Cheryl Wyatt in tow. 'Ty thought we'd find you here!' Cheryl exclaimed. But, as if she understood that Ruby had health problems, she was gentle with her too, and Phinn found she liked the other woman—if not the possessive way she was hanging on to Ty's arm.

'We'll leave you to say goodnight to Ruby,' Ty commented, edging Cheryl towards the door, and turning as though waiting for Will to join them.

Will didn't look as if he was likely to take the hint, so it was left to Phinn to look at him and say, as though making a general comment, 'I won't be long.'

They were a good group, Ty's friends, and time flew by until all but Will and Cheryl Wyatt made to depart. Apparently the departing guests all had properties out of London, either in Gloucestershire or one of the neighbouring counties.

Shortly after they had gone, Phinn took a glance to the lovely watch she had on and was amazed to see that it had gone midnight! 'If no one minds, I think I'll go up,' she said, to no one in particular.

'Do you have to?' Will asked.

'I shall be up early in the morning,' she replied, because he was so nice.

'Then so shall I,' he answered.

'Er—good,' she said politely. She would be getting up early to go and check on Ruby; she had no idea what Will intended to do.

By morning she discovered that he did, as he had said, love horses. He came into the stable at six o'clock to see Ruby anyhow. That morning Phinn was dressed in her usual jeans and a tee shirt, with her hair pulled back in a rubber band. It did not seem to put him off.

'Ever get up to London?' he enquired as she got busy with a pitchfork.

'Not usually,' she replied.

'If you fancy it, I'd like to take you to a show. You needn't worry about getting back. You could stay the night.'

Phinn gave him a startled look.

'Cheryl will be there too!' he hurriedly assured her, correctly interpreting Phinn's look. 'I didn't mean…'

Phinn forgave him. She was in the middle of thanking him for his invitation, but refusing, when Ty came in and joined them.

'Couldn't sleep?' he asked his friend Will.

'The bed was bliss,' Will replied. 'I was just asking Phinn to come to a show with me—Phinn could stay overnight with Cheryl and me, and…'

'Phinn wouldn't want to leave Ruby overnight.' Ty refused for her.

'You or Ash could look after her for one night, surely?' Will turned to Ty to protest.

Phinn shook her head. 'Thank you all the same, Will, but no way.'

'Mrs Starkey is making an early breakfast,' Ty cut in, and as Phinn got on with her chores, Will, so not to offend his host or his host's cook, went with him.

Will did not ask her out again, but came to find her when they all decided to go for a long walk—exercise needed after the previous evening's dinner and this morning's full breakfast. 'Do come with us,' he urged. 'Ash tells me there's not a thing about this area that you don't know.'

Perhaps because she fancied a walk, Phinn went with them—though was not too enamoured that more often than not Cheryl appeared to be walking with Ty, as though his partner.

Brother and sister left shortly after lunch, with Will kissing Phinn's cheek and saying he would be in touch. But as soon as Broadlands returned to normal, Phinn went to chat with Ruby.

Nobody wanted very much in the way of food at dinnertime. And with Ty spending time in his study catching up, and Ash in one of the other rooms watching one of his favourite programmes on television, Phinn went first to see Ruby, and then decided to turn in.

She was in her pyjamas, face scrubbed, body

showered, hair brushed out of the band it had been in all day, when she remembered the watch. Ty was staying tonight, but would be leaving very early in the morning for London. She was tempted to take it along to his room, but…

But why not? Ty was not averse to popping into her room when he wanted to leave her salary cheque. And anyway, he was in his study downstairs. It would only take but a moment, and she would by far prefer that the expensive watch was in his possession before he went off tomorrow. He was off on his travels again, so heaven only knew when he would be home again.

Not giving herself time to think further, and just in case anyone was about, Phinn threw on a light robe. She was by then aware of which room was Ty's and, picking up the dainty watch, she quickly left her room. At his door, for form's sake, she tapped lightly on the wood paneling, but not waiting for an answer quickly went straight in.

Only to stop dead in her tracks! The light was on, and Ty was not downstairs in his study as she had been so sure he was. Barefooted, his shirt unbuttoned prior to his taking a shower—or whatever was his normal night-time procedure—there he stood.

'I'm sorry—sorry!' Phinn exclaimed, flustered, realising she must have been in her bathroom cleaning her teeth and so had not heard him passing her door. She held out the watch while at the same time wanting to back to the door. 'I thought you were downstairs. Only I—um—wanted this watch in your safekeeping before you left.'

Ty didn't move, and made no attempt to take the watch from her but, as if women entering his bedroom was an everyday event—and she did not want to think about *that*—he invited, 'Come in and talk to me,' doing up a couple of shirt buttons as he spoke. 'I don't bite.' And when she looked at him, a touch startled by his invitation, 'Well, not usually anyway,' he said, the corners of his wonderful mouth picking up.

But Phinn, while she would have liked nothing better than to talk to him, looked down at her thin pyjamas and lightly robed self. 'What do you want to talk about?' she asked. It might be normal for him to chat the night away with women in their night clothes, but it was a first for her.

'Well, you might want to tell me how you enjoyed the weekend, for one thing?' Ty suggested.

'I did,' she replied. Ruby had picked up again, so all was right with her world.

'You liked my friends?'

He asked as if it mattered to him that she should like his friends. That thought warmed her, and Phinn for the moment forgot she was feeling awkward. Since Ty wasn't attempting to take the watch from her, she stepped further into his room and placed it down on top of a mahogany chest of drawers.

'Very much,' she answered. 'Kenneth made me laugh, and I thought his wife, Rosemary, was sweet.'

'You know you were a big hit with them,' he commented, moving casually to close the door.

Phinn looked at him, again startled, as the door closed. 'Er—you're not going to attempt to seduce me, are you?' she asked warily.

Ty burst out laughing, his superb mouth widening. 'What a delight you are!' he remarked, but replied, 'That wasn't my intention, but if you…?' He left the rest of it unsaid, but his mouth was still terrifically curved in a grin. 'I just thought we could have a private moment or two while you let me know what you're going to tell Will Wyatt when he rings.'

'What makes you think he's going to ring?'

'You know he is. He's totally captivated by you.'

She would not have put it as strongly as that. 'He's nice,' she commented.

'You're not going out with him,' Ty stated more than asked.

'As Your Lordship pleases,' she responded, and just had to laugh.

'Are you making fun of me?' Ty asked, coming a dangerous couple of steps nearer.

'Would I dare?' she asked demurely.

'I wouldn't put it past you to dare anything, Phinn Hawkins,' Ty answered. And, when she looked as though she would turn about and go, 'Do you want to go out with him?' he demanded, with no sign of a grin about him now.

It did not take any thinking about. The only man she wanted to go out with was the one standing straight in front of her. 'I'm not going up to London to go out with him, and since I wouldn't want to leave Ruby for more than a couple of hours, I can't see any point in him coming down here to take me out.'

'Which doesn't answer my question.'

'I know,' she replied impishly.

'You *do* know you're likely to drive some man insane?'

'You say the sweetest things.'

Ty looked at her mischievous expression, his glance going down to her uptilted mouth. 'You'd better go!' he said abruptly, and brushed past her as though to go and open the door.

But he did not make it because, her pride rearing at being thrown out—dammit, it was *he* who had asked her to stay!—Phinn at the same time moved smartly to the door. And somehow they managed to collide slap-bang into each other.

Angrily, Phinn put out her arms to save herself, but somehow found that she was holding on to Ty. And Ty, in his efforts for stability, somehow had his hands on her waist. And then, as they looked into each other's eyes, it was as if neither could resist the other.

Ty let out a groan, his words seeming to be dragged from him. 'I want to kiss you.'

Phinn shook her head to say no, but found that the person in charge of her was saying, quite huskily, 'If memory serves, you kiss quite nicely, Tyrell Allardyce…' The rest didn't get said. It was swallowed up as Ty's head came down and his lips met hers.

It was one very satisfying kiss, but at last he raised his head from hers. 'You don't kiss too badly yourself,' he commented softly, looking deeply into her eyes.

'I do my best,' she answered, mock-demurely.

'Want to go for seconds?' he questioned lightly, and, while she was unsure what Ty meant by that, what she did know was that to be in his arms was pure and utter bliss and she never wanted it to stop.

Unsure what to answer, Phinn followed her instincts and stretched up and kissed him. And that was all the answer he needed because, lightly at first, Ty was returning that kiss, and bliss just did not begin to cover it. Her heart rejoiced to be this close to him, to be held in those firm arms.

Her arms went around him and as he held her so she held him. She could feel his body through her thin clothing and loved the closeness with him. Yet even as Ty ignited a fire in her, she found she wanted to get yet closer.

She felt his hand at the back of her head, his lips leaving hers as he buried his face in her long, luxurious strawberry-blonde hair. And then his lips were finding hers again—and she knew that as she wanted him, so Ty wanted her.

With his arms around her, he pulled her to him. 'Sweet darling,' he murmured, and she was in a mindless world where she *was* his sweet darling.

For how long they stood, delighting in each other's kisses, Phinn had no idea, but only knew that she was with him wherever he led.

A small spasm of nervousness attacked her, nevertheless, when, compliant in his arms, she let Ty move with her to the inviting king-size bed. But, incredibly, he seemed to notice her hesitation, for, with his arms still around her, he paused and looked down into her slightly flushed face.

'Everything right with you?' he asked tenderly— and she was utterly enchanted.

She looked tenderly back and found her husky voice to say, 'Oh, yes,' and to add, 'But I do believe you *are* seducing me.'

Ty smiled into her eyes. 'Believe?' he echoed. 'Don't you know?'

She smiled back. She loved him. What else mattered? She wondered if she should tell him that she had never been this way with a man before, but did not want him to think her a fool, so instead she kissed him. And Ty needed no further encouragement.

Phinn was enraptured when he undid her robe and slid it from her shoulders. And she loved, adored him when, once she was clad only in her pyjama shorts and a thin-strapped pyjama top, his eyes travelled down over her.

Ty took her in his arms once more, and then she realised that they had been merely skating around the preliminaries, because with a gradually increasing passion Ty was teaching her what lovemaking was all about.

She felt his warm hands come beneath her thin top, felt those hands warm on the skin of her spine, and was drowning at his every spine-tingling touch.

When those same hands moved to the front of her and, seeking ever upwards, he at last captured her breasts, her cry of sweet rapture mingled with his groan of wanting.

He kissed her, moulding and caressing her breasts as his kiss deepened. But, as if tormented beyond reason at the sight of her, as if tormented to uncover the splendour in his hold, Ty pulled back. 'I want to see you,' he breathed.

Phinn swallowed hard to hide her shyness. 'I want to see you too,' she murmured huskily, and got her wish when, unhurriedly, Ty removed his shirt.

His chest was magnificent and she stared in wonder before leaning forward and placing a kiss there. And she was delighted when, as she leaned forward, Ty pulled her top over her head. Then, as she stood before him, her top half uncovered, he pulled back to study her. 'Oh, my sweet one,' he said softly, as he surveyed her creamy swelling full breasts with their hardened pink tips. 'You are totally exquisite.' And he took first one hardened pink peak into his mouth, then released it to taste the sweetness of the other.

Phinn swallowed hard when his hands went to the waistband of his trousers, and buried her face in his shoulders. Then she knew more bliss—utter bliss— when they stood thigh to thigh. His hands at her back, he caressed unhurriedly downwards.

His body was a delight to her, 'Oh, Ty,' she cried. 'I want you so much.'

'And I you, sweet darling,' he murmured, and moved with her as though to take her to lie down on the bed with him.

But while Phinn was unaware that she had made any slight movement of hesitation, Ty seemed to sense one. Because he paused, his glance gentle on her. Just that—no movement. Just waiting. If she had any objection to make, now—even at this late stage—was the time to state it.

And, looking at him, Phinn almost told him that she

loved him, but somehow felt that that was not what he would want to hear. So instead, foolish or not, she realised that in all fairness she ought to say something.

'Er…' she began hesitantly. 'I'm, er—a bit…'

The words seemed to stick in her throat, but Ty wasn't going anywhere. With his warm hands still holding her, he said gently, 'You want to make love with me, but you're a bit…?' And, as if he simply could not resist her gorgeous breasts, he bent to kiss them.

'Well…' She took a steadying breath as he pulled back to look at her. 'Have you any idea what you're doing to me?' she asked, side-tracked, the feel of his mouth at her breast still with her.

'If it's anything similar to what you're doing to me, I'd say it's pretty dynamic,' he answered, and smiled, and kissed her—but made no move to lie down with her. 'You're a bit—what?' he prompted gently again.

'Well, the thing is—I'm not at all sure how these things go…but I—er…'

'Tell me, sweet love,' he invited, when she got stuck again.

And suddenly she wanted it all said and done quickly. 'The thing is…' she began in a rush, then halted, got her second wind, and rushed on again. 'Well, I feel a bit of a fool because I've no idea whether you need to know to not but…' Oh, heavens,

so intimate, half undressed, nearly completely undressed, and still those private words would not
come! That was until, totally impatient with herself,
she burst out, 'I've no idea if you need to know that
I've never—um—been this f-far before.'

On the instant Ty stilled, his expression changing
from that of a tender ardent lover to disbelief at
what it sounded as if she was saying. Then his look
changed to one of utter astonishment as it started to
quickly sink in, and from astonishment to a look of
being completely shaken.

Ty was stern faced as he gripped hard on to her
naked shoulders. 'Just what, exactly,' he urged—a
little hoarsely, she thought, 'are you saying?'

'Well, I wasn't sure… That is, I don't know if I'm
supposed to say, or if it's all right for you to just—
er—find out, but…'

'Oh, my God!' He was incredulous. 'You're a
virgin!' He seemed stunned.

'Does it matter?' she asked, feeling more than a
touch bewildered—and heard Ty take what she
assumed to be a long-drawn steadying breath.

'Right at this moment,' he commented tautly, 'I
want you more than you can know.' His glance
moved down to her breasts and he gave a groan as
he ordered, 'For sanity's sake, cover yourself up!'
And when Phinn, more than a little confused at what
he was saying, was not quick enough, he swiftly

picked up her thin robe from the carpet and as quickly wrapped it around her. Then, running a fevered hand across his forehead, he said, 'I want you, Phinn. Don't mistake that. But I need space to try and think straight.'

Phinn stared at him. She felt even more unsure, which made her feel nervous—and a fool. And a split second later she knew, while the rest of her brain was just so much of a mish-mash, that the moment was lost! Knew with crystal clarity that she was never ever going to know the full joy of sharing her body with Ty, the man she loved.

And in the next split second, while everything in her still cried out for her to be his, her pride began to stir. And as her pride started to surge upwards because Ty needed to *think* whether to reject her *or not*—so her pride took off and rocketed into orbit. *Reject her!* 'Take all the time and space you need,' she exploded furiously—damn it, her voice was still husky. 'I'm leaving.'

'Phinn, don't—' Ty tried to get in.

'I won't!' she hurled at him, and was already on her way. 'Trust me—I won't.'

## CHAPTER EIGHT

THE hours until dawn were long and painful. Ty
might have said that he wanted her and not to make
any mistake about that. But that he'd had to *think*
about it showed that he could not have wanted her
as much as he had said he did.

Her watch—his watch—showed it was just
before four when Phinn heard the faint sound of Ty
leaving the house. She wanted to leave too, and
never to come back.

She had told him she had wanted him. For
heaven's sake, what more proof did he need that she
was his for the taking? She had stood—she
blushed—semi-naked in front of him. And he—he
had rejected her!

In fear and mortification that Ty might have seen
that she loved him, that she had given away her
feelings for him, Phinn wanted to run and hide. To
run and hide and never to have to see him again. But
she could not leave—there was Ruby.

Phinn spent many countless, useless minutes in wondering what, if anything, Ty thought about her. But in the end, with more scorched cheeks, she realised that from his point of view making love with her did not have to mean that he cared anything about her at all. Given that once the kissing had started they had soon established there was a certain chemistry between them, from Ty's point of view it did not have to mean a thing.

Nursing sore wounds, Phinn showered and dressed early and went to see Ruby. Phinn had sometimes wondered through Ruby's various bouts of illness if, for Ruby's sake, she was wrong not to have her put down. But as she spoke gently to her that morning, and Ruby nuzzled into her, Phinn knew that she could never do that.

That Monday was a busy day for phone calls. Her mother rang, and Phinn again promised to try to go and see her soon. And Will Wyatt rang, asking her not to forget him and telling her that he was working on a plan to get Ty to invite him for a long weekend soon.

In a weak moment Phinn wondered if Ty would ring. But that was fantasy, for he never did. And why would he, for goodness' sake? He lived in a fast-paced sophisticated environment, where sophisticated women abounded. He hadn't the time nor the inclination—obviously—to bring a 'village local' virgin up to speed.

Realising she was in danger of letting what was now firmly fixed in her head as Ty's rejection of her sour her outlook, Phinn turned her back on the memory of Ty's unbelievable tenderness and his heady passion with her, and concentrated on why she was there.

'Where are you off to, Ash?' she asked him, when she saw him setting off across the fields. He was so much better now than he had been, so much brighter all round, that she had begun to feel that her role in watching him was now more or less redundant. But Ty was paying her to be Ash's companion, and whatever feelings went on in her head about Ty, a job was a job.

'I thought I'd stretch my legs and think about farming matters.'

'Shall I come with you?'

That was Monday.

On Tuesday, with Ruby once more in fine fettle, Phinn again latched on to Ash when he said he was going up to Honeysuckle Farm with a view to checking out some improvements he wanted to make. By then, with Ty so constantly in her head, her aversion to going to the neglected farm where she had been brought up seemed to be secondary.

Bearing in mind she was being well paid to keep Ash company, when she saw him making for the pick-up on Wednesday, she went over to him. But before she could open her mouth to invite herself to go along too, wherever he was going, Ash beat her to it.

'Phinn—dear Phinn,' he began sensitively, 'as my honorary sister, I love you dearly. But would you mind if just this once I went out on my own?'

Phinn looked at him. He had put on weight, the dark shadows had gone from beneath his eyes, and he was a world away from the wretched, heartsore man she had known a couple of months ago.

She was not in the least offended, and grinned at him as she replied, 'Depends where you're going.'

For a moment or two he looked as though he wasn't going to tell her. But then—just a touch sheepishly, Phinn thought—he answered, 'If you must know, I thought I'd meander over to Geraldine Walton's place and see how she feels about having dinner with me on Saturday night.'

Phinn just beamed at him. 'Oh, Ash. I couldn't be more pleased!' she exclaimed.

'She hasn't said yes yet!'

She would, Phinn knew it. 'Best of luck,' she bade him, and went to chat to Ruby.

By the look of it, her work at Broadlands was done—and that was worrying. Matters financial were crowding in on her, but Phinn could not see how she could continue to take a salary from Ty when she wasn't doing anything.

By afternoon, however, Phinn had something

more to worry about. Ruby had stopped eating. Trying not to panic, Phinn rang Kit Peverill, who was out at one of the neighbouring farms but said he would call in on his way back. Which he did.

'Doesn't look too good, Phinn,' he said, after examining Ruby.

Phinn's low spirits dropped to zero. She clenched her jaw as tears threatened. 'Is she in pain?'

'I'll give her an injection to make her comfortable,' he replied. 'It should last her a couple of days, but call me sooner if you need to.'

Phinn thanked him, and as he went down the drive she saw Ash returning in the pick-up. 'How did it go?' she asked Ash, but had no need to. The smile on his face said it all.

'As you yourself have discovered—who could resist the Allardyce charm?' He grinned.

Who, indeed? But she had other matters on her mind just then.

'Was that the vet's Land Rover I passed in the drive?'

'Ruby's not so good.'

Sympathetically, Ash went back with her to see Ruby, who seemed to Phinn to be losing ground by the hour. Phinn had no appetite either, and spent the rest of the day with Ruby, only leaving when Ash came and said that Mrs Starkey was preparing a tray for her.

'I'll come in,' Phinn told him. No way could she eat in front of the sick mare.

Ash, Phinn discovered, had turned into her minder. He took turns with her in staying with Ruby. And, because Ruby had taken to Ash, with his gentle way of talking to her, Phinn left Ruby with him when she needed to shower, or to try to get down the sandwich Mrs Starkey had provided for her.

Phinn called in Kit Peverill again on Thursday— his expression told her what Phinn would not ask.

Phinn stayed with Ruby the whole of Thursday night. Ruby died on Friday morning. Phinn did not know how she would bear it—but Ash was marvellous.

Ash might not have been at his best in an office environment, but when Ruby died he more than showed his worth. As Ruby went down, Ash took charge. And Phinn was never more grateful.

'I'll go and phone the vet and make all the other necessary phone calls while you say goodbye to her, darling,' he said gently. 'Leave everything to me.' With that, he left the stable.

An hour later Phinn left Ruby. She saw Ash without actually seeing him, and, her face drained of colour, went walking.

For how long she walked over land that she had once ridden over with Ruby, she had no idea. She was miles from the house when she came to a spot where she and Ruby had unexpectedly come across a recently fallen tree trunk. She could feel Ruby's joy as they had sailed right over it even now. Ruby was not a jumper, and they had both been exhilarated. Ruby had given her a look that Phinn would have sworn said, *Hey—did you see me do that?*

When Phinn returned to the stable, hours later, the vet had been and gone—and so too was Ruby gone. The stable doors were open, the stable cleaned and hosed down by Ash, and Ash was coming over to her.

'They took her as gently as they could,' he promised. 'I've arranged to collect her ashes—I thought you might want to scatter them over her favourite places.' And, looking into her face, 'You look tired,' he observed. 'Come on, Mrs Starkey's got some of your favourite soup waiting for you.'

More or less on automatic pilot, Phinn went and had some soup, was fussed over by Mrs Starkey, and told to go and rest by Ash. Phinn felt too numbed to argue, and went and lay on her bed.

She thought she might have slept for a while, but she felt lifeless when she awakened. She took a shower and changed into fresh trousers and a shirt. She felt a need to do something, but had no idea what.

Brushing her hair, she pulled it back in a band and went outside. She did not want to go into the stable, but found her feet taking her there. It was where Ash found her some ten minutes later.

Leaving the stable together, they walked out into the late-afternoon sun. 'I don't know of anything that's going to make you feel any better, Phinn, but if you want me to come walking with you, want me to drive you anywhere, or if you'd like me to take you out somewhere for a meal, you've only to say.'

Phinn had held back tears all day, but as she turned to him her bottom lip trembled and she knew that she was close to breaking. 'Oh, Ash,' she mumbled, and liked him so much, felt true affection for him, when, placing a gentle arm around her, he gave her a hug. Needing his strength for just a brief moment, Phinn held on to him.

It *was* only a brief moment, however, because suddenly she became aware that there was a car parked in front of the house—a car she had not heard pull up.

It was Ty's car, and he was standing next to it, looking their way. Ash had not seen him, but Phinn could not miss the fact that Ty was positively glaring at her! Even from that distance there was no chance of missing that he was furious about something. Something so blisteringly anger-making that a moment later, as if he did not trust himself, Ty had swung abruptly to his right and gone striding indoors.

So much for her wondering, as she had so often since last Sunday, how she was ever going to face him again. Forget tenderness, forget gentleness—Ty had looked as though he could cheerfully throttle her!

With a shaky sigh, Phinn stepped out of Ash's hold. 'You've been a gem today, Ash,' she said softly. 'I'll never forget it.'

'I'm here for you, love,' he said, but let her go when she pulled out of his hold. 'I'm going to the office. Want to come?'

Phinn shook her head. She felt lost, and didn't know where she wanted to go. But the sanctuary of her room was as good a place as any.

Before she could get there, however, she had to run the gauntlet of one very thunderous-looking Tyrell Allardyce. She had hoped he might be in the drawing room, his own room or his study, and that she might be able to reach her room without seeing him.

So much for hope! Phinn had barely stepped into the hall when Ty, as if waiting for her, appeared from his study. His demeanour had not sweetened any, she noted. As was proved when, looking more hostile than she had ever seen him, 'In my study—now!' he snarled.

*Go to blazes and take your orders with you*, sprang to her mind. But, since he was obviously stewed up about something—forget 'sweet darling'—she'd better go and get it over with.

Phinn walked towards him, past him and into his study. But she had hardly turned before he had slammed the door shut and was demanding explosively, 'Just what the hell sort of game do you think you're playing?'

Phinn sighed. She really did not need this. Yet how dear he was to her. She wanted to hate him. But, furious with her or tender with her, she loved him in all his moods.

'I'm—not with you,' she replied quietly.

'Like hell you're not! How long's it been going on?'

She still wasn't with him. 'How long has what been going on?'

Ty gave her a murderous impatient look. 'Naïve you might be, but you're not *that* naïve,' he roared, and Phinn, having been spent all day, started to get angry.

'Don't throw that back at me!' she erupted, warm colour rushing to her face at his reference to her having disclosed to him, in a very private moment, that she was inexperienced.

'I'll do whatever I like!' Ty fired back. 'You're here to look after my brother, not to try and send him down the same downward spiralling road your cousin did!'

'That's most unfair!' Phinn charged hotly.

'Is it?' he challenged, with no let up in his fury. 'What's your plan? To trot into his bedroom one night when he's half undressed and have a crack at losing your virginity with him too?'

*Crack* was the operative word. Without being

aware of what she was doing, but incensed and in sudden fury that Ty could so carelessly demean something that had been so very special to her, infuriated beyond bearing that he could say such a thing, Phinn hit him! She had never hit anybody in her life. But all her strength went into that blow.

The sound of her hand across Ty's cheek was still in the air when Phinn came to her senses. She did not know then who was the more appalled—her or Ty. He by what, in his fury, he had just said—she by what, in her fury, she had just done. Either way, it was clear, as he stared dumbfounded at her, that no female had ever hit him before.

Phinn felt absolutely thunderstruck herself as she stared at the red mark she had created on the side of his face. 'Oh, Ty,' she mourned, tears spurting to her eyes, a tender, remorseful hand going up to that red mark. 'I'm so sorry.' Still Ty looked at her, as if speechless. 'I'm—a bit upset,' she understated.

'*You're* upset!' he exclaimed.

'Ruby…' she managed, and knew then that the floodgates she had kept determinedly closed all day were about to break open.

'Ruby?' Ty questioned, his senses alert, his tone softening.

Had he stayed furious with her, nasty with her, Phinn reckoned she might have been able to hang on until she reached her room. But when Ty, who obviously didn't know about Ruby but had sensed all was not well with her, started to show a hint of sympathy, Phinn lost it. She made a dive for the door, but before she could escape Ty had caught a hold of her.

'Ruby?' he repeated.

'Ruby…' The words would not come. Tears were already falling when she at last managed, 'Ruby—she died today.'

'Oh, sweetheart!' In the next instant Ty had taken her in his arms and was holding her close up to him—and Phinn's heart broke.

Sobs racked her as Ty held her close. He held her and stroked her hair, doing his best to comfort her as tears and sobs she could not control shook her. Having held her emotions in check all day, it seemed that now she had given way she was unable to stop.

Ty was still holding her firm when she at last managed to gain some semblance of control. 'I'm—s-sorry,' she apologised, and attempted to pull away from him. His answer was to hold her more tightly to him. 'I'm sorry,' she repeated. 'I—haven't cried all day.'

'I'm sorry too,' he murmured soothingly. 'And I'm glad I was here when you finally let go the grip on your emotions.'

Phinn took a shaky breath that still had a touch

of a sob to it. 'Ash has been marvelous,' she felt she should tell him. 'He saw to everything for me.'

'When he's on form he's good in a crisis,' Ty agreed.

'I'm all right now,' Phinn said, trying to shrug out of his comforting hold.

'You're sure?'

She nodded, wanting to stay exactly where she was. 'I look a mess,' she mumbled.

'You look lovely,' he answered, taking out a handkerchief and gently mopping her eyes, now red from weeping.

'You're a shocking liar,' Phinn attempted, and took a small step backwards.

Ty, still holding her, looked down into her unhappy face. And, oddly, it seemed the most natural thing in the world that they should gently kiss. Phinn took another step back and Ty, as if reluctantly, let her go. Phinn left his study to go up to her room.

It was not the end of her tears. Tears came when she least expected them.

Not wanting to break down again, should tears appear unexpectedly at the dinner table, Phinn went to tell Mrs Starkey not to make dinner for her and say that if anyone asked she had gone to bed.

'Can I make you an omelette, or something light like that, Phinn?' Mrs Starkey asked.

But Phinn shook her head. 'That's very kind of

you, Mrs Starkey, but I'm not hungry. I'll just go and catch up on some sleep.'

In actual fact Phinn slept better than she had anticipated. Though she was awake for a long while, and heard first Ash come to bed and then, later, Ty. She didn't know how she knew the difference in the two footfalls, she just did.

She tensed when Ty seemed to halt outside her bedroom door, but she knew that he would not come in. After last Sunday bedrooms were sacrosanct. That was to say she knew she would never again trespass into his bedroom. By the same token—remembering that chemistry between them—Ty was giving *her* bedroom a wide berth.

Having awakened early, at her usual time, Phinn felt tears again spring to her eyes when, throwing back the covers, she realised that there was nothing—no darling Ruby—to dash out of bed for.

Phinn dried her eyes and pulled the covers back over her, and thought back to yesterday. Not Ruby dying—that would live with her for ever. And, while she would always remember her gentle, timid Ruby, Phinn did not want to dwell on her dying. Instead she thought of happier times. Times when she and Ruby had galloped all over Broadlands, the wind in her hair, Ruby as delighted as Phinn.

Fleabitten old nag indeed! But now Phinn was able to smile at the memory. Ty had been pretty wonderful in finding a stable to make Ruby's last days comfortable.

He had been pretty wonderful to her too, when he had come home yesterday, Phinn considered, remembering how he had cradled her to him as she had wept all over him. He had mopped her up and…

And she had hit him, Phinn recalled. Not a tap, but a full-on whack! Oh, how could she? But she wasn't going to think about unpleasant things. She had been down in the pits yesterday and, while she knew she would not get over Ruby in a hurry, Phinn also knew, remembering the dark pit she had descended into when her father had died, that it would get better.

Meantime…Phinn was just thinking that she might as well get up after all when someone knocked lightly on her door and Ash, bearing a tray, came in.

'Mrs Starkey thought you might like breakfast in bed. I told her I'd bring it up and see how you were.'

'Oh, Ash,' Phinn protested, sitting up and bringing the bedclothes over her chest. 'Everybody's being so kind.'

'You deserve it,' he replied, and asked, 'Here or on the table?'

'Table,' she answered, thinking, as Ash placed the breakfast tray down on Grandmother Hawkins' table, that she would sit out as soon as he had gone and eat what she could.

'How are you this morning?' Ash asked as he turned back to her.

'Better,' she said.

'Good. I'll leave you to your scrambled egg before it gets cold,' he added, and on impulse bent down and kissed her cheek.

He meant nothing by it other than empathy with the circumstances of her losing her best friend. But the man who had suddenly appeared in the doorway to the side of him did not appear to share the same empathy.

'*Ash!*' he said sharply to his brother.

Phinn looked from one to the other. Never had she known Ty to speak so sharply to him. But, while she was wondering if the two brothers—whom she knew thought the world of each other—were on the point of having a row, Ash did no more than grin at her and say pleasantly, 'Ty,' to his brother.

As Ty stepped into the room, Ash stepped out and closed the door.

'Does Ash usually bring you breakfast in bed?' Ty demanded.

'*Now* what have I done?'

'Apart from showing too much cleavage?' Ty snarled.

Phinn glanced down to where the covers had just a second ago slipped down. Her barely pyjama-top-covered breasts were now on view. 'Had I known I was receiving visitors I'd have worn an overcoat!' she flared, quickly covering herself.

Ty did not care for her sarcasm. That much was plain. 'You're quite obviously feeling better this morning!' he rapped.

Phinn was fed up with him. 'You're never the same two minutes together!' she accused hotly, remembering the way he had tenderly dried her eyes in his study yesterday. 'Is there a purpose to your visit?' she demanded hostilely.

'Not the same as my brother's, clearly!'

'As you once mentioned, Ash has a sensitive side. He brought me breakfast for Mrs Starkey and stayed to ask how I was feeling.'

Ty was unimpressed. 'You just leave him alone!' he ordered.

'Leave him alone?' she echoed.

'I don't want to pick up the pieces when another Hawkins does the dirty on him!'

Phinn stared at Ty in disbelief. Was that what he thought of her? She took a hard pull of breath—that or weep that Ty could say such a thing to her. 'Close the door on your way out!' she ordered imperiously—and, oh, heavens, that was it!

She knew she had angered him when his expression darkened—and that was before he strode over to the bed. 'I'll go when I'm ready!' he barked, standing threateningly over her.

But in Phinn's view she did not have to sit there and take any more. In a flash she was out of bed and snatching up her robe from the end of it as she went.

'Stay as long as you like!' she snapped. 'I'm off to take a shower.'

Wrong! 'You don't care who you hurt, do you?' Ty snarled, whipping the robe away from her and spinning her round to face him.

Hurt? Him? Hardly likely. He must be referring to Ash. 'You've got a short memory!' she erupted. What had happened to *you're so good with him*?

'Not as short as yours!' Ty grated, and with that he caught a hold of her and pulled her into his arms. 'Less than a week ago you were mine for the taking!' he hurled at her vitriolically. 'Let me remind you!' And, without waiting for permission, he hauled her pyjama-clad body up against him. The next Phinn knew, his mouth was over hers. Not tenderly, not gently, but punishingly, angrily, furiously—and she hated him.

'Let me go!' she hissed, when briefly his mouth left her.

'Like hell,' he scorned, and clamped his lips over hers again. And while holding her in one arm, his other hand pushed the thin straps of her pyjamas vest to one side.

Then his lips were seeking her throat; his hands were in her long flowing hair as he held her still.

'No,' she protested—he took no notice. She pushed at him—that did no good either and in fact only seemed to provoke him further, because his hand left her hair, but only to capture her left breast. 'Don't!' she cried. She ached for his kisses, but not like this.

Ty ignored her 'Don't' but as if enflamed by the feel of her lovely breast in his hold, the next she knew her vest pyjamas top was pulled down about her waist and her pink-tipped breasts were uncovered and Ty was staring at her full creamy breasts as though mesmerised.

He stretched out a hand as though to touch one of those pink peaks and Phinn could not take any more. 'No, Ty,' she cried brokenly. 'Not like this.'

She thought he was going to ignore her, but then it was as though something in her tone had got through to him. Got through to this man who liked to keep his sensitivity well hidden. Because Ty pulled his hand back and stared at her, at the shine of unshed tears in her eyes. And some of his colour seemed to ebb away.

'Oh, God!' was wrenched from him on a strangled kind of sound, and in the next moment he had stepped away from her. A split second later, as if the very hounds of hell were after him, Ty abruptly spun away from her and went striding from the room.

It was the end, and Phinn knew that it was. She had no idea what had driven the civilised man she knew him to be to act in the way he had, and, while she might forgive him, she had an idea—with that agonised *Oh, God!* still ringing in her ears—that it would be a long while before he would be able to forgive himself.

And all, she knew, because of Ash. Ty had been rough on her when he had first known her on account of his protectiveness of Ash. But she had thought Ty had learned that she would never hurt his brother. But, no. Despite what had taken place between her and Ty previously, he had twice witnessed what he had thought to be a tender scene between her and Ash—yesterday, when he had arrived home and had seen Ash with an arm around her, and just now, when he had been passing her open door and had spotted Ash kissing her cheek on an impulse of the moment. As he had said, he feared that another Hawkins would 'do the dirty' on Ash again.

Feeling defeated suddenly, Phinn knew that she was leaving. What was there to stay for? By the look of it, Ty would clap his hands when she went. As he had said himself, when Ash was on form he was good in a crisis. Which meant that since Ash had taken over yesterday, when Ruby had died—tears sprang to her eyes again—Ash was back to his old self and was no longer in need of a companion.

With her appetite gone, Phinn ignored the breakfast tray that Mrs Starkey had so kindly prepared and went and took a shower.

She had almost completed her packing when she heard the sound of a car engine. She went to the window and was in time to see Ty's car being driven out of the gates at the bottom of the drive.

Pain seared her that she would never see Ty again. Not that she had anything that she particularly wanted to say to him, but… Perhaps it was just as well that she left before he got back.

Ten minutes later, acknowledging that she could not take all her luggage with her—not without transport—Phinn remembered how yesterday Ash had offered to drive her anywhere she wanted to go.

Phinn cancelled that thought when she realised that with Ty being so anti he would just love it when he got back to learn that she had made use of Ash to take her and her belongings to Gloucester.

She had no idea how her mother would take her arriving on her doorstep and asking to stay until she had found other accommodation, but, since her mother had stated more than once that she would like her to live with her and Clive, Phinn didn't think she would have any major objection.

Knowing that her mother would most likely cancel her golfing arrangements if she rang her and asked her to come and pick her up, Phinn opted to ring Mickie Yates.

Disappointingly, he was not answering his phone. She gathered he must be off somewhere on one of his various pursuits. She did think of asking Jimmie Starkey to take her, but that did not seem fair somehow. He was a hard worker, like his wife, and had earned a weekend to himself.

In the end she knew that she would have to try and make it to Gloucester by bus—if buses in Bishops Thornby still ran on a Saturday. Phinn would contact Mickie at some other time to collect the remainder of her belongings for her.

She left the watch Ty had loaned her on her grandmother's table. She gave a shaky sigh as she recalled Ty's kindness in bringing that familiar table up to her room so she should feel more at home. Then, with a last look around her room, she determinedly picked up one suitcase and left her room.

It was with a very heavy heart that she descended the stairs, but she tried to cheer herself up by reminding herself that her stay had only been going to be temporary anyway.

She had just reached the bottom stair, however, and hefted her case down into the hall, when a sound to her left made her jerk her head that way.

Ty! Colour—hot colour—seared her skin. She had thought he had gone out, and that she would never see him again! But her high colour came from remembering that awful scene in her bedroom earlier. 'I thought I saw you driving your car down the drive!' she said witlessly.

He ignored her comment, his eyes glinting when he could not avoid seeing she had luggage. 'Where do you think you're going with that case?' he demanded shortly.

'I'm leaving,' Phinn replied—and waited for his applause.

It did not come. What came was Ty striding forward and hefting her case up and away from her. 'We'll see about that!' he grated, and, leaving her to follow, her suitcase in his grip, he strode from her in the direction of the drawing room.

Phinn hesitated for a second or two, torn between a need to go and—oh—such a hungry yearning need to stay. Her need to stay—if only for a minute or two longer, while Ty presumably sorted her out about something—won.

'As long as you intend to keep your hands to yourself!' she called after him spiritedly, that lippy part of her refusing to die, no matter what.

A moment later she followed. She was unsure what Ty intended to have a go at her about now. All she hoped was that she would be able to get out of there without hitting him again or with her pride intact—preferably both.

# CHAPTER NINE

TY HAD not cooled down at all, Phinn observed when she entered the drawing room. Her case was on the floor a yard from him, and he had his back to her, but his expression when he turned to survey her standing there was most definitely hostile.

'You want me to apologise?' he queried, his tone quiet. But hostility was still there lurking, Phinn felt sure.

She shrugged her shoulders. 'Suit yourself,' she replied, and saw that her remark had not sweetened him any.

He walked by her to firmly close the drawing room door, then came back to stand in front of her. And off on some other tack, he demanded, 'Where do you think you're going?'

'Not that it's any business of yours, but—'

'Not my business?' he echoed. 'You waltz in here, disrupt the whole household, and—'

'Now, just a minute!' Love him she might, but she

didn't have to take his false accusations. 'For a start, *you* invited me here. Yes, I know I've had an easy ride of it…' Oh, damn. Those tears again, as a fleeting memory of her riding Ruby got to her. She looked down at the carpet while she gathered herself together.

But suddenly Ty had come closer, hostility forgotten. 'Oh, Phinn,' he murmured softly. 'My timing is, as ever, all to pieces where you're concerned. You are grieving for Ruby, and all I'm doing if giving you more grief.'

'Don't be nice to me!' Phinn cried agitatedly. 'When you're wearing your hard-as-blazes hat I can cope, but…'

'But not when I go soft on you?' he queried. 'I shall have to remember that,' he commented—a touch obscurely, Phinn felt, since after today she would not be seeing him again.

'Look, I have to go. I've—er—got a bus to catch.'

'Bus!' He looked scandalised, and let her know how he felt about that in no uncertain tone. 'You can forget that, Phinn Hawkins!' he told her bluntly.

'Ty, please. Look…'

'No, *you* look. I know this isn't the best of times for you. And I know you've had almost a year of one upset after another. And I so admire the way you have battled on. But, at the risk of upsetting you further, I'm afraid I cannot let you leave until we've talked our—problem through. And, whatever happens, you are certainly not going anywhere with that case by bus.'

'I'm—not?' What was there to talk about? Oh, heavens—had he seen her love for him and considered that a 'problem' to be talked through? No way was she talking *that* problem through!

'If you're still set on leaving after—' He broke off, then resumed steadily, 'I'll take you anywhere you want to go. But first come and sit down. I'll get Mrs Starkey to bring us some coffee.'

'I don't want coffee—er—thank you,' Phinn refused primly.

She wasn't sure that she wanted to sit down either. But, taking the chair furthest away from the one she thought he would use, she went and sat. Only to find that Ty, as if wanting to be able to read her expression, had pulled up a chair close by.

'I'm aware I'm in your debt,' she said in a rush. She did not want him reading any unwary, unguarded look in her eyes or face, no matter how fleeting. He was as sharp as a tack was Ty Allardyce. 'But I intend to get a job. Obviously I'll settle my debt with you as soon as—'

'For God's sake!' Ty burst in. 'Don't you know, after what you did for Ash, that I shall be forever in *your* debt?'

'This is about money. I don't like owing money,' Phinn retaliated, shrugging his comment away.

'Circumstances have caused me to accept you paying the vet...' She bit her lip. Darling Ruby again. 'Look, Ty,' she said abruptly, 'I know that you don't approve of my—er—friendship with Ash. That you fear I might hurt him. But I never would. Trust me, I never would. Apart from Ash not being interested in me in that sort of way—romantically, I mean—I'm not like my cousin...'

'Ash isn't interested in you that way?' Ty immediately took up. And was at his belligerent best, when he barked, 'You could have fooled me!'

'Why? Because you saw him with a sympathetic arm around me yesterday? He's sensitive. You know he is. He guessed I'd got Ruby on my mind this morning—and kissed my cheek in the empathy of the moment.'

'He doesn't normally go around kissing you?'

For heaven's sake! 'He leaves that to you!' Phinn snapped, then realised she did not want to remind him of how he had kissed her before—apart from earlier—and her willingness in that department. 'Look,' she rushed on, starting to feel exasperated, 'I know all this fuss is solely about your protection of Ash, and your fear I'm another avaricious Hawkins ready to hurt him, but I promise you the only way I can hurt him is in the way a sister might unthinkingly hurt her brother.'

Ty's eyebrows shot up. 'You see Ash in a *sisterly*

light?' he challenged sceptically, everything about him saying that he did not believe a word of it. And that annoyed her.

'Of course I do! The same way that Ash thinks of me as his honorary sister!'

'He thinks of you as his *sister*?' Ty's disbelief was rife.

'Don't you two ever talk to each other?' Phinn exclaimed.

'Apparently not. Not about our deepest emotions, obviously.'

Phinn guessed it was a 'man thing', because never had she known two brothers so close.

'What makes you so sure that Ash regards you only as a brother would?' Ty challenged.

'Oh, Ty, stop worrying,' Phinn said softly, knowing all Ty's concern was for his brother. 'Ash actually said so one day this week. Besides, Ash has someone new on his mind.'

Ty's head jerked back in surprise. 'You're saying he's interested in somebody else?' he asked, but was soon again looking as though he did not believe it for a moment. 'He didn't so much as glance at Cheryl Wyatt last Saturday, and I invited her especially to…'

'You were matchmaking?' Phinn queried, amazed, her mouth falling open. Ty had invited Cheryl on Ash's account! Phinn's jealousy of the beautiful Cheryl Wyatt eased somewhat. If Ty had invited Cheryl for Ash's benefit, then Ty could not be interested in her for himself. 'Er—wrong stable,' she announced.

'Wrong stable?'

'I don't think I'm breaking any great confidence— Ash has a date with Geraldine Walton tonight.'

It was Ty's turn to be amazed. 'He's…? Geraldine Walton?'

Phinn found she could not hold down a grin. 'So you've no need to worry that I'm going to let Ash down,' she remarked lightly. 'I just don't figure in that way.' Looking at Ty, loving him so much, she truly did not want him worrying any more about his kid brother. 'So you see, Ty, Ash truly sees me as a kind of sister.'

With her glance still on Ty as what she had revealed sank in, Phinn felt that he seemed to visibly relax. As if what she had just said was somehow of the utmost importance. As if a whole load of concern had been lifted from his shoulders. And it was only then that Phinn realised just how tense Ty had been.

Her grin became impish, and she just had to add, 'Sorry, Ty, that sort of makes me your sister too.'

But his reply truly jolted her. Shaking his head, he told her flatly, 'I don't think so. I don't want you for a sister.'

That hurt, but somehow she managed to hide it,

and as casually as she could she got to her feet, tears again threatening—but this time tears from the hurt that he had just so carelessly served her. 'Well, that puts me in my place,' she commented offhandedly. And, head up, pride intact, 'Well, if that's it—if that settles your concerns about Ash—I'll be off.'

She did not get very far! To her surprise, she did not even get as far as lifting up her suitcase before Ty was standing in front of her, blocking her way. 'That,' he clipped, 'in no way settles it.'

'It doesn't?'

He moved his head slowly from side to side. 'No, it does not,' he said firmly, to her further surprise. Adding, 'I've a more special place for you than that.'

More special than a sister? Hardly! 'You've heard how good I am in an office? You're offering me a job?'

'There *is* a job for you—if all else fails,' Ty replied.

'What sort of job?' A job where she stood a chance of seeing him again? No, thank you, said her pride. Oh, please, said her heart.

Ty looked at her for long moments, and then stated, 'When Ash goes to Honeysuckle Farm it will be more than a full-time job for him. I shall need an estate manager here.'

'Me?' she exclaimed. But, on thinking about it, 'You won't need anyone full-time,' she denied. 'You're selling Yew Tree Farm, I believe. And while it will take a couple of years for Ash to lick Honeysuckle into shape…' Her voice tailed off, guilt smiting her.

'Honeysuckle will be fine—with your input. Presumably with your local knowledge you know of someone who will show Ash the ropes?'

'Er—I do, actually,' she admitted. 'Old Jack Philips—he's worked on the land all his life. He retired about a year ago, but he's finding retirement irksome. He was saying, that lunchtime Ash and I went to the Cat for a drink, that he's itching to have a few days' work each week.' Ty smiled, and that was so weakening Phinn had to work hard not to wilt. 'But that still doesn't make an estate manager's job here full-time,' she stated firmly. 'Besides, I've no experience of being an estate manager.'

'Sure you have. You take a stroll through the woods and spot exactly which trees need taking out—know which new trees should be planted. You've an in-built sense of country lore. Not to mention you can deal with office work with both hands tied behind your back.'

Phinn had to smile herself. Yes, she could do all of that, and she would love to stay—would love to walk the estate, love to be his estate manager—but there wasn't even a couple of days' work here.

'And don't forget there are a couple of tenanted

cottages that would have to be kept up to date—their upkeep and running repairs to be contracted out.'

Phinn shook her head. She didn't want to go, she knew that she didn't, but... 'I have to go,' she said decidedly.

Ty stared at her, not liking what he was hearing. 'It's me, isn't it?' he challenged. But before Phinn could panic too much that he had guessed at her feelings for him, he was going on. 'You've had enough of my grouchy attitude with you on too many occasions?'

'Ty—I...' She was feeling out of her depth suddenly.

'Will you stay if I promise to mend my ways— apologise for every unkind word I ever said? Every—?'

'Oh, Ty,' she cut in. 'You weren't awful all the time!' She laughed lightly, ready to forgive him anything. She guessed that was what love was all about—forgiving hurt, real or imagined. 'Sometimes you have been particularly splendid,' she added, quite without thinking.

'Truly?' he asked, and seemed tense again suddenly. 'I wasn't very pleasant when I kissed you this morning, but—'

'I don't think I want to go there,' Phinn rushed in. 'I—er—was meaning more particularly your thoughtfulness in putting Grandmother Hawkins' table in my room. Getting Mr Timmins in to tune the piano. The—' She broke off. She had been about to say the replacement watch he had bought her—but she did not want to remind him of how her own watch had become waterlogged.

'Do the good times outweigh the bad, Phinn?' he asked.

'Yes, of course they do,' she replied without hesitation. It wasn't his fault that she had fallen in love with him. 'I just don't know what Ruby and I would have done if you hadn't come along and offered us a home.'

'It pales into insignificance when I think of what you did for Ash, and in turn for me.'

'We're going to have to stop this or we'll end up a mutual admiration society,' Phinn said brightly. And then, because she must, 'Thank you, Ty, for letting Ruby end her days in comfort and peace.' So saying, she took a step towards him, stretched up and kissed him.

It was a natural gesture on her part, but when she went to step back again, she discovered that Ty had taken a hold of her hands in his. And, tense still, he asked quietly, 'Am I to take it that you—quite—like me?' looking down into her wide blue eyes.

Phinn immediately looked away. 'You know I like you!' she flared. 'Grief—you think I—' She broke off. 'Time I went!' she said abruptly.

But Ty still had a hold of her hands. 'Not yet,' he

countered. Just that, but there was an assertive kind of firmness in his tone that Phinn found worrying. 'You accused me earlier of not ever talking to my brother. I think, Phinn, that you and I should start talking to each other—openly.'

Phinn was already shaking her head. 'Oh, I don't know about that,' she replied warily.

And Ty smiled a gentle smile, his tension easing as her nervousness increased. 'What are you afraid of?' he asked softly. 'I tell you now, all pretence aside, that while I may have unwittingly hurt you in the past, I will never knowingly hurt you again.' Her throat went dry. She tried to swallow. 'Come and sit down with me,' he went on. She shook her head, but found that Ty was leading her over to a sofa anyway. She still hadn't found her voice when, seated beside her, Ty turned to her and stated, 'Given that I was such a brute to you when we first met, you have a very forgiving nature, Phinn.'

'Brute doesn't cover it!' She was glad her vocal cords were working—thanks largely to Ty going off the subject of her liking him.

'I agree,' he conceded, his grey eyes steady on hers. 'To re-cap, and in my defence, Ash was doing so well here on his own, and I was going through a busy time in London. The obvious thing to do was to leave matters down here with him. The alterations were going well, with no need for me to try and find time to pay a visit, but when I did find time to come home I was shocked to my core by Ash's appearance—at how ill he looked.'

'You must have been. I was myself,' Phinn volunteered. 'He told you about Leanne?'

'I got most of it from Mrs Starkey. I supposed I grilled her pretty thoroughly. When she'd told me all that she could, I was in no mood to be pleasant to any member of the Hawkins family.'

'You ordered me off your land.'

'And to my dying day I shall ever be grateful that you ignored me bossing you about and came back again.'

Phinn had an almost overwhelming urge to kiss him again, but reckoned that she had done enough of that already. And in any case, he already knew that she liked him without her giving this clever man more to work on.

'I think you first started to get to me that day by the pool,' he went on when she said nothing. 'I could see you were upset about something, for all it didn't stop you being lippy, but I had no idea then that you were in shock.'

'I—er—started to get to you? You—er—started to like me, you mean?'

Ty stilled. 'It matters to you that I like you?' he enquired quietly.

She shrugged. She was getting good at it.

'Everybody likes to be liked,' she answered—and thankfully he let it go.

'It was more a personal thing for me,' Ty said carefully.

'Oh,' she murmured. Oh—heavens!

'And the more I got to know you, the more I got to like you,' Ty went on.

Her throat went dry again. 'Oh—really?' she managed, but her voice was quite croaky and unlike her own. She coughed to clear it, and was able to offer an offhand kind of, 'That's good.'

'Not from where I was seeing it,' Ty answered. She refused to say *oh* again. 'From where I was seeing it,' he continued, unprompted, 'that's when the trouble began.'

'Trouble?'

'Trouble.' He nodded. 'There was I, getting to like you more and more each time I saw you. And there were you, my dear Phinn, excelling in the job I hired you to do. Ash was coming on in leaps and bounds. So much so that you, as his companion, were doing things with him that I—I found I wanted to do with you.'

Phinn blinked. Open-mouthed, she stared. 'Really?' she gasped.

'Believe it,' Ty replied. 'I found I was coming back here every chance I could.'

'Because of Ash, of course.'

Ty smiled. 'Of course,' he answered. 'So, if it's all about Ash, why do I want you to take me fishing too—to teach me to tie a fly—to take me with you sketching? And why, heaven knows why, do I feel so cranky when Ash tells me that you think he's gorgeous?'

Phinn could only stare at Ty in amazement. 'You wanted me to think—you—were gorgeous too?' She didn't believe it.

'I think I'd have settled for kind, or nice—or even for half of the smiles you sent my brother's way.'

Phinn stared at him, feeling somewhat numbed. Her brain seemed to have seized up anyway. 'You—were…?' The words would not come. She dared not say it—and make a fool of herself.

'Jealous,' Ty supplied. 'The word you're looking for is jealous.'

'No!' she denied faintly, not believing it.

'Yes,' Ty contradicted.

'I—er—expect that—um—happens with brothers. A sort of brotherly—er—thing,' Phinn said faintly, not having the first clue about it, but still not believing that Ty meant what it sounded as if he meant.

'I don't know about that. I've never been jealous of Ash before. In fact, I grew up with it being second nature for me to look out for him, to protect him if need be.' Ty took a long-drawn breath then, but continued firmly. 'Which is why it threw me when I realised my rush to get home as soon as I could was not so much to check on how he was doing, but more because I wanted to see you.'

Phinn's eyes widened, and her throat went dry again. 'No,' she murmured.

'True,' Ty replied. 'You always seemed to be having fun with Ash. I wanted to stay home and have fun with you too.' And, while Phinn stared at him stunned, 'Work was losing its appeal,' he confessed.

She found that staggering! She had formed an impression that Ty lived, slept and dreamed work. 'You…' she managed faintly.

'I,' he replied, 'knew I was in trouble.'

'Trouble?' she echoed witlessly.

And Ty smiled a gentle bone-melting smile for her as he explained, 'At the start I wanted you here in my home for Ash. But the more I had to do with you, and the more I knew of you, the more—dear Phinn—I wanted you in my home not for Ash, but for me.'

She swallowed, her insides a total disaster. 'Oh,' she said huskily.

'And it was *oh*,' Ty said gently. 'Because of how Ash was, he had to be my first concern. He liked you, the two of you got on well—which was fine. What was not fine was that the two of you should start to care for each other. That,' he said, 'was not what I wanted.'

'You were protecting Ash when you were anti me?'

Ty looked at her steadily. 'Where you were concerned, Phinn, I was losing it.' And, as she stared at him, 'I was as jealous as hell where you two were concerned,' he owned. 'Logic fast disappearing.'

'Logic?' She suddenly seemed incapable of stringing two words together.

'Logic,' he agreed, explaining, 'I knew, logically, that there was absolutely no sense at all in my not returning to London on a Sunday evening—but there was no space in my head for logic when it came to my persistent need to want to be where you were.'

'Oh, Ty!' Phinn murmured. He had delayed his departure because of her! She found that staggering, and had to make one gigantic effort to get herself together—she owned she was in pieces. 'Look, I—um—know you're a bit averse to me leaving, but you don't have to—'

'Haven't you been listening to a word I've been saying?' Ty cut in sharply. 'No, I don't want you to leave. But that's only a part of it. You're in my head, in my—'

'No!' she denied—but that was when her memory awoke and gave her one mighty sharp poke. 'If you're going on to—' She broke off, running out of steam before she began. But, gaining her second wind, she snatched her hands out of his grasp, the better to be able to tell him, 'You had your chance with me once, Tyrell Allardyce. If you think you can sweet-talk me—only to reject me again—you've got another—'

'Reject you?' Ty cut in, staring at her, thunder-struck. 'When did I ever reject you?'

'You've got a short memory!' She had an idea she had gone a bit pink, but had to have her say. 'Less than a week ago, up in your bedroom, I wasn't so-phisticated enough for you. You—'

'For God's sake.' Ty chopped her off. 'I was off my head with desire for you!'

Her colour was definitely pink—high pink—and she began to wish she had not brought the subject up.

'Oh, Phinn, you idiot. Not sophisticated enough? Don't you know I treasure your innocence?' She shook her head, but Ty caught a hold of her hands and hung on to them when she struggled. 'Listen to me,' he urged. 'That night—last Sunday night,' he inserted, to show he had not forgotten a thing, 'I was already in a situation where I was more feeling than thinking. And then you go and throw a bombshell at me, and I've moved on to a totally new situation. I needed to be able to think clearly—but, dammit, I couldn't.'

'Hmph!' she scorned. 'What was there to think about?'

'Oh, Phinn—*you*, my love.' Her spine was in meltdown again. 'If you'll forgive me, we were both highly emotionally charged. I needed a few moments of space to think what was best *for you*.'

'For me?'

'Sweet Phinn,' Ty said gently, 'I knew I had to be away by four in the morning. Was unsure of exactly when I'd be back. I needed to be able to think, to judge—was it too soon to tell you how much you mean to me? How would you react if I did? I didn't seem to know very much any more. What I did know was that I wanted what was best for you. But did I have enough time to hold you in my arms and make you understand how very special you are to me? Fear gripped me—would I scare you away if I tried?'

'Special?' Phinn whispered, her throat choked. She gave a dry cough. 'Special?'

'Very special,' Ty answered. 'You were at your most vulnerable—I didn't want to go leaving you with any doubts. But before I have the chance to think it through, you and your massive pride are up in arms, and you're more or less telling me to forget it—and thereby solving my quandary for me.'

Phinn's head was in a whirl. 'Er—as you mentioned—we—er—should—perhaps—have talked a little more openly.' And, getting herself more together, 'Though since you went away there hasn't been any chance to…'

'I wanted to phone you. On Monday. On Tuesday. Countless times I had the phone in my hand—' He broke off to ask sharply, 'Has Will Wyatt been in touch?' And, when she was not quick enough to answer, 'I'll take that as a yes. He's been angling for an invite here all week. But…' Suddenly Ty halted. Abruptly—as if he had just reached the end of his rope. 'I'm done with talking,' he said impatiently. And then, taking what seemed to her to be a steadying breath, he said, 'Just tell me straight—if I promise not to roll in the aisle laughing, will you stand up with me in church and say "I, Delphinnium Hawkins, take you, Tyrell Allardyce"?'

On the instant, searing hot colour rushed to her face. She could not think, could not breathe. Though as Phinn recalled how Ty had said he did not want her for a sister, that he had a more special place for her than that, so her brain started to stir. He wanted her—not as a sister, but as his wife! Feeling stunned, for countless seconds Phinn could only stare at him. She had never for a moment dreamt that that special place was this! And, feeling winded, she was not even sure that she could credit having heard what she thought she had just heard.

Had Ty, in effect, just asked her to marry him? She felt trembly all over, but with her heart beating wildly she could not just leave it there. Staring wide-eyed at Ty, she saw he looked tense again—seemed to be waiting. He had asked a question and was waiting, tensely, for her reply!

Phinn took a deep breath. 'What…?' she began. But her voice let her down. She swallowed, and found her voice again. 'What sort of pr-proposal is that to make to a girl?' she asked with what breath she could find—and waited for him to roar with laughter because she had totally misunderstood.

But no! Looking at him—and her eyes were fixed solely on his face—she saw that he was looking nowhere but at her either. She saw him take another steadying breath, and came as near to fainting as she had ever done in her life when, after a moment of searching her face, Ty solemnly answered, 'Hopefully, should I be able to clear away my fears over you and Ash, the proposal I wanted to make—the one I rehearsed in ten different ways, but feared that you might laugh at—goes...' He paused to take a deep pull of breath. 'Goes: Phinn Hawkins, I love you so very much that I cannot bear to be away from you. I...'

'You—love—me?' Phinn whispered.

'I love you so very much, my darling Phinn,' Ty confirmed. 'Love you so that you are in my head night and day. You fill my dreams. Everywhere I go, you go too. You are there in everything I do—and it is my most earnest wish that you marry me.'

Ooh! The breath seemed to leave her body on a sigh. Numbly, she stared at him. He loved her! Ty—the man she loved—loved her. She stared at him, her breath taken.

'Well?' he asked when she said nothing, his hands gripping hers tightly. 'Have you no answer for me?'

Oh, Ty. Didn't he know? She tried to speak, but no sound came. She tried again, and this time managed to answer, 'I'm—not laughing.'

Her words were faint, but Ty heard them. 'That gives me hope,' he said.

'You *are* serious?' She started to have doubts.

'Loving you is not something I would joke about.'

'I'm sorry,' she apologised, her voice gaining strength. 'Your—er—what you've just said is such a surprise.'

'Is it?' Ty seemed surprised himself that she had not seen how things were with him. But his patience was getting away from him; tension and strain were showing in his face. 'Please, Phinn, give me an answer,' he urged.

She smiled at him, her answer there in her all-giving tender smile as she replied, 'If you don't mind if I whisper the "Delphinnium" bit in church, there is nothing I would like better than to take you, Tyrell Allardyce.'

Ty did not wait to hear any more. Joyously he gathered her into his arms and tenderly kissed her. 'I didn't make a mistake. That *was* a yes I heard?' he pulled back to ask—and Phinn realised that Ty, like her, could hardly believe his hearing.

'Oh, yes,' she replied softly.

'You love me?'

'I was afraid you would guess.'

'Say it?' he encouraged, with love for her in his eyes.

'Oh, Ty, I love you so,' she whispered.

'Darling Phinn,' he breathed, and, drawing her closer, he kissed her lingeringly. For a short while he seemed content to just hold her like that, close up to his heart. Then, 'How long have you known that you didn't just hate me, as I deserve?'

'You're fishing,' she accused.

'Why not?' He grinned. 'I've been a soul in torment.'

'About me?' she asked, her eyes widening.

'Who else? I asked you to stay here partly because there was nothing I would not do for the woman who saved my brother's life, and partly out of concern that Ash would brood on his unhappiness if I left him here on his own. Only to soon find that, when I should be rejoicing because Ash is staring to pull out of it, I'm a bit put out at the closeness the two of you seem to be sharing. I denied, of course, that I was in any way jealous.'

'Oh, heavens!' Phinn gasped.

'You noticed I was out of sorts?' Ty asked, kissing her because he had to.

Phinn sighed lovingly. 'I thought you were anti because you'd seen how well Ash and I were getting on and were afraid that another Hawkins was getting to him.'

'It wasn't so much you getting to him that was concerning me, but that he might be getting to you.'

'You *were* jealous!' she exclaimed.

'I acknowledged that on the day I found you in the music room. I held you in my arms—and wanted to hold you again.'

'You did hold me again. That same night—in the stable,' Phinn recalled.

'I was ready to grab at the smallest excuse,' Ty replied.

Phinn smiled at him. 'That was the night I realised that I was in love with you,' she confessed.

'Then?' Ty exclaimed.

'I tried to hide it.'

'You succeeded. Although…'

'Although?' Phinn queried, when it seemed as though Ty would leave it there.

'Last Sunday—in my bedroom—when you were so unbelievably giving to me…well, it gave me hope. All this week I've been tormented by visions of you, wanting to phone, afraid to phone. Had I read too much into your unawakened but eager response to me? Was it just some sort of awakening chemistry on your part? Or dared I hope—did you care for me?'

'What did you decide?'

Ty smiled. 'That was the problem. I couldn't decide—and it was driving me mad. I decided to get back home as fast as I could, the sooner to find out.' He gently stroked the side of her face. 'It was inappropriate for me to say anything yesterday, when you were in such distress over Ruby.'

'I'm sorry I hit you.'

Ty kissed her. 'Given that you pack a powerful punch, I thoroughly deserved it. I was as immediately appalled by what I had said as you were,' he revealed. 'I knew I had to leave matters until the morning—this morning—when I would try to gauge how things were and then, if the signs were good, put myself out of my misery by telling you how things were with me, hoping against hope that there was a chance for me with you.'

'It all went sort of wrong,' Phinn put in.

'You can say that again. I wanted to come to your room last night—and again this morning—to check how you were. I wanted to hold and comfort you. But, knowing how you in your scanty pyjamas can trigger off physical urges in me, I was unsure. Having managed to stay away, I was a little short of incensed when I saw your bedroom door was open, and as I look in as I'm passing, there's my brother, kissing you.'

'He was just being his lovely self.'

'I know, and I'm ashamed,' Ty confessed. 'Ashamed that I was for an instant jealous of him. And oh, so heartily ashamed of my behaviour with you afterwards.' Phinn leaned forward and tenderly kissed him. 'Forgive me?' he asked.

'Of course,' she replied, smiling, loving him, her heart full to overflowing.

'Ash knew in your room this morning that I was jealous—the wretch,' Ty said good-humouredly. 'I can see that now. Now that I know his interests lie in other directions, I can forgive him that he went off whistling, not a care in the world—leaving me stewing when I sent him off to Yew Tree Farm with some paperwork.'

'He took your car.'

'He can be very aggravating when the mood's on him,' Ty complained indulgently, his love for his brother obvious. And Phinn knew that Ty was heartily glad to have his brother back to his old self, no matter how occasionally aggravating he might be. 'So—having got Ash out of the way, having got the house to myself—I'm left waiting for you to come down, knowing that I want to marry you, if you'll have me, but still with concerns about how Ash feels about you and how you feel about Ash.'

'And I came down with my case packed.'

'I wasn't having that,' Ty answered, smiling. 'Whatever the consequences. I knew my timing was off, knew you were upset, but I had no more time to wait. I've loved you too long, darling Phinn, to be able to let you walk out of my door.'

'Oh, Ty,' she sighed, and loved and kissed him. She pulled back to ask softly, 'When did you know?'

'That I loved you?' He looked at her lovingly. 'I suppose you could say that the writing was on the wall when I ignored the social events I normally enjoy in London the sooner to get back here.'

'For Ash?' she inserted.

'Of course for Ash.' Ty grinned. 'Then, as Ash began to surface from his feelings of desolation and I saw that a bond was growing between you and him, I found myself thinking that if Ash was ready to join the dating circuit again, I'd find him somebody to date. I realised then that I had begun to think of you as *my* Phinn, and that in fact I was actually in love with you.'

Her heart was so full, Phinn just beamed a smile at him. 'Oh,' she sighed. And was kissed. And kissed in return. 'You—um—mentioned inviting Cheryl Wyatt…?'

'Much good did it do me!'

'It didn't do me much good either,' Phinn owned. And, when Ty looked a touch puzzled, 'Being jealous is not your sole prerogative,' she confessed.

'Honestly?'

'No need to look so delighted.'

'I'm ashamed,' he lied with a grin. 'Anyhow, that backfired on me, didn't it? There am I, hoping Ash might show an interest in Cheryl, not knowing that he was keen to date Geraldine Walton…'

'I almost mentioned how well Ash had been getting on with Geraldine that night I asked you if it was all right if I took a part-time job—only the moment passed.'

'I wish you *had* mentioned it,' Ty commented feelingly, and Phinn, realising that he must have known some mighty anguish over her and his brother, wished now that she had told him too, and Ty went on, 'Anyway, with Ash so much brighter than he had been, I invited the Wyatts—only to find it's not Ash I've paired up, and if I'm not careful my friend Will will be marching off with you.' Ty broke off, and then, taking her face in his hands, 'Oh, sweet love, have you any idea what I feel for you?' There was such a wealth of love for her in his tone that Phinn felt too choked to be able to speak. 'While you charmed everyone at dinner last Saturday, I looked at you, could not seem to take my eyes off you, and I have never felt so mesmerised.'

'I had to keep looking at you too,' Phinn confessed huskily.

They kissed and held each other. And then Ty was saying, 'So why do I find you entertaining Will Wyatt in Ruby's stable? You don't mind talking about Ruby?'

Phinn shook her head. 'I don't want her forgotten. She's been a part of me for so long.' Swallowing down an emotional moment, she said, 'Will Wyatt was outside smoking a cigar when I nipped out.'

'Cursed swine,' Ty said cheerfully. 'He stuck to you like glue as much as he could—Saturday *and* Sunday.'

Phinn laughed. 'I—er—take it you didn't give in to him angling for an invitation to Broadlands again?'

'Too true,' Ty answered ruefully. And, after a moment, 'Though I shall be delighted to invite him to our wedding.' Her breath caught, and Ty's expression changed to one of concern. 'You *are* going to marry me?' he asked urgently.

'Oh, Ty…' As if there was any doubt. 'I'd love to marry you.'

He breathed a heartfelt sigh. 'Good,' he said, but added, 'And soon?'

'Um…' was as far as she got before they both saw his car sail past the window.

'Right,' Ty commented decisively. 'First we'll tell that brother of mine that I'd like him to be my best man.' He looked at her to see if she had any objection—she beamed her approval. Ash was her brother too—that would be cemented on her marriage to Ty. 'Then we'll drive to Gloucester to see your mother.'

'We're going to see my mother?'

Ty nodded. 'My PA got married last year. Her wedding, with her mother's help, was eighteen months in the planning. I'm afraid, darling Phinn, I can't wait that long to make you Delphinnium Allardyce. We'll go and see your mother and hope to get her approval for a wedding before this month is out.'

'Ty!' Phinn exclaimed, her heart racing. Ty wanted them to be married in less than three weeks' time! Oh—oh, how very, beautifully wonderful!

'You're not objecting? You don't mind?' he pressed swiftly.

Phinn shook her head. 'Not a bit,' she answered dreamily.

'Good, my lovely darling,' Ty breathed. 'Ash may not need you any longer, but I cannot live without you.'

And with that he drew her closer to him and kissed her.

He was still holding her close when the door opened and Ash stood there. He at once saw them— Phinn in his brother's arms, Ty with a look of supreme happiness about him—and a grin suddenly split Ash's face from ear to ear.

'What's this?' he asked, grinning still.

'Come in.' Ty grinned back. 'Come in and say hello to your soon-to-be sister—by marriage.'

# ONE DANCE
# WITH THE COWBOY

BY
## DONNA ALWARD

MILLS & BOON®

All the characters in this book have no existence outside the imagination of the author, and have no relation whatsoever to anyone bearing the same name or names. They are not even distantly inspired by any individual known or unknown to the author, and all the incidents are pure invention.

First published in Great Britain 2009
Paperback edition 2010
Harlequin Mills & Boon Limited,
Eton House, 18-24 Paradise Road, Richmond, Surrey TW9 1SR

© Donna Alward 2009

ISBN: 978 0 263 86888 3

Harlequin Mills & Boon policy is to use papers that are natural, renewable and recyclable products and made from wood grown in sustainable forests. The logging and manufacturing process conform to the legal environmental regulations of the country of origin.

Printed and bound in Spain
by Litografia Rosés, S.A., Barcelona

**Dear Reader**

In 2008, our family moved from Alberta to the east coast of Canada. We left behind some very good friends, and also fond memories of the prairies. When I heard that my RWA chapter in Calgary was hosting a workshop, I knew I wanted to attend and reconnect. Around the same time I was doing some research on rescue ranches, and came across the site for Bear Valley Rescue Ranch. I sent an e-mail, and it was returned with an invitation to visit.

So, when I attended the workshop in October, I also spent a sunny fall afternoon with Mike Bartley. He and his wife Kathy run Bear Valley, and I am so glad I went. Mike clearly believes in what he's doing, and has a real affection for the animals—calling them 'sweetie' and rubbing lots and lots of noses. We also visited the donated quarter section where he keeps most of the herd, and in those few moments a story blossomed.

Writing stories set in Larch Valley has been special, because in a way it keeps me connected to the part of Canada I called home for over a decade. Little did I know when I wrote THE RANCHER'S RUNAWAY PRINCESS how much I would look forward to visiting this town again. I hope you enjoy Jen and Andrew's story, and come back in April to meet Andrew's brother Noah, and find out what happens when he meets the unstoppable Lily Germaine.

Until then

*Donna*

For John, Joyce, Gage and Dallas…we miss you.
Keep laughing.

# CHAPTER ONE

THERE were times in life you either had to go big, or go broke.

Jen's fingers paused on the pen, the cool tube turning warm and slippery in her hand as the room suddenly seemed hot and stifling. The loan papers sat before her and the numbers swirled in front of her eyes.

"Ms. O'Keefe?"

She looked up from the papers, her lightweight sweater cloying, the yellow silk scarf strangling her as her breath shallowed. It was such a *lot* of money, after all. The new bank manager's face frowned a little at her continued hesitation.

She took a breath, looked down, and signed her name—once, twice, three times.

She clicked the pen closed, feeling at once a euphoric blend of fear and excitement. Risk-taking was not her specialty. But over the years she'd learned it was a necessary evil at times. She'd run the numbers until she could cite them by rote. Everything she'd done told her this was a good move. A necessary move.

But seeing it in black and white, knowing that what she'd built so far could be swept away with one failure…it was enough to take a girl's breath away.

She would not hyperventilate. She would not.

She rose, shook the manager's hand. Not the same man who'd given her the first loan for Snickerdoodles; he'd been a friend of her father's and had retired last year. This man was in his late thirties, still exuding that air of big city rather than small town. It wasn't the same. It didn't give her the sense of security that she could really use right now.

Snickerdoodles Bakery was about to be transformed into Snickerdoodles Café and Catering, and if she'd miscalculated she'd lose it all.

"Congratulations, Ms. O'Keefe."

"Thanks." She smiled thinly, extricating her hand from his clasp. Watched as he slid her copy of the papers into a portfolio, handing it to her with a smile.

"Let us know if you need anything at all," he suggested, and she picked up her bag.

Need anything? There were enough zeroes on the dotted line that she hoped she wouldn't need a single thing more…ever.

She was nearly to the glass doors when the nerves hit full force.

She'd done it. She'd just remortgaged everything she had—including her house—to finance a complete refurbishment of her bakery.

She had to be crazy.

She scrambled to get outside, into some fresh air that might hold off the rising panic attack. If she could just get to one of the park benches lining Main Avenue she'd sit and put her head between her knees.

She pushed frantically through the doors, the vision of a bench swimming deliciously before her eyes. Except that halfway there her shoulder encountered a solid wall that took every last bit of oxygen from her lungs. The contact sent her staggering, the portfolio sliding out of her hands and skidding down the concrete sidewalk before coming to rest against a half-height barrel newly filled with petunias, lobelia, and some sort of trailing plant.

Warm, strong hands gripped her biceps, keeping her from falling on her rump in the middle of noon foot-traffic. She looked up, opened her mouth to speak, but instead fought to inhale now that the wind had been completely knocked out of her. Her mouth gaped and flapped as she fought for air to rush it back into her lungs. And if the jolt hadn't stolen her breath, the man attached to the hands definitely would have.

Finally blessed oxygen rushed in and she gasped. Her head tipped back as she looked way up into a too-familiar face. She saw the shock and confusion firing in his hazel eyes for just a moment, wondered if the same emotions were mirrored in her own. It seemed as if years of memories raced between them, though only a few seconds passed. His eyes cleared, cooled. Setting her firmly on her feet, he let her go briefly to retrieve her folder of papers and brought them back to her, holding them out as she fought to calm the hammering of her heart.

"Hello, Jen."

Somehow her hand slid out to take the folder from him, while the warm, slightly rough sound of his voice sank deep into her consciousness. His hands were gone from her arms now, and her skin felt cold in their absence, even though it was the first time he'd touched her in many, many years.

"Hello, Drew."

The moment she said it she felt the blush creeping up her neck, hoped that her scarf camouflaged her flushed skin. She'd been the only one ever to call him Drew. Everyone else had called him by his full name…Andrew. Not Andy, or any other shortened version. Drew had been saved just for her. They both knew it. And Jen saying it now had suddenly transported them to a place deep in the past. Somewhere she hadn't ever wanted to go again. Self-conscious, she raised one trembling hand to smooth the tendrils of hair that were escaping what had been her attempt at a sophisticated twist. When she realized what she was doing, she dropped her hand abruptly. She didn't need to preen for Andrew Laramie.

"Are you okay?"

She looked up into his mossy-gold eyes again, tucked the portfolio under an arm and resisted the urge to straighten her white sweater and matching skirt. *What are you doing here? Why are you back? How long are you staying?* All those questions raced through her mind, but she would not ask any of them—not after the way he'd treated her the last time he'd been home. The rebuff still stung. The answers shouldn't matter anyway. It was a public street. He had as much a right to be in Larch Valley as anyone. He owned half of the Lazy L Ranch, and everyone knew it. Just as they knew the place had been abandoned for the better part of a year.

"I'm fine, thank you." She brushed a hand down her skirt, simply to be doing something other than gawping at his too-handsome face.

"You're pale. Are you feeling all right?" He peered closer, his eyes clouded with concern.

The question erased the panicky thoughts about her bakery and a flash of annoyance flickered through her. What right did he have to worry about her now? None!

"I'm not one of your horses you can doctor, Andrew." This time she made sure she used his full first name. She adopted the most aloof expression she could and stepped back, adjusting the strap of her bag on her shoulder. "What are you doing here, anyway? Shouldn't you be getting ready for the Derby or something? I'd think the racing season'd be keeping you mighty busy."

She knew she sounded obnoxious and wished she could take back the words. It was petty and not her style. After all this time she shouldn't let him rattle her.

It was no secret in Larch Valley that Andrew Laramie had gone on to a sparkling career in veterinary medicine, working in the racing industry south of the border. His dad, for all their falling out, had been proud of him. He'd said so every time she'd gone to visit him. It was a low blow to throw it back at Andrew now, but she couldn't seem to help it now that she was face to face with him. Just seeing him, in the middle of town on a busy Monday afternoon, put her on the defensive.

Maybe when he'd been home for the funeral they might have talked, put things to rest. But he'd spurned any sort of conversation, deliberately ignoring her when she'd reached out to him, put her hand on his arm in sympathy. She had only wanted to help, but he'd barely acknowledged her presence, brushing by her after the final prayer with only a sidelong glance. It had confirmed the fact that she needed to stop making herself available for him to hurt her. Once had been more than enough. She tended to learn her lessons.

"I'm not working in Virginia any more."

That wasn't current news, and she struggled to hide her surprise. "Greener pastures?"

His gaze landed on her, the censure in it heavy, and she lifted her chin in response.

"The Jen I remember never copped an attitude."

"The Jen you remember was a long time ago." She said it quickly, doubting he knew how much she'd truly loved him back then.

His eyes softened, and he seemed almost resigned as he agreed. "Yes, she was. I'm sorry for that."

It was as if he knew exactly what she was thinking—he'd always had an uncanny knack for it, and the last thing she wanted from him was understanding. Not now. What was he sorry for? His remark? Or a whole lot more? The fact that she wanted to know was frightening enough, and sent up a warning siren. *No.* She had to get out of here. Whatever had brought him to Larch Valley, she was sure something more important would take him right back out again. He was probably out to sell the ranch. Goodness knows he didn't need it or want it. He never had. She'd seen how his determination to stay away had hurt his father; it had hurt *her*, knowing he had turned his back on all of them. Now he could pocket all his lovely money and keep on with his oh-so-important career.

"I should get back. I have work to do," she said, aiming for polite civility. She should just go her own way and get on with things, as she'd been doing for several years now.

"Me too," he replied, but his gaze still held hers trapped within it. He lifted his hand and she froze as one long finger tucked a stray strand of hair behind her ear. Goosebumps erupted down her arms, shivering against the cool early spring air.

Then he stood back, tucking his hands into his jeans pockets. "I'll see you around, Jen."

He went past her, continuing west on Main Avenue, while she was left standing in the middle of the concrete sidewalk. She highly doubted she'd see him again when all was said and done.

She straightened her sweater and squared her shoulders. Today was one of those freak encounters, nothing more. Tomorrow she'd still be here, and he'd be gone.

As she pointed her white pumps toward her bakery, a block away, she reminded herself that leaving was what Andrew did best.

This time wouldn't be any different.

"Andrew. Gosh, it's good to see you!"

Andrew smiled, and it felt good. But it was impossible not to smile at the red-haired pregnant woman coming down the steps toward him. He gave her a hug, and then set her back.

"Damn, you look good, Luce."

"You too. And you remind me of home. Well, the old home anyway."

He laughed at her impish expression. He'd met Lucy many years ago when he'd done some work at Trembling Oak and she'd barely been out of high school. When he'd been back late last fall he'd realized she was the one his good friend Brody had e-mailed about, and that she was a real, bona-fide princess. He'd nearly fallen off his chair.

But it was good to see she hadn't changed. And it was great to know Brody was so happy.

"It's good to be back," he said, looking up at the farmhouse, and he discovered he meant it.

"Come on in. Mrs. Polcyk's made a streusel cake and there's a pot of coffee on. Brody'll be back soon, and you can tell us about your plans."

He followed her into the house.

The first thing that greeted him was the scent, and he was reminded not of his own house, at Lazy L, but the afternoons he'd spent at the O'Keefes'. Molly O'Keefe had been a hell of a baker; where Jen inherited it from, he supposed. He'd always felt more at home there than he had at his own place, with just his dad and his brother Noah for company.

"Well, Andrew Laramie. If this isn't a touch of the prodigal coming home."

He struggled not to blush as Betty Polcyk rounded the cupboard and enfolded him in a hug.

"Hi, Betty."

"It's about time you got yourself back here."

"Yes'm." He'd learned long ago that no one argued with Mrs. Polcyk.

"Sit down. I'll get you some cake and coffee. Brody's on his way in too."

Slices of cinnamony cake were procured, along with coffee for Andrew and a large glass of milk for the pregnant Lucy. He'd taken his first meltworthy bite when the door slammed and Brody came in.

Andrew rose to meet his old friend and the two shook hands. Brody hadn't changed. Slightly older than Andrew, but still with the ready smile Andrew remembered, still big as a barn door, and still the kind of man who could be counted on. Andrew hoped he could count on him now.

"Good to see you, Brody."

"You too. Good to have you back." He went to the sink, washed his hands, and took a chair at the table as Andrew resumed his seat. "I was nearly thinking about making an offer on Lazy L if you hadn't shown your face around here again. But I figured you and Noah'd have to work it out first."

"I've bought him out."

The words hurt a little. Noah hadn't put up an argument, and Andrew knew the cash from the sale would be a nice addition to Noah's wages as a soldier. It was the fact that it had had to be done that had bothered Andrew. He hadn't been ready for the old man to go. But there was no changing it now. The important thing was that Lazy L was his.

"Hadn't heard that part."

"Half a ranch isn't doing him much good when he's overseas. I'm here to ask for some help."

Brody sipped his coffee while Lucy put down her fork. "What sort of help?"

"I'm using the land to start up a rescue ranch."

Brody's cup went back to the table and Andrew met his gaze squarely. He knew it wasn't what Brody had expected to hear. But Andrew knew it was what he wanted to do. Needed to do.

"There's no money in that, Andrew. How're you going to live?"

This part, at least, was the part he'd figured out. "What I've put by will keep things afloat. I'm taking the front third of the barn and converting it into a small clinic. There's no mortgage on the place, and I'll make enough to support myself. I've got a good reputation as a vet. I'm counting on word getting around that I'm back in business."

"And the horses you take in…no vet bills will be a help?"

"Yes."

Lucy folded her hands. "Still a lot of work. A lot of money for upkeep. And a big change for you."

It *was* a big change, and he knew it must sound and look odd. The truth was he was burnt out. He'd gotten the career he'd wanted but he'd tired of it. It wasn't all it seemed, and he'd seen more than he cared to. Had compromised his principles a few too many times to hold on to his self-respect. He swallowed, remembering the day he'd made the decision to walk away from it all. It had felt good, right. He'd bought out Noah's half of Lazy L and still had more than enough to sustain himself—thanks to some savvy financial decisions along the way.

He could afford to do this, but he wanted help. He wanted it to be bigger than the sum of its parts. He wanted it to be not only about him, but something that was meaningful to the community. The trouble was doing it now, when everyone knew he'd turned his back on Larch Valley and the people in it a long time ago.

"I've been away for years. What I need to do is build goodwill again. Memories are long, and people remember that I left and didn't come back." He thought of Jen, thought of his father, and both left an ache in his chest. His father was gone; it was too late to mend fences. But Jen was still here. Even if she acted like she hated him, he knew he had to try to make amends. Somehow.

"I thought…in a few weeks…when I get the house and barns sorted a bit, I could throw a bit of a benefit. Maybe a dance like your Dad used to throw in the summers—remember, Brody?"

Brody and Lucy shared a long, tender look. "It's still an annual event," Lucy said softly, and Brody's fingers came to link with hers.

Andrew stared at their joined hands, thinking of Jen again. There had been a time when they'd held hands constantly, naively thinking everything would be easy and glorious and perfect. How wrong they'd been. Seeing her at the funeral had been a blow, a reminder of his many failures when it came to people who mattered. He hadn't known what to say, had been so bound up in his grief that he'd been sure he'd get it all wrong. And yesterday on the street she'd made it very clear his presence wasn't welcomed. He was honest enough with himself to admit it had stung a little. He had told himself not to expect her to welcome him back with open arms, but he'd thought she'd be a little more civil. Jen had always been understanding and open.

But he'd worry about that later. Right now, it was all about picking Brody and Lucy's brains about holding a benefit.

"I was thinking you two would know who I

should ask…who to hit up for donating time or materials. I'd like community involvement to keep the ranch sustainable. Frankly, it's more about awareness than it is about the money."

Brody nodded. "I'll make a list…suppliers and farmers who'd be willing to donate feed and hay. Ranchers in the area, for sure. Local farriers, and definitely local media." Brody looked at Lucy. "Media might best be handled by you, don't you think?"

"I'll polish up the tiara," she quipped. "And I'll help with the party end too, Andrew, if I can. You'll need music and decorations—we'll get those donated, never fear—and food."

Andrew felt himself get swept up in the whirlwind of planning, realizing that he was actually doing this. He was throwing away his illustrious career in order set up an operation that wouldn't make him any profit. He had to be crazy. And yet for the first time in years he felt energized, excited. As if he were doing something worthwhile. Something bigger than himself.

"Food? What sort of food?" He knew Betty always did a huge spread for the Hamilton Barn Dance, but he wouldn't presume to ask her. "A barbecue?"

"No, I don't think so. Nights are still pretty chilly, and who's going to want to stand outside for that? I think you need finger foods, buffet-style." Lucy winked at him. "And these are ranchers. So none of those canapés and pâtés you and I are used to, hmmm?"

He laughed. It was good to come home and be welcomed. He hoped that by throwing this party more doors would open up for him. People tended to have long memories in small towns. Up until now it hadn't really mattered.

"Well, I'm sure not able to cook it. Who do you suggest?"

"Jen O'Keefe."

His grin froze. Brody barked out a laugh. "Nice one, honey," he chuckled.

"Did I say something wrong?"

"I saw Jen yesterday," Andrew replied acidly. "She'd rather poison me, I think." Poison. Hah! Of all the townspeople, Jen would probably be the hardest to win over.

"Jen's sweet," Lucy defended loyally. "She'd never poison anyone."

Andrew shook his head. "Oh, yes, she would, and I'd be top of her list."

"Whatever for? You just arrived."

That's right, he had. But before that he'd gone, and he hadn't kept his promise. She hated him and she had every reason.

"Because I'm an idiot, Lucy." He accepted the words for what they were—the truth. "She'll never agree, anyway. She doesn't even want to look at me, let alone allow me to hire her for some shindig. And doesn't she own the bakery?"

Lucy nodded, running a finger along her bottom lip. "Yes, but she was going to see the bank about a loan to expand. She's branching out into catering. Oh, it's perfect, Andrew. She'll be closed while renovations are ongoing. In the meantime she can cater for you, and it'll be advance advertising for her new venture."

It made sense. If it were anyone but Jen. But yesterday she'd looked at him as if he was dirt beneath her shoes. She'd been coming out of the bank…had she got her loan?

"She's a brilliant cook."

"I remember," he said without thinking.

Lucy raised an eyebrow.

Brody nudged her. "They go *way* back."

Andrew shook his head. "Don't get any ideas, Lucy. Whatever was between Jen and me has been over for a long time. And it'll stay over if yesterday is any indication." He ignored the twinge of regret he felt at saying the words. "The only way she'll agree is if maybe you ask her. She won't even speak to me." If he were going to mend fences he was going to have to take his time. Asking her for a favor wasn't going to put him in her good books.

But Lucy shook her head. "No way, buster. I'm not being a go-between. Time to grow up. Imagine a party and you saying *Tell Jen that I said…* and her answering with *Tell Andrew that I said…*" She set her jaw. "This isn't Junior High. Jen is the best person in this town to cater your party, and if you want her you're going to have to ask her yourself. Otherwise you're going to end up at Ready-Right buying deli trays and potato chips."

They almost sounded appetizing compared to having to face Jen's coldness and ask her to take the job. Eating crow had never been his favorite menu item.

But the bigger picture was making his objective a success and putting his best foot forward. And cubed cheese and crackers wasn't going to do that.

He was going to have to ask her. And she'd either say yes or no. One thing he knew for sure. He wouldn't beg.

# CHAPTER TWO

SNICKERDOODLES BAKERY lay in the middle of Main Avenue, a two story plain building painted brick-red and with the false front found on many of the other buildings gracing the quaint street. Its western character was part of what Jen loved about Larch Valley—the sense of timelessness and comfort that came with it. It was a town with heart, with soul, with family. And even though her parents had retired nearby, in the more convenient city of Lethbridge, Jen had made the decision to stay.

The truth was, she didn't want to let go of it. Nor did she want to let go of the business she'd built from scratch—much like the way she built her cakes and pies and breads. It hadn't taken long after Ready-Right built their store for Jen's business to suffer. She could either let it go, or decide to take a risk.

She'd risked. And, despite the moments of panic, it felt right.

But today, pasting the announcement in her front window, it seemed rather daunting.

After her bank meeting last Monday she'd met with the contractors, and then had spent the remainder of her afternoon poring over catalogs. New equipment, new furniture. New signage. And closing for nearly a month to make it all happen.

Yup. Definitely certifiable, she thought, turning over the "open" sign and unlocking the door. In a few days the ovens would be cool and this door would remain closed. But for today she'd take pleasure in baking her favorites.

It was a warm morning, and she opened the inside door, nudging in a stopper with her toe and letting the spring air through the wood-framed screen. She smiled as she went back to the kitchen to finish cooking the filling for date squares. The screen door would also let the smell of her fresh baking out…the best and cheapest form of advertising she knew.

She'd just slid the tray of squares into the convection oven and set the timer when she heard the slap of the screen door against the frame.

She wiped her hands on her cobbler's apron and left the hot kitchen, going into the main part of the bakery, cool with the breeze wafting in. She paused when she saw the tall figure standing next to a rack lined with fresh bread loaves. This made twice that he'd appeared this week, and each time her breath had caught at the sight of him. She resolutely pushed the reaction to one side, and reminded herself that he had been the one to walk away.

"Still here, then?"

He turned, and her heart stuttered in her chest.

She'd already seen him once; the shock of their eyes meeting should have been over. But it wasn't. Seeing him today, a brown Stetson on his head, his hazel eyes shining at her from within his tanned face, had the power to reach inside her and take hold. It was as if no time had passed at all and he was standing before her ready to ask if she'd like to go for a ride in his truck. The memory ached with sweetness.

It was a physical reaction, but it came from a heart that had never quite forgotten what it was like to be loved by him.

"I'm still here."

"Why?"

It struck her as odd that they dispensed with any pleasantries. No *good morning* or *what brings you back*? or even a polite *how are you*? Perhaps they were past the need for small talk. Perhaps they were past the need to pretend for each other. Either way, neither of them tried to make the meeting something it wasn't. He was here. She wanted to know why.

He stepped forward, his hands in the pockets of his brown farm jacket. The counter separated them; Jen was glad of it. He couldn't see how her fingers were fussing with the display case between them.

"I'm staying at Lazy L."

"You are?" He was out at his old farmhouse? But it had been vacant for six months—longer if you counted the time his father had been in the hospital. It could hardly be suitable for visitors.

"For good."

Those two words sucked the wind clear out of her sails. Dealing with Andrew being in town for a few days was one thing. Knowing he was going to be back here indefinitely was quite another.

It would be a daily reminder. It wasn't something she could just put in a box for a finite amount of time and forget about once he was gone again.

"What about your career?" The words felt strangled, coming out of her mouth dry with nervousness.

"My career has taken a different path."

She didn't know what to say. Any response she might have thought of left her head as he slowly lifted his hand and removed his hat.

His hair was short, the tawny strands just long enough for a girl to run her fingers through. While the Stetson had shadowed his eyes a bit, they now glowed the color of the timothy he'd used to pick for her— the kind they'd chewed between their teeth as they'd walked the fields west of town, going nowhere.

"What sort of different path? You never wanted the farm," she said softly. *Never wanted to be tied here*, she remembered. But the last thing she wanted to do was bring up their old history. She'd thought enough about it last night, tossing and turning until past midnight.

"I never wanted what my father had laid out for me. You know that," he answered. "But it doesn't matter now. I'm back, and I'm starting up a rescue ranch."

She wanted to know more. She wanted to ask him why now, why here. What had changed. But seeing him brought back a lot of old feelings that had already taken a long time to get past. Hurt, for one. Learning not to love him so much. And anger. She'd done a lot of being angry and she didn't want to do it again. It was a life-sucking emotion, and she needed all her energy over the next few months to restructure her business.

She was a girl who learned her lessons.

"Could you come out from behind there so we can talk properly?"

She swallowed, forced her fingers to still. Andrew Laramie had broken her heart over a decade before, and he wouldn't do it again. They'd find a way to coexist in this town, and she'd make peace, but that would be the end of it.

"No, I don't think so."

"Jen…"

She raised a hand, closing her eyes. "Don't say my name that way."

And suddenly she was aware that they both knew nothing was over. No matter what lies they'd been telling themselves.

Silence reigned for a few moments and Jen opened her eyes. He was still there, still waiting. Not disappearing. She wished he would. After so many months of wanting him to come back, she now wished he'd go away and take his complication with him.

"Do you want to talk about this, Jen? Because we never did, and—"

"No, I don't." She said the words strongly. She'd lived through it once. She couldn't survive it again.

His eyes cooled as he rested back on his heels. "I deserve that." He pulled a newspaper clipping from his pocket. "You read this week's paper?"

"Not yet. Why?"

He handed her the clipping and stepped back. She scanned the first paragraph and looked up. "A charity benefit?"

"Lucy works fast. I didn't expect to get any publicity so soon."

"You know Lucy?" This was rapidly growing bigger than she could have imagined. It almost felt as if he was coming in and hijacking her life—which was silly. She'd built a life, one without him in it, just the way he'd wanted.

"I met her in Virginia several years ago. And I've asked Brody for his help too."

She looked down at the picture of Andrew; it was a stock photo that had been taken a few years ago at Churchill Downs, when a prominent racehorse had been injured. He'd certainly chased his dream and found it, but now it appeared he'd paid a price for it. So had she. He couldn't expect her to forget it with a pair of gorgeous eyes and a smile.

"I still don't know what you're doing here, Andrew, so why don't you get to the point?"

He cleared his throat. "The point is, I need someone to cater the food for the benefit. And Lucy insisted on you."

Lucy insisted. Not his idea at all. She felt the wisp of gratitude for her friend's loyalty quickly overshadowed by an irrational annoyance at Andrew's ambivalence. "Meaning *you* would have gone with someone else?"

"I didn't say that." He started tapping his hand against his thigh. Swept it out to the side in an encompassing gesture. "*This* is why I didn't want to ask. I didn't want it to be awkward, or…or difficult."

She softened the slightest bit. "What else could it be after all this time?"

For a long moment their gazes caught, and in his she sensed apology. She had never been one to hold a grudge. Yet at the same time every nerve-ending within her warned her to protect herself. She would always have a weak spot for Andrew.

"Lucy said you were the right one for the job. And I trust her judgment."

He trusted Lucy, but not her. She lifted her chin a little. She wasn't sure what she'd expected. She *wanted* him to keep his distance. It didn't make sense for her to be the least bit wounded by the fact that she hadn't been *his* choice.

"I'm sorry, Andrew, but I'll be in the middle of renovations here." She pointed at the sign in the front window announcing her temporary closure.

"Which is why it's the perfect time." He stepped forward. "I understand you're branching out into a café, and a catering side business. What better way to get a head start than by catering a job for me? You'll have positive publicity before you even open. It will give you something to do besides fret and drive the workmen crazy." He grinned at her disarmingly and she caught herself nearly smiling back.

She aimed him what she hoped was a look laced with skepticism. It wouldn't do to admit it, but the idea *was* sound. If he was already getting coverage in the local paper, then she *could* readily promote the new business before her grand reopening. She shouldn't turn it down just because it was Andrew doing the hiring. Surely she had more business sense than that?

"I'll think about it." She delivered what she hoped was the world's most impersonal smile. But then he smiled back, wide and unreserved, and it lit up the room.

"I'd forgotten how you could do that," he chuckled. "Look, I'd have invited you anyway, Jen. The Christensen Brothers are playing, and heck, half the town and then some are coming. You'd be helping me and I'd be helping you."

"I don't want your help."

"Maybe I want to give it anyway. I owe you." He took a step forward, closer to the glass case that separated them, close enough that she could see the tiny wrinkles at the corners of his eyes. He looked tired.

She knew it shouldn't make a whit of difference to her.

He'd never needed her; he'd made that abundantly clear. She turned away as the oven timer went off, went to slide the squares out of the oven and onto a rack to cool. When she turned around he'd come through to the back and stood in the door to her kitchen. The screen door slapped again and she was trapped; she would have to pass by him to reach the storefront.

"You don't owe me anything," she said quietly.

"Maybe I want to make amends, too," he said quietly.

"Isn't it a little late for that?" She whispered it, torn between wanting to reach out and bridge the gap between them and wanting him to simply go away and let her get on with the life she'd built without him.

"Come out to Lazy L. It's not all done yet, but come out anyway. See what I'm doing. See if you don't believe in it. If you turn down the job after the tour, I'll accept it. I promise. Just give me a chance."

Promises were exactly what she wanted to avoid when it came to Andrew Laramie, but she heard the ding of the silver bell next to the cash register and heaved a sigh of frustration. She couldn't keep whoever it was out there waiting forever.

"Why does it matter to you what I think? I'd just be the caterer."

He looked her in the eye. "It matters. It's always mattered."

Her heart stuttered at that pronouncement just for a second. But the rustle of her customer picking up merchandise jolted it back to a regular rhythm and she knew she had to get a move on. "Fine. I'll come out for a tour. On Sunday. Now, will you let me get back to work?"

He stepped aside as she hustled out to the front, pasting on a smile for the customer who had come in.

She was making change when he came out of the kitchen behind her. Agnes Dodds from the antiques shop up the street snapped her eyes open as he passed, but that wasn't what got to Jen.

He'd put his hat back on, and as he went behind her to reach the door his hand ever so lightly grazed her waist, lingering for a second, before he turned the corner and shouldered his way out the door.

Try as she might to forget it, the band of skin where he'd touched her burned with remembrance for the rest of the morning. She'd go see the ranch. And she'd decide about catering. But whatever else Andrew had in mind was strictly off-limits.

The foothills were beginning to green up after the spring rain when Jen made the drive out to the Lazy L Ranch for the first time in months. The ruts in the dirt road leading to the farmhouse were different, but so many things remained unchanged that for a few moments she suffered a distinct feeling of déjà-vu.

Andrew spoke of making amends. She wasn't sure what to make of that. A lot of time had passed, and she'd spent a good part of it putting their relationship behind her. She wasn't even sure she was interested in *amends* when it had been so difficult to reach *acceptance*. Maybe this was what he needed to make it okay for himself. Maybe she should listen to what he had to say. She didn't have any desire to hurt him, after all. Maybe hearing him out would be best, and then they could both move on and the ridiculous flutterings that happened when she was near him would disappear for good.

She pulled up in front of the house and parked next to a new pick-up truck—a shiny red diesel with enough power to haul a good-sized trailer, like the one parked next to the barn. The house itself looked lonely. The paint on the porch was peeling, the front door was faded from years of sun and wind. The corral beside the barn was empty, a few of the railings broken and drooping.

He had his work cut out for him.

She got out of her car and immediately heard the sound of hammering coming from the barn. She followed the noise, taking in the brown dry grass of the previous fall that had never been trimmed. It seemed things had fallen by the wayside here even before Gerald's death. If Andrew was planning on holding a dance here in a few weeks he had a lot to do.

She found him in the barn. It had been swept clean, and he was working in a T-shirt and jeans, with a stack of two-by-fours and one-by-sixes by his feet as he repaired broken boards. A brown tool belt hung low at his hips, accentuating the curve of his bottom as he reached down for the lumber. Dust motes swam in the beams of sunlight as he raised the hammer and nailed a board into place, the muscles in his shoulders and back plainly revealed through the cotton tee.

Instead of his Stetson today, he wore a ball cap, and she could see the precise line where his hair met his neck, neatly trimmed. She had the absurd urge to run her finger along the shorn edge.

The house was a derelict, and there wasn't a lick of hay in the place, and yet he was determined to accomplish this. She couldn't help but be impressed by his dedication alone. It echoed back to what she herself was trying to achieve—how could she in turn discourage him?

"Andrew?"

He whirled at the sound of her voice and she tried a smile. "I told you I'd come. But if you're too busy…"

"Of course not." He put down his hammer and unhooked the belt, the nails in the pouch jangling as he put it on the floor beside the neat lengths of wood. "Your timing is fine. I was going to take a break for a drink anyway."

His boots made hollow noises on the bare floor as he made his way over to where she stood. "Excuse the mess. Things are in a bit of disrepair, as you can see."

"I didn't know…"

"Neither did I. I should have. I realize that now." He gestured toward the ladder. "I didn't think you'd come, though I hoped you would. I've got a cooler downstairs with some drinks. I'll give you the grand tour—what there is of it."

She went down the ladder ahead of him, and was treated to a tempting view of his backside as he followed. There was no denying the physical attraction still existed. He had lost the callowness of youth and grown into himself. She'd always found him handsome, and it was just her dumb luck that he was even more so now. But she'd learned the hard way that it certainly wasn't enough to pin a girl's hopes on.

She looked away and followed him down the corridor to what was meant to be a tackroom. It still housed a few old saddles and bridles, but they, like the rest of Lazy L, hadn't been cared for in quite some time. The leather looked faded and cracked.

He opened a small cooler and handed her a can. She popped the top, all the while aware that it was just the two of them out here in the relative middle of nowhere. The isolation of it lent itself to a certain intimacy. He cracked his own top and took a long swallow, his throat bobbing three times before he lowered the can. A small trickle of sweat gleamed at his right temple.

A bird sang outside in the wild rose bushes.

She lowered her can. He lowered his. And for a heart-stopping moment everything held, waiting, waiting. His gaze dropped to her lips and a rush of warmth flooded her body. All it would take was one step by either of them and…

And it was exactly what she didn't want. Her eyes

flickered away. It was only the memory of this exact spot, the place where they'd first kissed all those years ago. It did something to her, pulled her in. She needed to remember she was here as a businesswoman.

"How about that tour?"

Andrew put the can down on a dusty ledge and she froze as he stepped nearer. Her words had been steady but her heart was a traitor as it sped up at the proximity of his body to hers. She kept walking backward but misjudged, and her back found solid wall.

"A…Andrew." She stuttered his name as he took the can from her hands and put it down. "Don't do this."

He took her cold hands in his warm ones and searched her eyes. The low peak of his cap shaded the upper half of his face, darkly mysterious in the dim light of the tackroom. Their first kiss. She remembered it as if it was yesterday. The nervous tumbling in her stomach, the excitement, the naked yearning. What she'd thought were resolutions suddenly didn't seem so resolved anymore. All those feelings and more were the ones she was feeling *right now*.

His thumbs rubbed over the tops of her hands. "Don't do what?"

*Kiss me*, she thought, but pursed her lips together. She wouldn't say it. Wouldn't voice it. She'd long ago promised herself she'd never ask him for anything ever again. Along with the flare of attraction she felt the knife-sharp edge of pain—how she'd felt the moment she'd accepted he was not coming back. No, he couldn't kiss her again. Not now. She turned her head away, but he released one hand, reaching up to grip her chin and turning it back to face him.

Andrew looked into her eyes, so dark a blue they were almost black in the muted light. He was touching her again, her icy hand in his, her perfect chin cupped within his fingers. He wanted to kiss her. Wanted to taste her lips beneath his and see if they still tasted the same. If she still made that breathy sigh she always had when he'd touched the delicate corner of her mouth with his own. Wanted to know so badly that he nearly forgot why he'd asked her here.

And she was wondering too. He could see it in the way her chest rose and fell, almost frantically, the way her pupils dilated when he moved in a couple of inches.

And then he closed his eyes and heard the words he'd never been able to get out of his head. *"You owed us better."*

It hadn't been Jen who had said them, but she'd been included in the sentiment, and he knew now that Gerald Laramie had been right. What he owed Jen now was an added complication. He needed to somehow make it up to her. He'd been a coward for a long time. What he wanted to do now was show her the man he'd become. He wasn't proud of all the decisions he'd made along the way. He was proud, however, of what he meant to do *from this day onward*. And for some reason her stamp of approval was worth something.

"Jen," he said softly, shocked to see the glimmer of tears in her eyes as he held her chin. Dear God, had he done that to her? Was it possible she still cared for him? After all this time? Or had he hurt her that much?

Leaving her had been harder than she realized, but there'd been so much more going on at the time he hadn't known what else to do. He'd been eighteen, and faced with a burden he hadn't expected. He'd had dreams, hopes, but ones she hadn't shared. Coming back to Larch Valley had been impossible that first year, and had grown more difficult each year since as his pride got in the way. It had only been when Gerald had died last fall that he'd realized he'd let it go too long.

He cleared his throat, released her. "We made so many mistakes," he conceded. "I won't compound them today. It's just…seeing you after all this time. It brings back a lot of memories."

He couldn't help but admire her backbone as she straightened, her shoulders back and tall with confidence.

"You either give me the tour and try to convince me to cater your dance, or you get out of my way and let me leave." She tried to sound strong but the words came out with a distinct wobble. "This…" she waved her finger between the two of them, speaking more clearly "…won't happen."

Her flat denial grated on his pride.

"Even if you want it to?"

He hadn't been wrong about the longing in her eyes, about the way their bodies seemed to gravitate together without even trying. He wasn't immune either. He remembered their first kiss in this very room. The way she'd been joking around, sitting on a saddle, and he'd pulled her off into his arms. They'd been in a cocoon of privacy in the barn, and he'd been sure she could hear his heart beating through his chest.

Like it was right now.

"I don't want it."

He backed off. He didn't either. Not really. He wanted to start out on a new foot, not work backward. But he tended to forget his intentions the moment he saw the flush on her creamy skin, or the way two tendrils of hair always seemed to escape her ponytail and frame her face.

He gave her space to move, and move she did. She slid out around him and out the tackroom door into the main barn area.

He followed closely behind, watching her dark ponytail swing as she strode away. He knew two things for sure at that moment. Firstly, his intentions had been honorable. He did want to set things right between them. And secondly, honorable intentions didn't always work out the way one hoped.

Because he still wanted to kiss her. And he had no idea what to do about it.

# CHAPTER THREE

THE air outside the tackroom was blessedly cool and Jen inhaled several times, trying to slow her pulse. She shouldn't let him get to her. She shouldn't let memories of the two of them have any power. What she needed to be doing was focusing on how she was going to improve her business. The money she'd make catering this function would help carry her through the month she was closed, giving her a head start in paying back her loan. It would give her a chance to promote early. Summer was coming up. There were any number of functions she could cater: showers and weddings and family picnics. So she'd just ignore Andrew's hazel eyes and stay on course. For all she knew he'd play at this awhile and then be gone as fast as he'd arrived. But for now she'd play along.

"We've got room for several horses in here, if we need it, to house them in cold weather." His voice came from behind her, strong but somewhat mollified, and she was relieved that he wasn't going to pursue what had just happened between them. It was just old history creating atmosphere. It wasn't real—couldn't be. It would be much better if they stuck to business.

His boots echoed on the concrete, the sound ricocheting through the empty barn. "I'm taking the front quarter of the barn and adding a clinic. I've got some men coming over this week to do the building, and I've got equipment and supplies on order. I'll be able to doctor my own stock, as well as that of other ranchers in the area."

She stopped at the last stall and put her hand on the door, turning to face him now that she was back in control of her emotions. "You shouldn't have much problem with drumming up business once word gets around."

But for how long? He was prominent, successful. How long before he got bored with Lazy L and Larch Valley and went back to his real life?

"That is the hope." He nodded. "I can manage financially without it, but I don't think I'd feel like me if I weren't practicing, you know?"

It was surprising to realize he was financially secure at such a young age. Goodness, he was so much more sure of himself than he'd used to be, and it was a little intimidating—especially considering she was barely scraping by and had just gone into debt so substantially. "If you enjoy practice so much, then why come back? Why now? You were so successful in the States. Your dad was always talking about you."

His head snapped up, his gaze catching hers, and she thought she detected a flare of pain before it was quickly doused.

"My father?"

She wasn't sure how to answer the clipped question; clearly the mention of Gerald put Andrew on edge. She decided to tread carefully. "I used to visit him after you left. Take him cookies. He followed your career from the start, you know."

It had been hard for Jen, hearing all about the life Andrew had chosen instead of choosing her. But Gerald had been good to her, and she knew he had been lonely. It had always been clear to her that Gerald had been as hurt about Andrew's severing of ties as she had. They had had that in common, and when Noah had been deployed Jen had started taking treats to the older man every few weeks or so. Over the years she'd seen him less and less. That had all changed when he had been taken to hospital. Then Jen hadn't been able to stand to see the aging man alone, when his sons couldn't be bothered to come see him.

Andrew shook his head, as if he didn't quite believe her. "No, I didn't know that. He never told me."

Andrew gestured forward and they exited out into the bright spring light, walking toward the corral by tacit agreement. He seemed reluctant to spend any more words on his father, so Jen decided to try talking about the ranch and his project again.

"So why here, and why now?"

They ambled slowly while a red-winged blackbird flitted from bush to bush ahead of them. "The racing world isn't all glory," he said finally. "Ask Lucy. She saw lots at Trembling Oak, and it's one of the better places I've been. I grew tired of watching it all. Horses bred to excess and then disposed of when they're not profitable. It's that elephant in the room that no one wants to discuss, you know? The world only really sees the glamorous side. And it's certainly not limited to the racing industry by any means. It's everywhere."

He sighed. "There are no easy answers or quick fixes." He leaned against the fence surrounding the corral. "I didn't mean to jump on my soap box. I guess it just ate away at me a little more each day until I knew I had to get out." He sighed. "There came a time when it seemed like I was helping take more lives than I was saving. It eats away at a man. I wanted to do something more positive."

"So now you're trying to change the world? It's a big step, Andrew. Some would say foolish."

"Change the world? Hardly. Change *my* world,

definitely. Maybe it's selfish of me to retreat to some quiet corner of land rather than get out there and beat a drum."

"People handle things in different ways. It doesn't make them right—or wrong either." Who was she to judge? She'd made her own decisions and she'd lived with them. Tried not to regret them, or second-guess herself. She looked out over the empty corral, wondering what it would look like filled with horses, as it had been once before.

"So what did it for you? What was the moment you knew you wanted out?"

Once she'd said them, the words were like a knife with two edges, echoing back to that September morning when he'd gone away to school, never to come back. He'd promised he'd return. That she'd never be alone. She'd never understood why he hadn't at least offered an explanation.

Andrew picked at a splinter on the corral railing. "I put down a yearling simply because he wasn't going to be profitable for the racing operation. A beautiful, gorgeous sorrel." He turned, looked into her eyes, and once again she felt the jolt of aware-ness that somehow had never quite gone away.

"I cried, Jen. I did it, and I cried over that horse, and that's when I knew."

Her throat burned as she swallowed. There were times she wanted to find fault with him, to issue blame for how he'd hurt her. But not now, not at this moment. This moment all she felt was sorry, because it was obvious this was something that had touched him deeply.

"You did the right thing," was all she could say, but she wasn't at all sure. Because coming home to Larch Valley and Lazy L might not be the right thing at all. And then where would he go?

"I've had enough of the limelight. I made my money on the backs of those horses, Jen. Now maybe I can do something good with it. Find some peace of mind."

His impassioned words struck a chord with her. He'd always had such ambition. Now that drive was tempered by compassion, and her resentment toward him began to thaw. Maybe he wasn't all about the glory and the money and the greener grass after all.

And then she remembered how he'd been too focused on building that illustrious career to visit his ailing father. And the truth of the matter was she was a long way from trusting that he wouldn't pull a disappearing act again. What was to say this wasn't just some transition period? What if he was just going through some sort of personal crisis?

"But there's just you here." She looked around, seeing the evidence of many months of neglect. It was a large job for one man, and lent itself to the notion that perhaps he hadn't thought it through as much as he ought to have. "You can't possibly do this all by yourself."

"I don't want it to be just me, though, don't you see?"

His eyes lit up—a distinct change from the gravity of moments ago.

"I could afford to run this on my own. But I don't want to. I want it to be bigger than me. That's why I want to involve local businesses. Let them contribute to it so it makes it a community effort. Feed, hay, fostering—heck, even just helping out with the day-to-day chores."

She could see how his plans energized him, once again making her feel she hardly knew him at all. Had she ever—truly?

He reached out and took her hand. "I felt good about it the moment my decision was made. And then I thought, why keep that to myself? What right have I to it? I wanted something good to finally come out of Lazy L. Who knows? Maybe Noah will come back for a while after his tour is over."

She left her hand in his for a few moments, not knowing what to say. Something good *had* come out of Lazy L—him. Why couldn't he see it? Why did he run around chasing it? Frustration bubbled, but she had no idea what to say.

Why had he left it until now, when it was empty and abandoned? Gerald hadn't been able to keep it up either, and yet he'd refused to sell. He'd insisted the ranch be there for his boys. It was a sad thing when all was said and done. Noah didn't want his share and Andrew hadn't come home until Gerald had passed on. She wondered if that was on his list of regrets as well. She knew very well that Gerald would have backed his son in his project and been proud of it. He'd always been so proud.

"Do you ever wish you'd made other choices?"

Andrew let go of her hand. It felt too natural in his, and made him forget the reasons why he'd left her in the first place. He looked over at her, resting his arms on the top rail of the fence. The empty, dusty corral was before them. Other choices? He wasn't the second-guessing type. But seeing her these last few days, the beautiful woman that had grown out of the girl, he'd let himself wonder if all the years spent trying to prove himself had been worth it. In a way, she represented everything Larch Valley stood for. He wanted a chance to win her over, as he'd never been able to do with Gerald.

But he wasn't looking for a romantic attachment. Some things were meant to be left behind.

"I'm not in the habit of second-guessing myself," he remarked, knowing it wasn't entirely true. "If I'd made different choices I wouldn't be here now. And this is where I want to be. And what's the sense in wishing anyway? I can't change what I did. You don't get do-overs. You just make your decisions, hope they're the right ones, and get on with it."

He'd played the "what if?" game lots over the first few years he'd been gone. And he'd never received any good answers.

"But you learn from your mistakes…or at least a wise man does," she replied. A breeze toyed with the hair next to her face, pinning a strand to the corner of her mouth. He watched, fascinated, as she hooked it with a finger and tucked it away. She'd been eighteen when he'd left Larch Valley for university, but he remembered that motion as if he'd seen her perform it just yesterday.

"No matter how much we might want to, we can't turn back the clock."

Their gazes caught and held, and he sensed she had questions running through her mind that she wouldn't ask. It was just as well.

"I'm not doing a very good job at giving that tour, now, am I?" Attempting to lighten the mood, he stood away from the fence and pointed, forcing a smile when he felt none. "Over there I'm building a newly fenced area for horses I need to keep close by and monitor. The bulk of the herd will pasture on the quarter section west of the house. And I'm building a couple of shelters out there as well, so they have a place to huddle during bad weather."

"And what about you, Andrew? The house…"

The house was a weird place to be these days. It was full of ghosts, and not all the pleasant kind. It was too quiet, the silence filled only by the harsh words said several years previously. But it had a bed, and a bathroom, and a kitchen, and it was his. He wasn't sure he could ever exorcise the specters of his past from its rooms, but he was going to try. One of these days he'd get up the courage to go through Gerald's things. So far he'd been unable to make it past the doorway of his father's room.

"The house needs some work as well."

"And you want *it* in shape before the benefit too?

He ran a hand through his hair. Lord, there was so much work. Working from dawn to dusk was the only thing getting him to sleep these days; exhaustion was a powerful tool. But for the briefest of moments there were so many items on his to-do list it was overwhelming.

"In a perfect world. But there's so much else to do I can't see how it will happen."

Jen watched as Andrew walked away, over to the porch of the house, putting a hand on the railing leading up the step. He obviously felt very strongly about what he was doing. And he needed help. She was tempted to offer hers. Maybe because he seemed so tired. Maybe because it touched her that he was trying to build something fundamentally good. Maybe it was the fact that the place he needed most seemed to be home, whether he realized it or not. Maybe it was for the simple reason that they'd once been friends, once been lovers. Maybe it was all of those reasons mixed up together.

Her gaze dropped to the back pockets of his jeans as he made his way up the steps; the spit in her mouth pooled as attraction sizzled through her limbs. He'd invited her here to convince her to cater the dance. And it was working. If he asked her at this moment she knew *yes* would come out of her mouth before she could stop it.

"Jen…" He turned, looked down at her and her insides went all woozy.

"What?"

"Why don't you come inside? We can talk more about the dance."

Right. Business. That was exactly where her thoughts should be.

"I don't think that's a good idea." The house held too many memories of their time together. If she were going to do this it was going to be for business reasons, not because of a misplaced sense of nostalgia.

"Why not?"

It was too difficult to come up with plausible reasons without delving too deeply into the truth. Seeing Andrew, being with him, felt much too familiar for her to be comfortable.

"I need to get back. I have some work of my own to do."

He watched her for a few moments, and she felt as though his eyes could see right into her and through the small lie. "I see," he said quietly.

"I'm sorry."

"But you'll cater the party?"

How could she say no? It would be a deliberate snub and she wasn't capable of it. And his enthusiasm had touched her, whether she admitted it to him or not. "Yes, I'll cater," she decided.

He put his hand against the spooled porch railing. "We should talk about the menu, then, and your fee. You sure you don't want to come in for a few minutes?"

Oh, she wanted to. She wanted to spend more time with him, and she was curious about the house now that he was back in it. But she knew it would be a mistake. Especially after the little interlude in the tackroom earlier. She didn't want to be alone with him. Not until the newness of seeing him again had worn off. Right now it was far too fresh.

"Another time? Soon."

"Dinner? Tomorrow night?"

The suggestion came out so quickly she had no time to put up her guard. "Dinner?"

"Come out tomorrow and have dinner. Everyone has to eat."

First of all, unless something had changed over the years, Andrew couldn't cook. And dinner for two out at the secluded ranch was even worse than going inside now. "Why don't you meet me in town?" she suggested. "For pizza. Papa's is still there, you know." In town, in a public restaurant, she'd feel more comfortable. More on her own turf, in control of the situation.

"Papa's it is. I'll pick you up at—"

"I'll meet you there," she broke in quickly. "After all, it's not a date."

"I'll be there at six," he replied, pushing away from the column. He turned and went into the house, the screen door smacking against the frame behind him.

Not a date. Jen worried her lip with her teeth as she walked back to the car. It sure felt like one just the same.

Andrew was waiting for her at Papa's, seated at a table by the front window and scowling into a soft drink. Jen lifted a hand to Jim, the "Papa" behind the name, and exhaled, pasting on a smile. She'd been relieved yesterday to set up their meeting in a public spot, but later had realized the folly of it. She might say it was not a date, but she knew the townspeople of Larch Valley would think that it looked like one.

She sat down across from him. "You're early."

He looked up, a smile breaking out on his face.

"I had an errand in town and finished earlier than I expected." As Jen put her purse on the seat, Linda Briggs brought a plastic tumbler and put it on the table. "Andrew ordered you a Dr. Pepper," she said, but Jen detected a bit of steel in the words.

"Thanks, Linda. How's Megan? Last I heard she was down with this spring cold."

"On the mend, thanks for asking," Linda replied.

Jen couldn't help but notice that Linda kept her back half-turned toward Andrew. Had he done something to make her angry? Jen smiled, attempting to lighten the atmosphere that for some reason held a shimmering of tension.

"You kids ready to order?" Linda asked, poising her pen over her small notepad.

Jen looked at Andrew, who was doing a good impression of being relaxed, leaning back against the vinyl of the booth seat. "You still like everything?"

"Absolutely."

"A medium colossal, then. And could we get a salad to share too?"

"Sure thing, sweetie." Linda scribbled on the pad and went back to the kitchen.

"Wonder what I did to her," Andrew muttered, leaning ahead and picking up his glass. He took a drink and put it down again, moving it in circles on the scratched table top. "She was friendly enough when I came in, but when I asked about your drink she clammed up. You do still like Dr. Pepper, don't you?"

She felt a little uncomfortable, knowing Andrew had deliberately ordered her favorite drink from teenage years. Jen suddenly smiled as realization dawned. She'd known Linda since she'd been a girl. Linda's son Dawson had been friends with both her and Andrew. Linda, in her motherly way, was being protective. The whole town knew Jen had been heartbroken when Andrew had gone away. Her smile faded a bit, as she remembered. She'd been so sure he'd come back. In a town like this, everyone had known she'd been waiting. And they'd known when her heart had been broken too.

Linda was looking out for her, and Jen didn't have it within her to mind. The people of Larch Valley had always been there for her. It was the reason why she'd wanted to stay—even when she'd lost her reason to.

Linda came back with a Caesar salad and two plates, and Jen waited quietly until she went away again. She picked up the plastic tongs and served each of them a helping of the crisp salad.

"You want to know what you did?" Jen asked, picking up the thread of conversation. She looked up at Andrew, who'd irritably picked up his fork. "You didn't come back."

"You're joking. That was years ago." He put down his fork and frowned at her.

"You really have forgotten what Larch Valley is like, then. Memories are long."

"Including yours?"

She felt a little twisting in her stomach at the question. He really had no idea, did he? Maybe it was time he learned. "Especially mine," she replied quietly. "Don't be angry with Linda. She'll come around. I think she always kind of hoped that Dawson and I…"

"You and Dawson?" The question echoed through the eating area and both their heads turned quickly toward the kitchen area before moving back to each other. The gold flecks were sparking in his eyes and she raised her eyebrows.

"Are you jealous?"

He looked away. "Of course not."

Jen picked at her salad. "For the record, no. Not me and Dawson. He's a friend. That's all he's ever been. Linda is just being protective."

"And you obviously need protecting." There was bitterness in the words.

"Hardly. I learned to stand on my own two feet long ago. Anyway, we came to talk about this dance, right?"

She pushed her salad plate aside and pulled out a notebook. "What we're discussing here is business."

"And that's all there is?"

"That's all there can be. Don't you agree?" She felt a certain release in saying the words. "I can't dwell on the past. I moved on, built my own life. Just as you did."

"I know that."

Relief was tempered by a disappointment she didn't want to feel. "I took your job because it makes good business sense. Not out of any feelings of misplaced sentimentality or loyalty."

His throat bobbed as he swallowed and she saw a muscle tick in his jaw. Was he angry at her?

She wrote the word "*Menu*" at the top of a page, but Andrew stopped her with a hand on her arm. She looked up, mesmerized by what she saw in his eyes. Anger, frustration, gratitude…and something more that complicated everything.

"Is that all?"

"It's all there can be, Drew."

Linda chose that particular moment to deliver their pizza, hot and fragrant with tomato and cheese and toppings.

Andrew slid his fingers off of her wrist and looked the waitress square in the face. "Thank you, Mrs. Briggs."

She seemed to soften a little bit. "You're welcome. You kids call if you want something else."

Jen slid a piece of pizza on to her plate, and so did Andrew. "Do you suppose we'll always be considered 'the kids'?" She laughed lightly, trying to dispel the serious atmosphere. The last thing she wanted was for things to get heavy. Why couldn't they leave things behind and be friends? They were both adults.

"We did have some good times, didn't we?"

She took her fork and lifted a black olive off the pizza slice, popping it into her mouth. "Drew…"

"Oh, come on, Jen. How many times did we come here for pizza after a school dance or a movie?" He stared pointedly at her plate. "Do you still eat all the toppings first, and then the crust?"

She couldn't help the grin that crept up her cheek. "Yeah, I guess I do."

"Those were good times."

She would not cry, or sniff, or get sloppily sentimental. She couldn't. "Yes, they were," she replied, fixating on a mushroom buried beneath melted cheese. "Movie theater's closed now, though. And the high school is now the junior high. They built a new high school north of town. Times change."

"People change too, right?"

She gave up on the mushroom. Andrew hadn't even touched his pizza, she realized. He was looking at her as if wanted her to believe him. And she did want to. But she couldn't afford to. It would complicate everything.

But he was right. People did change. "Have you changed? You're back home, so I guess you must have. But I hope you realize that things here didn't necessarily stay the same. Me included."

He frowned, finally picking up his pizza and taking a bite. He swallowed, took his napkin and wiped sauce from his lips. "Oh, I think I've reached that realization," he replied.

Jen realized that several pairs of eyes were watching them now, and she forced a smile. As much as she appreciated the moral support, it had always been a challenge, being under the watchful eye of the town. "One thing that hasn't changed," she said quietly, "Nosy Nellies. I'd say the two of us together is causing a bit of a sensation."

"It's not really a date," he said, but she could see his earlier annoyance was dissipating. "We might as well get down to business and enjoy ourselves. This is way better than anything I could have cooked anyway."

His eyes glowed at her, and she felt a strange sense of accord with him. Perhaps they could move past their old relationship and be friends. Catering his event would be a good start to that.

She slid her plate to the side, took one more bite, and then clicked the top of her pen. "Okay, then. We're thinking finger foods, right? And nothing too fancy."

"Exactly."

"Hot, cold? Do you want dessert?"

"Definitely some sweets. Your brownies, for one. You know, the one thing that didn't surprise me was that you made baking your livelihood, Jen." He slipped another piece of pizza on his plate and smiled at her. "You were always a great baker."

Jen felt a pang of remembrance. She doubted that Andrew realized that his father's death had affected her as well. She could still remember visiting on Saturdays and watching Gerald at the sink, cutting up potatoes and carrots to go with a roast. The house of single men ate plainly, and she'd always brought something for dessert. Cake, or pie, or the banana bread that had been Noah's particular favorite. He'd jokingly said he was going to marry her someday, so she could cook sweets for him all the time. She could very nearly hear their voices, and see Noah's wink at Andrew as he said it, knowing she was Andrew's girl. Andrew had broken her heart, but she'd also felt the loss of her second family acutely.

She'd always promised herself that she'd be rational, sensible, if he came back. But the past had its claws in her and she had to fight to keep the memories from being too bittersweet. She wanted to look back with fondness. If they could just remember the good times, before it had all gone wrong…

"Remember the time Noah decided he was going to make pies? He was back from boot camp and had brought a whole box of fresh apples with him."

Drew laughed now, genuinely entertained. "He absolutely refused your help."

"And the pastry looked like a road crew had come through doing patch work."

"And we all ate it, even though it was tough and the apples were still hard."

"It was better with the ice cream."

They were smiling fully at each other, and when Jen realized it she dropped her eyes to her plate, stirred more than she cared to admit by the warmth of his gaze.

Andrew saw her gaze drop and his smile faded. She was still so pretty. Fresh and natural, as she had been as a girl, only now with a woman's strength and knowledge. At first he'd missed her so, but then over time it had faded, and he'd convinced himself it was a high school thing. But it wasn't. She still got to him. There *had* been good times before it all blew apart.

"Is it strange, being back in the house, then?"

Her soft voice drew him back from his musings and he sighed. Being in the house again was like looking at a room through a filter. It was a shadow of itself, dusty, faded, stuck in time. He'd walked in and taken stock: the tie-back curtains were limp and faded at the windows, the oak table was scratched and without a tablecloth, the old cushion floor hadn't been scrubbed and waxed in an age. And it was quiet. So very, very quiet.

"The house hasn't really changed," he replied

quietly, giving his lips a final wipe with the napkin. "I don't think Dad ever threw anything out. If there was an ounce of use left in it…"

"I know. Even when he went to the care home he took that awful old thirteen-inch TV with him. I tried to convince him to buy a new one, but he said that one was perfectly good. Wouldn't buy a DVD-player either—insisted on watching his old movies on that VCR you bought him for Christmas way back when."

It sounded so typically Gerald that Andrew nearly smiled. But it was that type of obstinacy that had kept them apart. He puckered his brow, wondering why Jen couldn't see that. "You spent a lot of time with him?"

"Not so much. A visit here and there. He was lonely. He missed you."

Andrew's lips pursed as he watched her reach up to tuck a stubborn piece of hair behind her ear.

"Would you like me to tell you about him? Maybe it would help."

He crumpled up the napkin and tossed it on the table. Having to hear about Gerald from Jen was like taking a stinging cut and then poring salt on it. "Help with what, exactly?"

Her eyes widened. "You must miss him."

He laughed soundlessly, little humor in his expression. "Yeah."

"He missed you too. He made sure that Elsie at the library kept tabs on…"

"Let's get one thing straight, shall we?" He lowered his voice, trying to keep the shake out of it, trying to keep the people at the nearby tables from hearing. Lord, he'd spent years trying to get his father's attention—to no avail. What did Jen possibly know about that? About how hard he'd worked to prove himself to the old man, to show that he'd made the right choice by following his own dreams? "I appreciate the sentiment, really I do. But talking about Gerald is a no-go zone."

"But…"

"I mean it, Jen."

"Can I ask why?"

He stood up, reaching inside his pocket for a few bills which he tossed on the table. "I don't know what you think you know, but Gerald Laramie didn't give a damn about what I did once I left Lazy L."

Without waiting to hear her response, he strode to the door and swung it open, walking out into the spring evening.

# CHAPTER FOUR

JEN hastily grabbed her purse and notebook. Her heart ached as realization struck. Was he so hurt by his father's death then that even talking about it was simply too much? She thought back to when they'd met after the funeral. He'd been alone. Noah had been deployed and hadn't made it back. She'd offered her condolences but he'd brushed by her as if she were nothing. But maybe he'd been too full of grief. Maybe it hadn't been about her at all.

She followed him out the door, taking quick strides to catch him as he made his way up the avenue toward the park. "Drew, wait," she called softly. His steps slowed but they did not stop. And she began to wonder if Andrew's sudden appearance at Lazy L, his sudden change of heart, hadn't been prompted by his father in the first place. She owed it to Gerald to tell Andrew some of the things his father had said during the last years. But not today. It would fall on deaf ears.

She caught up with him at the park, where he'd dropped onto a bench, staring out at the trees that were just starting to bud. The sound of laughter and the creak of swings came from the playground. She didn't know what to say to him now, so merely sat down beside him, considering the odd turn of events that had taken her life and turned it upside down over the past few months. Here she was, taking the biggest business risk she could remember, and sharing breathing space with Andrew Laramie on a spring evening. It was a stark reminder that she had her life now and he had his, and they weren't joined in any way. And yet it was so clear to her that he was hurting. How could she turn him away when what she really wanted was to help him?

"Today was a bit of a trip down memory lane, wasn't it?" She crossed her left leg over her right, all her senses tuned to his every move. His shoulders lifted up and down as he sighed. She marveled at how he could be as familiar to her as the scent of a summer rain kissing a dusty road and yet be a total stranger. Once upon a time she would have been able to read his thoughts.

"Perhaps."

She fought back the urge to sigh and tried an encouraging smile instead. "Maybe it would have been better if we'd just stuck to menus."

She wished he'd look at her, so she could see the

answer in his eyes. But he just stared resolutely out over the grass. His shoulders tensed slightly and she knew she'd struck a nerve.

"Undoubtedly."

"You know, I was mad at you for a long time, Drew."

"I know."

"But only because I was hurt."

She saw him flinch as her words struck home.

"I just want to be honest. We're not eighteen anymore. And while I've agreed to help you because of business…"

"We both know this is more than business."

His words were like lighting a match to kindling, the fire catching and burning. "I can't dwell on the past. I moved on, built my own life. Just as you did."

"I know that."

His throat bobbed as he swallowed, and she saw him clench his jaw. Was he angry at her? She almost smiled. It would be one of the first true indications that he had any feelings on the matter at all.

"But there's more to it, isn't there? Let me be your friend, Drew."

He turned his head, and for a few moments he seemed to be the man she remembered. "It was good, talking about some of the memories," he said quietly. "I know I hired you, but it was good having dinner with a friend."

What could she say to that? She couldn't read his

eyes; he'd dropped the shutters on them again. She wasn't sure they could actually *be* friends. Too much water under the bridge and all that. And yet to be more was unthinkable. He had already broken her heart once.

"Either way you slice it, you've got this benefit to think of first. We can talk about Gerald another time."

"Or not."

So cold. So cut off. She worried her hands together as she wondered about his determination to avoid anything to do with his father. Maybe all he needed was time. He hadn't been home long, after all.

"We didn't even do any menu-planning. Why don't I work up a preliminary list? That way you can veto anything that doesn't suit and we can come up with some alternatives."

"That would be good."

"Right." She got up, tucking the notebook back in her bag. "Thanks for dinner."

He rose too, and took a step toward her. "I'm sorry it ended the way it did."

She wanted to ask why, but knew she'd be faced with his stony silence again. She understood that whatever it was, he wasn't ready to talk about it. But the moment drew out, as if he was waiting for her to say something. And all the time she was trying not to look at his lips, or to remember the way they felt and tasted, or the way he'd always been pulling her ponytail elastic out to run his fingers through her hair. Her toes nearly curled just thinking about it.

"We'll talk soon." She offered a polite smile, though her heart was thumping. She spun and hurried off back down the street toward her car.

She got in, slamming the door. Friends, indeed. If that were true, why did she very nearly feel his kiss on her lips?

And why did she want it so badly?

Jen wasn't at all certain that the color she'd chosen for the interior—chocolate cherry—was the right one.

Paint smeared an old white T-shirt and dotted the tip of her nose as she peered up at the line where the white ceiling and the reddish-rose wall met.

The bakery kitchen was still a shambles as the contractors restructured and rewired for additional equipment, and the flooring for the café section wouldn't arrive until next week, but Jen was bound and determined that the walls be painted, so that once the flooring was installed the trim and crown molding could follow right away.

But she was getting tired. She was working double duty preparing for the benefit at Lazy L as well as at Snickerdoodles, and she would be glad when Sunday rolled around and the dance was over. She'd have her check and could make her first payment on her loan before she even reopened.

She sighed, retied the bandana over her hair, poured paint into the plastic tray and picked up her roller.

She was halfway through the first wall when knocking came from the front door. "We're closed!" she called out, but seconds later the knocking came louder. With a sigh she put down her roller and went to the door.

"I'm sorry, the bakery is—"

"Closed. Yeah, I know."

Drew, standing there in the shadows as the street-lights just started to flicker on. His grin was lopsided and boyish, and she lowered her lashes before he could see how happy she was to see him. She shouldn't be. She'd drawn a line in the sand that meant *strictly business*. Or at least *strictly friends*. She wasn't planning on crossing it. Heck, she'd even decided another meeting was not a good idea and had e-mailed him a tentative menu instead of seeing him face to face. All she'd been able to think about was the way he'd looked at her as they'd sat in the park.

She'd made some samples and delivered them when she was sure he'd be out of the house. And now here he was—live, breathing, and in her construction zone.

He stepped inside and looked around at the chaos. Jen had a moment of female vanity where she realized she was in her worst clothes, with an old bandana tied over her hair and paint smudges on everything. It quickly passed…she was simply a business owner working hard to stay afloat. She was proud of what she was doing. And certainly not too proud to do her share of the work. It shouldn't matter what she looked like.

"Did you need something in particular?"

The words came out slightly snappish. She was annoyed at herself for caring about her appearance. His booted feet left footprints in the fine film of drywall dust still sifting about on the floors as he walked the perimeter, casually examining it.

"I came to say thank you, actually."

Jen tried to ignore the persistent ache in her shoulders—the one put there from spending the day painting. When John, her painter, had called and explained that his young daughter had been in an accident and would be in the hospital for a few days, she'd never given it a second thought. The last thing she wanted him to worry about was work. And rather than fall behind she'd picked up a brush and roller and had started the café walls herself. The more she could pitch in, the faster it would all go.

The distraction of Andrew wasn't helping her accomplish that goal.

"Say thank you for what?" She had to stop standing there like a lovestruck idiot. Pasting a neutral expression on her face, she went back to her stepladder and paint tray, rolling an even coat on the sponge and stepping up to roll the top part of the wall.

"For dropping over all those samples this week." He followed her, stopping at the base of the ladder and tilting his chin up. She tried valiantly to ignore him. Tonight he wore a khaki colored T-shirt that should have been boringly neutral but instead brought out the greeny-gold of his eyes, so that one color nearly reflected the other. She made a point *not* to gaze into them.

"Did you make a final decision?" There weren't that many days left, and she needed to get shopping and cooking for the final menu. And perhaps manage a few hours of sleep at some point.

"I did." He patted his jeans pocket and her eyes were diverted to the worn denim. "Right here. I have to admit, your goodies pulled double duty."

"How so?" She bit down on her lip, intent on focusing on the wall.

"They kept me from having to cook a couple of times. And tasted better than boxed macaroni and cheese. Other than the pizza we shared, meals have been a bit sketchy out at the house."

So he didn't cook much for himself. She wasn't sure if she was pleased he seemed to have a weakness or annoyed with the fact that perhaps he'd never needed to learn.

She refilled her roller and rubbed it on the wall in

front of her. "If you want to leave your final choices on the ledge over there, I'll get them when I'm done," she said, weariness leaking through her tone.

"Done?" He took a step closer to the ladder. "You can't mean to do all this tonight. It's after nine o'clock."

"I need to get this coat on so it will be dry for the next one tomorrow. Even with the tinted primer it's going to take three coats."

"I thought you'd hired contractors."

"I did."

"Then why aren't they doing it?"

She inched over on the ladder, reaching for a spot on her right that she'd missed. "They are. I'm helping. The less time I'm closed, the better."

"Is money that tight, then?" he said quietly.

Every ounce of pride in her bristled. The roller ran faster and faster over the wall. "I'm just a small business owner, trying to keep up during a challenging financial climate." She smiled grimly, absurdly proud of herself for that sentence. "But that's not why, if you must know. I hired John Barker to paint for me, but his youngest is in hospital and he needed a few days off."

"Is it serious?"

Her shoulders relaxed slightly at the genuine concern she heard in his voice. They'd both gone to school with John since first grade. "I don't think so.

But the last thing he needs to worry about is the job, you know? He'll be back next week."

"No one could ever accuse you of being lazy, Jen."

"Thank you."

"They might accuse you of being a bit of a bleeding heart, though."

Bleeding heart? When it was simply a matter of neighbor helping neighbor? "Maybe you haven't spent much time in places where people help each other, Andrew. Where they look out for each other."

"A person doesn't like to assume he's welcome in a place. Maybe a fella likes to be asked."

She scowled. It was bad enough she'd taken his catering job to begin with; bad enough she had to see him as often as she did. And definitely awful to realize that she was just as attracted to him now as she'd been then. Maybe even more so. It was difficult to keep her mind on business when her thoughts kept leading her elsewhere.

"Maybe if a fella *offered* his help once in a while, he'd feel a lot more welcome," she retorted.

"All right." His voice was deep and oddly quiet again—the way it got when it could reach right inside her and turn things upside down. "Would you like my help, Jen?"

She swallowed. Yes, definitely. The gently worded question did soften her toward him considerably—even if she had been the one to practically script it for him and give him a nudge. Was she really so weak when it came to him? She hoped not.

"I'm fine. Really and truly." She lowered her chin and pinned him with what she hoped was a stern look. "I'm *always* fine."

"Yes. I know." He conceded her point softly, and she forgot her goal to avoid his eyes. Now his were soft and mossy-colored with understanding, fringed with his stupidly long lashes. Her tummy flipped over as the moment drew out. She did not want his understanding or his pity. He couldn't know, after all. He hadn't been here to see the damage he'd done. She'd be a fool to let him in again, wouldn't she?

"I did come to ask a small favor." He finally said something, though his eyes never left her face and her own were drawn down to stare at his full lips as he spoke. "Something special for the benefit."

"Something special?" She'd already pored over her recipe books trying to find the kind of foods his guests were likely to enjoy. Plain, substantial food, yet with a festive, elegant twist. It had been more difficult than she'd expected. Now, as she watched his lips move, she realized he was too close. She inched farther over on the step.

"A recipe." He looked as if he was about to choke on the words. "I thought maybe it would be a good addition."

She stared at him. "My menu wasn't complete, I take it?"

"No! Of course not. I mean, it was fine," he amended. "I just came across this the other night when I was going through the kitchen. I thought if anybody could make sense of it, you could."

He reached into his pocket and withdrew a small slip of paper, handing it over. "It was one of Gerald's favorites."

The confession was made so softly she knew it had been difficult for him to say. After his quick refusal to even speak his father's name at dinner, she knew it was a big thing for him to reach out even this much. She took the paper, scanning the faded handwriting.

"This is it?" There was hardly anything on it, just rudimentary ingredients, no measurements, no method.

"I know it's rough…but you're such a good cook, Jen. I felt certain when I saw it that you could adapt it for the function." He looked up at her, his eyes warm with confidence. "I haven't had it since I was a small boy. Mum used to make it for Gerald's birthday."

Andrew kept referring to his father as Gerald, and she wondered if it was part of the way he was handling his grief. The little bit of distance to make it easier. She wanted to ask, but he'd made it clear he didn't want to talk about it. She didn't want to start another argument.

And, as much as she wanted to help, there was the added work to consider. She'd have to experiment first—see if she could get it right.

"I don't know, Drew. It's not very complete, and I'd have to experiment a bit. And even if I did make it, it might not taste like you remember." A sudden thought struck her. Many of the selections she'd picked were make-ahead, with the consideration that she was without much of her bakery equipment. The old oven was gone and the new one ordered and not yet delivered. She was down to the stove in her house. If she adapted this recipe, it had to be with a mind toward her limited capabilities.

"I'm sure it'll be great," he murmured, fueling her doubts. He took one more imploring step forward, his booted toe bumping the stepladder as Jen tried backing up and found nowhere to go.

His boot hit one leg of the ladder and her weight was mostly over on the other. She watched as the paint started to slop in the tray hanging on the front of the ladder and lurched forward to steady it. She did, but then the center of gravity of the ladder shifted, throwing her off-balance once more. Her foot reached for the step that was no longer there.

She knew she was falling and powerless to stop it. There was a sense of weightlessness as gravity took over and nothing was beneath her feet. She braced herself for a big bump on the hard, concrete floor. Only it never came.

Instead she was caught by two strong arms, one unceremoniously hooked beneath her left armpit, the other tangled up between their bodies as he bolstered her weight. She twisted, opening her mouth to rail at him for causing the accident, then her gaze caught his and the words vaporized before reaching her lips.

Other than the once he'd touched her waist in passing, they'd avoided physical contact. Even in the tackroom it had been the one barrier not crossed. But now...now she was held in his arms, unable to avoid the strength there, or the hard, warm feel of his length against her in several places along her body. In his arms. The one place she'd never thought she'd be ever again. It was both sad and electric.

And, by the flare in his eyes, she wasn't the only one feeling the current.

His hot gaze dropped to her lips, and she felt them open slightly as her breath accelerated with acknowledgment. *He's going to kiss me*, she realized, while in her brain denial fought to be heard. It wasn't loud enough. For the briefest of seconds their lips hovered, only an inch apart. And then he tightened the arm around her ribs and his mouth was on hers.

Her heart slammed into her ribs, pounding against the biceps that held her so tightly against his body so hard that she was sure he must be able to feel it through his skin. His lips were warm and soft, yet controlling, demanding she return in kind. It was a demand she couldn't help but answer as her mouth opened beneath his.

The moment she acquiesced the world tilted sideways. Andrew turned slightly, unpinning his trapped arm and wrapping it around the top of her shoulders. His fingers gripped her neck beneath the hair cascading from her bandana. He shifted, planting his feet on the concrete, a solid place for her body to curve into as she melted against him.

His hand left her neck briefly to pull the bandana off her head, and she felt his fingers twine in her hair. And, oh, he tasted the same as she remembered. She shouldn't be able to recall the flavor that was simply *Drew*, but one touch of his lips on hers and it came flooding back with disturbing clarity.

Finally he broke the kiss, resting his lips against her temple with a sigh. Their breathing echoed through the empty space.

"Jen," he whispered, and her eyes closed as the sound of her name on his lips reached inside of her and held on. It was as good as she remembered. It was better.

His hand lay against her head, almost as if he was tracing the shape of it with his palm, and she leaned into the contact. The taste, the smell of him, the feel of his body against hers—those senses all lent themselves to a strange feeling of security, as if she'd never left.

And then she remembered. *She* wasn't the one who'd done the leaving. He had.

She pulled away out of his arms, stumbling backward past the ladder and the drop cloth. How could she have fallen under his spell so quickly? After she'd promised herself she wouldn't? After making her wishes perfectly clear that evening at the park? Platonic only! She ran her tongue over her lips, trying to wash the taste of him away and failing utterly.

"Jen," he cautioned, and the indulgent tone of his voice did absolutely nothing to comfort her.

"Was this your sales pitch, Drew?" She wished the words had come out strong and defiant rather than with a tell-tale wobble. In her consternation she'd forgotten she didn't want to call him Drew, and that aggravated her further. She forced herself to calm. "Did you think kissing me would convince me to help you? To take on more work?"

"That's not why I kissed you!" He took a step forward, eyes flashing, and she could feel the memory of his wide chest against hers only moments before. Her fingers itched to touch it again, to see if it really felt as strong as it had seemed.

"Then why did you?"

A hush fell over the room. Suddenly Jen didn't want to know the answer. The possibilities were far too frightening when she'd spent so much energy first getting over him and then building her own life without him.

"Because I had to know."

She swallowed. Fear fought with undeniable curiosity. "Had to know what?"

Was there really several feet between them? It didn't feel as if there was. Lord, even from this distance it felt like he was touching her, and she couldn't escape it. It was as if the space she'd attempted to put between them didn't even exist.

"If you tasted the same."

Every dying hope she'd had was suddenly resurrected and swelled into her chest. She tried beating it down. This wasn't what she wanted. She refused to fall under his spell again, knowing that in all likelihood it would end when he'd had his fill of home and went to seek his fortunes again. And yet her own reaction demanded she know the truth about his.

"And did I?" She lifted her chin.

And finally, finally, he broke eye contact. "Yes," he admitted, and she could clearly see that the result didn't make him as happy as it apparently had when they had been engaged in the actual activity.

"You left me," she whispered, shattered. "I haven't forgotten."

"Neither have I."

She supposed it was as much of an admission of guilt as she'd get out of him. It wasn't his fault she couldn't seem to shake her feelings for him. Clearly they'd never gone away but had only been put in storage, waiting for his return to be brought out and dusted off. Feelings were one thing. But letting him see them was quite another. And they'd both admitted there was no going back.

"I agreed to cater your dance for two reasons," she said, desperately trying to regain her emotional footing. "One being it's good for *my* business. Secondly, I think what you're doing is a good thing, and it's something I am proud to be a part of."

"Jen, I—"

"I'm not finished." She drew on all her inner strength. "This does not mean I'm interested in starting anything up with you. I'm certainly not a convenience you can use when you need something done."

He stepped forward and she knew she'd hit a nerve by the sharp angle of his jaw and the way his lips thinned.

"You have never been a convenience," he gritted out. He turned away, paced a few feet, and his shoulders rose and fell even though she didn't hear the sigh. He hooked his thumbs in his pockets before turning back, and some of the heat and panic drained out of her.

"You're insulted," he said. "You're insulted, and that was not my intention at all. When I thought of it, it was because of two things and two things only. One, you're the best cook I know, and if anyone has a hope of recreating this it's you. I'm certainly not Martha Stewart enough to try it."

She tried hard to keep her lips from twitching; the very thought of Andrew being anything like the domestic icon was laughable.

"And the second reason was that I'm coming to realize you were close to my father. Maybe closer than I ever was. I thought you might like to do it."

"Why? Because I'm a soft touch?"

He shook his head. "No, Jen. Because you're you."

It shouldn't have touched her, but it did. He understood. Perhaps he even understood that she could never willingly turn her back on someone in need—even him.

This was the first time he'd mentioned anything about wanting to connect with memories of his father, and even though a tiny voice inside her warned her it was a bad idea, she wanted to help him with that.

"Why is this so important to you? It's just one dish."

Andrew took his time replying, first walking over to the counter that had held the cash register not that long ago. Now it was covered with a cloth, and he ran his finger over it, leaving a trail and getting drywall dust on his fingertip.

"Lazy L is my home, Jen. But I can't live in the past anymore. I need to move forward. I just want to live in the present. To start over. And to do that I realize I can't keep ignoring my past. I need to accept it."

Boy, could she relate to that. It was a good reason, and one that made sense.

The welcoming feel at Lazy L had come from Gerald and Noah and Andrew. Now there was just Andrew, and who would welcome him? He was asking for her help, and she suddenly realized how difficult that must have been. The Andrew she remembered didn't like to ask anyone for anything. His kiss still tingled on her lips.

"If I do this, I expect to be reimbursed for everything I buy." She forced herself to keep the terms businesslike, so he wouldn't see how much his plea touched her.

"Naturally."

"And don't expect a miracle. I'm in the middle of renovations here, and already cooking for Saturday night."

"Of course not."

She had to be insane, the way she kept agreeing to do things for him.

"And you'll have to be available to taste test. I

can't possibly make something to taste like you remember if I don't know what that is." Belatedly she realized she'd just come up with an additional reason to see him. She couldn't seem to keep her distance from him even when she tried!

"Whatever you say."

*Hah,* she thought, *it's whatever* you *say when you're getting your way.* And yet she remembered Gerald saying to her, not long before he died, to go easy on Andrew when he came back. As if he'd known his son would return when Jen had known no such thing. She felt she should do this, just knowing it was one of Gerald's favorites from years ago.

"Then you have a deal." She turned away from him and went back to the ladder, heart pounding. "Now, get going so I can finish this up before midnight."

"Thank you, Jen. Again."

The sincerity in his voice touched her, and she closed her eyes briefly, knowing he was looking at her back.

"Don't thank me yet," she advised, picking up the roller and filling it with paint once more. "I might mess this up completely."

He came forward, put his hands on her shoulders, and placed a kiss on her forehead. The spot burned where his lips had been.

"Thank you anyway," he murmured, as she closed her eyes. His footsteps went away, and then she heard the shutting of the door. Only after he was gone did she put the roller down and hang her head, admitting to herself that he still had the power to put her heart in tatters.

## CHAPTER FIVE

JEN decided to use Andrew's house to experiment with the recipe, since her bungalow was home to many of the supplies from the bakery. There was barely enough space for her to put together a meal for herself, let alone try anything extra. On the night of the benefit she'd be using his kitchen anyway. She could use the time to get a feel for working in his space.

With only a few days left until the dance, she could also start taking some of what she needed out there, saving her trips on Friday and Saturday. No doubt Andrew thought it was a matter of throwing together a little bit of food, but she knew it was much, much more involved than that.

But the last coat of paint hadn't gone on until after four o'clock, so it was nearly dinnertime when she finally finished packing the car and headed west to Lazy L.

She noticed the difference in the property the moment she turned up the drive. The fences leading to the house and surrounding the corral had been repaired and painted a blinding white. Someone had made a first cut of the grass around the house, and the pale green spears bore the newness of spring growth. It no longer looked neglected. It looked like it had a purpose.

The front door was unlocked when she took the crock pot of roast inside. She put the pot down on the table. Whatever the improvements outside, they hadn't been extended to in here. It was bland, faceless, without a single stamp of personality and in dire need of updating. It was a house, she realized, but not a home. Andrew could say all he wanted about moving on. The old house was exactly as it had been left. She wondered why he hadn't seen fit to add his own belongings rather than keeping old remnants of his childhood. A shrine to happier times?

Shrugging, she went back outside. It wasn't her place to decide how Andrew did or didn't decorate his house. Her only immediate concern was Saturday night's success. She went back to the car and took out her supplies; the flatware and dishes she'd ordered for her catering business hadn't arrived yet, so she'd decided to make do with paper plates and napkins made from recycled paper. Thank goodness the chafing dishes had been delivered, and the platters. There'd be no need to worry about keeping the hot dishes hot and the cold, cold.

She was on her last few bags when Andrew came around the corner from the barn and she stopped, her heart skipping a beat.

He'd obviously spent the afternoon at some sort of manual labor. His boots were dusty and streaks of dirt ran up his jeans. His T-shirt was crumpled and carried the same film of dust as his boots. A brown Stetson was pulled low over his eyes, shading out the afternoon sun.

He looked hot, and dirty, and undeniably sexy.

Jen raised her head and stiffened her spine. It was bad enough she'd melted in his arms the other night. It wouldn't do to let it happen again. She wasn't the kind to turn her back on a friend, and it was obvious he was still struggling to come to terms with Gerald's death. There were just limits, that was all.

"I brought some things out. I hope that's okay." She called over to him, turning away so he wouldn't see the flush in her cheeks or the way her tongue wet her lips.

She'd help him get his feet beneath him. Be neighborly. Once the benefit was over he'd be reconnected with lots of Larch Valley people. He needed to make that connection. She knew that Linda Briggs wasn't the only one in town who had a long memory. It wasn't just her that he'd left. It was all of them. If he wanted the rescue ranch to be a success, he had to win the town over as well. And if she could forgive him for leaving, surely they could as well.

"That's fine," he called back, his voice low and gravelly. "Sorry I wasn't here to let you in."

He sidled across the yard and she exhaled, trying to will away the increase in her heart rate caused by nothing more than his proximity.

"The door was unlocked."

"Right. I forgot. Old habits." He smiled, the corner of his mouth quirking up the way it always did when he flirted. What other old habits could he be thinking of?

She walked ahead of him, taking the bags to the door. He held open the screen while she went in. People didn't tend to lock their doors around here, but she supposed they did where he'd been living.

She put the bags on the table. "I brought out the things to make your beef mixture," she explained. Cooking, at least, was one activity she could do where she felt very much in control. She looked up and smiled. "The beef is cooked. I'm going to pull it and mix up the sauce. Then it'll be your turn, once it has simmered."

Andrew looked down at his jeans and back up, a crooked smile creasing his lips at the volume of dirt marring the blue fabric. "Mind if I shower first?"

She swallowed. The innocent question was suddenly filled with innuendo, and she wasn't prepared for the heat that rushed through her body at the thought of his muscled limbs under the shower spray.

"Go ahead. This will be a while." She could do this without looking foolish. She adopted a bland expression. "Take your time."

He pulled off his boots and left them by the door, walking down the hall to the stairs that led to the second floor. She snuck a look at his rear view as he went. Lord-a-mercy, the worn denim looked as if it had been made just for him—complete with a streak of dirt right across his backside.

As he turned to go up the stairs she snapped her head back to the pot that held the roast, moving it to a countertop and plugging it in. She opened a drawer, finding two forks in exactly the same place they'd been over a decade earlier. Another drawer held a scarred old cutting board. She put the roast on it and covered it to keep it warm while she mixed the sauce mixture with the small amount of drippings in the ceramic pot. As she whisked it all together she took out a small bottle and measured out three tablespoons of brown liquid, adding it to the mixture.

As the shower started running upstairs, she took the two forks and pulled the beef apart, shredding it into small pieces. She added the tender meat to the sauce, the spicy tomato scent meeting her nose.

The shower stopped and she imagined Drew reaching for a towel…

Several seconds later she realized her hands had paused over her task and she shook her head, chiding herself. It wouldn't do to start thinking about him that way. A dry laugh escaped her lips. Start? She'd done nothing *but* think about him since that day on the street.

She took out a small container of mini brioche buns and sliced them in half, just to keep her hands busy.

She was getting out two plates when his steps sounded on the stairs. She stirred the beef that was soaking up the barbecue sauce, keeping her back to him as he entered the room.

"It smells good in here."

"Did you want to try the sauce? I can still tweak it."

She put the lid down on the countertop and held up a teaspoon. The rich smell wafted into the air, and her stomach rumbled. She'd hardly had time for lunch today, between painting and packing things up for Lazy L. And now, with food so nearly ready, her stomach was announcing its hunger.

Andrew took the teaspoon and stepped up to the pot, dipping it in and tasting the sauce.

He closed his eyes and she watched his throat bob as he swallowed, watched as he licked a remnant of sauce off his top lip.

"Well?"

"It's good. It's really close, Jen. Maybe…a little more something. A little more heat."

She took out a small bottle and added a few drops, stirring it around. "You won't be able to tell the true difference right away. It has to simmer in it."

But she could tell by his smile that she'd managed to decipher the recipe well enough. She picked up a mini-bun and spooned a small amount of beef onto it, covering it with the rounded top. "Try this. I tried baking these this morning to make them appetizer-sized. What do you think?"

He finished the bun in two bites, chewing and swallowing in a way that kept Jen's eyes glued to his face.

"That's delicious. I think…" His voice faded away and his throat bobbed once more. His eyes lost their impish gleam and Jen was at a loss to know why the sudden change had come over him.

"What is it? Is there something wrong with it? Too much Worcestershire?"

"No, nothing like that." He reached over for a paper towel and ripped a strip off the roll, wiping his hands. "I was just going to say I think even Mum would approve."

Andrew never talked about his mother. It had always been simply understood. Jen remembered her parents reading her the riot act one day when she'd come home from second grade, talking about how Andrew Laramie didn't have a mom. They'd made it clear that it wasn't acceptable to tease or taunt him about it in any way, shape or form. She'd felt sorry for Andrew then, and years later, when they'd started dating, he'd said very plainly that his mother had left them when he was five. Not since then had he ever mentioned her.

"How much do you remember?" she asked softly, hoping to keep the conversation going. *Casual, easy*, she cautioned herself.

"Not much," he admitted. "I remember her making this for my dad. I remember them laughing. And I remember them fighting." Defiantly he switched on the tap and got a glass of water, but then held it, forgotten, in one hand. "I remember coming home and realizing she was gone."

It was more than he'd ever admitted to her before, and her heart ached at the obvious pain he still felt about it. "I'm sorry, Drew," she murmured, putting her hand on his arm. "That must have been very tough for a little boy."

Andrew seemed to remember where he was, and snapped out of whatever reverie he'd gone into. He lifted the glass and took a long drink. "It doesn't matter now. We're all grown up, and I've got this place and my own life. I'm sorry I brought it up."

*I'm not*, she realized. What she didn't understand was, if he carried around so much hurt about his mother, what had possessed him to literally ignore the one parent who'd been determined to see him through? She longed to ask him. But she got the feeling she'd be faced with that stony brick wall again.

Without meeting her gaze, he reached out for another bun. "I didn't mean to make you uncomfortable. I'm usually not sentimental."

"You didn't. Of course you have memories here. This is your home." She reached for another bag on the table. "You don't have to nibble on those. You'll be all night filling up. Here."

She took out two Kaiser buns and put them on plates. "If you don't mind me joining you, I haven't had dinner yet either."

He cleared a space at the table while she heaped the buns with barbecue beef. She handed him a plate and took out one more container—a bowl with a snap lid. She took the cover off and made impromptu salad forks out of two soup spoons.

"What's this?"

"Spinach and cranberry salad."

Andrew sat at his seat, wondering what to do about the quandary he was now in. He was having a meal with Jen O'Keefe. Only she wasn't just Jen O'Keefe. She was Larch Valley's darling. He'd seen that clearly enough the other night at Papa's. She was the girl he'd lost his virginity with. And she was the girl he'd left behind without a word of explanation. How much more complicated could a guy get?

He couldn't stop thinking about her, about how he'd kissed her at the bakery when he had known all along he would have to go slowly, gently. Complicated.

"Aren't you going to eat?"

He marveled at how she could sit there as if this was something that happened any day of the week when his insides were twisting with nerves. It had nothing to do with the Tabasco in the sauce or the poppy seed dressing on the salad.

He'd made peace with so much over the last months. He'd been so confident he could come back here and start over. But he'd been wrong. This didn't feel like home. He felt like a stranger here. Jen was the one person who made anything seem familiar, comfortable. As if he belonged. And yet…he couldn't explain to her all the reasons. Not when he still didn't understand them himself.

"Aren't you hungry?"

She paused and looked up at him, her smoky blue eyes wide and questioning. She had no idea of the battle within him, of how he'd simply found himself worn out with it all and was seeking some peace. Maybe even a chance to put some ghosts to rest.

He forced a smile, not wanting to burden her with his troubles. "Just thinking about all there is to do before Saturday night."

"I've been thinking about that. Snickerdoodles is

having its electrical done tomorrow, and I'm not going to get my deliveries until next week. John's daughter is out of the hospital, and he's putting up my crown molding in the main room tomorrow. I'm basically off the hook for a few days. I can help."

The offer was at once a godsend and a nightmare. An extra set of hands would be mighty welcome. But the fact that they were Jen's hands threw a kink in the works. He wanted her around. He craved her company. She was like a ray of sunshine wherever she went. But it was harder and harder for him to think of making amends when he kept thinking about kissing her, thinking about the way her hair smelled or her skin felt beneath his fingers…

Definitely complicated.

"You don't have to…"

"Isn't that what you're paying me for? What's left to do?"

"I'm building the band stage in the morning. I've got to make a run into town for the drink supplies. And…oh, dammit, I forgot about coolers." He ran a hand through his hair. "I haven't even thought about decoration. Do I need it for a barn dance?"

She shook her head and laughed. "You didn't ask Lucy for help, did you?"

"No. She offered initially, but I figured she had her hands full with Brody and with the baby coming."

"The baby's not here yet, and Brody's probably

driving her crazy. I'll make a call. There's always washtubs out there you can put the beer in. What about lights?"

"Lights?"

"Twinkle lights. You got any?"

Lord, she was talking about twinkle lights? He was setting up a practice, getting in feed for the horses that would be arriving. "I had the fences painted…"

She made a sound in her throat that he didn't like at all. He'd had priorities other than *twinkle lights*.

"Straw bales?" She leaned over her plate and looked deep into his eyes. The way she blinked— the long lashes kissing her cheeks before lifting back up—could make a man lose his train of thought completely.

"Straw bales? Yeah, I've got some of those for bedding…"

She leaned back in her chair, laughing lightly. "Gee, Andrew, you don't need a caterer, you need an event-planner."

"Lucy looked after inviting the businesses and the ranchers and the media."

Jen shook her head and pushed her plate away. "You can't have them all coming here like this. A mowed lawn and some white paint doesn't make a party." She got up and went to her purse, pulling out her notepad and making a list.

"What are you doing?"

"Putting together a barn dance."

"Jen, I really don't—"

"Is there going to be anyone coming in here? In the house?"

"Probably. The bathroom's in here."

"Well, we can't have it looking like this," she remarked. "It's still stuck in the eighties." She jotted down something else, and his blood pressure went up another ten points. When had he suddenly lost control of the situation?

"Stop. Stop making your list."

She looked up, a mask of confusion marring her face and making a tiny, adorable wrinkle just above her nose.

"What's wrong?"

She folded her hands over her tablet and looked up.

Damn it all, now she'd gone and made him feel stupid. Like when he'd used to get mad at school and the teacher had worn that same *Let's just wait until you calm down* indulgent look. He took two breaths. "You're already doing enough."

"Andrew," she began, her voice steady but soft, "you need help. I'm offering it. It's as simple as that."

"It's too much." He knew she would think he meant too much for her, but he meant too much for him. Already he was feeling the lure of her, the soft sweetness of her generosity weaving its spell like it had all those years ago. She'd weave her way right in here if he wasn't careful. He'd find himself telling her things. Things he'd kept to himself for a long time. Things he was afraid for her to know.

"I don't plan on doing it by myself. I'm very good at delegating," she smiled. His unease multiplied exponentially. The last thing he wanted was for this to be a whole community production, especially when the welcome wagon hadn't been all that warm.

And yet…he did want Lazy L Rescue Ranch to be a community-type project. Not something he hid away and did, but something he could build and be proud of. Something Gerald would have been proud of. This was the launch. And she was right. He wasn't prepared for a party and it was rushing toward him like a freight train.

He looked around the kitchen with its many supplies. Already there were tables from the church sitting folded in his barn, waiting to be set up.

"Who else is going to do it?"

He scowled, hating that she was right. He needed her. There was no two ways about it.

"If you do come out…"

"Carry on with what you're doing. You won't even know I'm here." She sat back with a satisfied smile.

But *he* would know. And he'd get used to her being around. Worse, he'd miss her when she was gone. And she surely would be gone once she knew the real truth about why he'd left Larch Valley.

* * *

Andrew saw changes in the barn and the farmhouse, even though he'd seen little of Jen. He'd heard her car drive up after lunch, but he'd been so busy that he hadn't even gone up to offer her a greeting.

But coming inside now, the night before the dance, he could see she'd come and gone.

Her touches were everywhere.

The kitchen had changed drastically since Jen's appearance. The drab, limp curtains were gone, replaced by pristine white ones with pale yellow daisies dancing around the hem. A bit more feminine than he would have chosen, but they made the room look homier than he ever remembered it being. A yellow and white checked cloth covered the scratched table, and a chrome holder held white paper napkins in the middle. A new microwave graced a corner of the counter—Gerald had never conceded to the need of one—and there were matching white and yellow dishcloths and drying towels hanging over the old towel bar to the left of the sink. It was as if she'd let in a ray of sunshine to the drab old room.

There was a note leaned up against the coffee maker, and he ignored the welcoming beat of his heart at the sight of it. He should never have kissed her at the bakery. Or encouraged her with puppy-dog looks. She'd woven her spell and had him all wrapped up with a bow at the end of it. He had to be careful not to get caught simply because it was easy being with her. Jen wasn't the kind of woman you trifled with. She was the kind of woman who deserved to be treasured, cherished. And committing himself to Lazy L was about as dedicated as he was prepared to get these days.

She was still hurt by what had happened in the first place, he could tell. No matter what she *thought* had happened, she'd be wrong. And he had no energy to explain it to her, to see the look of disappointment and dismay on her pretty, generous face. It had been difficult enough, saying as much as he had about his mother. Seeing the look of pity pass across her face. Oh, she'd tried to hide it, but it had been there. She'd felt sorry for him. And pity wasn't what he wanted from her.

He'd spent a long day leveling the drive with a rented grader and fixing fences out in the quarter section, while the crew of students he'd hired had finished painting the barn. The progress over the last week was mind-boggling, but the dance was tomorrow and the electrician had just finished wiring up the clinical area at the front of the building. There was still equipment to install, supplies to unpack. The rented sound equipment to set up for the dance. Tonight he was bone-weary. And wondering if he was turning into some crackpot idealist trying to do this thing.

He went to the bathroom to wash his hands. A jar

of cinnamon-smelling potpourri sat on the tiny vanity, and a cheerful cherry-red handtowel hung from the round towel hook. Such small touches and even the tiny half-bath looked welcoming.

Hell, even the loft was transformed. He'd heard the syncopated sound of a staple gun and had returned to the barn tonight to see ropes of white mini-lights strung along the rafters and down the stair railing. Along one long wall she'd already set up the church banquet tables and laid them with white and red plaid cloths. He had no idea where they'd come from. The straw bales that had been downstairs were now upstairs, at right angles to the stage, artistically placed with a pitchfork next to one and an old saddle over the other. She'd lugged the heavy bales up there herself, he'd realized with wonder.

Long benches, something he thought would be more likely in an old schoolroom than his barn, lined the other wall as seating. She'd even thought to put a bucket of sand near the stage for the dance floor.

She was a miracle worker, and he tried very hard to resent her for it. But he couldn't. Because she was Jen, his Jen, who had always had a way of making people feel good simply by being around them. She was the kind of woman people relied upon, no matter what. A constant. It was no wonder the people of the town rallied around her.

Right now his stomach was speaking louder than

his conscience. He put a dish of the lasagna she'd left behind in the oven to heat. Tomorrow her official job would be done and the dance would be over. The work on Lazy L Rescue Ranch would begin. He'd settle up with her—adding in extra for her efforts in the house and barn—and they could go back to being contemporaries. No, friends. That was all.

That was all he had to offer. It was all he could expect. He certainly wouldn't become her lover. Even if he couldn't get her smoky eyes or her wistful smile out of his mind.

# CHAPTER SIX

THE Christensen Brothers were warming up in the barn and the twinkle lights were glowing faintly as the sun started its descent in the cool spring sky. Andrew greeted guests in the yard, directing the parking. He hadn't expected this good a turnout. Neighbors, old friends, townspeople were all arriving; ranchers and business owners shook his hand and asked questions about his venture. The smile he'd forced onto his face now stayed there all on its own. Normally he kept to himself, only socializing within the industry when called upon to do so and never hosting. But this didn't have the affectation he had become used to. It was friends and neighbors and a level of comfort he was surprised to encounter.

This was going to work. And his hope was that in it he'd find the satisfaction that had somehow been missing all these years. Tonight he felt as if he was *where he belonged.*

Jen passed him, going from kitchen to barn,

throwing a smile in his direction. The warmth in her eyes made his heart thump and he tried to push it aside. She only wanted to be neighborly. It was who she was, he realized. He knew without a doubt that she'd be doing the same thing for anyone who'd asked for help—she was that kind of warm, giving person. It was one of the things he liked most about her.

And yet as he watched her walk away, in a pair of faded jeans, he couldn't forget the way she'd felt pressed against him when they'd kissed at Snickerdoodles. She'd gone above and beyond getting ready for tonight. He wished there was a way he could return the favor. He knew she had to be struggling with the bakery. It wasn't easy, running a small business. Once things got settled he'd think of something as a thank-you.

"Andrew!"

A familiar voice calling his name drew his attention back from its meanderings. It was Lucy, followed by Brody and Betty Polcyk. Lucy's red hair rioted around her glowing face, and as she came forward to give him a hug her firm belly made a round barrier between their bodies. He laughed, kissed her cheek and stood back. "You look wonderful."

She looked down at herself and shrugged. "I look like an apple," she replied, but grabbed his hand and pressed it against the warm mound. "Look at this. Junior's ready to dance."

He had no time to react. His hand was placed on the crest of her belly and he felt several strong kicks against his palm. His eyes stared at the spot…dear Lord, he could actually see her stomach change shape. He was used to this in mares, but not in women. It had a way of humbling a man, even one who was just an old friend.

He tried a laugh. "He's already doing a two-step in there!"

Brody came up behind Lucy and put his hands on her shoulders. "I told her she had to take it easy. But she's determined to dance."

"And you never argue with a pregnant woman."

Jen's teasing voice came from behind Andrew and everyone chuckled. He slid his hand away, a bit reluctantly. He'd never felt an actual baby move beneath his hand before, and the miracle wasn't lost on him.

He tried to imagine Gerald touching his mother like this, but the picture wouldn't gel. The old man had held so much resentment for so long that he couldn't conjure up fantasies of marital bliss. Gerald had never been one to show affection, not to his wife and not to Andrew. But Brody and Lucy—Andrew smiled. This was how it should be.

He watched helplessly as Jen came forward and gave Lucy a quick hug. He swallowed hard. As teenagers they'd whispered in the dark about the kids they'd have someday, never imagining how far apart life would take them. Hell, he remembered one time when Brody's dad had thrown his annual dance and Brody had found him and Jen in a dark corner of the barn. Brody had teased him, saying Andrew and Jen would have a houseful of kids before he even got started. The memory of sneaking moments with her sent a rush of desire through him. Now they were all grown up, and it was Brody preparing for fatherhood. Andrew and Jen struggled to have an uncomplicated conversation at the best of times. Memories kept getting in the way.

Andrew stepped back, lifting a hand. "I'll see you all later. Have fun." He had other people to greet. And he had to stop letting the past take over. Look at Jen. She'd dusted herself off and carried on splendidly without him.

When the yard was full, and the cars had started lining up along the road, Andrew made his way to the loft to join the festivities. The floor was already vibrating with the stomping of feet and the pulse of the bass guitar and drums as the Christensens whooped it up.

The noise was raucous, and people he knew—and many he didn't—shouted to be heard over the band and others talking. A young girl bustled around the banquet tables, cleaning up empty plates and napkins, replenishing the paper goods, and organizing the platters as guests nibbled at the food Jen had prepared. Agnes Dodds waltzed past with Tom Walker, who'd owned the feed store before passing the reins to his son, Tom Junior. She threw an outrageous wink in his direction and he laughed, winking back. Some things in Larch Valley never changed at all. Sometimes he found it aggravating, like being under the microscope at the pizza parlor, but on a night like tonight he could see how that was just as it should be.

Jen returned, carrying a platter of what he recognized as Southwest Spirals and chicken and cheese taquitos. As much as he didn't want to admit it, she'd changed. She had grown into an independent, confident woman. Successful, beautiful, beloved by the town. She was happy. Once she'd told him her fears and wishes. But they'd made their lives without each other. He watched her work, smiling and chatting to neighbors as her hands flew over the trays. It wasn't just memories pushing him now. He was starting to care for the strong, independent woman she'd become.

She was talking to the girl behind the table when he approached. "This looks great, Jen. You've outdone yourself."

She smiled her brilliant smile and it caught him square in the gut. Lord, when she smiled like that it lit up a whole room. "Have you met Suzanne? She's a local girl, graduating this year."

He held out his hand and Suzanne looked up at him, wide-eyed. She took his hand and shook it, then smiled with a mouth full of braces. He couldn't help it. His own grin widened. "Thanks for helping out tonight, Suzanne."

Jen saved the poor girl from gawking. "Suzanne is going to wait tables this summer at the café, and help with the catering."

The band broke into a rowdy two-step, and Andrew's toe started tapping. "You're doing a great job," he called to the teen. "Could you spare your boss for a dance?"

He turned his gaze to Jen, who had just finished pulling the plastic wrap off a platter. "Me?"

"Care to take those boots for a spin, Miss O'Keefe?" He raised an eyebrow, challenging. Daring.

For a moment he thought she was going to refuse. But Suzanne nudged her arm and took the plastic from her fingers. "Go on, I'll be fine."

"O…Okay."

He held out his hand and she took it, coming around the corner of the table.

Her palm was warm and soft in his, and his chest constricted at the sight of her, slightly in front of him, in a pair of well-worn jeans that looked as if they'd been made for her figure. She wore a black form-fitting T-shirt that said "Snickerdoodles" on the left chest, in printing that matched the sign above her store. When she turned to him and placed her hand inside his, he placed his right hand on her waist. It felt warm and lean beneath his palm.

Maybe this was a mistake. A really big one. Because touching was touching, and it had the same affect on him no matter if it was in a room full of neighbors stomping to music or in a quiet, empty bakery late at night.

Jen fought to keep her smile in place and her hand in his as his grin faded and he stared into her eyes. What had she done now? Unless his touching her was causing the same internal reaction to him as it did to her. The moment she'd turned and assumed the dance position there'd been a change. Facing him was too much like when she'd fallen off the ladder straight into his arms. It made her chest hurt from breathing fast and shallow, made her body tingle from remembering being flush against his. And now it felt as if half the town was watching them.

For the first time in forever Jen wished she wasn't in a place where everyone knew her secrets. Everyone remembered that Jen and Andrew had been high school sweethearts. Everyone remembered how she'd mourned the loss of him. She knew that they couldn't even have a simple dance without there being speculation.

"Stop looking at me like that," she said, as low as she possibly could.

"What?"

And still their feet refused to move. She saw two more pairs of eyes dance past them, curiously peering over shoulders to see what was going on. She couldn't possibly repeat herself any louder. She put back her shoulders and lifted her chin. "Just dance with me, will you?"

He heard the command and picked up the beat, leading her backward at last. The motion of the dance at least kept their bodies from brushing too much, and after going around the floor once Jen started to relax. She had been staring at a point past his shoulder, feeling awkward. But the rousing music did its job, and before long she found herself enjoying it. He was a good dancer, smooth and confident. It seemed the simplest thing in the world when he looped her under his arm and back again.

She stopped staring beyond him and shifted her eyes to his face.

It was as if no time had elapsed at all. His gaze was warm beneath his favorite well-worn Stetson, his eyes laughing at her as their feet glided smoothly over the boards. A tan-colored shirt flowed over his broad shoulders, the color picking up the gold flecks in his hazel eyes. He was filled out, a more mature version of the boy she'd known, but he moved the same. Smelled the same. Heavens, he even felt the same, she realized as his hand tightened on hers like it had the dozens of times they'd danced before.

This bigger, broader, older Drew was far more dangerous than the boy she remembered.

The two-step ended, but Andrew didn't release her hand. "One more." He leaned forward and said it in her ear.

"I should get back…"

"Your helper can manage for five more minutes," he insisted.

She wanted to. She was beginning to realize that the attraction buzzing through her veins was based very little on the past and had much more to do with the man before her now. It made him seem like a familiar stranger, one who knew her better than most and yet someone so completely brand new that she was drawn to him. At first she'd only wanted to know why he'd gone, and had put up walls, trying to protect herself from the pain. When had that changed? When had she stopped being so angry? Now she craved to know about all the years in between. About the man before her now, who had made such a right-angle turn in the path of his life.

It was complicated. Despite the kiss, he hadn't said a single word about wanting to pick up where they'd left off. Not that they could. But she could have one more dance, here in front of lots of people, where nothing would happen. *Five minutes*. A safe five minutes, where she could be held in his arms and pretend. She would allow herself that.

A fiddle began to scrape and Jen heard the beginnings of a waltz. Deep inside, energy raced through her as they altered their hold and their bodies brushed. After tonight she wouldn't have the excuse of the job to see him anymore. They would only run into each other occasionally in town. As she held her breath and felt his chest touch hers, she knew she would miss him.

Their feet made shuffling sounds in the thin layer of sand that skimmed the floor. The fiddle sang out a lonesome tune to the one-two-three rhythm, creating an ache in her heart. As she let out a sigh, Drew's arm tightened around her, drawing her even closer. The backs of her eyelids stung. It was almost as if he were saying *I'm sorry* with his body. But that was silly, wasn't it? She was sure he wasn't sorry at all. She was just being fanciful.

Their feet took smaller and smaller steps, and her head rested against his strong shoulder. In a few minutes the music would stop and he'd walk away. She wouldn't be able to feel the muscle beneath her cheek, or smell his scent that was an individual cocktail of man and hay and soap, or hear the way his voice said her name softly, with the slightest bit of hoarseness in it, like sandpaper.

Like he did now.

"Jen."

She turned her head to look up at him and he looked down, his lips a firm line but his eyes a tangle of emotion. Her left foot stumbled and he righted her with one strong arm. For a bar of music everything seemed to hold, suspended. Then he lifted their joined hands so they were clasped between them and dipped his head to kiss her.

The song, the voices, the sound of boots on the wood floor all dissolved into a pleasant hum as Jen focused on the feel and taste of his mouth on hers. His fingers gripped almost painfully around hers, and she moved her opposite hand from his shoulder to curl it around his back, her fingertips grazing the short strands of his hairline beneath the hat.

This kiss was different than the last. This was a hello—light, soft, firm, and warm all at once. She didn't have to know the reasons to know that somehow she'd forgiven him. It didn't matter. What mattered was the man before her now. A man who had returned to face his demons, who wanted to resurrect Lazy L into something good. Who kissed like an angel.

Her heart tripped as he sighed into her mouth. She wanted to melt against him. To…

And then, like a thunder crash, she remembered where they were. In the space of a second she realized the music had stopped and that the barn was utterly silent. She stepped back, breaking off the kiss but unable to tear her gaze from his. His hands lowered and hung loosely by his sides, and a small, teasing smile flirted with the corner of his mouth, as if to say *our secret's out now*.

But she didn't feel like teasing. A hurried glance around her told her that every single person there was watching with morbid fascination. The blush started at her chest and worked its way north to her face in an instant, and she pressed her hands to her cheeks. Oh, Lord, what had they done?

As Andrew started to chuckle, so did the closest dancers to them, and before long most everyone was laughing and clapping.

Jen's heart tumbled. She felt utterly exposed, but she knew she had two options. Cut him and run, or pretend to join in the good-natured feeling and pretend it was no big deal. The last thing she wanted was to make a scene. She forced her lips to curve and delivered a mock curtsey to Andrew, who laughed and reached out for her hand. She let him tuck her under his arm for a few moments as they provided a unified front. But the smile felt brittle, and inside she was trembling. How could he have done that, in front of everyone? And why? She'd done a lot of recovering under the watchful eyes of the town. It felt wrong, working through those feelings in such a public way.

"I need to get back to work." She stood on tiptoe and said it in Andrew's ear as the music started up again.

He nodded and smiled, his hand resting along the small of her back just a little bit longer than she was comfortable with. "We'll talk later."

Their heads were close enough that his hat hid Jen's next expression. "Count on it," she replied quietly, then spun back to the buffet table to hide her flushed cheeks.

He had to be seven kinds of fool, kissing her like that.

Andrew avoided her for the rest of the night, instead talking to ranchers and business owners about the rescue ranch project and disappearing now and then to do an impromptu tour. Still, every time he turned a corner or returned to the loft and the dance, he looked for her. She'd felt so right in his arms. And the way she'd looked up at him... He'd just done it on impulse. Kissed her. Like a teenager at a school dance.

What had happened to the whole "pay her and go their separate ways" idea he'd promised himself just yesterday? She might fit in his arms like a puzzle piece, and kiss like an angel, but he couldn't let things go too far. She'd ask questions he didn't ever want to answer. He'd come home for a clean slate. He would have to apologize. Take a step back.

He danced with Lucy twice, and even with Agnes

Dodds. She watched him with a sharp eye. "Young man," she stated clearly as he took small steps in deference to her stature, "you better not be toying with that girl."

Clearly he hadn't been thinking at all. Because every single person in this room knew he and Jen had history. And if they hadn't known it before they sure knew it now. The tongues were wagging. He had forgotten what it was like here. For Pete's sake, the town would have them walking down the aisle before the night was over. A simple mistaken kiss would create all sorts of mischief.

And yet there wasn't much simple about it. His eyes kept seeking her out, no matter where she was. Presently, as he danced with the wife of a neighboring rancher, he found Jen across the room, replenishing a platter. He felt his heart twist as she smiled at a guest. Why was it that, as much as he told himself he shouldn't, he found himself going back to her time and again? Wanting to tell her secrets?

He hovered by the barn door in the cool air as the dancing reached a fever pitch. The evening, as far as the Lazy L went, had been a resounding success.

He shook hands and thanked people for coming, but a big surprise came when Clay Gregory, a nearby neighbor, made to leave.

"Thanks for coming, Clay."

"You got it. You know you can count on me for a spare set of hands, Andrew."

"Appreciate it." Andrew shifted his eyes, but Clay, who was more than a match for Andrew's own size and strength, didn't move on.

"Don't mess with Jen," Clay warned.

Andrew looked back. Clay's expression was as mild and relaxed as before, but the steel in his dark eyes told Drew he was serious. "I wouldn't."

Clay took a step back. "That's good. I'm not sure she could take it again."

Clay left, but Andrew's mind was working double-time. What on earth…? First Agnes, who he could see meddling because everyone knew she was a bit of a busybody. But Clay? He hadn't acted like he was jealous, either. More like…more like a big brother.

Kissing Jen had been a bigger mistake than he'd realized. He had been gone too long. And he knew if there were sides to be taken the whole of Larch Valley would line up behind her.

As a line of guilt snuck through him, he suddenly realized Jen wasn't the only one who had a right to a grudge. And, more than ever, he felt the walls of the town close around him—much as they had several springs ago.

Jen hadn't danced after the kiss—not even with Brody when he'd asked. She was there to do a job and that was exactly what she was going to do. To the mothers, grandmothers and starry-eyed lovers she mentioned weddings and babies and showers. To the local business owners she promoted the catering side of Snickerdoodles for functions and parties. That was the real reason she'd agreed to take the job tonight. She had to remember that.

Andrew spun by with a woman hanging on his every word, and Jen snapped the lid on a container firmly. She had a bank loan stating she had to make a go of this expansion. She had to keep her eye on the prize. None of this dreaming and romanticizing. This time she didn't have Gerald to co-sign the loan. Instead she'd had to put her house up as collateral.

Shortly after eleven, Andrew made a speech. Jen took the precious minutes to give herself a break, and she opened a bottle of water and perched on a bale of straw. He welcomed everyone, and then outlined his reasons for converting Lazy L into a rescue ranch. He was passionate, but not overly so, convincing without being preachy. Asking for help without begging. And her respect for him—as a rancher and as a man—went up a few notches.

But when he ended by thanking those who had already committed to helping, and then moved on to thank the Christensen Brothers for providing the music, her heart froze. *Don't thank me*, she thought.

It would be the beginning of what that kiss had meant, and she despised it.

His gaze turned her way. *Please don't thank me*, she pleaded silently.

"And another big thank-you to Jen O'Keefe, for helping with the decorations and providing the food tonight." Appraising looks focused her way, and she gritted her teeth beneath the professional smile she had to produce. "Jen's expanding Snickerdoodles, so I know you'll all want to grab a flyer and see what's happening with her Main Avenue location."

She wanted to sink through the floor. This was worse than she'd imagined. She'd wanted to cater tonight to get a jump in advertising, to get the word out. But not this way. Because everyone looking at her now didn't see Jen O'Keefe, business owner, standing on her own two feet. They saw that kiss.

She knew enough about Larch Valley to know that once a collective opinion had been formed it would take an earthquake to move it again. Everyone would be convinced that Andrew had hired her for personal reasons, not professional. She closed her eyes briefly, trying to think of the best way to handle things.

As Andrew encouraged everyone to have a good time through the final set, she steeled her spine. What was done was done, and she couldn't change it even if she did desperately want to take it back.

What hadn't changed was her objective. She was Jen O'Keefe, doing a job, and that was what she would do. Anything else she was—real or imagined—would have to wait.

And once the last car was gone she'd clear the air with Andrew once and for all.

# CHAPTER SEVEN

JEN carefully avoided Andrew until the last stragglers were packing it in. She sent Suzanne home and started tidying the mess herself. The table and counters were a mass of dirty dishes, empty containers and scattered lids. The pristine order and organization before the event had disintegrated into empty chaos, right along with her good intentions. But, like the dance, the adrenaline rush of earlier had worn off, the end was a let-down, and she wished she didn't have to take the energy to clean it up. At least the food had been a hit. Most of what she was packing in her car now was empty platters and containers, not leftovers.

She was washing out an empty chafing dish when Andrew opened the screen door and the last truck departed with a honk of the horn.

Her feet ached, there was a definite pounding beginning behind her temples, and right now nothing sounded better than a hot bath and a soft bed.

But they had things to talk about first, and if they didn't do it now she'd lie awake fretting over it all night. Sleep was too precious a commodity to waste.

"You're angry." His deep voice echoed through the kitchen, but he came no further than his spot just inside the door. How many times had she stood in this kitchen since he'd gone away, hoping he'd walk back through it? Now he had—but not for the reason she'd once wished for.

She took a deep breath and let it out, because she badly felt like snapping at him, or being sarcastic, and neither would be beneficial.

"I am, yes. And confused."

"Which one most?"

He stayed where he was, as if waiting for her answer would make up his mind if he should come in or not, despite it being his house. She rubbed the scoring pad over the steel with renewed vigor. Angry, yes, but perhaps not for the reason he thought.

Her hand paused in the dishwater. She half turned, faced him to answer his question. He still stood by the door, one hand resting on a dining chair. He had taken his hat off and the top spiky part of his hair was slightly flattened where it had rested.

"Why did you do it, Drew? In front of everyone?"

"I don't know." He shrugged, dismissing the question.

"Sure you do," she persisted, noting that he'd

shoved his hands into his pockets the way a small boy would when he got caught out.

"Maybe I got swept up in the moment."

She snorted softly and turned her attention back to the dish, scrubbing out dried-on bits of food.

"You don't believe me?"

"Believe that your brain suddenly left your body? No, I don't. Don't you know how it looked when you thanked me like that?"

"This is about my *speech*?"

There was no way he could fake the tone of surprise, and she abandoned the dishes, turning to face him. "What did you think I was angry about?"

The air hummed.

The answer floated through the kitchen even without words. Finally Jen said it, so softly it was barely louder than the hum from the lightbulb above their heads.

"You thought I was angry about the kiss." Even as she said it her insides curled with remembrance of how his lips felt on hers, the vibration of his body against her as he held her close.

"Aren't you?" He started to step forward, but then seemed to think better of it.

Was she? Yes and no. How could she be angry when she'd wanted to kiss him in the first place? And yet…

"I wish you hadn't done it in front of everyone, that's all. It created a scene."

Finally he stepped further into the room, his lazy stride easily eating up the feet between them. "It was just a kiss."

Jen lifted her face up to his. "It might have been to you."

"Are you saying it meant something?"

His eyebrows lifted. His face was a blank of innocence. Was he really so oblivious to her growing feelings for him? Her heart sank, heavy with disappointment. Clearly, while her feelings had grown his had not, or he wouldn't dismiss it in such a way or be so surprised.

He was too close; she backed away and put up her hands. "That is not what I meant. This isn't even about you and me now. It's about…about…" Her arm swept wide, as if encompassing the whole valley.

"You're worried what people will think? After one little kiss?"

The dimple in his cheek popped ever so slightly and his shoulders relaxed. He reached out and touched her cheek with one finger. "Don't worry, Jen, it'll be forgotten tomorrow."

"No, it won't. Don't you see?" She jerked her head away from his touch and grabbed a dishtowel, wiping the remaining moisture from her hands. "This isn't some big city party where people hook up one night and go their separate ways the next. You should know. The valley doesn't have that—

well, what you would call level of sophistication. They didn't see a kiss at a dance. They saw two of its own with a history, smooching on the dance floor. They saw you putting your mark on me in front of everyone. And then when you thanked me…don't you see how it looked? I didn't want *us* in the spotlight."

"So which is bothering you? The fact that it was in public, or the fact that I kissed you at all? Believe me, I've already been warned against hurting you again."

Heat blossomed in her cheeks and she avoided his steady gaze. The truth was she *had* wanted him to kiss her. She hadn't been able to stop thinking about it, even when she was painting or filling out purchase orders or lining up catering jobs.

She skirted around him and started matching plastic containers with lids. "So why did you? Really?"

This time he looked away. He didn't answer for several seconds.

"I did get swept away. With you in my arms, and the way your hand felt in mine, and your cheek resting on my shoulder… Dammit, woman, I'm not made of stone. I wanted to kiss you and I did."

She swallowed against the lump in her throat as her hands stilled. He was right in that the dance had spawned something between them that was irrefutable. Why had she let him hold her so close? Or put her cheek against him, closing her eyes? She was as much to blame. And now she didn't know what was real and what was fantasy.

"I can't do this, Drew." She knew she'd forgiven him for leaving all those years ago, but that didn't mean she'd forgotten how it had hurt, or that she was willing to set herself up again. And Andrew had *complication* written all over him. She couldn't afford to lose focus on the big picture. This time she had to use her head.

He came forward and put his hands on her upper arms, his fingers warm and sure. "Think about it, Jen. I've been back a few weeks and we keep having these conversations. I keep kissing you. You keep kissing me back. What does that tell you?"

"It tells me I need to stop being in the same room with you, that's what." She shrugged off his hands and gathered up the empty pans to take back to her house.

"It tells me we're not over," he replied, putting a large hand over her wrist, stopping her movements.

But it was exactly what Jen needed to hear. All the resentment she'd been carrying for over a decade was suddenly diffused, floating away on the night air, leaving her feeling strangely empty. Maybe Drew really needed to understand how he'd hurt her. Maybe then he'd realize why forgiving wasn't the same as forgetting.

"Oh, but we *are* over," she said sadly, twisting her wrist free and putting the pans together in a precise stack. "And you made sure of that. You sealed that deal when you made the choice not to come back."

"I am back."

"Twelve years is a tad bit late, in my opinion."

He ran a hand over his hair. "I had my reasons."

"Oh, I'm sure you did." She picked up the pans and headed for the door, balancing them and pulling the screen door open with one hand. She carefully descended the verandah steps and walked to her car. She heard his boots following her and sighed. "I'm not interested in your reasons. You promised me. You promised you'd…"

But words failed her as the lump returned in her throat, rendering her speechless. He'd promised her she'd never be alone, but he'd left her alone. That was exactly what he'd done. And then he'd turned his back on the one person who'd actually shown any faith in her. Gerald. He'd hurt both of them so badly.

"I promised to come back." His voice was low and filled with regret. She opened the back door to her car and put the pans inside, closing her eyes for a moment to gather strength. She shut it again, and forced herself to look at him as the wall of anger she'd erected long ago crumbled into dust.

"No, Drew. You promised you wouldn't leave me alone. But that's what you did. Less than a year after we graduated Mum and Dad moved to Lethbridge, so Dad could be closer to the hospital.

They signed over the deed to the house to me, but I was on my own."

"Why didn't you just go with them?"

He really didn't get it. The words hovered on her tongue but she couldn't say them. And then he spoke again, this time his words harsh and sharp as knives.

"You could have come with me. I asked you to."

"My life was here." She folded her arms across her middle, trying to keep warm in the chilly air, trying to protect herself and her core of hurt. Anything to keep him at a distance.

"And mine wasn't. You made your choice. Why is yours okay and mine wrong?"

"Because here was *home*! Why didn't you come back? You had Lazy L. Noah and Gerald. And me!" She lifted her chin as she felt tears spurt into her eyes, saying all the things she'd wanted to say for so long.

His lips twisted, as if he was in pain. "I couldn't. I just couldn't."

"Why? Don't I deserve to know why, after all this time? After what happened tonight? Do you want to know why tonight was different? Because those people were there for me when you left the first time. They remember." She shivered, suddenly feeling the evening chill. "I mourned you, Drew." Two tears gathered in the corners of her eyes slid down her cheeks. "The people of Larch Valley saw me with a broken heart. And they were there for me when I put it back together. If we're going to resolve what's between us, can't you understand that I'd rather not do it with the whole of Larch Valley looking on?"

"If you want me to apologize, I will. For the timing. I realized it right away. I'd forgotten what Larch Valley was like."

He wasn't apologizing for the actual kiss, and knowing it sent her pulse racing. She was so afraid to repeat past mistakes, and yet so attracted to the man before her now. "Who was it that warned you off? I think I'd like to know."

"Agnes and Clay."

Jen indulged in a small affectionate smile. Agnes was a gem and Clay was a good man. "So you know what I mean. For you to kiss me like that, after how hard I've worked to stand on my own—" She broke off, choking on the words. Her feelings for him were new and yet old, bound up in a history she couldn't erase. "You thanked me for catering, but you made it seem personal and not professional."

"I was only trying to make it up to you."

"Then help me put this behind us. I don't want to live with the past hanging over me any longer. With unanswered questions plaguing my mind. I want to move on. I've worked so hard to move on. So please, Drew. Put me out of my misery and just tell me *why* you left and never came back until your father's funeral."

The moon was behind him, casting a pale glow against his form. The night was cool enough that their breath made tiny puffs of cloud in front of their faces. And Drew looked like a haunted man, the hollows of his cheeks in sharp relief in the shadows, his eyes dark with pain.

"He wasn't my father."

Jen's heart dropped clear to her toes. She must have heard wrong. "What do you mean?" she whispered. Drew's face was in utter earnest. "What do you mean, he wasn't your father?"

"Gerald Laramie wasn't my father. I'm not a Laramie at all."

He spun on his heel and went back to the house. Jen stood for a moment beside her car, her mouth hanging open. For a fleeting second she considered getting behind the wheel and driving away.

But she couldn't. She couldn't drive away from the look of anguish on his face, from the man who had made her laugh, the one who had sent her heart soaring with a kiss. So she made the long walk back to the house and the man she was trying very hard not to fall in love with all over again.

Andrew's heart clubbed against his ribs as he walked away from her and back to the house. He couldn't believe he'd actually said it. Out loud. To *her*. Maybe it was for the best. There wouldn't be any more pretending. And she'd understand why he had felt he couldn't come home.

He never should have kissed her. He never should have come back here, he realized. It was too painful. He should have sold Lazy L, taken his half of the profits and set up shop somewhere else. Whoever the hell had said you could always come back home again needed a smack upside the head. It didn't solve anything. It just made life that much more mixed up.

He paced in the dark living room for a while. A broken heart? Had she really said that? It seemed impossible. He'd known she'd be hurt, but he hadn't realized the full extent. Now he could add that particular regret to his list of unresolved feelings.

He listened for the sound of Jen's engine and her car peeling out the driveway. It never came. Instead, he heard her footsteps on the verandah.

She came to stand in the doorway, leaning one shoulder against the frame, her eyes soft with understanding. How could that be, when she'd just told him how much he'd hurt her? Her ponytail had little bits coming out and they framed her face, adding a delicious softness. When they'd been dating he'd teased her by pulling out her elastic and running his fingers through her hair. He wished life were that simple again. But it wasn't. Never would be again.

"You should have told me," she whispered.

"I never told anyone."

"And neither did Gerald. I'm sure of it." She stayed where she was, but he detected a shimmer of tension in her posture. She had a soft spot where his father—where *Gerald*—was concerned. She hadn't seen him the way Andrew had.

"He sure made a point of telling *me*."

He heard the pain in his voice and hated it. It made him feel weak. Nothing was easy these days. Not even the anger he'd been carrying around since he was a teen.

"Are you going to tell me what happened, or am I going to have to pry it out of you?"

"Does it matter? I'm not Gerald's son."

"Gerald was good to me, especially when everyone else seemed to have disappeared." She boosted herself away from the doorframe. "So, yes, it matters."

She was right. They kept saying one thing and doing another. Keeping it professional but letting personal stuff creep in. What was the alternative? Love? Commitment? With Jen there would be nothing less.

And he couldn't give it to her. What they needed to do was talk it out so she could finally be free. Perhaps if she knew the truth it would make sense.

"You were the best thing about high school, you

know that?" He took a step toward her but stopped, unsure of whether or not he should touch her again. How could he possibly make her understand when he didn't even quite get it? "And the one good thing about coming home. Maybe that's why I keep hanging around. Because you're the one person who doesn't make me feel like a stranger in my own hometown."

"Then why did you come back? Why here?"

He wanted to touch her but was afraid. And if he held her now that wouldn't really help with the "set her free" part. He sighed. It was a damnable thing, wanting to hold a woman and yet knowing you were both better off if you didn't.

"Let's sit down."

He went to the sofa and sat, resting his elbows on his knees and rubbing his hands through his hair a few times. He felt rather than saw her sit on the couch beside him, saw her smaller boots next to his bigger ones, and smiled a sad smile.

"The truth, then," he conceded. "I had to come here," he admitted. "I felt I had something to prove, and I knew that here was where I had to prove it. At Lazy L."

"A connection?"

"Maybe."

"It was here for you all along."

"No, I'm not sure it was." He leaned back against the cushions and closed his eyes. He couldn't stand to see the sympathy on her face. "When I told Gerald I wanted to go away to school, to study and be a vet, he was so angry. Noah had already gone to boot camp, remember? And I didn't say anything until after I'd applied for pre-vet. He was furious. He wanted me to take over the ranch, you see. And I didn't want it. I was seventeen and I wanted to make my own way, not be stuck on the family farm for the rest of my life." He sighed, remembering the arguments. "I was cruel, and I said things. Oh, it wasn't so much that I said them, but how I did. One night the arguing got really heated, and I said I wished I wasn't his son. And he told me I wasn't."

"Oh, Drew."

The world had a hard brittle edge just now, and Andrew clenched his teeth against it. "I goaded him into it. But that wasn't the worst of it, Jen."

She reached over and took his hand in hers. He squeezed it, knowing that once she heard the rest her simple comfort would be taken away.

"He was the one that sent my mother away. He forced her to leave by saying he'd take her to court with a drawn-out custody battle. That by the end everyone would know what kind of a woman she was."

Jen gave a little gasp. Gerald would never have done such a thing! It certainly didn't gel with her memories of a man who'd been kind and supportive, who'd even co-signed her first business loan. Or the man who had missed his son and followed his career with pride. "Why would he do that? I can't believe it, Andrew."

Andrew's hand was still in hers, and she kept the connection. She knew he believed what he was saying, but he had to be mistaken. She couldn't believe Gerald would be so cruel as to take a mother away from her children.

"He did it because she was having another affair. I'd been the product of the previous one."

It seemed incredible. Things like this—sordid affairs and tawdry goings-on—just didn't happen in Larch Valley. Her heart seemed to pause for a minute as she asked, "Do you know who your real father is?"

He shook his head. "No, only that he was already married. And that he wasn't from the valley."

It almost seemed as if the world she knew was falling down, like a tower of blocks tumbling to the ground. "I don't know what to say."

"I didn't either. I was barely five when she left us, but I had memories of her. Good ones. He never let us talk about her, but Noah had heard arguments. He'd told me things that didn't make sense then but did as I got older. When I asked Gerald why she didn't take us with her he said she didn't want to split us up, and that Noah was his."

Her fingers trembled inside his cold grip at what the words implied—how he must have interpreted them. How destroying for a boy to hear that. Both about his mother's infidelity and then affirming that he didn't belong. She forgot about Gerald for the moment, and focused only on Drew's pain. "You must have felt awful. Unwanted."

"I felt like a consequence."

His voice broke on the last word and Jen scooted over, tucking her legs up on the sofa and curling against his side. "Oh, Drew," she said again, profoundly sad for the boy who'd lost his innocence. It didn't have to make sense for her to understand how deeply he'd been hurt.

"I tried for years to prove to him that I'd made the right decision. I studied hard so I'd be top of my class. I invited him to my graduation but he didn't come. I sent clippings of places I'd been, things I'd done. But nothing seemed to move him. I looked back and remembered how he'd never told me he loved me, not even as a boy. I wasn't his, Jen. I couldn't face coming home. I hated home. And I couldn't tell you."

"Why ever not? I loved you." She whispered it in the dark. A part of her mourned for what he'd lost; another part felt betrayed that he hadn't shared it with her. Had he felt ashamed? Angry? She wouldn't have cared a bit about it. She would have held him, and kissed him, consoled him as best she could. They might have been young, but for her those feelings had been real. It hurt to know perhaps his hadn't been as sincere as she'd thought.

"I thought you left because of me."

"No—never!" He turned a bit and she felt his hard gaze on her face. "But I was too ashamed to tell you. I was nothing. I was some bastard boy who'd turned out to be a disappointment. That was what he said. The valley became a place with walls that seemed to close in more every day. I couldn't stay."

"If you'd told me…"

"What? You would have gone with me?"

The question stabbed into her conscience. She would have understood, commiserated, petted. But would she have packed up and gone with him? "I don't know. Maybe if I'd understood…"

"I asked you to come. You kept saying you couldn't leave your father. You said your place was with your family."

His words opened a hollow space inside her. "Dad was sick. I couldn't just up and leave. I was so afraid if I did something would happen…"

"Can't you see how different or situations were? You were dedicated to your father and I suddenly didn't have one. When you refused me, that was it. I had to cut ties." Andrew pushed his way off the couch, leaving her sitting there alone.

Jen stared at his back. He'd understood how she loved her father but had felt eclipsed by his illness, felt like he was always in the background. For two years Drew had put her first. Listened to her, had fun with her when laughter was scarce. Had loved her.

Now that a piece of the puzzle was in place, she was starting to understand. Suddenly forgiving him seemed easier. How could she condemn a boy who'd had to face such a devastating truth?

"Did you ever try talking to him again? If you'd talked to him you would have realized how much he loved you. His talk of regrets makes sense now. He was so proud of you! He told me all the time about things you'd done in your career."

Andrew looked as if someone had ripped the earth from beneath his feet. "What are you talking about? I lived with Gerald my whole life. Words of love…of pride…that's not the man I knew. Lord knows I tried!"

"Tried how?"

Drew rubbed a hand over his mouth. "Letters. Articles, pictures. Even my university transcripts."

Jen wrinkled her brow. So much of it didn't make sense, and now Gerald was gone perhaps they would never have the answers. Maybe all she could do was try to make it easier for him. "All I know is that the man I knew was gutted that you never came home. He could have sold this place a million times but he didn't. He left it to his *sons*. Plural, Drew. Hang on to that. He did love you. I'm sure of it."

"And yet here I am, still trying to prove something. To a ghost."

The fact that he was still trying, the fact that he was hurting so deeply touched her, but she hadn't gone through heartbreak without it opening her eyes a whole lot wider. Drew had so much to work through on his own, things that had nothing to do with her. She could see that now. What would happen when he figured it out? Would he leave again? She just wasn't up to being collateral damage once more. She couldn't willingly set herself up to be hurt twice.

What Drew was dealing with now was bigger than her feelings for him. Feelings she hadn't necessarily wanted but that seemed to be growing all the time. And she couldn't trust his perspective either. He was going through so much. She was here and she was familiar, something for him to hold on to. Once he'd worked through the rest of his problems he might discover she wasn't what he wanted anyway. He would put her in the past, just like he would his father.

He could never know how much she was starting to care again. Her heart ached for the whole convoluted situation as tears slipped down her cheeks.

"I only know that from my perspective Gerald loved you. Was proud of you."

Drew's tortured expression was more than she could bear.

"And so am I," she whispered brokenly, and before he could say more, she ran from the room, out the door and to her car.

She wiped her hand across her face, clearing the tears as she drove away. Maybe it was good that they'd finally cleared the air about the past. Maybe it was best that she understood why he'd left her. But if it was, then why did it have to hurt so much?

# CHAPTER EIGHT

ANDREW threw his jacket on the passenger seat and backed away, slamming the door of the truck. "You ready to go?" he called out to Brody, who was just finishing off his coffee.

Brody lifted his mug for one last drink. "I'll put this inside," he said when it was empty. Andrew watched his friend stomp inside to deposit his cup. Brody had been more help than Andrew had expected. Anything Andrew needed Brody got it— or knew someone who could. Even today Brody had taken the day away from his own operation to go to Fort McLeod and the auction that was happening there. By the end of the day the three geldings already in residence would have new roommates.

Brody came back out of the house and shut the door behind him. "You tell Jen where we're going today?"

"Why would I do that?" Andrew checked the hitch one last time and straightened, regarding

Brody curiously. Brody opened his own truck door, but leaned against it for a few moments.

"Just thought after the dance and all…"

God, Jen had been right. The more Andrew thought about it, the more he realized that whatever was between them, whatever he had to work through, it had been a mistake to try to fix it in front of the eyes of Larch Valley. First Agnes, then Clay, and now Brody.

"Did Lucy put you up to this?"

Brody shrugged, got in his truck and rolled down the window. "She and Jen are good friends," he admitted. "But I've known both of you a lot longer, bro."

Andrew climbed into his own cab and hit a button, rolling down the passenger window, determined not to let his friend know how much his words troubled him. "Hey, Dear Abby, let's shelve the advice for the lovelorn and get on the road." Brody's answering laugh made him grin. "I'll see you at the Fort," Andrew called out, rolling the window up and hitting the power button on the stereo deck.

They pulled out of Lazy L, Andrew in front, Brody in the rear.

It was a good day for driving. A bit cool, but clear, with a sharp wind coming from the west that promised milder hours ahead. Andrew reached over and changed the satellite station. He turned up the volume, feeling the bass while the gravely voice of Chad Kroeger filled the cab.

Yes, a good day for driving. A good day for clearing minds. He was still trying to wrap his head around what Jen had told him about Gerald. How could it be that their memories of him were so drastically different? Who was right? Or did the answer lie somewhere in the middle?

At the junction he turned north, with the plan of going past Larch Valley and across to Claresholm before turning south again. He hadn't driven this route in years, and he looked forward to it today. The spring grass was greening up, the sky was an endless blue, and for once the stress that seemed to settle in his shoulder blades was gone.

He checked his side mirror, saw Brody tapping a rhythm on his steering wheel and smiled. The exit for Larch Valley appeared on his left, the old service station long forgotten as the sign for the new one heralded high above the trees. He braked gently as he came upon a transport hauling livestock. A peek through the slats told him the trailer was full of horses. His brow furrowed. Going to the same auction they were? Or straight to the slaughterhouse? Traveling this road, he wondered if they were horses being sent up from the States. Now that horse slaughter was banned south of the border, more and more animals were being sent north.

He sighed, taking a look at the road into town, knowing that on Main Avenue the morning was getting underway. What was Jen doing today? Baking, naturally. He could picture her there, behind her counter, wearing her plain white apron, her hair up in the perky tail she wore when working, smiling at her customers.

But she didn't smile at him these days. Since the dance she'd stayed as far away as possible. Not that he blamed her. He'd expected it to happen after he'd told her the truth. And now that they'd cleared the air—well, most of it anyway—he didn't know what to believe. He'd tried for years to get any sort of approval from Gerald, so that he would understand why Andrew had made the choice to be a veterinarian. To make Gerald see he wasn't a waste. To make him proud. According to Jen, Gerald had been all those things. Why, then, had he never showed Andrew?

He turned the radio down slightly, wiping a hand over his chin. He hadn't realized how much his leaving had hurt her the first time, and the last thing he wanted to do was hurt her again. He cared about her too much.

As that thought pulsed through his brain, he saw the trailer ahead of him shift and his stomach took an uneasy roll. Something wasn't right. He slowed down, giving the driver room to straighten himself out. But suddenly the load shifted again and the entire truck crossed the center line. The cab shifted back to the right, sharply. Too sharply.

"God, he's gonna go!" Andrew shouted it to the empty truck. It happened in an instant, even as it seemed to play out in slow motion: the sharp jerk, the dust swirling up off the shoulder, the trailer tipping, tipping…

Heart in his throat, Andrew slammed on the brakes and felt his own empty trailer sway behind him.

Jen put the last row of lemon cookies in the display case, already thinking of the chocolate cakes she had to ice for the lunchtime crowd. The café expansion was paying off; her menu was small, but varied each day, and she couldn't deny that catering Andrew's benefit had been a boon. More than one person had come in saying they'd been there and had her beef on a bun or her hummus dip. Suzanne came each day after school and worked the smaller supper crowd, but until then Jen was alone. It meant she was getting up at four a.m. each day to start the necessary baking of bread and sweets, in addition to making a different soup each day. There wasn't time left after opening to do much baking.

She was starting to face the fact that she was going to have to hire extra help—an added expense but a necessary one. She slid the glass case door shut and sighed. She couldn't keep this pace up forever.

In addition to the day's baking, at mid-morning she filled huge baking pans with some sort of hot entrée: lasagna, creamy chicken pasta, shepherd's pie. It was good home cooking and country baking her patrons asked for, and that was what they got.

But she was tired.

She couldn't get Andrew off her mind, not even when she was trying to sleep during the few precious hours she wasn't at Snickerdoodles. She turned what he'd said over and over in her mind, trying to puzzle it out. It had been over two weeks since she'd seen him, and they'd both said things… well, they'd said things that needed saying. She couldn't believe Gerald wasn't his father. If not Gerald, who? She stirred cocoa into icing sugar and butter, frowning. This was precisely what Andrew— and Gerald, for that matter—wouldn't want. Speculation and gossip. No one would ever hear his secret from her.

When the cakes were frosted, she went to the window and turned over the "Open" sign. She opened the inside door and put in the door stop, letting the scent of her bread announce the time, just as she'd done when Snickerdoodles had simply been a bakery. Now the smell of fresh-baked bread was joined by that of warm muffins and fragrant coffee. She'd get the coffee-breakers next, as she was building the day's entrée of baked penne pasta with Italian sausage.

Her first coffee break customer was Agnes Dodds, who had begun delaying opening her shop until nine-fifteen each morning. She briskly made her way into the bakery each day with an insulated mug that announced "I'm not old, I'm experienced" and bought a fresh brewed coffee and a cranberry muffin.

"Good morning, Mrs. Dodds." No matter how old Jen got, she couldn't quite seem to call her Agnes. It didn't match with the strict, shrewd teacher she'd once known.

"Why, good morning, Jennifer." Agnes didn't believe in shortening names either. She filled her cup from the urn, gave a satisfied sniff of the brew before putting on the cover, and marched to the cash register.

"Cranberry muffin?"

"It is Friday. I'm feeling adventurous."

Jen's lips twitched. "Then might I suggest banana nut?"

"Just the thing."

Jen tucked it into a small paper bag and rang in the sale.

"How is that young Laramie boy doing? I heard he's quite set up now, and even has a few new residents."

"I…I don't know." The mention of Andrew's name sent a fluttery feeling over her, and she looked down at the keys of the register before looking up again.

"Oh, come now. No sense playing coy, Jennifer." Agnes's eyes were shrewd as she smiled. "Everyone saw that kiss. It's about time he came to his senses. I always thought you two made a fine pair."

Jen gritted her teeth. "We're not a couple, Mrs. Dodds. It was just a kiss."

But Agnes wasn't deterred. "Oh, don't worry, dear," she said, reaching over and giving her hand a pat. "He'll come around."

Jen's hand shot across the counter, holding out Agnes's change as the bell above the door rang and her friend Lily Germaine came in. "Have a good weekend, Mrs. Dodds."

As Agnes's quick step took her to the door, Jen sighed and looked up into Lily's amused face.

"Don't you start," Jen warned. She brushed her hands on her apron. "Did you come in to buy something or just to pester?"

Lily's pretty blue eyes sparkled. "We are in a tizzy, aren't we?"

"That's been happening all week. The prodding, not the tizzy," she added as Lily's grin widened. "Do you know I spent a lot of money and elbow grease renovating this place, but nine times out of ten the people that come in don't comment on the changes, they mention Andrew?"

"Jealous? That Lazy L is getting more attention than you?"

Jen huffed and went to the back, returning with two apple pies she'd decided to make that morning.

She opened the display door and put them in, while Lily came behind the counter and opened another door, closing it again with a cookie in hand.

"Not jealous," Jen replied. "I want Drew's project to be a success." More than just his project. She wanted good things for him. She looked up at Lily. Her friend had missed the dance, but Jen had been certain to fill her in on the details over therapeutic glasses of merlot and double chocolate brownies. She hadn't filled her in on the rest. "But it's not the rescue ranch that's causing the buzz. It's that stupid kiss."

She broke open a roll of dimes, emptying them in the till drawer, feeling slightly helpless and relieved that it was only Lily in the shop at the moment. "It took me a long time to get over him the first time. I spent a lot of energy building this business and my own life. And suddenly the most important thing I've done lately is kiss a guy at a dance. It's frustrating."

"Jen, you kissed him. You didn't marry him and change your name or anything."

Lily bit into her cookie and tossed her dark hair over her shoulder. At twenty-seven, she was the best friend Jen had in Larch Valley. She taught home economics at the nearby high school and barely looked older than her students.

"In this town, kissing him in public is just about the same thing."

Lily laughed. "That's why I don't date cowboys."

Jen couldn't help it. She chuckled too. "You're good for me, Lily."

"Well, at least I'm good for something."

"Why aren't you at school?"

Lily's eyes twinkled again. "Professional Day. I have to be there, but not for sessions. I'm going in to reorganize the sewing patterns or something." She polished off the cookie and grabbed a napkin to wipe her hands. "Speaking of sewing, how'd your cowboy like the curtains?"

"He's a man. He didn't say anything, or take them down, so I figure they met with his approval. Thank you for doing them. And for putting together the fingertip towels."

"Anytime. The windows here would look fantastic with café rods and panels. I have some great material that would match."

The door opened once more and Jen nodded. "I trust your judgment, you know that. And I'd be glad of the help."

"You got it. I've got a couple of girls who could use some extra credit time. Hemming curtains would be just the thing." Lily sent a sly wink and a smile.

"Miss O'Keefe?"

The voice that said her name was bursting with urgency. Jen looked over at Mark Squires, the manager who had signed off on her loan. His tie was crooked, and it looked as if he'd run his hands through his hair several times.

"My gosh, what is it?" She scurried around the counter while Lily shut the screen door that had been left gaping open.

"I just came down the highway to work. There's been an accident at the junction into town. Your man…"

Her heart plunged. "Is Andrew okay? Was he hurt?"

"No, no, he's fine. It's the horses…"

Mark's face paled as he took a few deep breaths. "A tractor trailer overturned. It was full of stock. Laramie's there, as well as Hamilton's men. I just thought you'd want to know."

"Of course. There must be something we can do to help without getting in the way. Are the RCMP there yet?"

"They're directing traffic."

Jen went to the coffee dispenser and filled a large cup. "Here," she said, holding it out. "You look like you could use this."

"Thanks, Jen." He checked his watch. "I'm already late, but I thought you'd want to know, considering…"

Yes, yes, considering. The whole town expected it now, but under the circumstances Jen ceased to care.

"Thank you for telling me, Mr. Squires," she replied, trying to keep her voice calm. She was still shaking from the momentary thought that Andrew had been hurt. She saw him to the door and turned back to face her friend.

"What are you doing?" Lily laid a hand on her arm.

Jen knew what she wanted, and she didn't care if it made sense or not. She wanted to be with Andrew. She could already picture him there, working on the side of the road—dear God, a whole trailer full of horses. The past didn't matter. She wanted to support him now.

"You won't be able to get through to the school until they open that road, Lily."

"Jen…"

"I've got to go to him, Lily. If you knew—" Her voice broke off, catching as she thought of not only their last conversation but the reason why he'd chosen this line of work in the first place.

"What I know is he left you and broke your heart, and here you are running after him again." Lily's brow furrowed with disapproval. "Jen, think about it for one minute. Don't be stupid."

But Jen shook her head. "I have thought about it." She went to Lily and gripped her fingers. "I know him better than anyone. I knew his father too, and… Oh, Lily, I'm not at liberty to tell you about it. Believe me, I know he hurt me. It is not something a heart forgets."

But her voice softened as she remembered how he'd looked, sounded as he'd told her about Gerald.

She had given him space because that was what she thought he needed. But not today.

"I know why he left now, and I have to help him. My eyes are wide open, Lil. I know what I'm getting into. I will not leave him when he needs me."

Lily's eyes had filled with tears. "It's your choice," she whispered hoarsely. "You're a big girl and can make your own decisions. Just tell me what I can do to help."

Jen cleared her throat and took a deep breath. "Can you man the cash register? There won't be any lunch today, but if you could keep the bakery part open…"

"Consider it done."

Jen took a box of gloves and shoved them in a bag. "I've got my cell. Call if there's trouble and I'll do the same."

She didn't know what she could possibly do to help, but she remembered Andrew's face the day he'd told her about putting down that colt. The scene on the highway would be awful. She didn't want him to go through it alone.

By the time Jen reached the scene, the fire department was cutting through the top of the trailer. She swallowed as she saw the blood on the road; the men with grim faces trying to help as best they could. For a moment all she could do was stare at the chaos before her.

Everyone with a spare pair of hands in Larch Valley was now working to free the horses from the twisted wreckage of the trailer. Jen looked to her left; a man was sitting by the side of the road, looking dazed and stunned. The local RCMP detachment's vehicles were parked on either side of Highway 22, barring traffic. Jen craned her neck but couldn't see Andrew anywhere. She approached the closest officer, who was at the moment directing a tow truck to the front of the line.

"Grant?"

Constable Grant Simms turned his head at the sound of her voice. She would remember his face as long as she lived—drawn, tired, and clearly distressed. She put her hand on his arm. "Grant? Am I okay parked at the old service station? I'll move if I'm not."

She'd parked there because it was abandoned and off the side of the road, out of the way. "We don't need rubberneckers, Miss O'Keefe."

"I came to help."

After a slight pause, he relented. "Yes, your car's okay," he agreed, looking toward her car and nodding. "Nothing coming through here anyway."

"Have you seen Andrew Laramie?"

Simms sent an annoyed look over his shoulder. "He and Hamilton were setting up a temporary corral last I saw."

The flashing lights on the cruisers were meant to

warn away traffic, but Jen knew the highway would be closed at either end anyway. Right now, the air was filled with the squeals of panicked, injured horses and the shouts of men.

She watched, horrified, as two of the firemen cut open another compartment, releasing the horse inside. Tears stung the back of her eyes as she saw the animal try to rise. The men backed away from the flailing hooves, until one man came forward, fearless, skillfully moving so his body could guide the mare to the side of the road, where a portable pen had been set up. Andrew.

Jen watched, fascinated, as Andrew used only the presence of his body and movement to get the terrified horse to go where he wanted it to go. His dark blond head disappeared and reappeared again. Brody Hamilton was leading another horse through the makeshift gate. The scene seemed to take on more order as she saw groups working together.

She saw Andrew pause, lean over and place his hands on his knees, catching his breath. He looked so tired, so…worn. She took a pair of latex gloves from the box she'd brought, dropping the remainder on the hood of a nearby car. They weren't surgical quality, but beggars couldn't be choosers. She strode across the highway to Andrew, while the sounds and smells of suffering assaulted her from every direction.

When he looked up and saw her coming his shoulders relaxed and his eyes filled with gratitude—and something stronger. She wiggled her fingers into the gloves and went to his side. "What do you want me to do? I'm here to help."

"Jen." It sounded strangely like a benediction. He reached out and roughly grabbed her, pulling her close in a brief but tight hug. She rubbed his back, realizing just how awful this must be for him. He was in the business of saving animals, and anyone with two eyes could see that not every horse would be saved today. She held on while his fingers dug into her back.

"Hey, Doc!" A shout came from behind them, and she stepped out of his arms to see one of the Prairie Rose ranch hands waving at them. Andrew put a hand on her arm. "This isn't pretty. Be sure."

"What do you need?" she insisted, feeling misgiving swirling in her stomach but determined to see it through. There was suffering going on here, and she wanted to help.

"My bag's beside my truck. If you'll run to get it…"

"I'll meet you over by Hal," she responded, setting off for his half-ton at a trot.

When she turned the corner to where Hal had indicated, she watched, fascinated, as Andrew went to the side of a beautiful bay stallion which was struggling to get up and failing abysmally. The horse dropped to its side, and she hustled over as Andrew looked up.

"What is it?" she asked, giving the wounded animal a respectable berth and handing him the bag.

"Broken radius, both sides," he replied, his eyes never leaving the animal. "He has to have hit something straight across. A metal bar, maybe. The fractures are identical, right across here." Andrew motioned with his hand where the injuries were. He withdrew a syringe from the bag and measured out medication.

As Jen watched, he knelt by the animal, his hands patting the heaving neck. His fingers were gentle, soothing and yet capable, and for a flash she remembered how they'd felt holding her hand as they'd danced during the waltz. They were hands that knew how to heal.

"I'm sorry, old boy," he murmured, administering the needle. Moments later the horse stopped struggling and a second needle was produced. Jen's eyes blurred with tears as the horse stilled completely, Drew hung his head and gave the neck a pat. "It's better than having him suffer," he said quietly, and rose from his knees. She wiped her fingers beneath her eyes as she saw the slump of his shoulders.

And when Andrew lifted his head and looked right at her, his face etched with resignation and acceptance, her heart threatened to beat clear out of her chest.

His face was dirty, his hands streaked with mud and blood. His lips were a grim line as he paused for the shortest of moments, eyes fixed on her. He looked exhausted, and angry, and unreachable. There were so many complications in their way... choices she refused to make...but none of it mattered to her heart. Like the initials carved into the bench in the town square: JO + AL. It was just as true today as it had been then. She couldn't have stopped the feelings any more than she could have stopped this morning's accident. Both were forces out of her control.

A shout echoed and he looked away, reaching down for his bag and moving on. Jen made her feet move, following him. Feeling it was one thing. Letting him know was another. And it was better he didn't know. Lily's words echoed in her head: *don't be stupid.* And her response that her eyes were wide open. She meant it. Wanting to be there for him, caring for him and supporting him, that was one thing. Letting herself be vulnerable to him was another. She knew the difference.

Andrew turned a corner and disappeared, but for some reason Jen turned her head to the right. There, in the tall grass beyond the shoulder of the road, was a roan mare. She was lying on her side, but something told Jen she wasn't injured. She scrambled down the bank and went to the mare's side.

"Hello, beautiful girl. Oh, look at you." There was a small cut on the neck, but otherwise she seemed fine. Jen stripped off her gloves and reached out, rubbing her nose, crooning soft words. The dark eyes looked into hers, and then with one fast movement, the mare was up and staring at her through a shaggy forelock.

"Stay here. I'll be right back."

Jen climbed back up the slight shoulder and found Hal again. "Hey, Hal, you got a halter in there somewhere?"

"Sure." Hal must have assumed she was on Andrew's errand, because he handed it to her and said, "Tell Laramie there's room for two more in our trailer and one more in his."

She took the halter and went back down to where the horse waited. She was a calm, sweet thing, and Jen cautiously approached, knowing she could still be spooked so easily in the chaos.

"Hello, again." She kept talking in a low voice. "I'm going to assume you're halter-broke, pretty girl. Yes, that's it." She slid the halter over the nose and behind the ears. "Now, will you come with me? I hear there's room in a truck for you."

She gave a tug on the halter, but the mare didn't move.

Jen heard a frantic whinny from the highway and blinked. She didn't know what had caused the accident but the aftermath was horrible. How had Andrew been so close? Where had he been going? The questions came to the fore now that the rest had sunk in. All she knew was that these animals were extremely fortunate he had been close by.

She laid her face against the mare's neck. "I know, it's frightening. But I'm here to help you, beautiful." She stroked the smooth hide. "Come, now, there's a girl."

She gave another slight tug and this time the mare followed, across the brown grass, up the embankment, to the shoulder of the road next to the Lazy L trailer.

# CHAPTER NINE

ANDREW looked up and saw Jen leading a roan mare by the halter, her ponytail swinging behind her and the dirtied white apron looking out of place. His mouth dropped open as he both admired her willingness to help and despaired of her lack of judgment. She was a baker, not a rancher. It was clear to him that the mare was pregnant. He should have examined her before Jen had done anything. Besides, didn't she know that an animal of that size could hurt her if startled or injured? The last thing he wanted was Jen hurt. He'd do anything to make sure that didn't happen.

He set his jaw and strode over to where they were standing, just outside his trailer. "What are you doing?"

"Bringing you Lazy L's latest resident." She looked up at him and smiled. The warmth of it hit him in the gut, sending warning bells pealing.

"Dammit, Jen, these animals could be injured! Unpredictable! You might have been hurt."

"I'm fine," she responded calmly, but the expression of accomplishment faded from her face. Momentarily he felt small and petty, but he knew the danger was real. And he wouldn't see her hurt for the world.

She kept a firm hold on the mare's halter. "Hal said you have room for one more. She has a cut on her neck, but otherwise looks fine."

"Except that she's with foal." He bit the words out, hearing the sharp tone and yet unable to stop it. Maybe it was a delayed reaction to the accident. Maybe it was because he recognized his own weakness and fear and hated it.

Andrew watched the slow realization cross her face as his words sank in. Her fingers clutched the halter as if suddenly more protective, and her wide-eyed gaze strayed to the mare's belly. "She is?"

He nodded. He was so tired, with so many feelings running through him today he couldn't even think of categorizing them. His one thought as his own vehicle had threatened to jackknife had been of her. Just her. So much that when he'd seen her he'd wanted nothing more than to bury his face in her sweet-smelling hair and hold on. But below it all was a simmering anger so complicated he had to work very hard at keeping it there rather than bubbling out. It didn't all have to do with Jen, and he didn't want to lash out more than he had to just because she was there. It wasn't fair to either of them.

The plain truth was none of these horses should be here. He'd been tempted to have a go at the driver of the truck until the RCMP constable had stepped in, and he'd focused instead on the animals that were suffering. He realized it was lucky that he and Brody had been starting out for Fort McLeod with empty trailers and had happened along when they had. But it could have been him on that road, injured, and who would care?

He didn't like the answer that immediately popped into his head. Oh, he'd done a fine job of pushing away the people he cared about while he was pursuing his career. Including the woman in front of him.

"Let me load her up." He stopped snapping, knowing Jen was only trying to help. He tried to put the smile back on her face, feeling guilty for erasing it in the first place. "We're almost done here. I've got to get these animals settled."

"All of them?" She looked around. Brody's trailer was holding four and the mare would make four in Andrew's.

"More than this. Some are dead. They'll be disposed of. Others are injured and need care. I'm not set up for surgery. Doc Watts in Pincher Creek is looking after those cases." He gestured toward the portable corral set up on the east side of the road. He'd planned on coming back from Fort McLeod with maybe half a dozen horses. Not three times that.

"I can take the easier cases and the mare will need an ultrasound. Brody and I'll be making another trip each. That gives me sixteen head. There's twenty one that need putting up. He's taking the other five, and he'll foster them there until we decide what happens next."

Her mouth dropped open. He took the halter from her hand and gently urged the mare up inside the trailer and secured her.

When he came back, Jen had removed her bloody and dirty apron and was twisting it in her hands. Her hair had been ripped from her ponytail by the wind and exertion, and strands blew across her face in the morning breeze. His curt responses had done their work. The tender glances they'd shared minutes before were gone. He'd been cold and dismissive. The way he'd effectively taken her joy away just now…he hated himself for it.

The truth was, being with Jen was sometimes the one thing that didn't hurt these days. And he'd driven her away. In the two weeks since the dance she hadn't spoken to him. Not once. Not until today.

And then she'd come running to him, and he hadn't been able to stop the hope that had pulsed through him at the sight of her. Why had she come?

"How did it happen, Drew?"

At her soft question he started. For a split second it seemed she was reading his thoughts and asking how they had reached this point. *Well, I found out I wasn't a Laramie*, he thought, with more than a hint of bitterness. But then he realized she was asking about the accident.

"I don't know. The driver said a wind gust, but I doubt it. I was right behind him and I didn't feel a thing. He seems pretty young. I'm sure we'll hear more about it later. It's better to let the cops sort it out."

"All those animals…dead," she lamented, her voice breaking a little on the last word. She gestured with an arm at the scene which finally bore some semblance of order.

"They would have been dead tomorrow anyway," he answered coldly. When there was an accident everyone came out in force, but who was there in the abattoir? No one. "Every one of these horses was on its way to the slaughterhouse."

Jen reached out and put a hand on his forearm. He tried to ignore the warmth it provided.

"What will happen to them now?"

"I'll figure it out. They won't be going there, I can promise you that. I won't let that happen."

He lifted weary eyes to hers. There were too many details to attend to right now, and he wasn't exactly good company. The truth was, it was a good thing the Mounties had shown up. His fuse was particularly short, and he knew damn well there'd been no wind. He'd rushed to the cab of the transport and yanked the driver out. Brody had pulled him away and told the driver to call it in while they began getting the horses out.

"What can I do to help you?" The hand on his arm squeezed, and he felt her gentle reassurance tugging at him. The adrenaline was wearing off and he had a full day's work ahead and then some. It would be too easy to pull her into his arms and drink in the comfort he knew she was offering. But wouldn't she consider that taking advantage too? Like she had at the dance? No, it was better if they left things the way they were. He needed to focus on Lazy L.

"You've already helped. Thank you for coming, but you should go back to the bakery."

He could tell he had offended her as her chin flattened. "I'm in your way," she said.

"Of course not." But in a way she was. Having to euthanize the horses had meant reliving the day he'd made his decision and he hated it. It made him feel raw and helpless and he'd rather Jen not witness any more of it. She'd seen him as weak as he ever cared to be. She had a way of making him feel vulnerable. Arranging to transport the bodies wasn't something he wanted her to see, either.

"Yes, I am," she insisted. "But will you let me know if there's anything I can do?"

"Yeah, sure."

His cool tone did its work. Jen stepped back. "I'll

see you around," she said, turning her back on him and striding toward where she was parked.

Jen traveled up the long dirt lane for the first time since the dance, with the scent of supper filling the interior of the car. She'd returned to Snickerdoodles to find everything ticking along like a good watch. Lily had filled in like a champ, and Suzanne had come in after school. It seemed Jen wasn't needed anywhere. Andrew had made it very clear at the accident site that she was in the way. Perhaps she always had been. And with new recognition of her own feelings she wondered if he wasn't also in hers, constantly dragging her mind away from what she should be focusing on: her business.

But the feeling didn't last long. She'd really had no option than to go and offer her help. Now the nerves of the morning had started to die away and she felt exhaustion setting in. But who would give Andrew a break? His long day was just beginning. She'd kept picturing his face as he'd seen her walking across the road. As if she were the answer to everything. She was afraid to be that answer. And yet she wanted to be with him. To help him. To see him smile at her again, the way he had as he'd asked her to dance at the benefit.

She parked next to a strange truck and shut off the ignition. Lucy's SUV was already parked in the shade of a poplar, and as Jen got out of her car Lucy came out of the house to stand on the verandah. It had only taken one hurried phone call to Lucy for Jen to understand how the day would play out. Brody, Andrew, and several other neighbors would be working to get the horses settled at Lazy L. And that many working men meant big appetites. Lucy had said she was planning on cooking something, but Jen had insisted. She had the ingredients she'd abandoned this morning and the baking was done. And Lucy was growing rounder by the day.

She waved at Lucy, who stood next to the railing with her hand on her belly. "Hey, Mama." She smiled, shutting the driver's side door and opening the back one.

"Hey, yourself. Need a hand?"

Lucy came down the steps, looking cute this afternoon, dressed in maternity jeans and a light flowered T-shirt that had a tiny white bow just beneath her breasts. It had only been a little over a year since their wedding, and already they were starting their family. A twinge of longing struck Jen's heart. It wasn't necessarily the baby, she realized. It was that her friend looked so perfectly, peacefully happy. Would she ever have that?

She thought back to her conversations with Drew. There would never be anything perfect or peaceful with them, whether she'd fallen for him or not.

Maybe there was simply too much baggage they would never get past.

"I brought drinks," Lucy said as Jen held out a bag containing several dozen buns. "You wouldn't let me cook. I thought the least I could do was provide pop. And I brought my coffee-maker. We can make two pots at a time."

"Great idea." Jen reached in for the first box, containing the main course. She'd also packed bags of buns, three pies, and one of the chocolate cakes still left from the morning. "Any idea how they're making out?"

"They're getting there. We haven't been here that long. Brody brought Andrew's stock out here, but then he came home with our five and got them squared away. Clay and Dawson are here. And Tom Jr. brought out the feed he promised and stayed to help."

Jen followed Lucy inside and placed the box on the counter next to the sink. The room was neat as a pin, and cheerful with the gingham cloth still on the table and the curtains at the window. A dirty coffee cup sat in the sink and there were toast crumbs on the counter. It looked like a home. As she took the baking pan out of the box, still in towels, she frowned. Somehow, the more settled Andrew got, the more *un*settled she became.

Jen shook the thought away. "That makes five hungry men. And us. I hope it's enough."

They made another trip to the car, and Lucy unpacked the pies and cake while Jen heated the oven and put the pasta in to warm. This was a neighbor helping a neighbor. There was no reason why she should feel wifely simply because she'd cooked a meal and knew her way around his kitchen. The change in her feelings didn't mean *they* had changed. If anything, they were further apart than ever. He still didn't believe what she'd told him about Gerald. And she wasn't willing to trust her heart to a man who had no idea what he really wanted.

"I heard you went out to the scene," Lucy said conversationally, but Jen knew she was digging. Then again, there wasn't much to hide since the dance. Except the discovery that her old feelings weren't so old anymore.

"Lily watched the bakery."

Lucy laughed. "How is Lil? Do you know she showed up at the house with a whole crib set for the baby? Bumper pads, comforter, matching sheets. She claimed she had some leftover fabric."

Jen laughed. It sounded like Lily. "And you were thinking…leftover from what?"

"Exactly. What would *she* have baby material for?"

The women laughed. Lily made no secret of not being in a hurry for marriage *or* babies.

But Lucy was undeterred by Jen's attempt at diverting the topic. "Still…it's very telling that you went out there, don't you think?"

Jen's hands paused over the bun she was slicing. "I wanted to help. Isn't that what we do here in Larch Valley? Help each other?"

"And it had nothing to do with wondering if Andrew was okay?"

She paused, hiding her flushed cheeks as she put her back to Lucy, reaching for the butter. "Of course not. Mark Squires said Andrew and Brody were helping. I just went to lend a hand."

But she couldn't meet Lucy's eyes. Was this going to be the start of more gossip? Not from Lucy, of course. But there were lots of people helping today. How long would it take before it got around that she'd run to Andrew's side at the first opportunity? Probably only slightly longer than news of their kissing in public.

And she suddenly realized that their embrace today hadn't been private either. Oh, what a tangled mess when emotions had to get involved!

Lucy's hand was gentle on Jen's shoulder. "Do you love him?"

Jen wheeled around, knitting her brows. She understood that Lucy was incandescently happy, and wanted others to be the same, but it wasn't that simple.

"I can't love him."

Lucy waved a hand at her. "Why ever not?"

But Jen knew she couldn't go into the reasons. They were all tied up with Gerald now, and it wasn't her story to tell. "It's complicated."

Lucy smiled, unconsciously rubbing her tummy. "Oh, isn't it always? And look. Here they come."

Through the screen door Jen saw five dusty men in jeans walking up from the barn, gesturing with their hands and talking. One—Jen recognized the dusty figure as Clay Gregory—said something that caused the rest of the group to laugh, and in the middle of it all was Andrew, carrying his hat in his hand, looking tired, but with an air of happy satisfaction about him.

He spied her car and hesitated, then turned his head sharply toward the house. The other men clumped on to the verandah ahead of him and made a show of removing their boots. Andrew came last, entering the kitchen in stockinged feet and shutting the screen door gently behind him.

Lucy'd herded the helpers down the hall to the bathroom, so they could wash up, which left Jen in the quiet kitchen with Andrew.

"I didn't expect to see you."

She blinked with surprise. "Am I in the way again?"

He had the grace to look uncomfortable. "I didn't mean it that way, Jen. I'm sorry for the way I spoke out at the accident scene. I didn't expect to see you back here after the way I acted."

His apology went a long way to mollifying her defensiveness, and her lips curved up in an easy smile. "You've been away from Larch Valley for a while, Andrew." She took the basket of buttered buns and placed it on the table. "I thought you might have figured it out at the benefit, but maybe not. We help each other here. Through thick and thin."

She stood back and folded her hands in front of her. He had to know a few sharp words weren't going to send her scurrying away for good. Heavens, she understood he was dealing with a lot. "I know how difficult it was for you today. And I knew you'd have extra manpower here. Bringing in food to help isn't a big deal. It's just my way of being your friend."

She minimized it to him, but refused to lie to herself. Yes, she probably would have helped in any case. But with Andrew it went deeper than that. It always would. If he ever needed her, no matter if he wanted it or not, she'd be there for him.

"People will talk. Aren't you worried about that?"

She looked down, slightly uncomfortable. Yes. She didn't like the gossip that tended to follow this sort of thing. Her coming here tonight would be taken as a statement of coupledom.

"I came to help in the best way I know how," she murmured. "That's all. I'm going to help, and I can't control what people say."

The men were returning to the kitchen and Jen greeted each with a smile and small talk, catching up with what was new. Unimportant details about who they'd seen at the grocery store, who'd been out to karaoke night the previous weekend. Did people not do this where he'd been? Despite longing for privacy, she knew she'd miss it if she left Larch Valley. She took a spoon and started scooping servings on to plates. Everyone here was connected, and there was comfort in it. Andrew remained quiet, only murmuring a thank-you when she handed him a plate.

Lucy fixed Brody's plate and handed it to him with a kiss, before going to the fridge for cans of pop. As she paused by the table his hand rested on her hip for a few moments. Jen swallowed against the lump in her throat. It was the kind of touch that said, *Hello, I'm here. Just here.* The kind of touch that said just as much as any words possibly could.

"Aren't you eating, Jen?" Tom Walker piped up from the table.

She forced a smile in response. "I don't know, Tom, did you boys leave anything?" she teased, but her heart wasn't in it. As the guys laughed, she added, "I'll get something later. Who wants coffee? Cake or pie?"

"Both!" came the answer from Dawson Briggs, and everyone laughed.

Jen found a chair for Lucy, and made her sit down

with some coercing from Brody. It wasn't long before the men had finished eating. They lingered only a few minutes over coffee, and headed out the door with thanks for the meal. They had their own chores to do.

"I'll help clean up," Lucy insisted, but Jen shooed her away.

"No, you go home with Brody. If you're on your feet any longer he's going to fuss and flutter and drive you crazy. And he has your own stock to look after tonight."

Lucy looked at the pile of dishes and the sink—there was no dishwasher—and hesitated.

"Go," Jen insisted. "I'm going to have something to eat and these dishes won't take but a minute."

Lucy nodded, glancing out the door at Brody and Andrew, talking in the rosy light of sunset. "Talk to him, Jen."

"I don't seem to know what to say lately."

Lucy met her gaze evenly. "You know what? I thought that once too."

When the Hamiltons had gone, Jen filled the sink with soapy water and started washing up. Andrew had disappeared to the barn again. Was he avoiding her? She scrubbed at a plate. Maybe, despite the few kisses they'd shared, he'd sensed her feelings went deeper than she had intended to show and it was his way of backing off.

But a simple thank-you would have been nice.

She had everything packed into one box and a light left on over the stove when she stopped. She was so proud of him for all he'd done today. He'd shown strength and compassion and ability in the way he'd taken charge of the situation. She knew Gerald would have been proud of him too. Maybe that was what Andrew needed to hear. Was it worth one more try?

# CHAPTER TEN

OUTSIDE, Jen paused on the verandah, soaking up the evening. A mourning dove cooed a repetitive lonely call. The once empty barn echoed tonight with soft whickers and the stamping of hooves, instead of lying silent as it had for many months. Jen smiled a wistful smile, remembering when the ranch had been vital and alive, and pleased it would be so again. Even if it wasn't quite the same as before, this was what Lazy L needed. Purpose. The barn was meant to be full. The house was meant to be a home. It had lain fallow like the fields for too long. It was so sad that Gerald wasn't here to see it. To see his son where he'd always wanted him to be. Perhaps in time Lazy L would provide whatever it was Andrew was looking for.

A light shone through the window at one end— the one where Andrew had set up his medical area. Jen put the box down on the step and went toward the beacon.

Andrew sat at a plain desk, packing gauze and bandages into a steel box. She watched him for a moment in the shadows of the doorway. Despite their complications, he was a good man. Maybe that was why it was so difficult to let go. To realize their relationship would never be what she'd once hoped it would. Wondering if what they had was enough. Or too much.

"I'm taking off now."

He jumped at the sound of her voice, and then let out a breath. His gaze met hers, his unreadable. "I'm sorry, Jen. I meant to take a quick look at the stock after supper, but one of the geldings needed his dressing changed, and…"

He looked sincere, and Jen waved a hand. "It's all right, Andrew. I understand."

"Thank you for supper."

"You're welcome."

Silence drew out. He dipped his head and started rolling gauze again.

"Andrew?"

"Hmm?"

She paused, wishing he would look up, afraid of what would happen if he did. She was tired of fighting her feelings for him. She'd done a lot of self-talk lately, about all the reasons why she couldn't fall for him, but the truth was she had. Even when she knew it was a mistake. A part of her knew it was better if he stayed aloof. A bigger part wanted to feel the delicious jolt she knew would happen if their eyes met.

It would be a mistake to have him as a lover, but she wasn't sure she could bear to lose him altogether again.

"Do you think someday we could manage to be friends?"

That snapped his head up. He put down the gauze, rested his elbows on the table, propping his chin on his thumbs. "Do you? There's an awful lot of water under the bridge."

"So how are we going to manage?" She held her breath. How would they get by if every time they saw each other it was either to argue or gaze at each other longingly? It was no way to live. It wasn't how she wanted to live, she realized.

He gave the tiniest of shrugs. "We'll manage. People do. In time it'll get easier."

In time. Did that mean he was finding this as difficult as she was? The thought sent a strange turning through her chest. Why was it that the further apart they got, the more she wanted him? The more she tried to hold on?

Something had changed today, something vital and alive between them, in the moment he'd looked up and seen her crossing the asphalt. She was tired of running from it.

"I wish you'd had time to talk to Gerald," she began. His jaw tightened, but she plowed on, hoping to help him past some of the resentment he clung to so stubbornly. "Now that I know why you left, many of the things he said seem to fit. I know he regretted your estrangement. He would have been proud of you today."

"Jen, I spent a lot of years in a high-profile industry." He shut the box with a firm click of the latch. "And I learned that there are millions of ways to spin things. But this is one time that there is no spin. It just is what it is. I should never have come back. I realize that now."

Shock rippled through her at the casual yet firm way he said the words. And a glimmer of fear of losing him so quickly when they had hardly reconnected. "So you're leaving? Now?"

"Hardly." He picked up the box and stowed it neatly on a shelf behind him. "I've sunk money and energy into this place. This morning I had three horses under my care; tonight I have nineteen. Soon to be twenty." He faced her, hands on his hips. "I couldn't leave now if I wanted to."

"But you do want to?"

"I thought this would be starting over." Giving in, he tossed the pen down and leaned back in his chair. "I thought it would be one last chance to prove myself to him. But it's not starting over. It's more like reliving all the failures, and I should have seen it and didn't."

Jen's hope plummeted. Why couldn't he see the reasons he'd returned clearly, like she could?

"You have never been a failure! What would make you say such a thing?"

"You tell me." He watched her coolly, wondering how their impressions of Gerald could differ so utterly. "You tell me how I should feel, when I worked myself to the bone trying to show Gerald that I'd made a good choice. That I could make something of myself to—"

He broke off, swallowed against the sudden lump in his throat. "To be a son he could be proud of. And tell me what I should think when I never received a single letter in return."

She twisted her fingers. "I don't know, Drew. I swear. All I know is that when I saw him he talked about you. I wish I had some way to show you. To prove it."

"I don't know what I thought I'd accomplish by coming back here."

That hurt, because she knew that she'd factored very little in his decision to return. "Maybe you did it because there are loose ends that need tying up. Or a circle that needs completing. Things that need to be resolved." Their relationship was one of those things. He needed to make peace with himself since

Gerald was no longer here. She took a step forward. "I think you were meant to come back."

"Well, it doesn't seem to be working so well."

"How can you say that? Look at what you've accomplished! You have brought Lazy L back to life. You have rallied the community around a cause. You have saved the lives of several animals already." She tried a smile, but it felt bittersweet. If only he'd done it sooner. She wondered if he'd made the same wish too. "I *know* Gerald is proud of you, wherever he is." She held other words on her tongue, about him changing her. About bringing her back to life as well as the ranch. She was afraid to say them. It would be revealing too great a weakness, and now, when he was talking about his coming back being a mistake, she knew she'd been right to keep her feelings to herself.

"Can we change the subject? There's been enough doom and gloom today." He offered a smile. "Would you like to see the mare?"

She would, and she accepted the diversion—for now. She usually didn't get silly over animals, but today, when the mare had looked into her eyes, Jen had fallen in love. "All right."

His chair scraped back and he went to move past her at the door. She didn't get out of the way quite fast enough and their bodies nearly brushed—close enough—she could feel him without actually making contact. She caught her breath and held it.

He'd been working all day in the dust and dirt, and suddenly the only thing she truly wanted was to touch him. Everywhere. Right here, in the wedge of light coming through the doorway, in the barn that was scented with horse and the sweet smell of fresh hay and the fragrance of the spring nighttime trickling through the open doors. To feel his arms around her and the beat of his heart against her cheek, like it had been at the dance. To leave all the heavy, mind-bending stuff behind them for a few blessed minutes.

For a moment her fingers stretched out, very nearly grazing the fabric of his T-shirt.

But he brushed by her and she let out the breath she'd been holding. He led the way down the corridor to a box stall. A velvety nose appeared and Jen smiled, delighted as the mare stuck out her head to be petted.

"Hello, beautiful. You're looking much better than you did this morning." The mare lifted her nose, leaning into Jen's hand as she scratched, and she laughed.

She turned to Andrew, who was standing a few feet behind her, his weight resting on one hip as he watched her with some amusement.

"What's so funny?"

"Not a thing." He stepped ahead so he was beside her and lifted his hand, scratching beneath the mare's mane. "You two get along like peas in a pod. She didn't take a liking to Clay at all."

"That's because Clay Gregory is a flirt." She rubbed the soft nose and crooned. "Isn't he, sweetheart? Good for you, giving him what for."

Andrew chuckled softly beside her.

"And don't let this one off the hook either," she murmured coyly to the mare. "He just pretends he's forgotten how to flirt."

"Hah!" came his ineffectual defense, and Jen laughed softly. For several seconds they petted the horse together.

"Is the foal all right?" The mare was so sweet, and Jen truly hoped there would be no further suffering after the accident.

"Yes, it's fine. I did an ultrasound late this afternoon, once she'd quieted."

"When's she due?"

"Best guess, seven to eight weeks."

"A summer baby."

His voice warmed. "It would seem so, yes."

She'd stopped petting, and the mare nuzzled again, looking for more attention. Jen rubbed between the horse's eyes. "Well now, beautiful. Considering how your day started, it seems you've found yourself in clover."

"Jen?"

Hope blossomed in her chest as he said her name softly and she closed her eyes. Maybe the mare had worked miracles, because the underlying tension from before seemed to have dissipated into the May breeze.

"I'm sorry, Jen. It's been a hard day."

She turned then and went to him. He wasn't avoiding her gaze anymore, and his hazel eyes were dark with sincerity. Before she could change her mind, she put out her hands and rested them on his ribs—not quite an embrace, but definitely crossing the line into physical contact. He felt warm and solid beneath her fingertips, and she could tell he was holding his breath.

But he stayed his ground, and she did the most natural thing in the world: she stepped forward and leaned against his chest, her arms forming a light embrace.

"I know it has," she murmured. "I didn't try to make it more difficult for you by bringing up your father."

"You didn't." His arms went around her too, holding her close. "You helped when I least expected it. Even when I sent you away."

"You must have known I would."

His breath was warm on her hair as she stilled, waiting for the answer.

"No," he whispered. "Not after I was so unbearable."

For several minutes they simply drew strength and comfort from each other.

She bit down on her lip. He was as receptive now as she'd ever seen him. Maybe this was her chance to reach him, to make him see exactly what he'd come home to instead of run away from.

"Can I say what I think? Will you listen? And then just think about it. Please?"

He hesitated, but finally agreed with a slight nod.

"Come here." She turned out of his arms, already missing the heat of his body against hers, but knowing there was no better time to make him see.

She led him to the end of the barn, where the sliding door remained open. She leaned against the heavy wood frame and looked out over the corral and fields beyond. Andrew stood in the middle of the doorway, his stance square, his hands in his pockets. She'd never seen a lonelier picture in her life. Tonight she saw what she had missed since his return. Not anger. Tonight she saw regret in him, and it broke her heart, because she knew he thought it was too late.

"This is yours, Andrew. Lazy L, despite what you think, is your birthright. Gerald knew it, and you knew it too, even as you rejected it for another path. I think you're horribly bound up in regret, and you didn't expect it to be this difficult coming home. I think you stopped hating Gerald a long time ago, because if you didn't care you wouldn't have tried so hard. But you're still hurting over it. And I think seeing me reminds you of that time with too much clarity. And so being with me probably makes you feel better and worse at the same time, and you don't know what to do with it."

She saw a muscle tick in his jaw. He refused to look at her, and instead she tried to see what he was seeing. Rolling hills of grass, black now in the growing darkness. Fences and the shadowed figures of horses beyond. Young ones, old ones, ones that were ill and others healthy. All horses he was trying to save.

And that was it, wasn't it? He was trying to save them all. To make up for what?

"You are doing a good thing here, Drew. And please don't interpret what I'm going to say as a criticism, but who are you really trying to save? The horses? Gerald? Your mother? Or is it yourself?"

She saw him swallow, and knew instinctively that she'd gone as far as she dared.

She moved from the door and half turned, facing his profile now. "There are some things, Drew, you are never going to be able to fix. But what you've got here is possibility. Opportunity. Don't waste it by worrying about things that can't be changed. Just think about it, okay? That's all I ask."

She started to walk away but paused, knowing there was something else she needed to say.

Something else he might need to hear. Her eyes stung as she let out a trembling breath. Their backs were to each other, but her voice resonated like ripples through the spring air.

"I still believe in you, Drew."

It was as close as she could get to admitting her true feelings and the urge to cry swooped in, fresh and brutal. And yet her feet refused to move. The reasons why she should go were still there, but they had somehow ceased mattering.

His choked reply sounded behind her. "Then you're a fool."

"No!" She spun then, rushing back to him, putting her hand on his arm. "Don't say that. You're a good man." She thought again of the haunted look in his eyes when they'd been working at the accident, his undisguised relief at seeing her and holding her close. "Everyone made mistakes, Drew. Me, you, Gerald, your mother. It's so easy to look back after the fact."

She took a step over, so that she was directly in front of him. She lifted her hand and put her fingers on his cheek. "I might hate that you left me all those years ago, but, Drew, you were eighteen. You did what you thought you had to. I might not like it, but I know you didn't do it to deliberately hurt me."

Drew closed his eyes, but behind them all he saw was the way she'd looked as he drove away that morning. Small and alone, and with the tracks of tears glimmering on her cheeks. Dammit, why was she being so generous? Couldn't she see her words were cutting him in half? And he didn't have the energy to fight her right now. Not tonight. Not after everything that had happened today.

He would rather die than hurt her again, and yet he needed her. She was the one person who knew the truth and she hadn't run away. Instead she was here. With tears in her eyes and her fingers on his skin.

He placed his palm over her hand and turned his head slightly, pressing a kiss on to the pad of her thumb. This morning he had come so close to losing her. Another few seconds either way and he would have been part of that accident. The trailer had started to go, and he'd nearly gone with it.

"Drew." She whispered his name and it reached inside of him and held. Everything else faded away, except her and the need rushing through him.

He reached out his right hand, commandeering the back of her neck, pulling her close as he kissed her. The sweet heat of her mouth was a surprise, and her fingers dropped from his cheek and instead dug into his biceps, holding on. He nipped her lip and heard her gasp against his mouth, prompting a satisfied smile. Renewed energy pulsed through his veins, bringing with it desire and hunger. His other arm pressed her close and lifted her so that her toes were off the floor, and he took the scattering of steps necessary to find a stall door. With the solid wood behind her, bolstering, she freed her hands and ran them through his hair. The sensation, coupled with the way she moaned into his mouth, only added to his greed.

She made him feel alive.

He wanted to scoop her up, take her inside the stall and lay her down on a blanket padded with fresh straw, with the sounds of the peepers for music and the glimmer of the moon and stars for light.

His mouth slid from her lips down to the hollow of her throat, where her heartbeat pulsed against him. It would be so easy, he thought. She was the one thing that hadn't changed, that made sense, that *still fit*.

*"Drew…"*

She whispered it, the syllable sliding through the air like silk.

He paused, and the doubt was enough to cool the passion roaring between them. He couldn't do this. As much as he wanted to, he couldn't.

And he did want to. Badly.

"What is it?" she said gently as he eased back from her. Her toes touched the floor once more. He could see the quick rise and fall of her breasts as she struggled for breath.

"We need to stop."

He watched as her face fell and the light went out

of her eyes. And here he was, letting her down again. It seemed impossible that she could be upset. She'd been fighting him every step of the way. In the bakery. At the dance. But not this time.

She stood before him, her cheeks pale, eyes wide with what looked like disappointment. "Why?" he asked. "Why aren't you fighting me now? What's changed?"

She lifted her chin, while the corners of her mouth turned up wistfully. "We've both changed. Can't you see it?"

Something about her tone set him on edge. Not angry, but unsettled, uncomfortable, like when he put on a T-shirt that was just a bit too small.

"I'm not sure what you mean."

"The chip on your shoulder. It's gone. I'm not sure when it disappeared, but you're not so…defensive," she finished, as if searching for the right word. "Hurting, yes. But angry, not so much. And neither am I. I hadn't forgiven you, you see."

He knew exactly when that chip had taken a hike. It had been this morning, when he'd hit the brakes. Administering medicine to wounded horses, seeing death and destruction, had driven it even further away, and it had disappeared over the horizon the moment he'd seen her coming toward him. Even as he knew she deserved better, even as he knew he had so little to offer, she was the puzzle piece that had been missing. He hadn't expected forgiveness. The fact that she offered it to him was an unexpected gift.

"I was very nearly a part of that accident." He sighed, and shifted so they were both leaning with their backs against the door. He could feel her eyes on his face when she turned her head to look up at him. All evening his mind had played those few seconds over and over. All evening the feeling associated with the memory was exactly the same. A life of missed opportunities and regrets.

"I thought you just happened by."

"No, it was right in front of me. Something wasn't right, and then it was happening, and all over before I could barely take a breath. I stopped, and Brody stopped, and we went into function mode."

"Oh, Andrew. It must have been so difficult for you. I know how much you're dedicated to saving lives." She leaned her head back against the faded wood, looking up with sympathy.

She thought it was about the horses.

He gave a little laugh of irony, the chuckle catching on the lump in his throat.

"I'm so tired of having to prove myself and coming up short," he sighed. His gaze held hers, caught in the smoky depths that had always been able to see more than he liked. "It's exhausting. But I have no idea where to go from here. Kissing you solves none of it. And it's not fair to you. I can't give

you what you want from me, Jen. You'd be better
off getting in your car and going home."

"Is that what you want?"

He turned his head so that he was facing her, like
two heads on a pillow. "No."

"What do you want?"

That was the million-dollar question—and one he
had no answer to.

"I can only see today. But I know you, Jen, and I
know you won't be happy unless you have everything. And I just don't have everything to give. I
don't know if I ever will."

"Did I ask for that?"

"Yes."

Her back came away from the stall. "I did?"

"Yes." He, too, stepped away from the wooden
barrier behind him. He reached for her and cupped her
cheek. "Every time you kissed me in twelfth grade
you wanted it all. The day I said goodbye it threatened to pull me in. And when I came back every time
I looked in your eyes I knew you were a woman who
would settle for nothing less than what you deserved.
But that's not me, Jen. I'm not strong enough to let
you go completely. And that's unfair to you."

"Why don't you let me decide that?"

He was so surprised at her question that he fell
silent for the space of two beats, his lips dropping
open. "Jen, I'm not ready for what you want. I don't

know if I ever will be." The last thing he needed was to repeat the mistakes of the past. He refused to let Jen be a casualty of that again.

But she persisted, and her tenacity chipped away at the chinks in his resolve. "So don't be ready. Let's just take it bit by bit. Even if it means simply admitting that we're not as over as we thought we were. Being friends to each other. And going a day at a time."

It sounded good. It sounded almost too good. In a place where loneliness abounded and friendship seemed in short supply it was an offer he couldn't refuse. The idea of living in the moment felt liberating. When was the last time he'd done that?

"A day at a time I can do." He tried a smile, found it more ready than he'd expected. He pulled her close, letting his hands rest on the hollow of her back, his fingers trailing along her tailbone. He dipped his head and tasted her lips again, then a third time, longer, deeper.

"This day doesn't have to end yet." He knew what he was suggesting. He wanted her with him longer.

"Mmm," she replied lazily. "But if I stay…"

The thought hung in the air, and he finished the sentence in his mind. He had no doubt that she'd done the same.

"If you stay…"

She blinked, sighed, and took a small step back.

Physically she'd barely moved half a dozen inches, but he felt the distance between them just the same.

"That might be best saved for another day. I'm not sure I'm ready for that yet."

He accepted it. This morning he'd snapped at her, and now they'd just somehow managed to forge a new peace. They'd started something…not quite a relationship, but something. All of that and sex added in probably wasn't the wisest choice.

And, if anything, he felt that he needed to make careful choices with Jen. What they had now was precious, tenuous at best. One day at a time.

"Then why don't I walk you to your car?"

"I'd like that."

He took her hand in his, the simple gesture touching him in unexpected ways. Together they left the barn, flicking out lights as they went, until they stood beside her car.

He opened her door, but as she went to get in he tugged her back.

"Will you come out again soon?"

She smiled softly as the moon went under a cloud, creating shadows on her face.

"Of course." She smiled again. "I'll want to check on the mare, now, won't I?"

"Just the mare?"

"Oh, there might be one or two more that I could spare some attention."

Her teasing smile lit all the dark places in his heart. If he wasn't careful he was going to fall head-first in love with her again.

One day at a time.

"Drive carefully."

He watched until her car made the turn from the lane to the main road, the sound on gravel inordinately loud in the clear evening.

# CHAPTER ELEVEN

"SHE'S doing well, don't you think?"

Jen leaned her elbows on the edge of the fence, watching the mare—now officially christened Beautiful—snip at pieces of lush grass. It was a Sunday, Snickerdoodles was closed, and she'd refused to play the "should I or shouldn't I?" game when it came to Drew and Lazy L. She had a need to feel the air on her face and she wanted to check on the mare. They had said one day at a time. What better day could they have than this?

"She's doing great. So are most of the others." Andrew leaned against the railing beside her, lazily shredding a thick blade of grass with his fingers. "Pokey's still on antibiotics, and a couple are skittish, but on the whole they've settled in."

"And have you settled in?" She was sure he hadn't meant to build his herd quite this quickly. But the question wasn't quite as intrusive as it would have been a week ago. There'd been a change in him—subtle, but noticeable. He was growing into his role at Lazy L and it showed.

"I'm getting there." His fingers finished the last strand of grass and it fluttered to the ground. "I'm glad you came out today."

"Me too."

He turned, putting his back to the horses in the pasture and leaning on the fence, hooking one heel over the other. His hat shaded his eyes in the spring sunlight, the denim jacket over his wide shoulders warding off the chill of the unseasonably cool day. He looked irresistible, standing there, and on impulse Jen stood on tiptoe and touched a quick kiss to his lips.

"What was that for?" He raised an eyebrow, seemingly unperturbed, but with a twinkle lighting his eye.

"Do I need a reason?"

Andrew laughed then, a solid, warm, feel-good laugh that filled her to her toes. Right now she didn't need to probe into what the future held. They could just exist in today and know it was okay. Jen wanted to leave the worries of the business and the spectre of the past behind them.

But his laugh drifted away on the breeze and his eyes softened to a troubled golden color. "I wanted to do something today, and I didn't have the courage. But now you're here maybe…" He paused. "That sounds stupid, doesn't it?"

"What do you want to do?"

"Go through Gerald's things. I haven't yet. Haven't even gone into his room. And it's time. Someone should go through his clothing. I'm sure the goodwill could use it. Leaving it as it is feels wrong."

Jen smiled softly. It was a huge step for him, and one she was glad to see happen. "Of course I'll help you." She placed a hand against his chest and looked up into his face, understanding that he felt a little foolish asking. "No one should have to go through a parent's things alone."

They went inside. The house was so quiet it was disturbing, like walking through a church sanctuary. Andrew gave her hand a squeeze. "Why don't you go up? I'll grab a box for the clothing."

When Drew reached the top of the stairs, he took a breath. He had gotten as close as opening the door and standing on the threshold once, but that was all. He stepped forward now, relieved to see Jen inside the room. Her mere presence took away some of his anxiety.

He put the box at the foot of the bed. "Where do we start?"

They began with the dresser, taking out clothes and folding them into the bottom of the box. Drew tried not to think of the last time he'd seen Gerald wearing a certain shirt, or the several pairs of knitted wool socks his father had insisted upon wearing in the winter, but he couldn't escape the memories completely. Of the gruff working man who had been on the opposite side of arguments more times than Andrew could count.

"Oh, Drew, look." Jen pulled a tiny framed picture out from between two plain white undershirts. "You were so small. Look at the blond hair! And there is your mother."

He took the snapshot from her fingers, swallowing hard. It was a picture of the four of them: Gerald, Julie, Noah and himself. Everyone was smiling. Drew was sitting on Gerald's lap, one pudgy hand lifted up and placed on his father's cheek. He couldn't have been more than two. Dimly he remembered there had been some happy times. But the memories were faded, and sometimes he wondered if he'd only imagined them.

And Gerald had kept the picture hidden away in a drawer, like a dirty secret. Drew put it down on the dresser's surface and stepped back. "I don't remember it," he murmured.

"Then consider it a gift," she replied softly. "A real reminder that there were some good times. Look at the light in Gerald's eyes. He loved you, Drew."

Drew tried to hide a telltale sniff and turned away, so she wouldn't see how her words had affected him. "Let's do the closet next, okay?"

He opened the closet door, immediately hit by the

scent of Gerald's aftershave. He closed his eyes as the spicy smell enveloped him. For a moment it was almost as if Gerald was there with him. He reached out and touched a flannel shirt. The cotton was worn and soft beneath his fingers, and tears stung the backs of his eyes. Gerald would never wear it again. He would never be back, and Drew would never have the chance to ask him all the things he'd wanted to. He was gone, his death a cruel and final blow to their estrangement.

"Let's take them off the hangers, Drew." Jen's voice was near a whisper as she placed her hands over his, gently slipping the top button out of the hole and sliding the shirt off into her hands. Her gentle encouragement kept him going until all that was left was the hollow tinkling of the hangers on the rod.

"There's a box up top. Can you reach it?"

Drew looked up, seeing a curious plain brown box, the kind that boots came in. He reached up and slid it off the shelf.

"Let's take it to the bed and open it," Jen suggested as Andrew wiped a thin film of dust from its surface.

They sat on the edge of the bed with the box between them. Carefully Andrew slid the tabs from the slots and lifted the cover.

What was inside sent his heart racing. Not the boots he'd expected, but clippings, letters, pictures. With trembling fingers he sorted through them, although they were meticulously organized. All the letters he'd mailed and never had a reply to, the envelopes opened and the pages wrinkled from frequent handling. Newspaper clippings, the paper yellowed but each one a highlight of Andrew's veterinary career both in Canada and in the U.S. His graduation announcements. It was all there.

"Drew?"

He realized several minutes had passed, and Jen was there, simply waiting for him. He reached out and took her hand. "He cared. He really cared."

"Yes, he did."

He looked up at her and saw her eyes were brimming with tears. He blinked and released her fingers, wiping his hand over his face.

"What's in the bag?" She nudged him on, picking up a small cloth bag tied with a drawstring.

With a deep breath he untied the fastening and turned the bag out on top of the papers.

Glittering white stones tumbled into the box, clattering loudly in the reverent silence. Andrew stared at the misshapen lumps, picked one up in his fingers, turning it over.

"What is it?"

"Quartz." He caught his breath after saying the single word, fighting to keep his composure.

"Why quartz?"

He closed his eyes, took a deep breath. This was

Jen. She'd stuck with him throughout the whole afternoon. He could get through this part.

"When I was a boy we had a game. We would find quartz and keep the brightest pieces. Gerald told me that quartz was supposed to bring wealth and prosperity. I kept all the best ones in a shoebox in my room." He paused, his stomach sinking with guilt. "I threw them all away the day I left. But he…he carried on, didn't he? Without me." His voice broke at the end. Here was the proof he had been sure didn't exist. Seeing it, touching it, had caused the dam to finally break. Clutching the stone in his hand, he lowered his head and cried.

Jen slid the box backward on the bed, moved over and knelt on the quilted spread, putting her arms around him. For a few minutes he simply let himself grieve. And when the worst was over he pulled her down into his lap and held her close. She had always believed. He was profoundly grateful she'd been here with him today. That he hadn't had to go through it alone.

"I wasted so much time," he murmured when he was back in control. "I should have come sooner. Why didn't he ever write back?"

Jen shook her head as it rested on his shoulder, releasing the scent of her shampoo, something light and feminine and familiar. "I don't know."

"I'd trade all my money for one more afternoon searching for rocks with him."

Her arms squeezed around his middle and she turned her face up to his. She'd been crying too, and in that moment he felt closer to her than he ever had.

"Why don't we? Let's go find some. You and me. Where was the best place?"

The idea suddenly sounded brilliant, and he smiled. "The creek bed by the west pasture."

"Wonderful. It's a beautiful spring afternoon. Take me there. It's been so long since we wandered the fields. We'll find new stones, and you can show me where you've pastured the rest of the herd. Tell me your plans."

He nodded, sliding her off his lap and standing. "We can leave the rest for later." The idea of being outside in the air and the sun grabbed hold. "Do you have a jacket? It's cooler today, and there's a cold front on its way."

As Andrew grabbed his jean jacket from a hook, Jen retrieved her coat from her car—a blue-on-blue nylon jacket that kept out the wind. Together they set off to the west and the far quarter section, where Andrew had pastured the healthiest members of the herd. The creek ran through the middle. The horses would be undisturbed there, with acres of luxurious grass to graze on and room to run and be free.

When Jen thought of the cramped quarters they'd

endured in the transport truck, she couldn't help but feel happy for the animals in their new life. And proud of the man who had made it happen. A man who had finally found a measure of peace this afternoon. She pushed back the tiny voice of caution in her head. She would not listen today. Today was about more important things.

They walked in silence, but each footstep they made somehow drew them closer together, as if their hearts were speaking though their tongues were quiet. Jen was taken back by a startling sense of déjà vu, of afternoons when, as teenagers, they'd walked this very path just for precious moments alone.

She had memories of that time, bittersweet ones, of the intensity of young love and how much it had hurt knowing it was over. Walking those paths again, she realized that they were not the same people. They were Jen and Drew *now*. Jen felt the reassuring presence of him walking beside her and remembered how he'd kissed her the night of the dance, how he had held her just this afternoon, how he had turned to her when he needed help. She would have fallen for him anyway. It was the new Drew that had recaptured her heart.

Drew's boots made scuffing sounds in the dirt as he ambled along beside her, and their elbows bumped. Nerves of anticipation quivered through Jen's belly as Drew clasped her hand in his. Today they had turned a page, and she no longer knew what was ahead for them. She only knew it was different from anything that had gone before.

They finally reached the far gate of the section, and Jen sighed as he slid the latch open and they went inside. "Oh, Andrew. I'd nearly forgotten how beautiful it is here."

The mountains spread out in a white-capped line as far as she could see to her right and to her left. This section of fencing sat atop a small rise, so that more of the foothills lay before them, the density of the trees increasing until they formed a solid greenish black line against the gray stone. To their right she could hear the faint gurgling of the creek.

"Me too." He kept her hand in his and she squeezed, turning her head to look up at him. He squeezed back. "The first time I felt like I was really home was when I came out here."

"Do you still wish you'd never come back?" She held her breath, waiting for the answer. Coming out here today marked something important: a willing sharing of time together simply for the purpose of being together.

"Not after today. Today changed a lot of things."

"The good times…what do you remember?"

He pulled with his hand, so that her body jostled the side of his. "You. Being here with you. How you'd bake us cookies on a Saturday afternoon and we'd go for walks like we are today. Hanging out with Noah and having him sneak me a beer when I was underage. That sort of thing."

"The not so good times—they have to do with Gerald, don't they?"

He pulled his hand from hers and took a few steps away. He nodded; she saw the back of his cowboy hat rise and fall along his neck.

"We were so angry at each other. We never managed to be on the same page. For a while I thought it was just typical teenage 'he doesn't understand me' stuff. And then when he told me I wasn't his I thought I had it all figured out. I held on to that resentment for a long time. And now I'll never be able to ask him about it. Finding that box today made me realize I was the one with the closed mind. I don't like that about myself very much."

They followed the sound of the creek and stood on the rocky bank, watching the gray water bounce and race over stones.

Jen knelt, trailing her fingertips into the frigid water. "You are very much like him, you know. In good ways, strong ways. I think if he pushed you it was because he wanted good things for you. He accepted you as his son, I know he did. I think he wanted you to accept him as your father."

Andrew reached down and picked up a crystal-white stone, holding it up to show her. She smiled, and he tucked the rock into his pocket and hunched his shoulders against the rawness of the wind. "I did. I always did. I wouldn't have wanted him to understand so much if I hadn't."

Jen went to him and laid her cheek against his back. It was a comforting place to be, secure in his warmth and strength. "You deserved to know the truth, Drew. It is unfortunate that it came to light in anger. And it is sad that it caused so much regret for everyone."

The wind picked up, and tiny sharp snowflakes started dotting the air around them. Jen looked up, surprised to see how quickly the dark cloud that had been to the northwest had closed in. She shivered in her coat and put her fingers in the fleece-lined pockets.

Drew mirrored her movements. "I can't change what's past, as much as I'd like to. I have to look forward. I set up this project and I'm committed to it. It's a lot of work. I'm not playing at ranching."

Jen pursed her lips, wondering how on earth he could be so blind. She had feelings for the man he'd become. But she realized he was still stuck in the past, and she wondered if when he looked at her he saw the girl she'd been or the woman she'd become. She wanted him to see the new Jen. The Jen who had been shaped by the past and had built herself a good life. That was the woman she wanted him to care about, not the girl he'd left behind.

"I go through the same thing with my business. People act like it's some sort of hobby when I put in longer hours than most people with regular jobs." She looked up at him, hoping he would understand her side of it. "And with you too. We grew up. But people think that because we were high school sweethearts we'll just pick up where we left off."

"But that's not true."

She shook her head. "How can it be, when both of us have changed so much?"

Drew looked into her eyes, grayish blue and questioning. She had changed. She was stronger than before. More beautiful. His gaze dropped to her lips, full and red against her flawless skin. More stubborn too. She hadn't given up on him. And, while it had gotten him through today, there was still a part of him that wondered if she didn't expect too much.

"So why *are* we here?" he asked, not moving any closer to her, but feeling a sense of contact just the same.

"I…" But her voice faltered and she lowered her lashes. Andrew's heart bumped against his ribs.

His lips curved up just the slightest bit as he closed the remaining gap between them and tipped up her chin with a finger. Delicious color bloomed in her cheeks and he thought about kissing her in the barn. "I know why I'm here."

A small laugh bubbled from her lips. "You're

impossible." She shivered suddenly. "And it's got cold fast."

The snow had started coming down harder. A thin layer settled on the green blades of grass. He should have known that word of a cold front didn't mean anything. Spring snowstorms were common, and by the bite of the wind this one was settling in to stay. Meanwhile, they were a long way from the house at Lazy L. And he'd been standing here staring into her eyes like a fool, hoping to God she didn't expect too much out of him at the same time. What a damn mess.

"We need to get back, Jen." The weather was suddenly more important than feelings. "This isn't going to blow through."

He saw her shiver, and chafed her arms with his hands. She was only wearing light sneakers on her feet, no gloves, and just a T-shirt beneath her jacket. "Come on, we've got to get moving. The way the wind's coming up, you're going to be frozen by the time we reach the house."

They were only about halfway back and his toes were cold in his boots; Jen's had to be freezing. Her hair was coated with snow, and she walked briskly with her arms wrapped around herself. He stopped them, brushed her hair off with his hands and took off his hat, settling it on her head. At least it would keep her a little bit dry, and he took her hand as they set out again.

At a fork in the road he made a decision. "Jen, it's coming down fast, and it's too far to the house." He cursed himself for getting caught up in their time together and not seeing the signs in the clouds. He'd thought it would be hours before they'd see any significant weather. "I have an idea."

She looked up at him, her teeth chattering. "The shack?"

"Yes. It's only around that bend, and we can wait out the snowfall."

"Can't someone come and get us?"

"Yes, but not until after the snow stops." He looked past her shoulder. The flakes were larger now, and coming down in a thick blanket. "The visibility is terrible. But it's May. It won't last that long. Okay?"

She nodded, and he felt relief fight with anxiety. He hadn't forgotten the other night in the barn, and how close he'd been to taking things further. How much he'd wanted to. But there was no time to think of those things now. The storm was worsening and they were getting too cold. They had to get out of the elements.

"Come on," he called against the wind, and tugged her hand. They jogged down the vee in the path and around a bend beyond some straggly spruce trees.

They took the snow-covered steps at a trot, and

Andrew lifted the iron latch on the door. He gave it a shove with his shoulder and the wood gave way with a creak. They stumbled inside, shaking their clothes and shuddering against the cold. Jen took off his hat and placed it on an old table; Andrew stomped his feet and looked around him.

He'd been out here a few times already. The first time he'd been working on the shelters, and curiosity had gotten the better of him. The door had stuck, as it always had, but the place had been neat but dusty. Someone had kept it up during the years he'd been gone. The memories had caught him from every corner as he'd taken the rugs and blankets and aired them out over the rickety rail outside the door. At the time he'd wondered why he was doing it. Now he knew. This shack was going to keep them comfortable while they waited out the storm.

But it wouldn't keep them safe from the desire that kept flaring between them. Or the fact that they were going to be alone for several hours with precious little to keep them occupied.

"I'll start a fire," he said quietly, slipping back out into the snow for an armload of wood.

Jen watched him through the dusty window, tramping across the clearing to a rudimentary lean-to holding wood already split. In the sudden fury of the storm the shack had seemed a wonderful reprieve. But now that they were here it was different. The intimacy of it was threatening. Who knew how long they would be here? The day had started out as carefree and easy. Now they were stuck together, assaulted not only by memories but by the events of the afternoon and their blooming attraction.

As she watched, her fingers curled into her palms, Andrew reappeared, carrying an armload of wood and a hatchet. She hurried to open the door for him, letting in a blast of cold air.

"Thanks." He opened the small woodstove and arranged several sticks, then took the hatchet and began chipping off strips for kindling. When he had it all to his liking, he opened a small tin box and took out matches. Within a few seconds the beginning of a fire was crackling.

"Can you watch this? I want to get more wood before the snow gets deeper."

Jen's unease multiplied. Surely they weren't going to be here that long? Reason warred with sudden panic. She'd seen this kind of storm often enough this late in the year. One odd system coming over the mountains that brought a sudden burst of heavy wet snow. Not flurries, but a full-on storm. One that wouldn't be over in an hour. And soon it would start growing dark, eliminating the possibility of rescue until daylight.

She added a stick to the fire, sighing. The taking it slow, one day at a time principle was about to be blown to pieces. She was pretty sure that spending the night in a secluded one-room cabin wasn't taking things slowly.

Drew came back in three more times, constructing a neat stack of wood along one wall that should keep their fire going for several hours. When he was done, he rubbed his hands in front of the stove while Jen sat at the drop-leaf table in a chair that had been cast off from the main house.

"So now we wait?"

"Yep."

Warmed, Drew stood and made a trip to the cupboard. First he took out several candles and stuck them in tin holders. He lit them one by one, the flickering glow adding a homey touch to the rough setting. Returning to the cupboard, he pulled out a teakettle, a tin, and two mugs, depositing the lot on the table with a grin.

"You've been in here already!" Jen's head snapped up in surprise. The candles and matches were new, and the kettle and mugs were free of the fine film of dust that coated the furniture. He couldn't have planned for the storm, but the knowledge that he'd been here since his return did funny things to her insides.

"I remembered it when I was out here building the shelters. It's been vacant for a while, but it *has* been used since…"

The fact that he let the words trail off told her where his mind had gone, and heat rushed into her cheeks. *Since we were here* was how that sentence would have finished.

"I'll fill the kettle with snow." She scraped back her chair, in a hurry to escape the warm glow of his eyes. The cold air stole her breath as she ran out and scooped snow into the kettle, then ran back in again.

He took the kettle from her and put it on the stove, the moisture on it hissing as it touched the iron top. "Take your shoes off and let your feet dry," he advised, opening the tin and putting a teabag in each cup.

She wanted to ignore him, not be told what to do, but she knew he was right, and the middle of a blizzard was no time to argue. She slid off her sneakers, putting them closer to the heat of the stove. As the snow began to melt in the kettle he moved his chair closer and lifted her legs, putting them up on his lap. She bit down on her lip. Now that they were storm-stayed, every little touch suddenly took on extra meaning.

But her toes were warming a little and she tried to relax.

"I cleaned it up a little, that's all. It's a good place to be with yourself." He looked around them, and then back into her eyes again. "And you never know when bad weather is going to crop up. A thunder-shower, a freak blizzard. It pays to be prepared."

But nothing had prepared her for this.

It didn't take long for the stove to heat the tiny space, and the coziness lulled them against the howling storm outside. The kettle hissed quietly as the water heated, and Drew's hand stroked her calf lightly. Jen was painfully aware of the bed behind them. Gerald had built the frame, and the mattress was an old one from the house. The first time Drew had brought her here he'd explained how his father or the hands sometimes spent nights here when it was convenient.

The last time had been just before he'd left for university, when he'd told her he'd be back.

And the times in between… She closed her eyes. She wanted him more now than she ever had then.

"Jen?"

She tried to focus on his face rather than on the fantasy she'd briefly indulged in. "What?"

He held out his hand, took hers. "It's going to be okay. We're going to be fine. These storms don't last forever. We've got shelter and a fire, and tea, and I even have a few protein bars in the tin box. It's not much, but it will at least keep us going."

A thought struck her—of the herd being out in the middle of such a storm. "What about the horses?"

He reached inside the box and took out a foil-wrapped packet. "I managed to get the shelters serviceable. They'll huddle in there together, snug as a bug. Don't worry."

But she *was* worried. "Sometimes people die in these storms."

"Yes, but they aren't stranded with a Laramie." His grin flashed at her and he patted her hand. "The water's hot. Here."

He handed her half of a protein bar and went to get the kettle. She took the rectangle and nibbled on a dense chocolate corner, wondering if he'd realized he'd referred to himself as a Laramie after all. She didn't want protein bars. And, to be truthful, it wasn't dying she was afraid of. It was the intense desire she felt and what they might do to relieve it that had her in a spin. It was as if everything was conspiring to make it happen—their growing attraction, the storm, the forced intimacy of being stranded together in a room with nothing more than a bed for decent furniture. One bed. The possibilities made her swallow thickly.

She dipped out her teabag and sipped the hot brew, feeling its warmth radiate from her belly outward. He was so strong, so capable. She stared over the rim of her mug at him, watching his fingers as he pressed his teabag against the side of the cup before removing it to an old square of newspaper.

She wanted what they had started the other night in the barn. She wanted him. All of him. Now, in the place where they'd stumbled over their first time together. Her heart beat so loudly she was sure he could hear it over the storm.

They were not children anymore. She was a woman, with a woman's heart and hopes and dreams. And, no matter how much she protested and agreed to taking it slow, it wasn't what she wanted in her heart. She wanted him to love her. *Heart and soul, can't live without you* love her. She wanted to see his face in the morning on the pillow beside hers, and she wanted to walk the corridor of the stables with him at sunset. Realizing it left her reeling momentarily, until Drew put down his cup, watching her with a strange expression on his face.

"What is it?"

The sound of his voice jarred her out of her stupor. She placed her uneaten bar back in the wrapper on the table. This afternoon he had finally taken giant strides to getting past his history with his father. A history that had been standing in their way ever since his return. Was it possible there was room for her now too? She was terrified, but she refused to look back. Life was full of chances. She didn't want to miss out on this one. Even if it meant risking her heart in the process.

# CHAPTER TWELVE

SHE stood, went around the corner of the table until she was before him, took his face in her hands and kissed him.

It was a full-on, nothing held back kiss, one filled with longing and passion and urgency, and it exploded into the tiny room, expanding into something bright and alive. Andrew's hands gripped her hips as she commandeered his head. Her fingers tangled in his hair as she abandoned any reserve she'd been holding on to. Ever since that moment he'd nearly knocked her over in the street this was what she'd truly wanted, and she poured all of her love and hopes into it.

She slid her hands down beneath the denim jacket, pushing it off his shoulders into a crumpled pile on the chair as he stood, pulling her close. Their breathing grew heavy, echoing around the space, and Jen removed her own jacket, feeling goosebumps erupt on her skin even though the fire kept the room warm.

She reached for the hem of her T-shirt and pulled it over her head, sending an unmistakable invitation. Her breasts tightened as his gaze dropped to the simple bra she wore. With trembling fingers she slowly undid the buttons of his shirt, all the while feeling as if what was left of her clothing was shrinking. The moment his shirt was untethered he stripped it off and dropped it on top of his jacket. He reached out and pulled her close, and she gloried in the feel of his skin finally against hers.

They blindly shuffled to the bed, stopping when the backs of her legs hit the frame. Jen broke the kiss long enough to turn down the blankets. The action felt so private, so intimate, that her body trembled. She was preparing for her lover. The only lover she'd ever known. The only lover she'd ever wanted.

When she turned back, Andrew lifted his hand, trailing a single finger down her cheek. "Be sure," he whispered.

"Are you?"

He nodded slowly, his gaze stopping at her lips briefly before lifting to her eyes. The gold flecks seemed to reflect the candlelight. "I have been unsure of a lot of things lately, but this is one thing I know I want. I want you, Jen."

She wanted him too, and was so tired of fighting it. Tired of worrying what people would think, tired of having to keep repairing the wall she'd built around her heart. She was tired of being careful and weighing all the options. For once she wanted to simply listen to what her heart was saying, and right now it was saying that the time for wasting her love was past.

She removed the rest of her clothes, slid between the quilts, and bade him come home.

Jen opened her eyes by degrees, adjusting to the light coming through the window. A gust of cold air had her burrowing back under the blankets. It was followed by the shutting of the door. She peered toward the foot of the bed; Andrew was adding an armload of wood to the coals left in the stove.

Tears stung the back of her nose as she watched him. Last night had been more than incredible. She'd given him her body, and, more than that, he'd given her his. As his hands had gripped hers on the pillow, images had flashed through her mind. Memories of their first time that had been branded on her so long ago they would never go away, resurrected by his strong and gentle touch. The way he'd touched her, as if she were precious. The look in his eyes at that crucial moment, the mixture of love and fear and awe of it all glowing out of his face. How she'd quietly cried simply because he had touched her body and soul and how he'd held her in his arms afterward.

She'd felt all that and more last night, held fast in

his arms while the wind gusted and the snow blew around the tiny cabin. But this morning something had changed. Though she couldn't put her finger on it there was a coolness, a tension in the air that hadn't been there before.

"Good morning."

He jumped a little, then turned to face her. "I didn't mean to wake you."

She dropped her lashes, then looked up again, patting the quilts. "It's not the same without you in here."

Again the uneasy feeling crept through her as she watched his movements. He came to sit on the edge of the bed, but made no move to get back in it. She felt at a disadvantage because he was fully dressed and she was wearing nothing at all.

"The fire burned down. I had to go out for more wood."

She frowned a little. There was no intimate smile, no good-morning kiss. Was he even going to mention the little detail of them spending the night together? She said the only thing she could think of. "The snow has stopped?"

"Yes. I called Clay from my cell when I was outside. He's rounding up Dawson and some winter clothes and they'll be here in an hour."

An hour? Yesterday she'd been worried about spending too much time shut up with him, and now it seemed precious minutes were ticking past so quickly. She started to reach out for his hand, then pulled back, unsure. "That's good, then."

"Yes."

Still no mention of what had happened between them. After last night she'd expected at least a chance to be held in his arms before the real world came crashing in again. Instead she was faced with this stoic stranger, and uncertainty rippled through her.

She had known being with him was a risk, but she hadn't thought he'd shut her out completely.

"Drew, we don't have much time so I'm just going to come out and say it." She leaned forward, holding the covers to her chest. "Do you regret last night?"

His gaze seared her, and she reveled in the heat, clinging to it like a beacon in a storm. "How can you ask that?"

"Because you're acting like it never happened."

Andrew looked down at her, torn between needing to escape and wanting to climb back into the blankets with her. He'd thought he could handle this. And last night it had seemed so clear. But this morning he'd watched the shadows on her face as morning dawned, watched her steady breathing, her sweet scent filling his nostrils as he rubbed her soft hair between his fingers. Now it was complicated. He couldn't ignore it any longer. With Jen, there was only one choice—everything.

And everything scared him to death.

"Of course it happened, and it was wonderful." He forced a smile, reached out and touched her cheek with a knuckle. "But we can't stay. Surely you know that."

"We have an hour," she suggested, sliding forward a few inches, and he felt his body respond.

"Jen…"

The smile slid from her face and her eyes dimmed. "What is it, Drew? I don't understand."

He got up from the bed and paced a few steps. "Maybe it's all too fast for me."

"You weren't running away last night."

"Where would I have run to?"

He instantly regretted the words as she slid back against the pillow, hurt etched on her face. He'd made it sound like she'd trapped him into something he hadn't wanted, and nothing was further from the truth. "I'm sorry," he added quickly. "I didn't mean it the way it sounded."

"I know. One day at a time. That was what we decided."

He looked at her, knowing from the dull light in her eyes that she was saying it because it was what she thought he needed. But he wasn't blind. Making love changed things in a relationship. Especially one like he had with Jen.

The heat from the stove began warming the air

again, and Drew brought a chair over closer to the bed rather than sit next to her. He needed that space. Needed to slow things down, make her see.

"Jen," he said softly, hating that what was coming next was likely to hurt her, but knowing he had to be honest. "The truth is I'm not sure I'll ever be ready for a committed relationship, and it's not fair to you to pretend."

Jen slid out of the bed, treating him to a delectable view that nearly had him groaning aloud. She pulled on her clothes with no muss or fuss, and then in the heavy silence straightened the blankets and pillows on the bed. Almost as if they had never been there. His heart sank. He'd hurt her after all, and that was the last thing he'd wanted to do.

"Stop," he entreated, as she made her hands busy over the table. He spun in the chair. "Stop." He reached out and stilled her hands. "Would you rather I lied to you?"

"No. Of course not." She pulled her fingers out of his grasp and poured the leftover water from the kettle into the teacups, rinsing them out.

This wasn't going well.

"Will you sit so we can talk about this?"

Her head sagged, and he felt as low as he ever wanted to. And yet he knew he had to be fair. And making her believe he was something he was not was wrong. Because in the thin light of morning, seeing her head on the pillow had nearly over-whelmed him with responsibility. He'd felt the need to run.

And he wouldn't put Jen through that.

She took the chair opposite him, and when she finally looked him square in the eye he realized exactly how much damage he'd done. For the first time she looked defeated, and it was all because of him.

"Last night was wonderful," he began to explain. "But after yesterday, finding out the things I did… You don't know what it meant to me to have you there. And I got carried away."

"I believe I made the first move."

Her courage in admitting it took him by surprise. "I didn't stop you. I wanted you too. But I can't do this." He swept out a hand, encompassing them, and then dropped it into his lap again. How many mountains was one man supposed to climb, anyway? He'd had to face a lot of demons to get even to this point. There wasn't much left of himself to give. "I still have things to work through. And if I let you, you'll wait. And I don't know if I'll ever be ready. I don't want to make false promises."

"If you *let* me, I'll wait?"

Jen's harsh, bitter laugh cut through the air as she repeated his words back to him. Had he actually just said those words? Yes, she'd decided last night what she wanted, and that was every single inch of Drew Laramie. But if he thought she was going to be the pathetic girl waiting by the gate again he was wrong.

"You don't know me at all, do you, Drew?"

"What do you mean?"

Oh, he could sit there in his chair, acting all wounded and confused, but there was too much at stake now for her to back down. "You think that just because I waited for you before I'll do so again? Do you think I started my own business because I sat around and pined for you? Or planned the expansion by sitting on my thumbs?" She huffed out a sigh. "You said I wasn't the same girl that you left behind. So stop treating me like it!"

"I never said you sat on your hands. Are you honestly telling me that you would walk out this door and let me go?"

She shook her head sharply. "No. But neither would I sit around and wait."

"I'm not following." His forehead wrinkled.

Jen let out an exasperated breath as she leaned forward. "I fight for what I want these days."

Silence fell, dark and uncomfortable. And uneasy words. "Then you have changed. Because you did not go after what you wanted all those years ago. I asked you to come with me."

"You asked me to leave behind my family when we were eighteen. So we could what? Live together in some dingy apartment while you paid tuition and we scrambled to pay the rent?"

"If you had loved me…"

"Oh, you're grasping at straws now, and playing dirty." This wasn't about the past any longer. It was about the Drew that had returned to Larch Valley, and he was covering. "I could say the same words back to you. You know what your problem is? You are so bound up in the fact that Gerald did not reply to your letters! Did you ever think how he felt every time you got in touch? You were so bent on proving to him that you were right that you didn't see that it was throwing your success in his face!"

He paled, took a step back. "Don't say that."

"How would *you* feel, Drew? The son you love rejects you, rejects the farm, and rubs your nose in it by reminding you of all the ways he is better than what he left behind!"

Silence fell, heavy in the tiny cabin, and Jen already regretted the words spoken so furiously in hurt.

"I'm sor—"

But he cut her off with a wave of his hand. "Don't be. I already figured that much out for myself, so you can't make me feel any worse than I already do." His gaze gripped hers, so that she couldn't look away. "You could have gone to Lethbridge with your mum and dad. No one forced you to be stuck here. Why didn't you go with them?"

He might as well know the truth. There was nothing hidden from each other in the cold light of morning.

"I was waiting for you."

Silence fell in the tiny cabin, and a spark popping in the stove caused them both to jump. That was the simple truth she had been clinging to. She had waited, hoped he would come back every school holiday, every summer. Until she'd realized he wasn't coming and she'd got on with her life.

Jen took a step forward, entreating. "That's right. I waited rather than going after what I wanted. You want to know why this town acts so protective of me? Because they were there for me when you weren't."

She hooked her thumbs in the pockets of her jeans. "If you had told me about Gerald and how hurt you were maybe I would have reconsidered. But we'll never know. And do you know why?" She rushed on, feeling the hurt and anger pour over her in painful waves. "Because you never trusted me. You could have told me a million times about Gerald and I would have understood. I would have been there for you. But you didn't let me in. Do you know how much that hurts me? To know you thought so little of me, when I loved you with everything I had? But now I realize you've never trusted me. You came up with the benefit idea to help my business… Did you not think I could make it work on my own? You embarrassed me at the dance in an obvious effort to drum up clients, when I'm already pretty well versed on how to advertise myself. You overpaid me and I didn't say anything, because we were friends and I knew deep down that you meant well."

"I was trying to help!"

"I never asked for your help!" She shouted it, feeling her blood pressure rise, her muscles tighten as the argument built. "I built that business on my own. *I* did it. Just me. No one else. For a while I kept thinking that the whole town only saw me as half of us, but that's not true. They know exactly how hard I've worked to make the bakery succeed. Everyone in this town gets it. Everyone but you. Because to you I'm poor Jen who got left behind. Except I'm not."

She lowered her voice, but her words were deep with meaning. "I'm Jen that stayed. I'm Jen that faced her life instead of running away from it."

"Stop it," he growled, spinning away and staring out the window, his hands bound into tight fists.

But she had gone too far to pull back now. She didn't even care if he saw her cry or not. He was brushing her aside as if what they had didn't matter. "It's true. And you know what else, Andrew Laramie? You say if I'd loved you I would have gone with you. And perhaps that is my cross to bear. Maybe I did fail you. But don't ever accuse me of not loving you. I did love you. I love you now. I never stopped."

Her voice started to break but she pushed on. "I have always loved you. Even when you make me furious, even when you make me stark crazy, I'm in love with you. And you're too much of a damn coward to take what has always been yours!" She finished with her hands on her hips, the sound of her harsh breathing filling the air, hot tears streaking down her cheeks.

She sucked in a breath, trying to regain a little control. "I'm not going anywhere. Don't you get that?" She said it quietly, a whisper that filled every corner of the room.

He turned around then, his honeyed eyes dim and bleak. "But I am."

The adrenaline swept out of her body in an instant, leaving her weak and unsteady in the void. Why hadn't she seen it coming? But after the other night he'd made it clear he had too many obligations to leave again. Oh, nothing made sense. All she could think of to say was, "Where?"

He shook his head. "I don't know. But someday I will. It'll all be too much and I'll be off again. Because you're right, Jen. You're the one that stayed, and I'm the runner. It's what I do." His lip curled as he continued in a voice filled with self-hatred, "Things got bad and I took off. Just like my mother. And I won't hurt you the way she hurt all of us."

Jen rushed forward, grabbing his arm. "How can you possibly know what happened if you haven't even spoken to her in twenty-five years? You should try to find her. Get her side of the story. Finally put it all behind you." She had to convince him. She couldn't have risked it all for nothing. She couldn't let him walk out of her life again. "I'll even go with you."

"No."

His withdrawal was clear. Jen felt it open a gulf between them and knew she'd lost. Gerald didn't matter. Their night together didn't matter. He had closed himself off to her once again. She'd told herself she had her eyes wide open where he was concerned, but she had been wrong. She'd let herself hope, that was all. She'd seen what she wanted to see.

He grabbed his jacket from the foot of the bed and shrugged it on as the hum of snowmobiles filled the air. He jammed his hat on his head and went to the door.

"Stay here. I'll be right back."

He slammed out the door, leaving her standing in the breach of stunned silence.

What had just happened?

Last night had been exalted, glorious, mesmerizing. How had they gone from that to here in the rising of a single sun?

She sank into a chair, taking deep breaths. She had to act as if everything was normal in front of

Clay and Dawson. She couldn't cry. She had to pull herself together.

"Hey, O'Keefe!" A shout sounded from the ramshackle porch, and she pasted on what she hoped would pass for a smile. Clay Gregory clumped in with a backpack in his hands.

"Well, if it isn't the cavalry to the rescue." She stood up and went to take the pack from his arms.

"Brought you some winter gear, courtesy of Dawson's sister."

"And I appreciate it."

Clay's keen eyes took in the neatly made bed, the stove and the clean mugs on the table. Jen raised an eyebrow and cautioned, "Don't even."

"Did I say anything?"

"Do you ever have to?"

He laughed. "True enough."

As she took boots, gloves, hat and a ski jacket out of the pack, Clay looked closer. "You okay? Do I need to take Andrew aside? I told him to watch his step with you."

She snorted out an emotional laugh. "I'm fine. Just hungry and ready to go home."

She had to look away as she said the word home. Going back to her house, away from Lazy L, looked as if it would mean the end of her relationship with Drew. Just thinking about it felt like a crater opening up in her center.

"If you're ready, then, let's get out of here," Clay suggested.

Jen looked around the shack, made sure the stove was closed up and the damper turned. Drew wasn't even going to come back in, she realized. Swallowing thickly, she shoved her hands into the thick gloves and clumped out behind Clay to the snowmobiles.

Drew approached from the woodpile and climbed on behind Dawson without a word. Jen got on behind Clay and put her arms around his waist as he gunned the throttle. The sun was out, sparking glittering crystals of light off the new snow, and the air was growing milder by the moment as they sped back along the path toward Lazy L. At any other time Jen would have thought it a beautiful day. But not today. By tomorrow most of the snow would be gone—melted away just like her hopes for herself and Drew.

# CHAPTER THIRTEEN

THE daffodils and tulips had weathered the storm, their cheerful golden blooms nodding along the edges of the fenced garden. The grass was green again, the air perfumed with spring, the resilient branches that had drooped under the weight of snow now stood strong, displaying their leaves. The potentilla and spirea were beginning to spread along the iron fencing. Gardens all through town were dark with freshly tilled soil and newly planted flowers. It was almost as if the blizzard had never happened.

Drew waited by the gate for several minutes, unsure. Finally he took a big breath and went inside. It didn't take him long to locate the stone; he'd been here for the interment the previous fall. Then the ground had been brown and dreary. Today, as he stopped by Gerald's grave, it was carpeted with green and decorated with a colorful arrangement of daisies and bluebells. He wondered briefly who might have placed them there, knowing somehow in his heart that it was Jen. She'd been a better daughter to Gerald than he'd been a son. He reached out and plucked out a single bluebell, turning it over in his fingers before tucking it into the front pocket of his jacket.

He knelt before the grave, reading the name, date of birth—today—and the date of death. It said nothing else. The other stones nearby said "*beloved wife*," or "*cherished father*," but not Gerald's. Gerald had died probably feeling unloved. It was a horrible burden for Andrew to bear now—now when he understood and could not tell him so.

"I'm sorry," he whispered brokenly. Whispering was the only way he could form words; his vocal chords were constricted, prohibiting true speech. He reached out and placed a hand on the cold granite, wondering somehow if Gerald could hear him, wherever he was. He wanted to think so, wanted to think that somehow his father knew he was here. That somehow, beyond his understanding, perhaps it didn't have to be completely too late.

"I was wrong and I was stubborn. It wasn't your fault."

He stared a long time at the stone, long enough for the sun to disappear under clouds, for the air to lose its benevolent warmth. Gerald had never treated Noah any differently than himself. He had simply been a man unused to sharing his feelings. Drew had been so blind. So he knelt, making peace, asking for forgiveness. When he could manage it, he cleared his throat. "You were a good father, Dad. I know I disappointed you. I hope you're proud of me now."

But he knew that while Gerald would have been glad to see him come home, he'd have been disappointed in how Drew had treated Jen. She had walked out of his life, just as he'd wanted her to. Because he'd been too afraid to reach out and accept what she was offering. Too afraid of failing her to trust in her love.

He'd all but ignored his brother too, the one person he'd always counted on in childhood. The phone call this morning had sent him reeling. Noah was in hospital. He'd been wounded in action, and was recuperating in Germany until he could be sent home.

But leaving Jen that morning in the cabin had made him face a lot of ugly truths. One being that he was following a pattern of hurting the people he loved most and then hating himself for it. Gerald, Noah, Jen. He looked down at his father's grave and knew he could never take back the things he'd said and done, could never change the years he'd wasted. But he could look forward. He didn't have to be doomed to making the same mistakes. He knew that now.

He was tired of making the wrong choices, trying to prove the wrong things. Even a few days without her had been empty and pointless. The loneliness had given him the courage to take the final step.

He reached into his coat pocket and withdrew the lump of quartz he'd picked up that day at the creek and he placed it next to the daisies and bluebells. Then he pushed up off the ground and brushed at the damp dirt on the knees of his jeans. He swiped at his eyes, kissed his fingertips and pressed them to the top of the stone.

"Happy Birthday, Dad," he whispered. As the first raindrops fell, he turned his back and made his way back out of the gate.

Jen hurried back along Main Avenue, hustling her way between bank and bakery through the rain that had sprung up so suddenly. She'd met with the realtor and a "For Sale" sign now hung outside Snickerdoodles. She'd hated watching the stake going into the ground, but knew inside that a Larch Valley with Andrew in it wouldn't work. He could say all he wanted about leaving, but Jen knew he was committed to Lazy L. As long as he remained, she would never be able to move forward, to be happy. But the decision, and every step toward the day she would leave, was ripping her heart to shreds, strip by strip.

She slowed briefly, allowing a young mum with a toddler to skirt past and into a storefront. And then there he was. Standing across the street, hair dripping, his oilskin jacket beaded with rain. Her feet stopped as their eyes clashed, as her heart leapt at the simple sight of him. This was why she had to go.

A splash of blue caught her eye, right there in his breast pocket. She knew even from this distance that it was a bluebell. He had been to his father's grave. He knew she had been there. Her lip quivered. She didn't want any of this. She didn't want to sell the bakery, she didn't want to leave Larch Valley, and she didn't want this distance. And still he gazed at her as her eyes filled, bereft by the gulf between them.

Drew saw her standing there, soaking wet in the rain, and his heart went into overdrive. In the space of a second the "For Sale" sign over her right shoulder registered. The bakery was up for sale. But the bakery was everything to her! Had he pushed her out of her home, then? Had he hurt her that much that she couldn't stand to be near him any longer? He pushed away the sense of guilt and shock. There was no time for that now.

He couldn't lose her. Not now when he'd finally put it all back together. Gerald. His mother. And her. It all made sense. But the pain in her eyes tore at him. At what cost? It couldn't be too late. He wouldn't let it be too late.

And then her lip trembled. He stepped off the curb toward her, mindless of traffic and rain. For the space of a heartbeat she hesitated, then her feet moved…one step after another… her gaze locked with his. They met in the middle of Main Avenue, moved straight into each other's arms. Their mouths clashed, a meeting of despair, hurt, apology and hope, cold with the wet of the rain and heated by the strength of love.

And when he finally took his lips from hers he closed his eyes and simply held on.

"I love you."

Jen's heart rejoiced and wept at the same time. Oh, just when she thought she couldn't cry anymore, that did it. Those three little words caused her to become completely undone inside, flooded with love and utter relief. She sobbed into his jacket, her fingers curled into the stiff fabric.

His soft chuckle sounded in her ear. "Shh, it's okay," he murmured. Then quieter, stronger. "It's going to be okay."

She struggled to stop crying. There was a shushing sound, and then a loud beep as a car swerved out around them. "We're in the middle of the street." His voice was a sexy rumble that she'd never get tired of hearing.

"I don't care."

"People are probably staring."

"Let them," she decreed, and his arms closed tighter around her.

He put his hands on either side of her head, kissing her forehead tenderly. "Yes, but I have things to say, and in the middle of Main during a spring shower wasn't what I had in mind."

"My house." Jen stepped back, touched his face and took his hand. "It's the only place we'll get any privacy."

They ignored the curious faces of neighbors and strangers on the street and took two left turns, heading northwest into the residential part of town. When they got to the gate of Jen's house Andrew paused. "I haven't been here since…"

"It doesn't matter. Not anymore."

She unlocked the door and they stepped inside. For a few awkward moments they took off their wet coats and shoes, ordinary movements in a day that was anything but usual. Still in the tiny foyer, he looked down into her eyes. "I want to kiss you again."

"No one is watching." She smiled a little then, a slight tease, stepping into his embrace. His fingers found the elastic holding her hair in its tail and he slid it out. Then he plunged his hands into the strands, cradling his head as he kissed her…and kissed her…until they'd had enough to satisfy them. For now.

"Tell me again."

"I love you."

She swallowed thickly, determined that her earlier tears were the last of the day. "You're sure?"

He squeezed her hand. "I've never been more sure of anything in my life. I saw your face across the street and I just knew. This is home. *You* are home."

He lifted her fingers and kissed them. "Come sit, and I'll explain everything."

She followed him into the living room, the one she'd completely redone after her parents had moved. No more eggshell paint and floral furniture. The walls were a honeyed brown, the sofa and chairs a rich chocolate. Drew sat on the sofa and drew her down on the cushions beside him.

"You went to see Gerald today."

"Yes. But I wasn't the first. You left the flowers, didn't you?"

She nodded. "This was the first year I didn't make him a cake, you know. It felt sad when I got up this morning."

"I realized something today. You were a good daughter to him, even though he wasn't your father. And I need to thank you for that. Because without you he would have been alone."

"Blood isn't the only thing that ties families together, Drew."

"I know. And sometimes blood isn't enough to hold them, either. I was wrong. And I can't go back and fix it. I thought running from it would make it go away, but it didn't. In all the ways that counted, Jen, he *was* my father. And I'm ashamed of how I treated him and ashamed of how I treated you. You were right. I didn't trust you. I was too afraid. You said you loved me. But my mother said that too and she left. Gerald never said it, and when he revealed I wasn't his son I thought I understood. I was so afraid you'd leave that…"

Jen sighed, feeling her heart break for him. "You left me first."

He nodded, looked down at their joined hands. "I thought you saying you wouldn't go with me was the proof I needed. And when you told me you loved me again, the only thing I knew was that I would end up hurting you again. Because that's what I do. I leave. I hurt people and I leave. Like my mother did."

She slid closer, rubbed a hand over his back. "Don't you know by now you are safe with me?"

"I went to see my mother. You were right about that too."

"Oh, Drew." She lifted his fingers and kissed them. "I'm so sorry for what I said that morning. About how you hurt Gerald. About everything."

Andrew looked down at her bent head, feeling nothing but love for her flooding through him. "I kept working—kept trying to show him that I was worth it, you know? I never thought about how else it might seem. Like I was throwing it in his face."

"I'm sorry I said that." Jen looked up at him with the smoke-gray eyes he loved so much, not judging, just accepting.

"No, you were right. I couldn't put it back together until I had all the pieces. So I went to see her."

Andrew held her close, needing to feel her next to him. The trip hadn't been easy, even if it had been necessary. Julie Laramie—Julie Reid now—was a shell of a woman who'd never found the happiness she'd looked for. There hadn't been room in his heart to be angry. All he'd felt was pity.

"She's living in an apartment. Divorced again. She looks old and tired, like a faded ghost of a woman."

"Do you want to help her?"

He sighed. "I doubt she'd accept my help. She hasn't had an easy life, Jen. She told me why she left." He sighed, remembering the bitter woman who'd smoked cigarette after cigarette in her kitchen when he'd gone to her for answers. "She wasn't happy with him. She said she tried but that it wasn't working, and that she'd had an affair. The affair produced me. Things never got better with them."

"He never forgave her?"

"I'm not sure now it was about forgiveness. He wasn't as hard a man as I convinced myself. He wouldn't have tried again if he hadn't loved her, you know? He just didn't have the words." He reached out and touched her cheek with a finger. "I don't want to be like that. I want you to know how I feel."

"Oh, Drew," she sighed, closing her eyes against the gentle touch of his fingertip.

"But when she stepped out again Gerald put a stop to it. The sad thing of it is, Jen, in her way she loved him. I could tell. She kept saying that he was a good man, that it was her fault. How can I hate her for that? How can I possibly judge when I've made so many mistakes of my own?"

Jen curled her legs beneath herself, leaning up against him so that their two bodies only took up one third of the sofa. "I'm so sorry, Drew."

"He was a good father, and she knew it. He told her he was keeping *his sons*." The words were flavored with regret. "She said she didn't fight for us because she knew he was right. That we would have a better life with him than with her. He wanted both of us. *He* didn't want to split us up. And I shut Noah out too, because we were only half-brothers. Now he's—"

When he stopped abruptly, she squeezed his hand. "He's what?"

"He's been wounded. I got a call this morning. They didn't tell me much except he'll be okay. But if there's one thing I'm sure of it's that he's going to have a place to come home to."

Jen sighed, and a new worry settled in her chest.

Noah had been like a big brother to her—a strong, laughing young man.

He shook his head, stroked her hand. "My mother spent her life looking and looking and coming up empty. I don't want to be like that, Jen." He cupped her face in his hands. "I don't want to look beyond what's right in front of me just because I'm scared. I'm not like her."

"No, you're like Gerald. You love strong and you love deep."

"I was so wrong. I should have believed in you all along. You were so right. About everything." He tucked her head under his chin. "It's not too late, is it? Please don't say it's too late. Don't sell the bakery. You can't sell it. It means everything to you."

Jen turned then, sliding up and back until she was sitting on his lap, in the shelter of his strong arms, feeling his heart beat against her palm as she had the night they had waltzed. She looked into his eyes, the hazel eyes she'd adored half her life, and shook her head. "Not everything. It was too difficult to think of a life here without you in it. I would wither away, Drew. And I thought we were over for good. How could I stay? I needed a reason."

He gazed into her eyes and she saw in them what she'd hoped to see that morning in the cabin. "I haven't stopped loving you in nearly fifteen years," she stated with a wistful smile. "I'm not likely to stop now." She drew a line along his bottom lip with her thumb. "Your heart is safe with me, Drew."

"Then it's yours. I'm yours. Heart, body and soul, if you'll have me. Is that reason enough?"

She blinked back tears—no, she would not cry anymore today! But his own eyes gleamed suspiciously as he cupped her hand and pressed it to his cheek.

"Have all of me, Jen. Marry me."

"You and Lazy L?"

"Yes, I'm afraid you'll have to put up with my strays and unwanteds." His lips threatened to smile.

"Snickerdoodles?"

"We'll take down that stupid 'For Sale' sign the moment after you say yes."

"Babies?"

His Adam's apple bobbed as he swallowed, the green bits of his irises lighting as the smile widened. "Lord, woman—of course. Your babies. *Our babies.*"

She threw her arms around his neck. Okay, so maybe she wasn't going to keep her promise not to cry again, but proposals like this one didn't come along every day.

"Is that a yes?"

"Yes. *Yes!*"

His arms came around her hard, rejoicing, clinging, renewing. Finally the grip eased into one of comfort, strength, acceptance.

"Jen?"

"Hmm?" She hummed it into the hollow of his neck, where her head rested against him.

"Tell me again, Jen."

"I love you, Drew."

He let the words wash over him, knew he'd repeat them every day of his life now that he had her in his arms. He kissed the top of her head and closed his eyes.

"I love you, too."

# ROMANCE 2-in-1

## Coming next month

### CINDERELLA ON HIS DOORSTEP
#### by Rebecca Winters

When Dana arrives on location at Chateau Belles Fleurs, she becomes the star of her own real-life fairy tale. Complete with handsome prince, irresistible chateau owner Alex.

### ACCIDENTALLY EXPECTING!
#### by Lucy Gordon

Dante doesn't believe he has a future to live for. So he knows the spark between him and Ferne can be no more than a holiday romance. Until Ferne discovers she's pregnant!

### AUSTRALIAN BOSS: DIAMOND RING
#### by Jennie Adams

Fiona's sunny smile and bouncy enthusiasm are a breath of fresh air in Brent's office and his ordered world. Is Fiona the woman to finally release Brent's fears and the secret he's lived with all his life?

### LIGHTS, CAMERA...KISS THE BOSS
#### by Nikki Logan

Growing up, Ava was like a sister to TV producer Daniel. Now she's a stunning woman and ratings winner. Dan can't take his eye off the ball now and risk losing a promotion, or can he?

**On sale 5th February 2010**

Available at WHSmith, Tesco, ASDA, Eason and all good bookshops.
For full Mills & Boon range including eBooks visit
**www.millsandboon.co.uk**

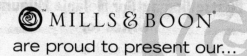

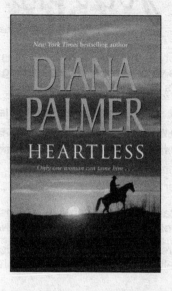

# millsandboon.co.uk Community

# *Join Us!*

The Community is the perfect place to meet and chat to kindred spirits who love books and reading as much as you do, but it's also the place to:

- **Get the inside scoop from authors about their latest books**
- **Learn how to write a romance book with advice from our editors**
- **Help us to continue publishing the best in women's fiction**
- **Share your thoughts on the books we publish**
- **Befriend other users**

**Forums:** Interact with each other as well as authors, editors and a whole host of other users worldwide.

**Blogs:** Every registered community member has their own blog to tell the world what they're up to and what's on their mind.

**Book Challenge:** We're aiming to read 5,000 books and have joined forces with The Reading Agency in our inaugural Book Challenge.

**Profile Page:** Showcase yourself and keep a record of your recent community activity.

**Social Networking:** We've added buttons at the end of every post to share via digg, Facebook, Google, Yahoo, technorati and de.licio.us.

## *www.millsandboon.co.uk*

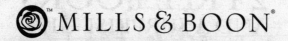

R/

# 2 FREE BOOKS
## AND A SURPRISE GIFT

We would like to take this opportunity to thank you for reading this Mills & Boon® book by offering you the chance to take TWO more specially selected books from the Romance series absolutely FREE! We're also making this offer to introduce you to the benefits of the Mills & Boon® Book Club™—

- **FREE home delivery**
- **FREE gifts and competitions**
- **FREE monthly Newsletter**
- **Exclusive Mills & Boon Book Club offers**
- **Books available before they're in the shops**

Accepting these FREE books and gift places you under no obligation to buy, you may cancel at any time, even after receiving your free shipment. Simply complete your details below and return the entire page to the address below. You don't even need a stamp!

**YES** Please send me 2 free Romance books and a surprise gift. I understand that unless you hear from me, I will receive 5 superb new stories every month including two 2-in-1 books priced at £4.99 each and a single book priced at £3.19, postage and packing free. I am under no obligation to purchase any books and may cancel my subscription at any time. The free books and gift will be mine to keep in any case.

Ms/Mrs/Miss/Mr_____ Initials _____

Surname _____
Address _____
_____
_____ Postcode _____

Send this whole page to: Mills & Boon Book Club, Free Book Offer, FREEPOST NAT 10298, Richmond, TW9 1BR